# Unexpecting

## Holly Kerr

Three Birds Press

# Unexpecting

-A Novel
(Formerly Baby! Baby? Baby!?)

# Chapter One

"A woman's prime period of fertility occurs between the years of twenty-two and twenty-eight, with each year decreasing the chance of a happy and healthy conception. After the age of thirty-seven, a woman should not attempt to conceive."

*A Young Woman's Guide to the Joy of Impending Motherhood*
Dr. Francine Pascal Reid (1941)

**B**ULLSHIT, I KNOW.

But for some reason, that passage has stuck with me for years. You know what it's like to have one of those repetitive songs stuck in your head? Years ago, it was that "Umbrella" song—not that it was a bad song; in fact, it's a pretty good song, but when I'm still silently singing "ella, ella," days after I hear it, it gets a little tiring.

If you think having a song stuck in your head is bad, imagine silently repeating to yourself again and again, "After the age of thirty-seven, a woman should not attempt to conceive."

Most of me will agree I'm being silly in taking the words of a long-dead doctor to heart, but an itty-bitty part of me is still listening and using my fingers to count the months on the calendar until I hit the De-Fertility Zone. Silly, I know, but I can't seem to help it.

Yes, I am fully aware that in this day and age there are countless women over thirty-seven who conceive and successfully deliver happy and healthy babies. I know that. You can't pick up an issue of People magazine without knowing that. But for me, thirty-seven has been something of a deadline, and it's looming ever closer these days. Here I am already at thirty-five, pushing headlong into thirty-six, which will inevitably lead to thirty-seven, the age when Dr. Francine Pascal Reid tells me I shouldn't attempt to conceive. So how am I supposed to have a baby?

Going to a wedding yesterday certainly didn't help.

Yesterday marked the seventeenth wedding I've been to in the last five years, and the ninth in which I've played the role of a bridesmaid. I remember reading something long ago, some old wives' tale about three times a bridesmaid, never a bride. I guess I'm screwed three times over then.

To make things worse, it turned out that the entire bridal party—other than me, that is—were all pregnant. Of course, being basically a nice person, I was sincerely happy for them, but can you imagine how my own desire to have a baby might make me a tad resentful? The anticipation I had felt toward being part of the wedding dimmed a little as I was forced to listen to all the little baby comments and pregnancy stories, not to mention names and dates and crib styles. I had had just about enough when Darcy's aunt Fran popped her head into the room where the five of us had just finished getting into our dresses (horrible green with, yes, a big butt bow). Once she'd cooed over us all, Aunt Fran announced that she thought it was just hilarious how Darcy had picked an entire bridal party of pregnant girls, assuming I was as pregnant as the others.

Mistakenly assuming a woman is pregnant is probably one of the worst gaffes a person can make. It just ends up embarrassing both parties, and there's really no delicate way to get out of the situation. So when Darcy's aunt said her little bit about how all the girls in the wedding party were pregnant (with a particularly poignant glance at me), Darcy's mother came to my defence about how of course I can't be pregnant because I don't even have a husband. I'm sure she meant well, but it really didn't help. It also didn't help hearing Michelle and Priya (six months along, with the most adorable little baby belly poking out of the dress) try to stifle their laughter.

If you haven't already got the point, my most fervent desire is to have a baby. Having my own baby is something I've always dreamed about. I still have my Rub-A-Dub Dolly, my six Cabbage Patch Kids, and the doll that cries when you squeeze her stomach all packed away in the basement. I never did the Barbie thing because Barbie was always too busy trying to get it on with Ken and didn't need taking care of. I babysat my way from ages twelve to eighteen, and I only stopped because I went to university and discovered that drinking and guys (unfortunately in that order) were a much more entertaining way to spend Saturday nights.

I've been teaching kindergarten for the last four years. Before that, it was grade three, and before that I worked as a nanny in the summers to help pay for university. I sound like I'm reciting my résumé, but it's just shoving the point across with my typical subtlety about how much I love kids. I love being with them, playing with them, and especially teaching them, and I've been hoping for years to finally have one of my own.

What's the problem, you ask? Not me, or so I hope. Knock on wood that when I do find the right man to have a baby with, I'll still be able to conceive—Dr. Francine Pascal Reid or no Dr. Francine Pascal Reid. No, for me the problem is finding the right man. Or any man, actually. Well, no, that's not quite right—I have no problem finding men. For some reason that boggles my mind, men practically flock to me, which is all good if you're going for quantity and just out for a good time. Not that there's anything wrong with that, but I want quality, and that's where I have had absolutely no luck.

Just yesterday morning, I left my apartment to take part in Darcy and Ethan's wedding, full of hope that I might have actually found one. I'd only been dating Mike for twenty-six days, and I thought things were progressing well. He's smart and funny, has a great head of hair, and as far as I can discover, there's been no history of diabetes or heart problems in his family, which kept him open as a candidate for baby-making. Things had progressed so well that I had plans to jump the gun on my hard-and-fast rule of not sleeping with a man unless I've known him for at least a month. Of course, exceptions are made, but usually the head manages to rule the heart and other body parts in these matters. There's no way I need a black book rivaling Kim Kardashian's.

I've been steadily wading through the pool of eligible bachelors for years, with absolutely no luck. And it's not like I'm looking for the perfect man—all I want these days is to find one with certain attributes that I would like to pass on to a child. Over the years, I've pared my requirements down to the basics: intelligence, relative physical attractiveness, sense of humour, and a family history with few or no unpronounceable illnesses or diseases. Unless I set out to get pregnant by some random man I pick up in a bar (yes, I'm getting desperate and have thought of that countless times, but I like to think it's a measure of the respect I still have for the male race and myself that I haven't been able to bring myself to go through with it), nothing seems to be working.

I know very well how these things usually happen: girl meets boy, girl makes boy wait patiently for three years while she sows some wild oats and then agrees to marry him—no, wait, that's how it was with my sister, Libby. How about girl meets boy and then relentlessly nags him until he proposes? Nope, that's the story of my friend Brit.

Anyway, I know how it's supposed to work even though I don't have many good examples to learn from, especially not my own parents. Until I was fourteen, I lived with Ed, the alcoholic asshole father, and Teresa, the quiet, holier-than-thou, I'll just keep my mouth shut and let my husband verbally abuse my daughters kind of mother.

And then everything changed when Ed died because he was too dumb not to wait until he got home to start dipping into his bottle of Jim Beam. He screwed up trying to navigate the exit of the parking lot for the Liquor Control Board of Ontario and crashed into the building. He would have been fine actually, had it not been for the heart attack. Everyone said it was the heart attack that caused him to crash into the building, but I don't believe it. He was a dumb drunk. Good riddance, if you ask me. My mother obviously shared my opinion about him since after she was sure he was dead (a week after the funeral, a more-than-suitable mourning period), she did the whole moth emerging from the chrysalis and became... well, let's just say the words prim, proper, and self-control around the opposite sex would never describe her.

But you don't need my family history right now. You just need to understand that I'm romantically challenged.

Things were going well with Mike and me, but because I was a member of the bridal party, I thought twice about bringing a date. No one likes to be stuck eating with strangers while his girlfriend sits at the head table surrounded by friends. Turns out I should have thought three times about bringing him.

The ceremony had just ended, with the priest pronouncing Ethan and Darcy as husband and wife, and the guests had gathered outside in the early June sunshine to heap congratulations on the happy couple. Being part of the bridal party, I was one of the first ones outside. After a couple of minutes looking for Mike in the crowd, I popped back inside the church to see what had happened to him and found much more than I expected. I found Mike—boyfriend of twenty-six days—in the coatroom of the church. Not that this is a bad thing, but the fact that he was performing a sexual act of an extremely intimate nature on the twenty-one-year-old stepdaughter of the matron of honour certainly was. A bad thing, that is. Even though Mike and his new friend were obviously very excited about finding each other, suffice it to say, I wasn't too thrilled about it.

"Do you mind?" asked the girl in a snotty tone as I stood there staring at my boyfriend doing what he was doing to her. If someone walked in on me in her position, I don't think I'd take the snotty route. I'd be pretty embarrassed, to tell the truth, and possibly apologetic if the person walking in on us was the girlfriend of the guy. But not this chickie.

"Do you?" I retorted incredulously. "He's my boyfriend! Or he was."

I then proceeded to tear a strip off of Mike—actually not really, since I couldn't get over the shock of my discovery that quickly and because I'm not good at confrontations at all. I did tell him I was taking his name off the present, however. I know, what's the point, especially since I bought the silly gift, but it's really difficult to come up with anything pithy when you're in that situation. I would have really liked to make a few comments about his sexual prowess or size of his member, but since I have no knowledge of the former and I couldn't help but notice the bulge in his pants happened to be fairly sizable, I was left with nothing. So I had no choice but to let them be, barely managing to paste a smile on my face as I left the church and headed to the waiting limousine. I guess the car was waiting for me, because the rest of the wedding party was already inside and the Bentley that Ethan hired to drive him and Darcy had just pulled away.

Once the car started, I turned to Michelle, the matron of honour/stepmother of the boyfriend-stealing tramp I found with Mike. I didn't know her name—the name of the girl I found with Mike, not the matron of honour. I think it's something like Mindy or Mandy, or it could be Mambo Betty for all I care. Michelle was sitting in the rear seat across from me with her hand resting on her great lump of a belly. Remember she's about eight months pregnant, not just lumpish.

You get the picture that I wasn't having the best of days? Seeing matron of honour Michelle, the laughing, pregnant stepmother of the tramp, lounging in the seat of the limousine with hand resting on her great pregnant belly with the smuggest of smiles—it just pissed me off. I vividly recalled her laughter at my expense earlier. I'm not normally a bitch, but like I said, it had been a bad day.

"Did your stepdaughter ever go to Sunday school?" I asked Michelle, with an innocent expression as the car pulled away from the church.

"Why?" Michelle looked bewildered.

"I would have thought going to Sunday school might have taught her a little respect for the church," I said conversationally. I couldn't help but notice that Michelle had kicked her shoes off, and her toes resembled little stumpy sausages. I fervently hoped she wasn't able to get her shoes back on.

"What? Amelia?"

"Oh, is that her name? I'm sure Mike didn't know either. Just so you're up to speed, I just walked in on Mike—who was my boyfriend as of about four minutes ago—going down on her in the coatroom at the church. And unless she stuck a very tiny coat up her who-who, I really think they were in the wrong place to do such a thing. And, sorry, but I really wasn't impressed with her attitude about being caught in the act, but what can you do? She's still young."

Michelle's smiling face transformed into an "O" of shock. "You saw her what?" she asked in a strangled voice.

"Being a very dirty little girl with my boyfriend. Who isn't my boyfriend any longer, so she's welcome to him, but it might have been nice to have a little advance notice."

"You can't be serious!"

"Oh, I'm pretty serious. I can give you the details if you like. I know she's wearing pink underwear—I think it might have been a thong, but I can't be sure since it was dangling off one of her ankles."

Michelle looked to the other bridesmaids as if asking for help defending her stepdaughter's honour. I found it interesting no one stepped forward.

"I'm just letting you know what went on. So when she brings him over to you as her new guy, you'll know how she got him." I gave her my best and biggest fake smile. "Wow, your ankles are really swollen. Or is that their normal size?" There was a muffled cough from somewhere in the car.

"Could I have the champagne, please?" I asked brightly.

Ari, one of the ushers, held up the chilled bottle. "Why don't you let me do it, just in case the cork takes somebody's eye out?" He expertly maneuvered the cork out with his thumbs. Then he handed the bottle over to me, and I proceeded to take a huge glug out of it. "Not much for sharing, are you, Casey?" he asked me with a wink.

I took another big drink, then another, conscious of the nervous glances of the rest of the wedding party floating around. "I'm a kindergarten teacher," I told Ari after another mouthful, trying to avoid burping aloud. "I'm all about sharing. Except for champagne or boyfriends." And that was about the extent of the conversation in the car until we got to the reception.

I like to think I behaved myself during the rest of the evening. I pasted another smile on my face during the endless picture-taking, laughed at the appropriate times during the speeches, and even enjoyed dancing with Ari the usher. I did manage to sneak a piece of cake onto Mike's chair just as he was sitting down to dessert, which left a lovely butter cream icing smear on his fine ass for the rest of the night, forcing him to keep on his jacket to hide it, when I know he sweats a lot.

Boy, was I wrong about Mike. I can't get over how wrong. And the worst part is how utterly stupid I felt. I had no idea he was such a fast-moving player. I met him at Second Cup, for goodness sake. Although I did agree to go to dinner with him the same night we met, so maybe that should have told me something. I just thought I was particularly irresistible that day, what with having a good hair day and wearing my lucky unders. I had no clue he'd turn out to be such an ass. He never once apologized either, and I was blown away that he actually stayed at the wedding. He even looked like he was having a good time, before the buttercream icing incident, of course. My night, on the other hand, was pretty much ruined.

You know how sometimes the idea of getting drunk is just the best option? That wedding was a perfect example. I like drinking to begin with—something that I do take care to watch, with the whole father being an alcoholic and such—but there's something about a wedding that really brings the party animal out in all of us. Maybe it's the free bar, countless bottles of wine on the table, and numerous champagne toasts. Plus, unless you're family, there's a good chance you won't be seeing these people ever again. In any event, by the time Darcy and Ethan took the floor to sway to "You Look Wonderful Tonight," I was well on my way to becoming quite shit-faced.

# Chapter Two

"Conception occurs when there is the least amount of pressure on both individuals. Lovemaking should be easy and enjoyable, with the eventuality of procreating the furthest thing from the mind."

*A Young Woman's Guide to the Joy of Impending Motherhood*
Dr. Francine Pascal Reid (1941)

I KNOW THERE ARE many women out there who are happily married and unable to have a baby for whatever reasons. I feel for them, I really do. If I ever find myself in that situation, I can console myself with the thought that I do have my kindergarten students and my sister's kids to lavish my affection on. Some women don't even have that. But some days, when I see one of my students run out to meet his parents with a huge smile on his face, and the parent swoops down to grab him in the biggest hug, I get this ache in my chest. And then when I'm with parents talking to them about their children and I see on their faces an expression of pride and awe for a child's accomplishments, the ache gets even more painful.

The worst is when I'm not even at the school, but just walking down the street and see a mother holding a child's hand. I want that. I really do. I know I must sound like such a selfish person to be so concerned with having a baby—like some spoiled child desperate for a new toy—especially since there are so many women who aren't able to conceive or carry a child, but truthfully it's the only thing I've ever really wanted. I feel like I have a hollow spot in my soul, and I know that having a baby will fill that spot. It's my dream, and in my mind, you should always follow your dreams, right?

I took a cab home from the reception and fell asleep on the way there. At least it was better than falling asleep on the subway because I've done that before and it's not fun. This way the only thing I had to worry about was the cab driver sneaking peeks at me and running the meter up as I snoozed.

"Miss? Miss?" was how the driver woke me. It was a lot politer than how some of my previous boyfriends woke me.

"Yes, thank you, sorry, thank you," I mumbled and threw a wad of bills over the seat at him as I fell out of the car. Luckily, J.B. was just getting home from work, or I probably would have flopped down on the postage-stamp-sized lawn and finished my nap right then and there.

J.B. Bergen was my roommate. Well, technically, he's not my roommate because he shared the upstairs apartment with Cooper while I lived on the main floor, but it feels like we all live together in one big happy house.

"Looks like someone had a good time," J.B. said as I stumbled across the lawn toward him and the front door. I tripped over a terracotta container of yellow tulips and purple pansies (Emma's doing—she's Cooper's girlfriend) and stumbled into a freshly dug flower bed, falling with my hands in the dirt halfway up to my elbows. J.B. came to my rescue and hauled me to my feet. I wiped the dirt off the skirt of my dress.

"It was the shittiest wedding ever," I told him. Then I smelled my hands. "Even my hands smell like shit." Then I burst into tears.

"Hey," J. B. said with concern. "Don't do that!"

To his dismay, I continued to stand in the front yard in my dirt-covered, ugly green dress, on which I spilled wine several times, and began to wail loud enough to wake the neighbours. I probably would have stood there for a while had J.B. not hustled me inside to my apartment.

"Hey, c'mon now," was the only thing he said as he unlocked my door and got me inside on the couch. "It's not that bad. Where are your shoes?"

I looked down at my feet, noticing for the first time that I was only wearing my nylons and they had definitely seen better days. "I don't know!" I wailed and started crying even harder.

"We'll find them, we'll find them." J.B. backed away nervously. "I'm going to get you something to drink, okay? Something nonalcoholic," he muttered as he headed into what constitutes my kitchen.

When Coop moved into the house, the main floor was already set up as a separate apartment, but missing most of the amenities, like a fridge and stove. Because it was me moving in and I can't cook to save my life, Coop asked if it was okay if he didn't put a full kitchen in, adding that I could use the one upstairs whenever I wanted. I was fine with that, and so I've only got a little bar fridge and a microwave in the kitchen area.

I guess I should back up a minute. My name is Casey Samms. I live in a house owned by one of my dearest friends, Cooper Edison. It's a pretty good setup because of the sweet deal I get on rent and the fact that my apartment is awesome. Plus, Cooper feeds me quite a lot. The house is one of those huge old ones that had been split into a duplex. I have the main floor apartment, which is on the smallish side because I share the floor with the laundry room and huge storage space. Coop and J.B. (and unofficially Coop's girlfriend, Emma) live on the upper two floors, which are beautiful and spacious. But because we're all such good friends and my apartment isn't furnished all that well, plus the whole no-kitchen thing, I spend a good chunk of my time upstairs.

I met Cooper about five years ago when he was the executive chef at a winery in Niagara-on-the-Lake and I had a summer job working in the tasting room. When he moved into Toronto four years ago to work at the restaurant Galileo and moved into his grandparents' huge three-storied house in the Annex, Cooper offered me the apartment on the main floor. So far it's worked out great. I'm hoping to be able to buy my own place soon, but there's been this little problem of a credit card debt I've been trying to clear up. It's almost cleared up thanks to me working two jobs—I teach kindergarten in the mornings and manage a wine boutique in the afternoons and evenings, as well as taking the odd shift waitressing at Cooper's restaurant when they need an extra pair of hands. Emma works at Galileo as well—she and Cooper have been together almost two years. I'm sure they'll be telling me she's moving in any day now.

J.B. returned to the couch with a bottle of water. "Do you want me to go get Emma or Coop?" he asked nervously. "I think they should be home by now." He hovered anxiously above me.

J.B. and Cooper met years ago when they were both working at some restaurant. J.B. is originally from this little place in Saskatchewan, but there is nothing small-town boyish about him. Maybe there was when he first got into the city, but these days he's all smooth and cool and pretty popular with the ladies. Not in any sleazy way, mind you—he's too nice of a guy for that—but he is quite the operator.

"I'm fine," I told him, getting dizzy from looking up. I leaned back and closed my eyes.

"Right," J.B. said as he sat down beside me and took off the top of the bottle of water for me. "Drink. You'll thank me in the morning."

"Ah, morning," I crooned. "Has to be better than today was." I took the bottle from him and obligingly took a mouthful.

"Probably will be. So it wasn't a good wedding?"

Instead of answering, I gave a sniff. "You smell like a bar. Beer, and," —I gave another sniff— "and tequila." This made perfect sense since J.B. is a bartender and manager of a nightclub downtown.

"You don't smell so fresh yourself," he replied. I took the edge of my skirt and tried to wipe the dirt off my hands and arms. "You're ruining that dress, you know."

"Ugly dress. Would you want to wear it again?"

"Green's not my colour," he said, which makes me laugh through my tears. "Are you going to tell me what happened at the wedding, or do you want me to guess?"

"Guess."

"You didn't catch the bouquet."

"Didn't want to. I'd probably have to marry Mike. Or maybe I should rename him asshole. But that might be too kind a name for him."

"That was my next guess." Even in my unobservant state, I couldn't help but notice J. B trying to hide a smile. "Another one bites the dust. What did he do?"

"Have you ever had sex in a church?"

"Can't say I have. I take it you weren't the one with him in the church having the sex?"

"It wasn't even sex—it was more than sex. The sex that Clinton said wasn't real sex, but is so sex, especially when I catch him doing it to her and..."

"I get it. You don't have to draw me a picture," J.B. grimaced. "Nice guy."

"I thought he was." I shook my head morosely. Tears started trickling down my cheeks.

"Hey, none of that," J.B. said gently, wiping away my tears, but they were falling faster than he could wipe. "He's definitely not worth it. I don't think I've ever seen you cry, except watching dumb girl movies."

I gave a halfhearted laugh, but it didn't stop me crying. J.B. gave me a hug. He gives good hugs. He's got a nice chest and good shoulders, and if I nuzzle into his neck, his cologne masks the bar smells. It's nice to have a friend like J.B. If I could have just stayed there for a while more, then I was sure everything would be just fine.

But then we started kissing.

I want to say I don't remember who kissed who first, but I really think it might have been me who initiated it. I know J.B. was only trying to make me feel better. And he did—much better in ways I wasn't expecting. But even though I was glad I wasn't crying any longer, there was a part of me that knew I should tell him to leave. Maybe I should also mention this was not the first time this had happened. After the last time, I said that was it, especially since Cooper was so upset about it—walking in on two friends going at it would do that to you; it was post-coital, but on the way to pre-coital, second round—and the last thing I want is to cause problems between J.B. and Cooper, since they're both so important to me and...

Fuck it. I'll deal with the aftermath later.

# Chapter Three

"The decision to have a baby should not be taken lightly."

*A Young Woman's Guide to the Joy of Impending Motherhood*
Dr. Francine Pascal Reid (1941)

I woke up Sunday as the early morning sun was peeking through the curtains I forgot to close and realized my life was slipping away. Okay, maybe that's a little too dramatic, but that's what it felt like. Discovering Mike was no better than the other assholes I've met was the straw that broke the proverbial camel's back. After almost twenty years of dating, this back had gotten quite good at carrying things, but now it had had enough. I really thought there might be a future with Mike, but once again, I was as wrong as a kid eating yellow snow. I can't say my heart was broken, but the ego did take a bruising, especially when last night was going to be the first time I had sex with Mike, not him going down on a skinny little twenty-one-year-old in the coatroom of the church.

Once I start wallowing in self-pity, there's no turning back, so with a firm shake of my head, I decided that was enough. Mike was so not worth it. In fact, no man had proven to be worth me lamenting the fact that it never seems to work out between us, and then moaning to everyone about how I have the worst luck in men. I needed to end the losing streak once and for all.

I am romantically challenged, plain and simple. Either that or I'm only capable of attracting losers. But since there have been a couple of good ones—only a couple, mind you—I'm still optimistic enough to hope I've still got a chance.

I glanced over to where J.B. was still asleep beside me. He was on his stomach, his face turned away from me and both arms stretched up like he was about to dive into a pool. Just so you know, J.B. is one of the good ones. Not that I'm involved with him—other than being friends, living in the same house, and on occasion, having sex with him, but that's it. Definitely not involved. So he's certainly not the reason I had the brain wave about giving up men.

And that's what I decided. I needed to give up the dating aspect of my life. It was clearly not doing me any good, and I hadn't proven to be very good at it, despite having years of practice. I meet a man, get interested in him, and think possibly, just maybe he might be the one, but then wham, out come the asshole tendencies. And it's not like I'm meeting Joe Stud at a bar or club. Over the years I've refined my meeting-men techniques to concentrate on the places one would assume the average, decent men would congregate. I've had success at various sporting events, restaurants, and a Bon Jovi concert, not to mention a fitness centre, a rock-climbing class, and plain old walking in the park. Plus, I think just about everyone I know has tried to set me up with a man, including one of my ex-boyfriends, who thought I'd be perfect for one of his friends. I'm also finding that the older I get, the quicker I go through men. In my twenties, I would keep them around for a while, thinking I could change them, help them, or just become the woman they so desperately needed. These days, with me hitting the mid-thirty mark, it doesn't take much for me to give a guy the heave-ho. Even if he just forgets his wallet without a suitable excuse, I'll say see you later.

I may be a slow learner, but I've definitely learned my lesson. No more getting stranded in Montreal and having to pay a three-thousand-dollar hotel bill. I know now how the words "I'm not ready to be exclusive" can often translate into "the other girl I'm sleeping with just gave me a dose of chlamydia, which I've just passed on to you." And I will never forget, nor will my roommates, how a man being sweetly possessive one day can quickly turn into a serious nut job and result in me having to get a restraining order against him.

And so I decided that's it. Keeping with the drama, it was like a bolt of lightning out of the blue. That was it. I had had it. No more men. No more dating. No more of the first flush of infatuation, which inevitably leads to another disappointment. Now I sound like a bitter old shrew, so I'll move past that. I am removing myself from the dating pool before I end up floating face down.

While my vow to remove all potential suitors from my present and future was a terrific idea—other than facing a future of celibacy and a lifetime of loneliness—it really didn't help with the whole I-want-to-have-a-baby aspect of my life. And yes, we all know the man is a pretty important part of the baby-making process. So I'd just have to figure out how to get pregnant without having a man in my life.

You might think it was ironic that I was seriously contemplating how to have a baby after engaging in sexual intercourse. You just have to know J.B. The last thing J.B. would want is a woman wanting to have a baby with him. And I don't—I want a baby, but not a baby with J.B., even as much as I like him. He's just not into things like commitment or planning a future past the third date, let alone the life-altering aspect of a baby in his life. Since I've known him, the longest relationship he's had with a woman was six weeks, and then only because she was one of those pseudo-celebrity types and the publicity from the lurking paparazzi helped the nightclub that he manages.

So how do I get pregnant without having sex with a man?

Again, it's like a sudden shock hit me. I took biology in high school. I only need one part of a man to get pregnant—really, only a tiny little essence of a man. And getting that little bit shouldn't be too difficult. It's like a flashing red neon sign—get thee to a sperm bank.

All I had to do was find the nearest sperm bank and make an appointment. It's a big city—there should be a number of clinics in the vicinity of the subway line. That's what I was going to do. I'd use the sperm of an anonymous donor to get pregnant. It may not be my first choice, but right now, I didn't see any other options. I'd get myself inseminated and have a baby. And it's not like I'd have to wait to get married or even meet the right guy. I could go and do this tomorrow! Well, maybe not tomorrow, but next week. I could be a mother. Soon!

I lay awake thinking about this for a couple of hours. I knew this was a decision that was going to not only affect my life, but the life of others, including my not-yet-conceived baby. Would I have wanted to be raised without a father? Hell, yes. Do I think I could do a good job as a single parent? It may seem arrogant, but I really think I'll do okay as both mother and father. And it's not like the baby won't have his share of male role models—my brother-in-law Luke is terrific, and Cooper and J.B. would be around. The more I thought about it, the better it sounded.

The possibility of conceiving sooner rather than later got me all excited. I really don't know how I managed to fall back asleep. But I must have fallen back asleep because the numbers on my clock said it was after ten when Cooper called to me from upstairs.

"Casey? You down there? I'm making breakfast, so c'mon up if you want to eat!"

I heard a grunt from somewhere beneath the blankets beside me in response to Coop's call.

"What the—what time is it?" J.B. grumbled, rolling over onto his side and taking most of my covers with him.

Maybe it's a fantasy of some women to be called for breakfast by one man while another one sleeps beside you, but not me. It's actually gotten to the point where I prefer not to have my guests sleep over—not that there's been the potential for that for a while. I'm not into the whole snoring aspect and having to share my bed space and cover-hogging and things like that. I'm surprised I let J. B. stay.

Actually, I'm surprised that I slept with him at all. Admittedly, I wasn't in the best frame of mind—okay, I was drunk and cheated on and sorely in need of comfort—but still. Maybe I used to be in the habit of collecting casual hookups like notches on my belt, but that was years ago. I like to think I've grown out of that. And J.B. has never been just a casual fling. But I guess when you take the disastrous time I had at the wedding, J.B.'s sympathetic shoulders to cry on, plus the fact I do find him extremely attractive, sex is what you get. And it had been awhile, so who could blame me?

"Time for you to get out," I told him, giving the blanket a hearty yank and uncovering a pair of bright red striped boxer shorts. Luckily J.B. was wearing them. "Cooper called me for breakfast."

"Go eat and leave me alone." J.B. pulled the blankets—we had a regular tug-of-war going on—and attempted to burrow back under the covers.

A weight like a small boulder landed on the bed, and my cat, Sebastian, gave his throaty meow—the one that announces he's hungry and wants to be fed now. But this morning finding something infinitely more interesting than just me in bed, Sebastian began to climb over J.B.'s inert body toward his head.

"Get off me, animal," J.B. growled.

"He thinks you should leave, too," I said. "There's no way I'm leaving you down here alone for Cooper to find you. You know he got all weirded out the last time." I sat up in bed and yawned.

"That was two years ago." With a deep sigh of displeasure, J.B. gave my cat, who was now partially resting his twenty-five pounds on J.B.'s shoulder, a shove and sat up. "Cooper needs to get over it. Besides, is he in the habit of coming down here?"

"He might have some laundry to do. You never know, and I don't feel like listening to him go on and on about it, so just go," I told him. Quickly, I grabbed enough of the sheet to pull it up around my bare breasts. "Don't you want breakfast too?"

J.B.'s hair was mussed as he glanced over at me. "You feeling better now?" he asked gruffly. "About the wedding and everything?"

"Yeah," I admitted shamefacedly. "I didn't mean to go all girly and cry on your shoulder like that. Sorry."

He gave a shrug and stood up. My breath caught as he stretched his six-foot-three frame. His abs and pecs and the... whole package was pretty amazing. "Anytime." Then he turned and gave me such an obviously lascivious wink that I had to laugh. "And I mean anytime."

I'm not in the habit of sleeping with my roommates. Definitely not Cooper since we've always had a great brother-sister relationship going on. But J.B. has always been different. We actually dated way back when Cooper first introduced us—if you can call three dates dating—but then Cooper offered me the apartment in the house, and we thought it would be too strange to be involved and living in the same house but not really living together, so we decided to keep it just friends.

I've always enjoyed being friends with men. They're easy, no pettiness, and let's face it, sometimes guys are just fun to hang with. But Cooper and J.B. are definitely two of my best friends, and so while I've always had a twinge of "what if?" with J.B., I'm really glad to have him as such a good friend. One night, about six months after I moved in, we got together, and things happened. And again the next night, which Cooper discovered by walking in on me in J.B.'s bed. He wasn't happy, but because we both love him, we agreed not to continue anything. The interest was pretty strong on my part and I think for him, too, but tempting as it was, I knew what J.B. was like. He doesn't do relationships or commitments or long-term anything, and I had no preconceptions that I was going to be the one to change him. It might be fun for a while, but I knew it wouldn't last, so why go through the heartache and screw up a really good living arrangement?

I threw my pillow at J.B., which is difficult to do while trying to keep covered. "We agreed it shouldn't happen again," I reminded him. "For Cooper's sake."

J.B. shrugged again and began hunting for his pants. "You decided that. Not me. Coop's a big boy. He can find someone else to walk in on if he really puts his mind to it." He pulled on his pants and found his shirt lying crumpled under the bed. As he was putting it on, he came over to my side of the bed. Before I could think to move away, he leaned down, cupping my cheek in his hand, and gave me a kiss.

I told myself the light-headedness I felt was just because I was still foggy from lack of sleep. J.B. is talented at a great many things, and kissing might be top of the list. I didn't say keeping it friends-only was easy.

"Still want me to go?" he whispered as he pulled away. His lips were a breath away from mine.

"Yes... no..." I murmured with my eyes still closed. "Maybe..." Then as I remembered my vow from earlier this morning, "Yes," I said clearly and pulled back. J.B. had a big smile on his face. "Don't do that again. Moron. Go."

"Ask me nicely," he said, still grinning. Was he trying to make this more difficult than it already was? Why on earth did he have to be so good-looking? At least he was pulling on his pants because those boxer shorts were becoming somewhat distracting.

"Go! And that's as nice as you'll get from me."

"I'm going, then," he said. "Your loss." But just as he turned away, his eyes lit onto something sitting on the nightstand next to my bed. "What's that?"

The way he said it made me think there was some sort of rodent sitting there quietly watching us. "What!"

"That!" He was pointing at a book, A Young Woman's Guide to the Joy of Impending Motherhood. It looked a little worse for wear; the spine was cracked, and there was a drink ring on the cover, but there was nothing about it that should get J.B. that excited.

"It's just a book. Sometimes I read it before bed. My mother gave it to me a few years ago. I'm not sure why. It's really old, too, from the forties, and I don't know if she thought it would be useful—not that she's ever given me much that's of use, especially recently, but..."

"Why do you still have it? You're not...?" J.B.'s eyeballs were practically popping out as he goggled at me.

"No. Not yet, anyway. But I want to have a baby. You know that," I told him calmly. "I've told you that."

"But... this wasn't... we used a condom... you didn't..."

"What are you trying to say?"

"But you want to have a baby!"

"So? Not like this! Not with you! That was just sex, not me trying to conceive! God, your ego..."

"Well, what am I supposed to think?"

"Think about how I was upset and drunk and you took advantage of me," I told him sarcastically.

"I did not!" he blustered.

"See how it feels?" I gave him a good teacher glare. "I did not sleep with you to intentionally get pregnant. I would never do that to you. I wouldn't do that to anyone! If I could and would, then I'd already have a baby. And if you continue this line of nervous babbling, I'm going to get upset, and that won't be good for either one of us."

J.B. just looked at me as he took a few deep breaths. In all the years I'd known him, he was always so cool and calm. I'd never seen him this close to freaking out. If it wasn't almost offensive, I might have laughed. But it also showed me I was making the right decision. I couldn't get involved with anyone else. I was going to do this on my own.

"Casey!" Cooper called down the stairs again. "You want to eat or what?"

"I'm going," J.B. said hurriedly. He held my gaze for a long moment before he let out a small sigh. "I know. Of course, you wouldn't. I'm sorry I thought... what I thought." And then he was gone, still buttoning up his shirt as he headed for the door and before I could tell him any more about what I'd decided. Who would have thought he'd get so bent out of shape about a book? I couldn't help but feel a twinge of unease about what he might say about me deciding to have a baby by myself.

It had nothing to do with him, I told myself staunchly. J.B. was a friend, and if he wanted to remain my friend, then he'd support me. And while our romantic interludes—that sounds so much better than calling them simple hookups—were definitely enjoyable, it wouldn't happen again because I was giving up men.

No more men—no more dating. J.B. was the last of them, and while it's always nice to go out with a bang, I didn't regret him being the last man I'd be with for a while. At least until after I managed to become a mother. And because I'd decided to use the artificial way to go about it, there wouldn't be a chance of sex getting in the way of anything. Sex always gets in the way of things—especially with J.B.

# Chapter Four

"The expectant mother should attempt to cultivate a constant support system, including family and friends, to allow a reprieve from the demands of the newborn."

*A Young Woman's Guide to the Joy of Impending Motherhood*
Dr. Francine Pascal Reid (1941)

I DIDN'T BOTHER GETTING dressed to go upstairs. But apparently, I'd taken too long because my cat, Sebastian, eventually struggled off the bed to wait by the door leading to the kitchen on the second floor. He likes Coop's breakfasts as much as I do, so to make both of us happy, I headed upstairs. The heavenly smell of coffee mixed with the unholy stench of burnt eggs assaulted me as I opened the door. The smell of the eggs could only mean Emma had again beaten Cooper into the kitchen.

It was a sweet gesture—Emma sneaking out of bed without waking Cooper in the hopes of preparing him breakfast in bed. But even sweet gestures have a downside when the person attempting them is as terrible a cook as Emma. I'm no Nigella Lawson myself, but poor Emma is truly horrible. Like unable to boil water properly horrible. (FYI, she doesn't understand that water boils quicker if you turn it on high and put a lid on the pot. It takes her about forty-five minutes to make pasta because she's afraid to turn up the burner.) It's a good thing Emma hooked up with a chef, or the poor thing would be forced to exist on takeout and salad from a bag. She's so tiny, the girl needs a great many square meals under her belt, or she might fade away to nothing.

"Morning," Cooper said from his position at the stove poaching eggs, which would soon be covered with his most delicious hollandaise sauce for eggs Benedict. I saw the handle of a frying pan already poking out of the sink and the remnants of brown, rubbery-looking egg bits still strewn over the counter.

J.B. was already sitting at the table, with his shirt buttoned but untucked. "Hey," he said casually, just like he does every time we have breakfast together. But when I sat down, he gave me a ghost of a smile.

"Hi," I said, unsure of where to look since all I could picture was the image of J.B. wearing only his red striped boxer shorts and I could still feel his lips against mine. It might have been an enjoyable night, but it's hard keeping secrets!

"How was the wedding?" Emma asked me as she poured coffee into my oversized Piglet mug. I turned to her gratefully. I always thought she looked like an elf. She's very cute with her pixie haircut, doe-like brown eyes, and sweet little heart-shaped face. All she's missing are the pointed ears.

Getting up for breakfast when Emma is over (which is more often than not these days) not only means Cooper will cook, but Emma will play waitress. It's definitely worth waking up for. It's like going for brunch in your jammies and not having to brush your teeth.

"Horrible." It was worth admitting to Emma what happened with Mike so I could stop trying not to look at J.B. I gave Emma a brief recap of the wedding and the discovery of the cheating, and she gave the perfect reaction of disbelief and sympathy. She also put a plate of food in front of me. Nobody makes eggs Benedict like Cooper. He and J.B. are planning to open their own restaurant in January, and I've told them countless times their place should just do brunch. The hours would be better as well. Sebastian was rubbing himself into a frenzied state weaving around my ankles, waiting for me to share breakfast with him. I didn't think he was going to get much this morning.

"Yeah, but you weren't really into him," Coop commented from his position at the stove when I finished telling my sad tale of the wedding.

I often wondered why I never tried crushing on Cooper. Coop is madly in love with Emma, so it's really a moot point, but he's pretty cute. And his shaved head is the perfect shape for baldness. I've been trying to get him to have laser eye surgery forever because his glasses hide the most amazing pair of grey eyes, which are by far his best feature. The grayish-brown soul patch under his chin, however, is his worst. I keep hoping Emma will shave it off one night when he's sleeping.

"That doesn't mean I want him to get off with someone right in front of me!" I protested with a mouthful of eggs. "This is so good," I added.

"I still don't know why you bothered with him," Coop grumbled. "I never thought he was good enough for you."

I guess the main reason Cooper has managed to stay in the just-friends mode is that he looks out for me, sort of protects me, just like an older brother would. And the way he teases me is just as annoying. But it's nice. He's three years older than me, but I don't have an older brother and Cooper lost his little sister to cancer when he was a teenager, so when we met, we sort of clicked into those roles. It was like we both realized we were missing something.

"Definitely not good enough if you found him going down on another chick in the church," J.B. commented. "There are much better places to hook up." He glanced at me, his meaning clear, and I could feel myself blush. J.B. and I definitely do not have a brother-sister relationship, unless you're into icky Flowers in the Attic weirdness.

"You've got to stop it with those guys," Coop instructed, pointing a finger like a disapproving teacher and oblivious to what was going on with J.B. and me. "Can I remind you about some of the more memorable ones? You've had to change your number because of one guy and take out a restraining order because of another. There were a couple who cheated on you, one got arrested, and one got into an accident with you. Need I go on?"

"It's only because we care." Emma smiled sympathetically as she refilled my cup with coffee. "We don't want you to get hurt." She looked pointedly at J. B., which made me think she was aware of everything that went on last night. She may be young, but she's a smart girl.

J.B. snorted. "No, we're sick of you being stupid."

"Thanks." I made a face at him. And there went my image of J.B. clad only in his boxers and any postcoital glow I might have had left.

"Well, I think it's definitely a good thing you gave Mike the boot." Emma gave me another smile, showing all of her pearly white teeth straightened by years of orthodontics. "I hope you're okay?" I nodded, because my mouth was still stuffed with food. "Any new guys on the horizon?" she asked fearfully from beside the stove, where she was holding a plate for Cooper, giving J.B. another glance.

"Nope," I said firmly. "I think it's time to take a pass on men for a while. No dating. No boyfriends. No more dating even if he's fantastic. I'm just going to concentrate on having a baby."

"What? What baby?" J.B. asked in a strangled voice. There were no winks and nudges this time. "I thought you said you didn't, you're not—you're pregnant?"

"No," I told him patiently, thinking he's really not getting this through his thick skull. "There is no possible way I am pregnant right now. Nor have I recently done anything to get pregnant," I said firmly, hoping J.B. didn't let anything slip. "There is no possible way I can be pregnant."

"There's always a possibility," Cooper pointed out. J.B. looked like he was ready to pass out, and I couldn't help but stifle a giggle. My birth control pills plus a condom meant J. B. was pretty safe, but obviously he was still scared. I guess talking about having a baby the morning after you sleep with someone isn't the nicest thing to do. Maybe I shouldn't have kicked him out so quickly.

"Not right now. I've wanted a baby for how long, and I've never once had an oops. Or an almost oops. Or I-think-it-might-be-an-oops-but-really-just-a-false-alarm."

"But you're having a baby?" J.B. was still goggling over this announcement and seemed to have completely lost interest in the food left on his plate.

"I want to," I told him. "I told you that—I've told everybody that. I think it's a good time to have one, but no, I am not pregnant at this time. I'm fairly positive about this, so..." Don't stress yourself out about it, was what I wanted to say, but obviously didn't. Darn Cooper and his not wanting to create tension in the house, or whatever his reason was behind not wanting J.B. and I together.

"But you say no dating, so how...?" Cooper wondered.

"I was thinking anonymous donor insemination," I announced.

Dead silence met my words this time. J.B. was the first one to find his voice.

"Anonymous what?"

"Really?" Emma asked curiously. "Like at a sperm bank? I know someone who did that."

"Casey, you can't be serious?" Coop asked. "C'mon. There's got to be another way."

"Tell me how," I challenged. "Right now that's the only way I see it happening. It may not be my first choice, but unless I have an eager and fertile man drop into my lap with his biological clock already ringing, then..." I shrugged. "You feel like filling a Dixie cup for me?" I had to laugh at the expression on Cooper's face.

"Uh, no, thanks. Really, no."

"Don't even think about asking me," J.B. warned. I noticed he still didn't look very happy about the direction the conversation had headed.

I'd wait until later to explain how I came about my decision and tell him he had nothing to do with it.

"Are you sure there's no ex-boyfriend who might be willing..." Emma's question was drowned out by Cooper and J.B. laughing.

"Don't even go there," Cooper said.

"See? If I want a baby, what other choice do I have?" I looked to each of them to see if one had a great idea popping into their head.

"Sorry," J.B. said rudely. "Have to say it—don't have a baby. Seems pretty easy to me."

"Unlike some, I happen to believe a baby is a good thing. Probably the best thing that could happen to me. The idea of not being a mother has never been an option," I told him earnestly. "And I don't want to wait for someone. I'm not getting any younger. If I have to wait around for the right guy, then who knows how long it will take? I came up with this idea, and it seems pretty good to me."

"But isn't there anyone you could use?" Emma wondered. "A friend, an ex-boyfriend... your brother-in-law? Any good man who would help you out?"

The name David Mason immediately popped into my mind, but I hadn't seen him in years. I met David my first year at university, and we were together four years. While David was the best relationship I'd ever had, hanging the hopes of having a baby on a man I broke up with twelve years ago is too desperate even for me.

"I went through the list early this morning after I had this brain wave," I told Emma instead, "and there's no one I would feel comfortable enough asking. I mean it's one thing to ask for some—you know—but then basically to tell him to get out of my life so I can do it alone? I'd probably end up losing a friend that way."

"And you really want to do it alone?" Cooper asked skeptically.

"Well, no, but what choice do I have? Sure, I'd like the whole fairy tale, but at this point, I really doubt that's going to happen. I'm thirty-five now. Even if I met the right guy tomorrow, I might still be looking at waiting a few years. I don't have time to wait. And this is what I want—a baby. It's what I want to do with my life, and so I'm going to go ahead with it." There was a sudden silence as I scraped the last of the eggs off my plate. "I don't expect any of you to get it," I finished.

"I get it," Emma told me wistfully. A little too wistfully for your average twenty-six-year-old, but before I could mention how she sounded, Coop came to stand beside her.

"Of course, we're here for you," he said firmly. "And we understand why you feel you need to do this."

"I think it's a wonderful idea," Emma said, sounding herself again. "You would make a terrific mother, and you've wanted it for as long as I've known you."

"I've known her a lot longer, and lemme tell you, she never shuts up about it," J. B. grumbled. "Are you sure this isn't like one of your other hobbies?" His smile widened. "Like the knitting thing?"

"That was knitting," I told him scornfully.

"Then what was rock climbing?" Cooper put in with a laugh. The teasing older brother was back. And when both of them get on my back... "Or making your own wine? The basement stank like rotten grapes for weeks. And didn't you want to go back to school and get some degree in Russian history at one point?"

"My favourite was cardio-striptease," J.B. laughed. "You honestly wanted Coop to put in a pole for you!"

"They were hobbies," I told them as sternly as I could, despite J.B. practically rolling on the floor, no doubt picturing my attempt at pole dancing. "I was trying to better myself, exercise my mind and my body. And meet people," I added. Meet men was what I didn't say. I had some success with the rock climbing. Of course, there were no men in the cardio-striptease class, but I did improve my flexibility and my upper body strength during my little sojourn. "I know having a baby is much more serious than that."

"Might be more fun if it was more like the stripper stuff," J.B. muttered.

"And that's why I would never ask you to be the father," I told him snidely. "What do you think?" I asked Cooper. Despite his continual teasing, frequent lecturing, and prying into my personal life, Cooper's opinion mattered a great deal to me.

"Doesn't matter what we say," Cooper shrugged. "If it's important to you, then it's important to us. We'll deal with it."

# Chapter Five

"The second child should be conceived not immediately, as it would place undue stress on the body, but so as to arrive within twenty-two to thirty-eight months of the first. This is to ensure the least amount of resentment and jealousy between the children and for them to feel secure in their place in the household. It is also beneficial to have one of each gender so as to ease any rivalry that may possibly occur."

*A Young Woman's Guide to the Joy of Impending Motherhood*
Dr. Francine Pascal Reid (1941)

T HE IDEA OF JUST going ahead and having a baby by myself was swirling madly in my head and making me so excited that I hadn't had a chance to figure out the logistics. But I would. Even if it meant paying a visit to the friendly neighbourhood sperm bank, which was really not something you ever plan on doing. I mean, I've dreamt of having a baby for years, and in none of those dreams have I ever gone up to the counter and said, "One cup, please, and a turkey baster to go."

That's not how they do it—at least I hope not. I needed to really look into this option if this was how it was going to go down. Maybe it would seem more appealing once I learned a little more. Because really, I couldn't see any other way to do this.

But before I did anything, I went over to my sister's to tell her what I'd decided.

My sister, Libby, has two beautiful children and therefore considers herself to be my superior when it comes to anything related to children. This is despite the fact that I have been a teacher for almost ten years. To Libby, if they didn't come out of my womb, it doesn't matter what I do with them. The main problem about this attitude—other than the annoyance factor—is that it's my younger sister who has this wealth of experience with which she loves to regale me. I should have been the one who got married first, bought a house first, and had babies first, seeing as how I'm two years older. But, of course, things didn't work that way for me.

Libby and I are pretty close considering how often sibling rivalry gets in the way. It's not a big issue, just something we're both aware of. We compete over everything. How many Christmas presents did you get? How old were you when you lost your virginity? How often do you go out partying? With the exception of the third, Libby's had me beat for almost everything our whole lives. It's quite tiring coming in second-best your whole life. If I didn't feel such a huge wave of sisterly love at times, I'd put an end to Libby and I being friends and just do the whole see-you-on-the-holiday thing. But as strange as it sounds, I adore my sister. And her husband, Luke—who is the same age as me, and therefore should have married me—and especially her two kids, Max and Madison.

To me, Libby has the perfect life. It seems I may be a glutton for punishment since I spend so much time with her, but the truth is I'm closer to her than just about anyone. We may have fought constantly as children, but we were always there for each other during the Ed-the-alcoholic father years, and as Mom became Terri-with-an-I and began the rounds with her countless boyfriends. Libby even lived with me for a couple of months between school and marrying Luke.

"You just missed our mother," Libby greeted me sourly as she opened the door.

"I'm devastated," I said sarcastically. "Was she alone?"

"Do you think I'd let one of her boy-toys in my house?"

Libby and I have some issues with our mother.

My mother has spent every day since my father died celebrating being a single, attractive woman. It might be okay if she just decided to celebrate life and being alive by taking cruises with other single fifty-somethings or trying skydiving. Even canoeing down the Amazon would be preferable. But no, my mother decided she likes men more than anything else. To say she's fun-loving is missing the point. My mother, formerly Mrs. Teresa Samms, now Terri-with-an-I, discovered she likes sex. She likes sex in a big way. While the feminist part of me thinks that's always a good thing, the daughter part of me wishes Mom would keep her legs closed. The worst memory of my childhood wasn't the day my father died, but the day six months later when I came home from school early to find Terri entwined in bed with Aaron, the sixteen-year-old boy who cut our grass and whom I had a huge crush on. What can I say? Mom likes them young.

Terri at fifty-three is still a good-looking woman. She had an almost instantaneous transformation from plain Jane Mom to voluptuous cougar when my father kicked the bucket, and for some reason, a great deal of men find cougars attractive. Unfortunately, these men are becoming closer to my age than hers.

Libby refuses to condone our mother's lifestyle and won't take her kids to visit Grandma anymore since there's usually some evidence of this week's "boyfriend" at her townhouse. Like when little Maddy found a vibrator—one of three, Terri confessed with a coquettish smile—underneath a cushion one Christmas morning. Terri didn't even bat a false eyelash.

"What did dear Terri want?" I ask Libby, following her through the house. I left the new set of markers and a board book I brought for Maddy and Max on the kitchen counter and helped myself to an iced tea before heading outside, cringing as I looked around. Libby gives Martha Stewart a run for her money. It's so perfect it's nauseating. Everything matches, from the dishtowels hanging on the oven handle, to the magnets on the fridge holding Madison's artwork, to the Kleenex boxes and the curtains she made herself. I almost sigh with relief when I get outside, but the backyard is just as perfect. Libby describes herself as type A with perfectionist tendencies, but I say she's anal retentive with a vengeance. It's scary how we came from the same mother.

"She said she was in the neighbourhood. She positively reeked of CK One, so I bet she came from a sleepover. Eww. You can tell she was dying to tell me about it, but I didn't ask. I had to give her lunch." Libby sank to her knees on the lush green lawn to weed a patch of white and pink flowers. I think they're called impatiens, but my gardening skills are very limited so I can't be certain. Libby, of course, has five green fingers on both hands, and her gardens are works of art. But at least my knees don't need constant exfoliation from crawling around on the ground like Libby's.

"Well, I'm sorry I missed her." I giggled inside. "Where's Luke?" I asked as I pulled the lawn chair closer to Libby.

"He ran off to Home Depot while Terri was still here." I noticed Libby had the baby monitor clipped on her belt. "We're building a playset for Maddy." Luke is deathly afraid of our mother, which is pretty funny to see. He's such a sweet guy, sort of like a modern-day Luke Skywalker, without the lightsaber and super-cool Jedi powers. You just know he'd stick around to help blow up the Death Star with you. Unless he has to face off against his mother-in-law, and in that case, he's out of there.

I watched as Libby separated the flowers with confident fingers, pulling only the intrusive weeds out of the soil. She and Luke bought the house in Leaside two years ago, doing extensive renovations to create the home they wanted. And, of course, while lots of couples constantly bicker and may even split up over the stress of DIY (do-it-yourself renovations), the experience only brought Luke and Libby closer together. My sister definitely has a charmed life.

"The kids?" I began hesitantly, not knowing exactly how to broach the subject of me providing a cousin for them. It was easier telling Cooper and J.B. With them, I just blurted it out and enjoyed their confusion. With Libby, because she has kids, it's a lot more serious. Plus her opinion holds a little more weight because she's family. "The whole mother thing—that's a good thing, right?"

Libby sat back on her heels and looked at me like I was on crack. "Why?" Her blonde hair was pulled off of her face into a thick ponytail, enhancing her heart-shaped face and sprinkling of freckles. No one who meets us believes we're sisters. Libby is small, blonde, and cute, with a figure that automatically stretches back into shape only weeks after giving birth. On the other hand, I am tall, with real-woman-size hip and chest measurements, which easily expand without constant vigilance.

My best—and worst—feature, depending on how much time I have when I'm getting ready, is my hair. I've been blessed—or cursed—with masses and masses of red curly hair hanging below my shoulders, like that Scottish girl in Brave. And like Julia Roberts in Pretty Woman. Actually, not to brag, but when that movie came out, I heard a fair number of comparisons between myself and the lovely Ms. Roberts. Not that I'm at all beautiful like she is—Julia Roberts is gorgeous, and I'm just me. I may not be Top Model material, but I don't make dogs howl when I walk by. Anyway, there are some similarities—I'm about the same height, and I've got one of those huge, wide mouths with the upper lip a little fuller than the bottom one. I don't think Julia Roberts's face and body are covered with freckles, though. I consider them the bane of my existence.

My most interesting feature, I think, is my eyes. They're perfectly almond-shaped with thick black lashes—uncommon in a redhead—and one is blue and the other is hazel, like one of those Siberian husky dogs.

I guess I'm okay to look at. But I have to admit that I have a set of spectacular breasts. I really think that's why I get all the male attention I do. They look at the chest first and stick around to check out the rest of me.

I stopped comparing myself to Libby since she was still staring at me, waiting for a response. "It's, well, because I want to have a baby," I told her quickly.

"Yes, I know." Libby's tone told me everyone in the known universe must know of my desire to have a baby. "What else is new?"

"What do you think about me having a baby now?" I asked as casually as I could.

"You're pregnant?" she cried loud enough to wake the baby inside the house.

"No! Not yet anyway. But last night I went to this wedding and found Mike hooking up with someone else, and then I got all drunk and came home and started blubbering on J.B. and then ended up having sex with him—"

"Really?" Libby asked gleefully.

"Don't sound so happy. It wasn't my finest moment. But it made me realize that I'm just wasting my life. There's no one out there for me—no one that I would want to have a baby with. And then I thought, what am I waiting for? I'm just getting older, and it's going to get harder to meet decent men because they're all either emotionally warped or divorced or both..."

"And you think you can manage to have a baby by yourself?"

"Thanks to the advancements in science, there are options these days. It makes sense, you know."

"What does? I think you lost me when you said you had sex with J.B. What was that like?" Libby asked, practically drooling for details.

"It was lovely, but don't get me off topic when I'm on a roll. I got thinking about everything last night, and then it just came to me—I'll go and get artificially inseminated and then..." I trailed off when I realized

Libby was looking at me with something akin to horror. "What? It makes sense!"

"Why on earth," she whispered, "would you want to have a baby now?"

"You have a baby," I pointed out. "You have two of them, actually, and you seem pretty happy."

"Yes, but you're not me." Libby yanked out a few blades of grass that dared to invade her flowers with enough vengeance to send nuggets of dirt flying over her shoulder toward me.

"What's that supposed to mean?"

"It means," Libby said heavily, sitting back on her heels, "that you're a single woman."

"So?" So much for thinking it might be a good idea to talk to my sister!

"I mean, Casey, you have so much freedom in your life. You can do whatever you want! You can move to England for a year if you want to, you can sleep-in all day and not worry about feeding everyone and doing the laundry, and you can go out any night and hook up with whomever you want! You've got it all—you're still young and pretty and you're not tied down to anyone."

If I didn't know better, it might have sounded like Libby was somewhat jealous of my life.

"It's not all it's cut out to be," I told her awkwardly. "It's hard, dating and meeting guys, and..." Again, I trailed off.

Now Libby's eyes looked like icy blue slits, and her whole expression resembled one I'd seen our mother make on occasion. Not that I would ever tell Libby that if I hoped to have her speak to me again. "Are you complaining about being independent? About not having to answer to anyone, not being responsible for anything but feeding your cat? Have you seriously thought about how much work is involved in raising a child? And how much it would change your life? Sure, you love them and all, but it's hard work. Seriously hard. And frustrating—so frustrating that you'll find yourself crying in a closet or screaming your head off into a pillow when no one will go to sleep. Not to mention keeping a marriage going with two kids. And you think you can manage on your own?"

"I think I can. I see you—"

"You don't see anything!" Libby burst out. "You don't see me getting up five times in the night and still have to be bright-eyed at 7:00 a.m. to get ready for work. You don't know how expensive kids' clothes are; you don't know what it's like to buy new shoes every other month! You've never had to discipline your own child, and you don't know how it breaks your heart when you make them cry because they've done something bad! You have no idea what it's like to be totally and absolutely responsible for not only the well-being of a child, but their entire life—if they get hurt, get sick, anything horrible that may happen to them! You just swarm in and spoil them and think you know what it's like to raise kids. Well, you don't, not until you have to go through twenty hours of labour and then, that's just the beginning! You think it's another hobby, something you want now, but wait six months from now, and you're all fat and miserable, or two years from now when you've got a toddler screaming at the top of her lungs in Toys R Us."

Libby went back to pulling out weeds. I didn't say anything until I saw her pull out a pink flower by accident.

"So you're not happy with being a mother?" I asked cautiously.

"Of course, I am," Libby barked. "How can you say such a thing?"

"Well, from the sound of it..."

"I love my kids," my sister said firmly. "I love my life, but I need you to know that it's not a bed of roses all the time. It's hard and it's frustrating, and sometimes it just saps the energy out of you."

"But it's worth it?"

"Of course it is," Libby sighed.

"Well, then, why are you trying to scare me off?" I cried. "You know it's what I've always wanted. I've been ready for years, spending all this time trying to get the right guy, and you know what? I'm sick of it! Sick of dates and having to be all cute and likable and listen to guys drone on and on about what super studs they are in the bedroom and the boardroom, when all I want to do is find someone who likes the same things as I do and will take me to a stupid movie or dinner at a place I like. And then get me pregnant."

"Just like that, you think? It's no wonder they all run screaming when you mention the word."

"They don't go screaming," I argued. "Well, maybe some, but others are long gone before I even think of them as a father."

"I have to tell you, Casey," Libby continued as if I hadn't spoken, "after having a baby, your body never

goes back the way it was."

"You are just trying to scare me."

"I'm trying to make sure you know what you're doing," Libby corrected, speaking as though I were no older than Maddy. "If you're going to go have a kid, I don't want you to go off half-cocked and then start yelling at me that I never told you anything. So I'm telling you—your vagina will never be the same. Sex will never be the same. Jumping up and down on a trampoline will never be the same, because you'll be too afraid of accidentally peeing yourself because you didn't do enough Kegel exercises while you were pregnant and you'll be freaked out you're going to be incontinent when you're old."

"Oh." What was I supposed to say to that? "Really?"

"I haven't even started on the labour yet, let alone what it really feels like to grow to the size of a small humpback whale."

"So you don't think it's a good idea?" I prompted. As much as Libby and I argue and get on each other's nerves, there's not a lot we won't support each other with.

"I think you're nuts," Libby said reluctantly, pulling out a weed with a little too much vehemence and spraying dirt over her smooth tanned legs. "But it might be nice for Maddy and Max to have a cousin to play with."

"What do you think of the insemination thing?" I asked.

"I'm not keen on having a niece or nephew and not knowing who the father is."

"It's not about you, Lib, you know," I told her quietly. "It's not my first choice, but what other options do I have?"

Libby looked seriously at me. "Isn't there someone you know who could donate and then step back and let you take over? What about one of your friends? An ex-boyfriend?"

"It's funny. Emma asked the same thing and all I could think of was David Mason."

"Oh," she said wistfully. "I remember him. I liked him. You were really stupid back then."

"Thanks. It's always nice to be reminded."

"Well, you were. So, is there anyone else you could get to do it?"

"Most of them are already involved with someone, and it seems strange to ask. It sort of crosses the line of friendship, you know? I thought it all through, and I don't see any other way."

"Well, there's always the not having a baby right now option," Libby reminded me, echoing J.B.

"That's what J.B. said," I told her. "But I don't think that's an option right now."

"You've made up your mind then?" Libby asked, crawling along on her knees to another part of the flower bed. No wonder her knees need serious help. "About this donor stuff?"

"Pretty much. Unless you have a better idea."

"I don't," she sighed. "So go for it, I guess. But don't say I didn't warn you."

# CHAPTER SIX

"The expectant young mother should cherish every engagement with her friends, since the arrival of the baby will drastically change those relationships, perhaps beyond repair."

*A Young Woman's Guide to the Joy of Impending Motherhood*
Dr. Francine Pascal Reid (1941)

EVERY MONDAY NIGHT, I meet my two best girlfriends for drinks or dinner or a movie. We've done it for years, and it's a way we can make sure to stay connected with each other. A girl needs her friends. Despite the not-so-positive reactions I was getting, I was still looking forward to running my idea of having a baby past them.

"I can't believe I found the perfect shoes for my wedding dress!" Brit shrieked as we settled in at one of the high round tables surrounding the bar. Tonight we were meeting for drinks at an upscale martini bar close to Brit's office, and it was already quite crowded. I'm sure the adjoining tables were just as excited hearing about Brit's shoe purchase as I was.

Brit and I have been friends since grade nine, when we realized that discussing painful menstrual cramps in a loud voice could get us out of participating in Mr. McDonald's gym class. Unfortunately for Brit, her last name is Spears. She dropped the "ney" in 1999, when the "imposter," as Brit still calls her, became famous. The two of us have both weathered some storms over the years—Brit's parents' divorce, my mother's lifestyle, living in different cities during university, and a disastrous attempt at being roommates after graduation—but the thing that's always remained constant in our lives is our friendship. Brit at thirty-five may be a totally different person than she was at fifteen and we might not see eye to eye about everything like we used to, but she's still my best friend and we do have a ton of history together.

I also know that underneath all the me-me-me talk, my old friend Brit is still there somewhere. She'll return someday. It's like how I keep hoping someone will make a sequel to The Wedding Singer.

I think Brit, more than anyone, will understand my desire to have a baby since she shares an equal obsession with getting married. She's been doodling hearts and Mrs. So-and-So in her notebooks since she was twelve. Her little fixation extended out of high school, into and past university, and well into her thirties. Like me wanting to find the perfect guy for baby-making, every time Brit dates a new guy, she's mentally measuring him for the dove-grey morning coat and keeps slipping in comments over drinks about how "Wind Beneath My Wings" is her favourite song. I'm sure it's pretty frightening for a guy only looking to get laid.

Lucky for Brit, she finally met Tom Smith, who fully indulges her obsession. He good-naturedly tolerates her five-foot-high stack of Today's Bride magazines and even sits through endless sessions with Brit's three scrapbooks filled with wedding ideas. And to top it off, he even proposed last year. I guess he is perfect for her since every other candidate turned tail and ran when confronted with the scrapbooks. They're getting married Labour Day weekend.

"...five-inch heels, which I know will make my feet ache by the end of the night, but they look so sexy; and you know, Tom is a good six inches taller than me so we'll be a little more equal. Just think how good we'll look standing together saying our vows! It'll be perfect!"

"You didn't tell her the best part," Morgan interrupted eagerly.

I met Morgan during my first year at university. When we met, Morgan was quiet, a little shy, and a bit overwhelmed moving into the city from the small town where she grew up. Plus she'd never had a serious boyfriend. Not that I was some urbane sophisticate, but at least I was familiar with Toronto, having grown up in the west end. Morgan and I lived across the hall from each other in residence, and since we both loved eighties' music, watched Beverly Hills 90210, and drank Long Island Iced Tea, our friendship was inevitable and instantaneous.

Like all of us, Morgan has gone through a few changes over the years. This gorgeously groomed woman sitting across from me is a far cry from the shy nineteen-year-old with the outdated haircut and the denim overalls she wore practically every day. Now, Morgan is almost clapping her hands with excitement over a pair of shoes. Did I mention the effect Brit has had on Morgan over the years?

To start with, the clothes. I used to be into shopping as much as the two of them—which was the main reason I got into debt so deeply—but while I finally managed to learn to control myself, Morgan was borderline out-of-control. Sure, both Morgan and Brit have way better incomes than I do, but wasn't buying a thirteen-hundred-dollar suit from Holt Renfrew just because you like the colour of the lapels on the jacket a bit much? Tonight, Morgan had on the exact outfit I saw in this month's InStyle, the one they called the "academic look"—even the fake glasses and the silver earrings she had to order online. Last month, we had to scour the city for every piece of the weekend-on-a-boat look.

"I know, I know—they're Manolo Blahniks! Can you imagine?" Brit was still shrieking. "I know I paid too much, but I had to. They're perfect. I love them. The straps are cream leather, but the heel—the heel! —is the best part. They're blue! A beautiful periwinkle blue, and I think I'll match the ribbon of my garter to them. How perfect is that? I've never felt so much love toward one thing—no, not even Tom, but don't tell him that!" she laughed.

You'd never know it from listening to her talk, but Brit's a CFO for a midsize accounting firm downtown. She loves her career and has a huge amount of responsibility offset by an even bigger salary, but can easily sound like a 'tween gushing about High School Musical.

"Perfect," I told her between sips of my martini. I couldn't help but wonder if I'd get a chance to even mention the baby thing tonight. Brit seemed to be on a roll.

"They are simply beautiful!" Morgan assured me. "Super expensive, but so worth it. I really hope I can find a pair to go with my dress when it's my turn."

To think that only yesterday I was listening to my sister rant about the expense of children's shoes. It was almost like I'd jumped into an alternate reality with these two.

"Of course, you will," Brit promised. "I'll help you look." She smiled reassuringly at Morgan. "And I'm sure it will be any day now that Anil pops the question."

Morgan has been with Anil for six years now. They share a house together, and Morgan has been impatiently waiting for Anil to ask her to marry him so that she can acquire the status of "being engaged" and all the benefits and privileges that go with it. Having watched Brit stress herself out needlessly for the past eighteen months trying to plan the perfect wedding, I saw no benefits or privileges of "being engaged."

"How is Anil?" I asked politely. I don't think Anil is amazing. He's okay but wouldn't be my first choice for a husband. Morgan loves him for some reason, so therefore I tolerate him for her sake and keep my true feelings to myself like the good friend I am.

"He's been working so much lately," she complained. "He's never home."

"He's working to pay for the huge rock he's going to get for you—just wait," Brit told her before turning to me. "You look good tonight. Have you lost weight?"

"Not that I know of," I said with surprise. I tucked a stray curl behind my ear. Brit may have morphed into one of the most self-absorbed people I know, but when she deigns to pay attention to you, it's like the sunrise breaking over the mountains. She's got that type of personality, which is probably why I put up with her selfishness. When Brit is nice, she's very, very nice. Plus there's the whole being-friends-for-twenty-years thing.

Brit gave me an approving nod. "I think you must have. You can help me. I've got to lose three and a half pounds before the wedding, or my dress will not zip up." And then she was off again.

"Yes, the wedding I went to on the weekend was fine," I said into a pause a little later when it didn't appear either Brit or Morgan were about to ask me anything about my weekend. I knew I'd be able to grab their attention with the word wedding.

"Oh, that's right, Ethan and Darcy got married. Was it nice?" Morgan asked. Brit sniffed not so delicately, and then when I didn't comment on her sniff, she sniffed again. See, Brit is good friends with Ethan's ex-girlfriend Denise, which is how I met him. We hit it off right away—Ethan and me, not Denise, whom I really couldn't stand, although I never told Brit that—and when Denise walked out on him, I didn't shun him like Brit, but kept in touch. Then he met Darcy. Darcy and I clicked right away—obviously since I was one of her bridesmaids. I don't think Brit likes it when I have a friendship that doesn't include her. She can be a bit possessive. It's sort of like having a small dog that growls when anyone walks by.

"The wedding itself was lovely, but Mike and I broke up," I said offhandedly.

"What?" Brit shrieked loudly. "Oh, Casey, not again! Breaking up is so drastic, don't you think? Are you sure that was the right thing to do? Mike isn't perfect—no man but Tom is, really—but let's face it, Casey, he is your best chance of getting a ring on your finger before you're thirty-six."

I believe I've mentioned Brit's obsession with getting married. Well, it also includes Morgan, me, and the rest of the single world.

"Mike is the very last person I want to marry," I told them empathically. "I'd rather take on Charlie Sheen with his porn and prostitute predilection than marry a man even remotely like Mike."

"You can be honest with us," Brit said. "You must be miserable."

"Did you break up before or after you slept with him?" Morgan asked sadly. "I don't know what would be worse."

"It was before. He found someone at the church." Even though Morgan knew of my plans for Mike and I told her about the little scene I interrupted in the coatroom, for some reason I didn't disclose what happened later with J.B. Morgan, like my sister, thinks J.B. is terrific and hot and would want too many details.

"What an ass!" Brit declared. "Did you at least get in a good swift kick when you caught him?"

"Tempted to, but no. I decided he wasn't worth the effort. Plus I was wearing heels, and you know how shaky my balance is when I have them on."

"Good for you," Morgan said loyally. "If that's what he's like, then you're better off without him. There's plenty more fish in the sea."

"Actually, I think my fishing days might be coming to an end," I told them. "The way I look at it, it's a good thing this happened, because it's finally made me wake up and realize there's no reason I need to be waiting around for a man. I'm just going to have a baby by myself."

"A baby what?" Morgan asked in an odd voice, sounding as unacademic as she possibly could despite the outfit.

"A baby baby. You know, goo-goo, gaa-gaa. A baby—remember, what I've always wanted?" Morgan and Brit were staring at me like I'd just announced the colour magenta was the new wedding white.

"You're pregnant?" Brit gasped in horror.

"No. No! Not yet, anyway. I just want to have a baby. I'm thinking, now's the time to just get with it and do it by myself."

"Yourself?" Brit repeated. "You've always had this crazy idea you need to have a baby, but by yourself? You need a husband or at least a suitable, committed boyfriend for that, so he can marry you after you lose the baby weight." She shook her head disdainfully, her blonde waves falling perfectly back into place. "Be serious, Casey." She tapped a manicured nail against her martini glass. This week's colour was plum, which matched her eye shadow quite well. The one time I went for a manicure with Brit, I almost lunged across the table at the girl when she tried to push down my cuticles. It wouldn't hurt, she informed me rather prissily, if I had learned proper grooming techniques, especially for my nail beds. I never knew nails had a bed. Needless to say, I didn't leave a tip.

"I don't understand," Morgan said dumbly. She kept adjusting her fake glasses like she wanted to take them off but was afraid of spoiling the look she was going for, the successful-woman-who-reads-Homer-in-the-original-Greek look. It was a stretch since the only Greek Morgan knows is opa! She looks better without the glasses. "Why would you want that? And who would the father be?"

"Well, that's the issue here," I confessed. "I think the only option I'm left with is to go with artificial insemination, but I'm still not too keen on that. I was wondering if either of you might have any ideas?"

"Don't have a baby," Brit told me bluntly, echoing J.B.'s words and tone exactly. It was probably the first time the two of them had ever agreed on anything, but I doubted either of them would find the humour in that. "Besides, I don't think this is the best time for that. You are going to be pretty busy for the next couple of months, you know."

"I am?" School was ending at the end of the month, and July and August were normally the most relaxing time for a teacher. I couldn't remember planning anything that might keep me too busy for conceiving a child.

"My wedding!" Brit shrieked, loud enough for several tables to glance over at us. "How could you forget that?"

"I have no idea," I told her sarcastically, which was lost on her. I saw Morgan lean back from the table, distancing herself from this conversation. Morgan and I might be closer these days, but Brit and I had more history than The History of the Decline and Fall of the Roman Empire.

"I don't either," Brit said staunchly. "I would think that might be forefront in your mind these days. Best friend getting married. Living lifelong dream."

"Exactly. Which is why I thought you of all people might take an interest in this. Having a baby has been my lifelong dream, if you remember."

"Yes, but it's not fair to have a baby to compensate for the lack of a man in your life," Brit lectures. "Get another cat if you're lonely. A baby can't compensate for lack of sex, you know."

"I do know that," I said with exasperation. "One has nothing to do with the other."

"Well, they kind of do," Morgan cut in, trying to lighten the mood. "Normally you have sex in order to have a baby, and from what I've heard, once you have a baby, you don't get to have much sex."

"I'm not trying to compensate for anything," I said angrily to Brit, ignoring Morgan's efforts. "That's a mean thing to say. I'm perfectly happy without a man. I'm not lonely. How can you say that? I'm never lonely—I'm always busy and…"

"I'm not trying to be mean," Brit said. But she couldn't look me in the eye, and she took a tiny sip of her pomegranate martini. One thing about Brit—like it or not—is that she's always honest. I don't think she's ever learned how to pull her punches. And while it's helpful to have her around to tell me truthfully if my bum looks too big in a pair of pants, I'd rather do without any frank assessment of whether I am lonely or not.

Morgan cleared her throat. "Is this a sure thing?"

"Well, no, since I'm not pregnant. But I hope to be soon."

"And this is how you want to do it? Are you sure?"

"Of course not!" Brit exclaimed before I could answer Morgan. "That's just crazy, post-breakup, desperate talk. If she's going to do this—which I have to repeat, is not a good idea—at least get a proper man for the job. Who knows what you'd end up with if you go to some clinic?" The utter disdain in Brit's voice made me smile. It was exactly the same tone of voice that she used when I once told her I bought a pair of sandals at Payless.

"I'm sure they screen the men properly. I doubt too many serial killers manage to get through," I told her.

"Isn't there anyone ...?" Morgan continued. "Cooper, or your brother-in-law, or ...?"

Brit gave an impatient sigh. "If you're looking for the right man to get you pregnant, then obviously you should have Tom do it."

I glanced at Morgan, who was wearing the same expression of amazement as I was, before I answered Brit. "Do you know exactly what you're proposing?" I asked slowly. "You're suggesting I have a baby with your husband-to-be?"

"Well, it wouldn't be his baby," Brit scorned.

"Uh—yes, it would!"

"It sort of would, Brit," Morgan echoed.

"Oh." Brit was silent for a moment. Caught up in her pride and smugness in landing such a fine specimen of a man, she obviously didn't think this through. "I'm just saying that Tom would be the perfect choice if I were willing to allow him to father another woman's baby. That's all."

"And if Tom were okay with the whole situation," Morgan put in with a tiny smile.

"Why wouldn't he be?" Brit asked seriously. "If I asked him, then that would mean I thought it was fine, so why wouldn't he?"

"I'm going to forget you suggested it," I told Brit, once again taken aback at Brit's utter conviction that the universe revolved around her. "But now, can you see why I'm considering insemination?"

"I say you hold off for as long as you can," Morgan told me. "It's not that we don't think you'd be a great mother, but I don't know why you'd want to do it yourself. It just seems like an awful lot of work. I think you should wait a bit more. There's still time. You could meet someone tomorrow, you know?"

"The thought just makes me so tired."

Morgan patted my hand. "It seems a shame that we're both so happy," she indicated her and Brit, "and you haven't been able to find someone. I always think it was a shame things didn't work out with you and David."

"Who?" Brit demanded.

"I was just thinking about him the other day," I admitted slowly, remembering my conversation Sunday morning with Cooper and Emma.

"Who are you talking about?" Brit repeated, her voice increasing in volume like it always does when she thinks she's being ignored.

"David Mason. Don't you remember?" Morgan asked her. "When Casey and I were in university, she went out with David. He was so cute," she swooned nostalgically. "And nice and…"

"He was perfect," I admitted ruefully.

"Didn't you break up with him when we went to Europe?" Brit asked, interrupting my inner reminiscing about the very best boyfriend I ever had. So what if I was only nineteen when we met? We had four wonderful years together until graduation.

I nodded. "Stupid move on my part."

"Not at all," Brit argued. "We had a great time in Europe without him. And if he was so important, he should have waited around for you."

I really don't think Brit understands the concept of breaking up with someone. Or else she has a slew of ex-boyfriends waiting in the wings in the hope that she might change her mind. Considering how truly gorgeous she's turned out, it might actually be possible, if they forget about certain aspects of her personality, which is actually possible to do when she's having a nice day. It also explains how I'm still best friends with her.

"See? There is someone out there for you," Morgan assured me enthusiastically. "And he would be perfect to have a baby with. Now you just have to wait until David pops back into your life. Maybe he'll show up at your school tomorrow, picking up his kid... well, maybe not his kid, because that would mean he has kids and possibly a wife, which wouldn't really help, but maybe someone else's kids! Maybe ..."

I couldn't help laughing at Morgan's animation. "I don't think I'll hold my breath. If I wait for that, I'm sure my eggs will all dry out, and I'll never have a baby. But it's a nice fantasy."

# CHAPTER SEVEN

"When a woman is in her childbearing years, her ovulation cycle must undoubtedly be taken into consideration when engaging in sexual intercourse."

*A Young Woman's Guide to the Joy of Impending Motherhood*
Dr. Francine Pascal Reid (1941)

AFTER I DROPPED MY not-so-dramatic bombshell on Brit and Morgan, the conversation inevitably returned to Brit's upcoming wedding until she left to meet Tom. Morgan and I stayed for another drink, and our conversation returned to the university years we spent together and David.

While Morgan might not have the amount of fond memories I have, there was a distinct note of affection in her tone when she talked about my former boyfriend, which isn't surprising, since she had once been interested in him herself. But it was surprising that Morgan would bring up David's name when I myself had been thinking about him. Strange. I guess that shows why we're such good friends.

When I got home some time later, J.B.'s motorcycle was parked right by the side door as I pulled into the driveway. There's room in the driveway for three vehicles if one is J.B.'s bike and we snuggle in together. Snuggling a car often results in me giving whoever parks in front of me a tiny tap, and as a result, my license plate now has a slight bend to the bottom. Today, it was only the bike I had to worry about, so I was okay.

I bypassed my apartment and headed right up to Cooper and J. B's place with the hope that there might be some food around.

The smell of garlic, ginger, and sesame oil filled the kitchen, mingling well with the sounds of Green Day from J.B.'s iPod. Cooper has created an amazing kitchen. It was the first room he renovated when he inherited the house from his grandparents. Three weeks after he got the place, the rest of the house was still looking like a reject from the seventies, with green and brown shiny wallpaper and matching carpet, but Coop's kitchen was already immaculate. It's all stainless steel appliances and frosted glass cabinets and granite counters. I know he paid a fortune for it, but even I—the only non-cook in the house—think it's worth it. The only thing marring the perfection is the kitchen table. It's one of those old turquoise Formica tables speckled with silver—truly ugly. But he wanted to keep something of his grandparents around, and the table was it. So now the table stays put in the kitchen, making the room look like a page from a what-doesn't-belong-in-this-picture book.

J.B. was in the kitchen with the counter full of vegetables, a cutting board, and a couple of Cooper's super-sharp knives, which I am afraid to use. J.B.'s not nearly as good a cook as Coop is, but he's pretty good. But then, anyone is better than I am. Usually, I can arrange a fair trade of me doing J.B.'s laundry for him feeding me. Cooper, on the other hand, feeds me out of the goodness of his heart.

"You're home early," J.B. said. "Thought you had your little hen parties on Mondays," He looked like he just got home from a soccer game or the gym, wearing baggy shorts and a faded grey T-shirt with his longish brown hair pulled back into a tiny ponytail. He's got lovely calves. An image of J.B. standing by my bed in just his boxers flashed through my mind again, and I closed my eyes, hoping it would go away.

"Brit had to meet Tom, so we just had a couple of drinks." I pulled open the refrigerator looking for a bottle of wine. "What're you making?"

"Spicy pork stir-fry. I've got a big pile of dirty clothes upstairs waiting for your spray and wash," he tempted me.

I could hear faint scratching at the door leading down to my floor and opened it to find Sebastian. He, of course, ignored me and immediately began to swarm J.B.'s ankles. J.B.'s hands were full, but he gave the cat a good scratching with his big toe. Such a multitasker.

"As long as there's no smelly hockey clothes, that's a fair deal. Is it just you home, or have you got some anorexic chickie stashed upstairs?" I poured myself a glass of wine and watched him julienne a pile of vegetables, his hands and the shiny, sharp knife moving intricately together. I tried to avoid watching J.B. caress my cat with his bare feet, because J.B.'s feet are fairly funny-looking. At least some part of his body is. No one should be that perfect all over. "Or is she coming over later?"

"I'll have you know..." J. B. began before he noticed the teasing expression on my face. "What gives with all the interest in my sex life, anyway?"

"What's with the interest in mine?" I countered.

"Only when I'm part of it, which isn't very often to begin with and apparently not going to happen again, especially if you're looking for a specimen cup to get you knocked up. You pregnant yet?" J.B. asked over the music as he chopped.

"Yep. It's called Immaculate Conception, and in all recorded history, it's only happened once, thousands of years ago. I should make the history books, don't you think?"

"Smart-ass. Speaking of which, I'd really like to give you a kick for dropping that little bombshell about wanting to have this baby right after we...you know. That's not a nice thing to do to a guy, you know? Makes a guy really think twice about a repeat performance, you know?"

"I'll give you some warning next time, okay?" I smiled at him.

"Ah, but I thought you said there wasn't going to be a next time."

"I did," I agreed, trying to keep the regret out of my voice. "Sorry."

"You'd be sorry if I wasn't tightly bagged the other night." J.B. gave a bark of laughter.

J.B. and I have been friends for years—good friends, I think—and have slept together three times, so I guess that makes us lovers. Occasional lovers. But never had we ever talked about the fact we've been intimate like we were now, casually and comfortably, sort of like an old married couple discussing a romp in the bed they both enjoyed. I kind of liked it, but then I started feeling guilty for liking it so I tried to stop thinking about it.

"So what gives? Did I somehow make you feel all maternal or something?" he continued in a curious voice. He turned toward me, leaning against the counter. "Can't say I meant to."

"It wasn't anything about you," I assured him. "It was—it just happened. Something that won't happen again."

"What—the sex or the wanting-to-have-a-baby part?"

"I always think about the baby part. I've wanted to be a mother since I was a kid, which is surprising considering my less-than-stellar role model. The sex—it happened, it's over, and it's not going to happen again."

"So you've said." J.B. gave me his slow smile, which had the effect of making the tiny twinge of regret blow up into a big balloon. He continued to scratch Sebastian with his ugly toe, and I concentrated on his unattractive body part. I also started singing the Kelly Clarkson song "I Do Not Hook Up" in my head. It would be so easy to fall into something with J.B. But the problem with that is that I'm not looking for something and I know he wasn't. So what would be the point? It's easier just to keep my distance—emotionally and physically.

"Whatever. I just woke up Sunday morning feeling all sorry for myself—"

"Feeling sorry for yourself? After sex with me? Can't say I've heard that one before. Thanks."

I had to laugh at his annoyed expression. "I said it wasn't anything about you. You were—fine."

"Fine? I'm telling you, Casey, you do wonders for a guy's ego."

I laughed again. "I don't think you need any help from me with your ego department. I'm sure there's a huge lineup if you're looking for gushing compliments." I sat down at the table. "I was feeling sorry for myself because of Mike and came to the conclusion that I've been wasting all this time trying to meet the right man so I can start a family. I'm not getting any younger—"

"No, you're not," J.B. said, which I'm sure was in response to my fine comment.

"Hey, I'm only thirty-five. You're what—almost forty, and—"

"Eh, eh, eh," J.B. interrupted, pointing his knife at me. "We don't say the F-word around here."

"Thirty-eight," I relented. "I was thinking that if someone doesn't come along soon, I'm going to have to settle for someone like Mike to have a baby." J.B. turned his head, but not before I caught sight of him wincing. "So why not do it alone? I think I'll be better off in the long run: I'll have my baby and not have to deal with some slimy, cheating bastard trying to break my heart."

"Not all guys are slimy or cheating, you know."

"I know. You're not. But then, you don't want a baby or any sort of commitment, so that leaves you off the list." J.B. grimaced again, and I laughed nervously. "Don't tell me you want to be on my list."

"You wouldn't know what to do with me if I was."

Oh, yes, I would, I found myself thinking to myself.

"You know it won't be easy," J.B. was saying, turning back to his pile of vegetables. "You have your teacher's salary, you live here—"

"I have two salaries, and you live here, too," I retorted.

"I have no desire to have a baby," he reminded me.

"Is that ever, or just for now?" I couldn't help but wonder.

J.B. shrugged his shoulders without turning back to me. "I don't know. Things are pretty okay the way they are. I like keeping things casual, especially with the restaurant opening next year. And I don't have anyone knocking down the door trying to get me to be a father, which makes it easier."

"Maybe because you never keep them around long enough so they can find out what a good guy you are. A little big in the ego department, but still okay," I teased. "Don't you have a biological clock or anything? Ticktock, ticktock?"

"That's a female thing. Guys aren't that stupid."

"Charming." I shook my head and began to go through the pile of mail sitting on the table. Magazines, flyers, bills, more bills, an envelope that looked suspiciously like a wedding invitation. "You've got a card here," I told J.B., holding it up. "Paris Flats, Saskatchewan? Isn't that where you're from?" J.B. snorted and ignored the card. "Don't you want to open it? Isn't it from your family?"

"What's the date today?"

"June 7."

"It's from my ex-wife. She sends one every year," J.B. told me casually.

"But—why? It's not your birthday, that was in April, wasn't it?"

"It's the anniversary of the divorce." I know about J.B.'s divorce, even though it took him two years to tell me. He doesn't talk about it. The only thing I know is he married young, just a few years out of school, to the proverbial high school sweetheart. Happily ever after for a while, and then bad stuff and splitsville. J.B. went to Calgary and then Toronto, met Cooper, and the rest is history. I really don't know much about J.B.'s early years.

"It's the—how long ago did you get divorced? And she sends you cards? Who does that? And what does it say? Yippee skippee? Thanks a lot, you big jerk?" I wondered with amazement.

"Open it if you want," J.B. said.

"I can't do that!"

"Go ahead. I know what it says." J.B. put down his knife and leaned against the counter. "'Dear J.B., I can't believe it's been twelve years since we agreed to go our separate ways. I still have fond memories of our life together and hope you will somehow be able to forgive me for my actions. I still love you,'" he recited. "Sometimes she gives me details of her life, like when she got married again or had her kids. Or sometimes just gossip about what's going on at home. Go ahead; read it. I don't care," he finished carelessly.

I waited for a moment to make sure he really didn't mind, then carefully ripped open the lavender envelope. The card had a big bouquet of flowers on the front. "Thinking of you," it said. "Pretty card," I commented.

"She's big into cards. Sends me one every birthday, Christmas... Groundhog Day if she could," he said, turning back to his vegetables. I heard the sizzle as he slid them into the hot frying pan.

With a last glance at J.B., I opened the card. He was right—the sentiment written was almost exactly word for word what he had said.

"What did I tell you? Anything interesting?"

I scanned the words. "She says you're hard to forget. And—oh. There's a bit about her—her son," I faltered. "Do you want to read that yourself?"

"Go ahead, Case," J.B. said quietly. "It doesn't bother me. I'd probably just throw it out."

"Well, she says that she can't believe her son will be starting high school in September, and she can still remember her first day and meeting you and how she fell in love with you... Oh. Maybe I shouldn't be reading this," I said quickly. I tried to hand the card to J.B., but he just shook his head.

"It's okay. It's the same every year. She misses me, will always love me..." J. B's words were casual, but the catch in his voice was telling me different. "She named her kid Jeremy," he told me.

"After you?" I asked, shocked. Quickly I did the math. "If he's starting high school, then he'll be thirteen or so, and if you've been divorced for twelve..." I looked, horrified, at J.B. "It's not yours, is it?"

He shook his head. "No. He's the reason that we broke up. The final reason, actually. I think she named him after me for some sort of appeasement or something. To make me feel better. It's—complicated. Messy. And she still sends me a card every year."

I can't see the reasoning for a woman to send a thinking-of-you card to her ex-husband twelve years after they divorced unless she was still in love with him and trying desperately to get back into his life. Not even I would pull a stunt like that. "Do you—?" I wondered aloud.

"Dinner's ready." And with that, J.B. firmly shut the door to any further discussion about his past.

Of course it practically drove me crazy—both the not knowing and J. B.'s unwillingness to answer any of my questions. I tried—really I did, but the sixth time I attempted to bring the conversation back around to his marriage, J.B. bluntly told me he didn't want to talk about it. Which, of course, made me suspect that he's still in love with the ex-wife but can't forgive her for her actions. What actions? Obviously, something to do with her having a thirteen-year-old son and only being divorced for twelve years. I watched J.B. eat his meal, as attractive but as inscrutable as always. To say he doesn't like to talk about his feelings is an understatement. I'm surprised I got this much out of him.

Is this why he goes through women like he does—keeping them around for a night or two and then discarding them with a smile? It's not like he doesn't tell them upfront—everyone who knows J.B. knows he's not into anything serious and long-term means a long weekend. I've seen women chase him relentlessly, convinced they are the one who can change him and be the one he ultimately settles down with, but up to now, no one has come close.

"Are you happy?" I blurted out as I played with the final two peppers on my plate. Instead of answering, J.B. took his empty plate to the sink. "J.B.?"

"About what? Being divorced?" he retorted with his back toward me.

"About everything."

I watched as his shoulders rose. "I miss having someone to love," he said so quietly I barely heard him.

"You—do?" My voice cracked at the word. "But you—you never want a relationship?"

"I haven't met a woman I can trust," he admitted, turning to face me. "I'm sure it's because of the divorce, but I'm not into all that psychobabble. I don't need to be fixed. All I want is to meet a nice girl and get to know her slowly. There's always so much pressure, and it's so much worse now that I'm older. They always want to talk about marriage and babies and a future. I just want to take my time. There's no hurry, but women always think you're distant and noncommittal when you want to take it slow, and there's no point in explaining to them because they start jumping to conclusions..."

"I had no idea," was the only thing I could say.

"Why would you? Sorry, Case, but you want the same thing as everyone else. Get married, have a baby... do you even want to take the time to get to know someone? I knew her like the back of my hand, and it still didn't work out. I'm not going through that again. If I ever find someone to settle down with—if, a really big if—I need to make sure she's the right one this time." He turned back to the sink before I could respond.

"What about me?" I asked through a suddenly dry mouth. I had to ask. The memory of being with J.B. was strong—sitting across from him, having dinner, our first date. The first time he kissed me after he brought me home, and we laughed because we had the same address. When he showed up unexpectedly at the store one afternoon, bringing me a tiny, perfect cherry cheesecake because I had told him it was my favourite dessert.

"What about you?" he replied with some hesitation as he turned slowly to look at me. "I knew what you wanted before we even hooked up, so there was really no point. I didn't want marriage and a baby right away, but I thought... anyway, it's a moot point, isn't it? You backed away quick enough when Coop said something."

"What if I hadn't? What if I—I don't know. What if I had told him to go to hell?"

J.B. smiled then, but it didn't reach his eyes. "He's your best friend, same as me. You wouldn't have told him that. Besides, Case, you wanted the same things as every other woman seems to and you weren't willing to wait for some guy to catch up. You would have gotten sick of the pace in a few weeks. A month, tops, and then put the pressure on me to do something about it, which I wouldn't have been ready to do. Never would have worked out."

"Never worked out..." I trailed off, feeling dazed. Is that how J.B. sees me? Lumps me together with every other woman who's marriage-crazy like Brit? How different am I from Brit after all? That's all I was ever looking for—a good man to get me pregnant. I really didn't care about any other factor, only that I got what I wanted.

"What does it matter?" J.B. asked. "It was a long time ago. Maybe it's better this way. Meant to be."

I couldn't ask him if he really thought that. I was having a difficult time taking in the information I'd just received. I didn't think I could take any more. To think I had backed off so easily because I was afraid of J.B. breaking my heart when all the time he had been thinking the exact same thing. What if...?

I really couldn't go there tonight.

"So that's why I like the ladies." His voice brought me back to the kitchen. "There's no harm in meeting people. It's the only way I'll find someone who might be right for me."

"Someone who wants to take it slow. Not rush into anything."

"Where there's no pressure. Someone who doesn't care how old she is, or that all her friends are married or having kids, and who can't hear that damn biological clock all the time." He took a step to where I was still sitting at the table and dropped a kiss on the top of my head. "And that's not you, Case, as much as I wanted it to be."

"Is that my problem?" I asked him after a long silence where I found my eyes filling with tears. J.B. had started loading the dishwasher. "Too much pressure?"

"For some. For others, it's just because they're assholes. You're a great girl and you know what you want, and when a guy doesn't want the same thing, he's going to get the hell out of there."

And that was the end of that discussion.

I told him good-night and thanked him for dinner. I headed downstairs to my apartment. I decided to see what I could find out about artificial insemination. If a baby were the only thing that would make me happy, then this was my only option, and I'd better find out what I was in for. Unfortunately, I couldn't seem to concentrate and ended up downloading a bunch of songs from iTunes and clearing out my inbox.

Maybe I do put too much pressure on myself and the men I meet, but I want a baby. And while I was thrown by what sounded like J.B. expressing feelings for me that I had no idea he had, I can't dwell on that. J.B. Bergen and I would not have worked out, and there's not going to be a second chance because both of us realize that.

I just have to take that big feeling of regret, stick it somewhere, and get on with things.

# CHAPTER EIGHT

"The sight of other babies will undoubtedly bring about maternal urges in the expectant mother, along with excitement and possibly panic."

A Young Woman's Guide to the Joy of Impending Motherhood
Dr. Francine Pascal Reid (1941)

B RIT WAS RIGHT ABOUT one thing: during the next few weeks, I was too busy to do more than think about having a baby.

I've been teaching for over ten years, but when I decided to switch to kindergarten from grade three about four years ago, I could only find a morning class to teach. This unfortunately corresponded with my determination to get my credit card debt under control. So now I was teaching my little four- and five-year-olds in the morning at a nearby school, and in the afternoons and some evenings, I was the assistant manager at a wine boutique downtown. It's interesting keeping the two jobs straight—ABC's, 123's, and runny noses in the morning, and pushing bottles of full-bodied chardonnay in the afternoons—but so far it's worked out pretty well. I'll have everything paid off within the next few months, but I'll keep both jobs until I can find a full-time kindergarten class.

There was a lot to do at the end of June, and I was constantly filled with the usual bittersweet emotions I have at the end of another school year. All my little five-year-olds would be heading into grade one come September, and I could only hope that what I'd taught them would make that transition an easier one. I was sad to see the end of June roll around—although it's great to have two months' vacation from teaching—and have to watch all my little birds fly away from the nest of kindergarten.

But I got through it, like I do every year. This year the whole two-month vacation had kind of lost its meaning since I'd still be working at the store for the summer, with some extra shifts thrown in. But it did take my mind off the whole baby-making thing, which was good since I'd decided I needed to wait until my period came so I could start figuring out my cycle. I bought one of those ovulation kits, but I hadn't opened it yet. I also made an appointment with my doctor for the first week of July so I could make sure the clock was ticking correctly. And then it would be off to the sperm bank, unless, of course, Morgan was right and the perfect man walked right through that door and was prepared to sweep me off my feet. Unfortunately, the more time that passed by, the more I suspected it would take a serious amount of sweeping to get me off my feet.

Being so busy made it easy to stop thinking about J.B. Not that there was anything to think about, but after our talk in the kitchen, I couldn't help regretting how things had worked out. And I felt kind of bad about it too, sort of guilty, without knowing why. I finally managed to give myself a good talking-to, about how there's no point in regretting because there's nothing to regret; chances are it wouldn't have worked out between us anyway. There's nothing to do but get on with my life, which was exactly what I was doing before J. B. said anything. If I kept dwelling on it, it was going to affect my friendship with him, which was the last thing I wanted. Nothing had changed; we're friends and that's it.

As much as I wanted it to be.

But I couldn't get what J.B. said out of my mind.

In any event, it was two weeks before anything exciting happened, but when it did, it sure was a kicker. And it also managed to take my mind off my "sort of" roommate.

The end of school fell on Wednesday this year, and the next day I spent the morning clearing the classroom. For the next few weeks, I kept my usual schedule at the wine shop—which is Tuesdays, Wednesdays, and Fridays from two to six, and then on Thursdays, I go in at one o'clock until nine. I don't mind working two jobs. I mean, I love teaching—people tell me I was born to be a teacher—but going from full-time to part-time was a bit of a strain financially.

I haven't minded working two jobs, but having the summer off from school will make it easier to get to work on time in the afternoon. Like today. I spent too much time in the classroom, and then in the staff room, finding out about everyone's summer plans, so I was pushed for time when I finally got to the subway, leaving no opportunity for lunch. Usually, I take the subway down to the store in the afternoon. It's at Church and Wellington and the parking down there is nonexistent, so transit is the better way.

Almost falling down the escalator to get to the train before the doors slid closed, I managed to swing into an almost empty car. Unfortunately, the day was a hot one, and the car was not air-conditioned. I could smell the residue of sweat and even more unpleasant body odors still lingering. I quickly considered hopping out and trying another one, but then the train began to move. And I noticed the cute guy seated by the door. If I had to be trapped in the hot and smelly car, I might as well have something nice to look at.

I took a seat across from him. He was tall, blond, and built, sort of youngish and reading Harry Potter. Aha. Cute, intelligent (he reads), imaginative (he reads Harry Potter), and very cute.

As if he could read my thoughts, the guy looked up and smiled. I gave him my most cheerful smile. (I find it difficult to do sexy. I make more of an ass of myself, so I just focus on being friendly and cheerful.) "Which one are you reading?" I gestured at his book.

"Goblet of Fire."

"I like that one."

"It's pretty good."

"Have you read the last one?"

"I'm trying to read the others first."

Of course, the thoughts racing through my mind had nothing to do with Harry Potter. All I could think of was that this guy might very well make a good father for my baby.

I must be desperate. Also, borderline obsessed and possibly insane if I'm looking at every male in sight as a potential father. This perfectly cute, seemingly nice man was sitting here having a conversation with me about Harry Potter, and all I could think of was getting into his pants. Literally.

The train suddenly screeched to a stop in the middle of the dark tunnel and knocked me off balance. I think it must have knocked some sense into me as well. I laughed uneasily as I pulled myself upright.

"Someone's not paying attention."

"Nope." He looked down at his book, still open on his lap, with the bookmark sticking out. I'm losing him. He wants to go back to his reading. But the bookmark—I like people who use bookmarks rather than fold down the page. "Normally you don't see men reading Harry Potter. Not that there's anything wrong with men reading Harry Potter..." I trailed off. What was I saying? "Not that there's anything wrong with it," I said stupidly.

"My girlfriend got me into them," he explained. Ah, the mention of the girlfriend. A kiss-off if I ever heard one. I smiled ruefully. There was no response to that.

The train pulled into a station, and a woman got on pushing a stroller and all but collapsed in a seat beside me. I smiled at the mother. At least I thought she was the mother. She looked old enough to be a grandmother, or possibly the nanny.

"How old is your baby?" I asked. At the sight of a baby, I lost all interest in the cute guy. I felt like telling her I wanted to have a baby, but that would make me look like some weirdo. Not that I didn't already look like a weirdo—for some reason, I enjoy talking to people on the subway. For most transit travelers, the rule is no eye contact, and shoes are checked out a lot, as well as the ads on the walls. But I find it nice to smile and wish a good day to my fellow passengers, especially if it's not too busy. Just one of my quirks, I guess.

"Three months," the woman said. She looked exhausted and bedraggled, and there was a stain on her shirt that might be baby spit-up. I thought she might be pretty if she lost fifteen pounds and covered up the horrible dark circles under her eyes. Was this what was in store for me? Would I look as bad as this? I'd never be able to talk to cute guys on the subway again.

I took a quick peek into the stroller. It was one of those where the baby lies down, so I couldn't see much, only the corner of a pink and purple blanket. "What's her name?"

"His," she corrected abruptly. "Hector."

"Oh. Sorry." I see pink; I assume girl. I gestured to the stroller. "May I?"

"What?" Now she looked irritated.

"Just have a look."

"Oh." She leaned back in the seat and closed her eyes. "Go ahead."

I fixed a smile on my face as I rose and peered into the stroller. Cute, girly blanket, stuffed elephant shoved beside him, little sweet face... "Ah!"

"What?" The mother was on her feet.

"No, no, sorry. It's just..." That was the ugliest baby I'd ever had the misfortune of laying eyes on! But you can't tell a mother that. She'd probably try to push me off the subway platform for saying such a thing. "Ah-dorable," I said with such false enthusiasm I was almost yelling.

My Harry Potter cutie looked up with a frown, and the woman scowled at me. "Please don't wake him up."

"No, no, of course—sorry."

After that, I stayed huddled in my seat. I was sure my cheeks were as red as my hair since they felt warm to the touch. I'm glad I never mentioned I was thinking of having a baby, or the mother might have cursed me with ugly baby syndrome or something. What happens if I have an ugly child? Will I still love it? I'm sure all these offers of help would dry right up if the baby came out being green or something. I'm sure Elphaba's parents (from Wicked, of course—such a good show!) were avoided like the plague when she came out looking a little funny and green. Everyone is always worried about having a healthy baby. Is it totally shallow and selfish to want your child to be good-looking as well?

But I was getting way ahead of myself. I shouldn't be concerned with having an ugly baby before I've figured out exactly how to conceive one on my own. And how am I supposed to do that? I've got to hit a sperm bank unless I can find a nice man to loan me some sperm. I wondered what Harry Potter-reader would say if I suddenly asked him. Hey, there, my name's Casey, and I'd really appreciate it if you filled this cup for me since you're so cute and I like the fact you can read! Don't worry, once I've got what I want, I'll never bother you again.

Sure. He'd hit that emergency bar and hop off the train so fast, probably with both hands protecting his family jewels as he ran screaming toward the nearest exit.

When the subway hit my stop, I slid off as inconspicuously as possible. The mother was sitting with her eyes closed, and the cute guy had gone back to his book without giving the weird woman who talks to strangers in the subway another thought.

It's a short walk from the subway to my store. When I got there, I found Hannah, who also works part-time, looking strained at how busy the store was. The afternoons are usually fairly quiet, but this weekend was Gay Pride Weekend and the wine store was located smack-dab in the centre of the alternative lifestyle district.

The afternoon flew by until Hannah left at seven. I let her go a few minutes early so that she could bring me back something to eat, and during a short lull in customers, I sat hunched on a box of wine behind the cash register eating my falafel as fast as I could. It's not my first choice of food and it always gives me heartburn, but beggars can't be choosers, can they? I was concentrating on not dropping sauce on my shirt, so that when the bell on the door dinged, I didn't look up with my usual welcoming smile until I heard voices.

"I see a head over there—is that my favourite wine goddess?" trilled a male voice. An effeminate voice, but male nonetheless.

I glanced over the counter. "Hi, Cory." Cory is one of my favourite customers. He's big and black and beautiful and very, very gay. "Let me just finish here..." I swallowed one last bite and stood up. Then I almost choked when I saw who had just walked into the store behind Cory.

How the hell did Morgan know this was going to happen?

# CHAPTER NINE

"Heartburn is a common ailment during pregnancy."

*A Young Woman's Guide to the Joy of Impending Motherhood*
Dr. Francine Pascal Reid (1941)

"FUCK A DUCK," I breathed.

"Well, I've never tried that," Cory simpered, "but if you insist, I'll give it a go."

"Casey? Casey Samms?" asked the man standing beside Cory. The man I was staring at with an expression of amazement, disbelief, and complete shock.

"How..." I couldn't even finish the thought.

"Oh, my God!" David Mason exclaimed. "Is it really you?"

Cory's bald head swiveled between me and his friend. "Do you two know each other? Did I do a good thing?"

"David?" I whispered. "Is that really you, or is this some sort of weird falafel-inspired daydream? I knew I shouldn't have eaten it so fast because now I'm going to get the worst heartburn in the history of the burning of the heart if the heart really can burn from eating a falafel." I noticed Cory looking at me with a strange expression, but David had a look of amusement and—could it be? —affection mixed with surprise on his still-handsome-but-now-with-some-wrinkles-in-the-corner-of-his-eyes face. It made me feel warm all over. "Sorry. Babbling."

"You always did that." David smiled wistfully I hoped it was a wistful smile!

"Oh, how fun!" Cory clapped his hands with a deafening smack. "You do know each other! Let's have a reunion!"

"I can't believe this," David said, shaking his head. "How long has it been?"

I shook my head as if I were mimicking him. "I don't know."

Before I could start firing off questions, a woman entered the store and came straight to me to ask a question. I had to yank my eyes away from David to help her, which was hard because all I cared about right now was drinking him in.

I last laid eyes on David Mason twelve years ago, when I told him in no uncertain terms I planned on traveling to Europe that summer unencumbered by any sort of involvement. Those were pretty much the exact words I used as well. I ended the healthiest, longest relationship I've yet to have with a thirty-second speech two hours before my plane was due to take off. To say it wasn't the smartest move is like saying we Canadians are well on our way to becoming Americanized by today's culture—you can argue how much, but there's no doubt that it was a dumb move. Especially considering how I'd spent every day of my twenty-three years planning on having a baby, and when I finally had in my sights a great guy who had his eyes set on a future with me, ending things for two months of freedom wasn't my best move.

"This... wow!" I finally said after I'd sent the woman on her way with three bottles of Chardonnay. "How, how are you?"

"A wine store?" David asked with confusion. By this time, he and Cory had set bottles on the counter, waiting for me to ring up their purchases.

But I didn't want them to go—well, Cory could leave, but not David. "I thought you were going to be a teacher?"

"Oh, I am. I teach kindergarten, but only part-time. I used to teach grade three.... Long story," I trailed off. "Yesterday was the last day of school," I added unnecessarily.

"So how do you know each other?" Cory interrupted bossily. He marched up to the counter and leaned against it, ready for the dirty details.

"We, actually..." David was stammering now.

"University," was the only thing I could say.

"Were you boyfriend and girlfriend?" Cory exclaimed, clapping his hands again. "Oh, how sweet!"

David and I glanced at each other, both with silly grins on our faces.

This couldn't be possible. There was no way that David could have just strolled into the store unannounced, unexpected, and even more unbelievably, so soon after Morgan and I had a conversation about him. Then of course, since the filter in my head that normally stops me from blurting out things didn't seem to be working right now, I said just as much to David.

"I really can't see how this can be happening," I said in amazement. "Because if you're really here standing in front of me, then that means Morgan is some sort of psychic, which she is definitely not because how on earth could she predict that it would be you walking in here today? Not that she said today, and not that she said it would be you either, since how..." I trailed off again when I noticed both men were looking at me like I'd grown an extra head. I clearly had an issue with verbal diarrhea today.

"Are you okay, hon?" Cory asked with concern. "Is this too much of a shock for you?"

"It is a bit of a shock," I admitted weakly. I gave David a glance under my eyelashes, but he was looking delighted now.

"Morgan!" he said. "How is she?"

I gave him a quick rundown on Morgan, and then myself after he asked what I'd been up to. Cory finally started wandering around the store again, collecting a variety of bottles as David and I talked. As I talked actually—David didn't offer much except an endless supply of questions.

"So you know Cory?" I finally asked. It's not what I wanted to ask, but I figured if I started probing with the are you married, any kids, want to get back together queries, I might just send him running for the door. Besides, I'd been surreptitiously checking for any sign of a wedding ring, and I'm happy to report there was no sign of one, not even a tan line. Of course, that didn't mean anything since some men choose not to wear them, but it did produce a fluttering in my stomach to think David was still single.

It's been twelve years since we broke up, and I'm a different person now. There's no way I would even consider getting back together with him, even if he wanted to, which I'm positive he doesn't. For sure I don't. What's done is done. I've gotten past my regret of losing David, of missing him so much my heart literally ached and I would bring up his name in any conversation with mutual friends, desperate for any tidbit about his life. Having David step back into my life is just a momentary blast from the past, a poignant memory come to life, a—

Bullshit!

Who was I trying to kid? Inside, my heart felt like it was bouncing around on one of those jumpy castles the school rents for the spring fair, and I couldn't stop smiling.

"We work together," David told me. "I'm over at City Hall."

"But didn't you move to Vancouver? I heard something about that."

"I did," he said with an amused smile. "I moved there after... I came home about six months ago."

"Oh. Oh! That's, that's nice. Um." Frantically I searched my head for a nonthreatening question to ask. I noticed there was a line waiting impatiently behind David.

"Look, Casey, I'd love to stay and catch up with you, but there's probably going to be a bunch of legs crossed at my place if I don't get home. I have dogs," he explained. "I have to get home to let them out."

"Oh. Dogs. That's nice." I knew my face fell when he said that, but I couldn't help it. Did I have to sound so lame? This was worse than the subway this afternoon. Then I focused on David, because like the sun moving from behind the clouds, what he was saying took away the dismal grey in my life.

"You look pretty busy here, too." He stepped to the side so that I could ring up the next person in line.

"Uh, a little." I swiped the customer's Visa card and gave it back without checking the signature.

"I'd love to get together," I could hear David say, although it was a little hard to believe. "If you'd like to meet and catch up and all that good stuff, that is."

"I would! I really would! That would be good—great. Everything's good tonight," I said embarrassedly. I could feel my face flush. "Thank you, enjoy the wine," I told the customer happily as she left.

"Well, that's good," David said in a bemused voice. "Look, I'm busy tomorrow, but how about Saturday night?"

"Or Saturday during the day?" I eagerly suggested and then kicked myself. Saturday night would be like a date while getting together during the day said let's just keep it casual—but I didn't want to wait any longer than I had to. "I mean, if you're not busy? I don't have any plans, and I thought it might be good—"

"That would be great. Why don't you come down to my place and..." His place!

"I live down by the beach, and we could go for a walk, grab some lunch, and hang out for a bit. Sound good?"

"Sounds wonderful," I told him with stars in my eyes. I was officially a loser, and now a whole line of customers knew it because they were all listening with rapt attention. Most of them were grinning now, including Cory, who brought up the end of the line, three people away.

"Great. Give me your number, and I'll text you the address." After which I apologized to the next customer in line and rang up David's wine. Then he gave me a big smile and said he'd see me Saturday about eleven. Then he was gone, vanishing as quickly from my sight as he popped into it. In fact, if it wasn't for Cory standing in front of me with four bottles of merlot and a gleeful expression, I might have thought I dreamed the whole thing.

"Well, that was fun!" Cory said loudly from the end of the line. "Fancy seeing each other after so long like that."

"Old boyfriend?" asked an older woman in front of him, just a little too eagerly.

"How could you tell?"

"Oh, you can totally tell," said a thin guy who wasn't much more than twenty. When he smiled, the ring in his eyebrow stuck out. "You're all flustered and smiley."

"She can't stop smiling," the older woman said with a smile of her own.

"She's glowing," Cory announced.

"Well, now I'm just embarrassed," I told them as I felt the colour mount on my cheeks. But I couldn't seem to get the smile off my face for the rest of the night, despite the wicked heartburn I ended up getting from that falafel.

# Chapter Ten

"Friendships will undoubtedly change at the onset of a pregnancy. Mothers-to-be will be preoccupied with the changes in their body and the impact a child will have on their future. They will have less inclination to deal with the petty problems of their friends."

*A Young Woman's Guide to the Joy of Impending Motherhood*
Dr. Francine Pascal Reid (1941)

I DID REALIZE IT was horribly pathetic to hold a candle for someone this long, but especially pathetic when you hadn't had any contact with him for years. The big question was, why was I still hung up on David Mason? Because ever since he walked into the store Thursday night, he was all I could think about.

In my defense, I don't consider that I've been holding the candle for him for the entire twelve years. I had a bad time of it when I came back from Europe, but I got over that in a couple of months. And except for the odd Google or Facebook search for him in the last year or so, I haven't given much thought to David.

Until I was canvassing my list of past loves, of course, searching for someone who might be a good fit for the daddy-and-dump role I needed to be filled. I hit on David—a quick hit, not a dwell—because we had a decent, stable relationship. But when Morgan brought him up out of the blue, with no idea he had also been on my mind, of course, I started thinking about him a little more, especially now that I'm given to analyzing every man I see for a possible sperm donor. And then David just showed up at the store, like some weird vision. Just seeing David made all my old, forgotten feelings fall into a perfect line before me, and I realized that, yes, it can be said that I've been hung up on him since we broke up. Pathetically so.

I fell in love with David when I was nineteen years old. At least I'm pretty sure I was in love with him, but the ease with which I surrendered the four-year relationship to go gallivanting off to Europe with Brit left many wondering. In my defense, though, Brit and I had this trip planned since we were sixteen. And it was an amazing trip. We were twenty-two—it was the summer after we graduated with our bachelor's degrees, me from the University of Toronto and Brit from Queens. Both of us were headed back to school in September—me for my bachelor's of education and Brit for her master's of business (I later completed my master's, just so you know)—but both of us felt we needed one last summer of fun before entering the real world.

Brit and I started off with one of those Contiki tours, the ones where you see seven countries in twenty days, drink copious amounts of alcohol, and get little or no sleep. And, oh yes, have sex with as many people as you can. Well, in Brit's case anyway. I'm sure not all the tours are like that, but I just happened to see it from Brit's point of attack. I think her final total for the tour was four, and I think she threw in a couple more when we were in Italy before we headed home. This, of course, from the girl who had only ever had sex with one person before we landed on foreign shores and who was on the cusp of becoming her now-gorgeous self. Brit traded away her relative lack of experience (not that there's anything wrong with experience or relative lack of it) with a vengeance on that trip. Not to sound condescending, but two of the four guys she slept with on the tour had just gotten out of the Navy and were trying to get as much action as they could.

I, on the other hand, stuck with quality rather than quantity and spent half the trip sharing the bed of our tour manager, a hunky Australian named Butch. There are much more interesting stories to tell about my travels with Brit other than our sexual escapades, but this isn't the time to get into it. I'll finish with how we ended up in Greece three months after setting off from London, seeing a lot more of Europe than we had planned.

But back to David, since that's what got me started down memory lane. When I got back from Europe, with every intention of throwing myself at David's mercy and begging him for another chance, I found he was gone. Moved-to-Vancouver gone. I don't know what it is about the western shores of this country, but they do attract a lot of single Torontonians. Anyway, David was gone and I was on my way to Kingston to finish my education, so it wasn't like I could go chasing after him. I thought about it for a while but decided against it. So that ended the history of David and Casey.

Was the trip to Europe worth sacrificing David? I have to say—absolutely. I did miss him, but I didn't have to be miserable about it and I did enjoy my freedom. Did I regret breaking up with him? Again—absolutely.

That was twelve years ago. Since then, I've heard the odd tidbit about him from mutual friends, and when Facebook came out, I took the opportunity to check for him a couple of times. And I've Googled him a few times, but it's not like I was stalking him or anything. And that's about it. I don't think I've been doing the whole holding-of-the-candle thing. It was just such a shock to see him after so long. And it was nice that he wasn't bitter or anything about me ending things. And it was exciting that he wanted to catch up with me as much as I wanted to catch up with him.

More than anything, David had transformed from my first serious, non-high school boyfriend into an almost mystical symbol of the best boyfriend ever. I know things weren't perfect between us (early twenties, still in university—when is a relationship at that time in your life perfect?), but I do remember it as pretty good. I'm sure I've romanticized it, but really, who can blame me with my disastrous stream of boyfriends? Thinking about David made me realize it might just be possible for me to find love.

All this went through my head on Friday, so I was a bit of a basket case by the time I got home—anticipation and nerves were creating havoc in my stomach. After work, I met up with some friends I've known from university, and I had the hardest time not announcing to all that I had a date with David for the next day. Or was it a date? I was meeting him at his house, which could mean David considers his home to be a nonthreatening, neutral place; he wants me to meet his wife or girlfriend or whoever he's sort of involved with—or he wants me to meet his dog. I have to say, I'm hoping for the dog, unless he wants me at his home to be closer to his bedroom so there won't be a logistics problem if he decides to seduce me then and there. That, of course, is my favourite option, and I know it's the least plausible.

You've probably noticed that I've conveniently forgotten that I'm giving up on dating and men. I've decided to justify my excitement by vowing to give up on new men. David, being part of my past, obviously doesn't fit into that category, and therefore it's all right for me to go on a date with him, if a date is what he has planned. Besides, the guy just walked back into my life—or at least my wine store—after twelve years; it's not fair to take that away from me!

I had just gotten home and settled into the couch upstairs to watch Letterman when Cooper and Emma came home.

"Hey," I called out. Emma followed Coop into the living room. "You're home early."

"It was pretty slow tonight. Nice weekend, everyone heads to the cottage." Coop sank into the chair opposite me. Before he could say anything else, the sound of my cell phone sitting on the table started ringing and interrupted. Sebastian had been curled up on a magazine on the table and jumped off like a shot. Cooper handed me the phone with a glance at the call display.

"One of your hen friends," he said.

"No one appreciates being referred to as poultry, thankyouverymuch." It was Morgan, and I could barely understand her through hysterical crying.

"Morgan, what is it? Did something happen? Are you okay?"

"It's Anil," Morgan finally managed to choke out.

"Oh my God, is he okay?" I sat up straight on the couch with my hand on my chest. "Was he in an accident?"

"He should have been. I wish he were dead! He broke up with me!" Morgan wailed so loudly I was sure Cooper, sitting across the room from me, could hear her. "He told me he didn't see a future with me! Now, I'll never get married! I was with Anil for six years, and now all I have is six wasted years. That bastard, that fucking bastard! You know, he knows, everyone knows I'm expecting a ring from him! I put so much time and effort into this relationship, and then the asshole goes and says he doesn't see a future with me. What kind of bullshit is that? I can see a future—you can see a future. Everyone can see a motherfucking future! How does that fucking bastard not come to that same conclusion? Six years—I'm thirty-five years old, for Chrissakes! The asshole is supposed to marry me! He needs to marry me!"

"Everything okay?" asked a concerned Emma from across the room. I was sure she could hear every word. I rolled my eyes at her and nodded. Then I gave them both a wave and walked down the stairs to my apartment without turning on the light. This was going to take a while.

"What am I supposed to tell people? It's so humiliating!" Morgan screeched so loudly into my ear, I stumbled down the last stair, which is about an inch higher than the others and always trips me when I go down in the dark. I practically fell into the door of my apartment.

"Oh shit," I mumbled.

"I know!" Morgan wailed. "It's such a shitty thing to do!"

"What exactly did he say?" I asked patiently, having regained my footing. I switched on the kitchen light so I didn't impale myself on something. My question started her off, and Morgan proceeded to go into gory detail about what Anil told her, what room this all took place in, what they had for dinner earlier, and even that he was wearing the Ralph Lauren sweater she gave him last year for their anniversary. I only had to say a few "uh huhs," murmur "wow" once or twice, and wish I had thought to bring my glass of wine downstairs with me.

Note to self: stop drinking whenever I get pregnant. I wonder if I drink too much. Probably. It's hard to be interested in wine and not drink it. I distracted myself with that thought for a few minutes.

"Maybe he'll change his mind?" I thought to suggest when Morgan took a breath.

"Huh! You think I'll be taking that bastard back after this? I told him, you walk out that door, you asshole, you won't ever be walking back in. And the son of a bitch left! He actually left!" I never realized Morgan was capable of so much profanity. "The prick never loved me. And after all the sex I gave him. He just couldn't get enough of me, and I never said no, not tonight. I was always into it. But no, the asshole's lost that for good. No more of this body curled around him to keep him happy at night!" I could almost see her snap the C, like in some Beyonce video.

Just as I was about to say something congratulatory for Morgan being so strong, her voice took a drastic switch. "What am I supposed to do now?" she all but whispered. "Look at how old I am. Thirty-five is old, no matter how much they say forty is the new thirty. I'm going to be forty in less than five years, and I won't even have a husband! I'll never be able to get married! I'll never have children." She broke down into noisy sobs.

I might have mentioned how firmly ensconced Morgan is to Brit's "Let's Get Married School of Worship." I wonder if I'm an anomaly—a woman in her mid-thirties not getting an ulcer because she's not married. Maybe if I wasn't so concerned with the baby thing, I might be. Then again, I might not.

"I don't know what to say," I admitted when the sobs abated. And I really didn't. Normally I'm the one doing the breaking up, and I'm usually not too upset about it. There's no need for words of comfort from the girls at the end of my relationships. Usually, it's high-fives and a drink to celebrate.

"You have to help me find someone new," Morgan instructed, really doing a Sybil with all of her mood swings. I guess grief does that. She'd gone through the whole denial, anger, and acceptance of life without Anil pretty darn quick. "You have to help me find someone so much better than Anil. I have to make the prick see what he's missing."

"Um, okay?"

"I have to find someone before Brit's wedding. There's no way I'm going by myself to that."

I probably will be, I felt like telling her.

"I'll call tomorrow, and we can begin to strategize. You know where to meet all the men. I don't care if I find an asshole either, as long as he looks good. I'm going for purely superficial here. He's just going to be a rebound guy, so it doesn't matter. And if he gives good head, more the better. Anil always ..."

I heard another sobfest coming, and I braced for it. With the choice of crying or intimate details of their sex life, I think I'll take the crying. I love Morgan to bits, but there is a limit to friendship. I still remember the time I had an adjoining hotel room to Morgan's when we were in Florida on vacation and received firsthand knowledge—through a very thin wall—of exactly what she likes in bed. What she likes, how much she likes, and where she likes it.

"Anyway," Morgan said after a ragged breath, "I have the worst headache. Damn Anil-the-fucking-bastard for making me cry. I'm going to go put some Preparation H on my eyes and take enough Vicodin to pass out. Talk to you tomorrow." Click.

I went back upstairs to retrieve my glass of wine, and I was not surprised to see Cooper cuddled on the couch with Emma, with Sebastian snuggled in between them, both of them petting him. I think my cat loves everyone more than me. He never lets me cuddle him. I'm just there to provide nourishment and a clean litter box.

I'm also not surprised that one of them—Coop, probably—has drunk my wine while I was listening to Morgan rant in all of her potty-mouthed glory.

"Do you know why someone would put hemorrhoid cream on their eyes?" I asked Coop and Emma.

"For puffiness," Emma promptly replied.

"Does everyone know that but me?"

"I don't want to know that," Cooper said emphatically, rolling his tired-looking eyes. "Was that a Brit or Morgan crisis?"

"Morgan. Anil broke up with her, and she's a little pissed. They were together six years, and she really expected them to get married soon."

"And now she's got to start over with someone new," Emma said sympathetically. "I'd be pissed too."

I never looked at it that way, mainly because I'm usually the one starting over with every guy I meet and I'm used to it by now.

"You going to bed right away?" Coop asked me.

I didn't bother to conceal the yawn that cracked my face. "I would have been fast asleep if Morgan hadn't called. What's up?" Cooper shot a guilty glance at Emma, and I could tell what was coming. "If Emma moves in, are you kicking me out?" I asked before he could say anything. "That's what this is all about, isn't it?"

Emma's laugh seemed relieved. "It's a big house," she told me. Emma has gone pink, an endearing trait of hers, which makes her look even more adorable. If I was ever thinking of being into girls, I'm sure Emma would be my type. Of course, I'd never tell her that and should probably not even be thinking it, but whatever.

Coop still looked guilty. "I guess J.B. got to you first. Sorry. Anyway, yes, Emma is going to be moving in, and no, I'm not kicking you out. That's your place downstairs, and really, the way our three schedules are, I don't think one more person living here will make much difference to you."

"Well, congratulations. I think it's great. I take it you're not kicking J.B. out either?"

"No," Emma smiled at me. "Do you want him too?"

"Well, sometimes..." I wheedled.

Emma shook her head. "I really think the two of you should get your stuff together. I think you'd be perfect," she said.

Cooper gave a choking cough.

"I don't think so," I said seriously. "Where is he tonight?"

Normally, Cooper and J.B. (and usually Emma lately) would come home together since the restaurant and J.B.'s nightclub are only a short walk away. Emma used to work at J.B.'s club, but J.B. got her a job as a waitress at Coop's and the rest is history. She also does quite a bit of acting—in local theatres and once as part of the chorus in Mama Mia. She's pretty good, but not quite up to making-it-in-the-big-time standard, but I think she came to terms with that a while ago.

"Still hard at work?" I added, already guessing the answer. Not that it bothers me or anything. J.B. can sleep with whomever he wants. It doesn't matter that last Saturday night he was in my bed, and now, less than a week later, he may be... not that it's any of my business.

"Well, no." Cooper looked embarrassed. "I think he offered to give someone a ride home."

That stung a little, even though there was no reason for it to. I looked pointedly at Emma. "Not that it's any of my business. But that's why it would never work with me and him. He likes the ladies too much."

"So did Cooper," she noted.

"Yes, but Coop was fairly easy to domesticate. Getting J.B. to settle down would be like trying to teach a cat to pee in the toilet."

"Thanks," Coop said wryly. He gave a great yawn and made a move as if to get off the couch. "You coming up?" he asked Emma.

"In a minute. I want to ask Casey what's going on with the baby thing. Did you give it some more thought?"

This was strange. I narrowed my eyes quizzically at Emma. "Yes, but why..." Why are you so interested? was what I didn't say since that would be rude.

Emma gave me a sad smile and looked sideways at Cooper. "I can't have babies," she told me in a soft voice.

"Oh, Emma. I didn't know. And I kept going on about it ..." Suddenly I felt horribly guilty being so selfish and so obsessed with it, when all the while... "How?"

"I found out about five years ago. A case of HPV left untreated..." She looked resigned. "Apparently I should be a poster girl for getting regular Pap tests."

"Oh, Em, I'm so sorry." I leaned over Cooper and gave her a hug. "I'll never talk about having a baby again."

"It's okay," she assured me. "I've had a while to get used to it. And you know who was great to talk to? J.B."

"The one who lives here?" I asked stupidly.

"The very same," Emma said with a smile. "When he was married, I guess his wife lost a few babies." She glanced at Cooper for confirmation.

"She had two miscarriages."

"That's why he's so against having kids," I breathed.

"Probably," Emma agreed. "It would be so horrible to go through anything like that and I feel so bad he had to, but he was great with me.

And Cooper. I've come to terms with it, and there are other ways to have a baby, you know."

"If I didn't want my own so much, I'd be a surrogate for you!" I offered, still feeling bad for her.

"Someday we might take you up on that," Coop said. This must be hard on him as well. Amazingly enough, Cooper has a fifteen-year-old son, whom he never gets to see. There was a lot of bad blood between him and the mother and her family when Dominic was born. I think they live in Montreal now. I'm sure he wanted to rectify things by having a baby with Emma someday.

"Another reason I think you should have a baby," Emma explained. "If you could get yours out of the way, then you could have one for us." She said it with a laugh, but there was a note of seriousness to her suggestion.

"You'd really want me to do that?" I was flabbergasted. And very, very touched.

"There's nobody else we'd even think about asking," Coop told me in a gruff tone.

"Really? Awww..." I leaned toward them and engulfed Cooper and part of Emma in another hug.

"Well, don't get too excited," Coop hastened. "It's not for a while yet. I think I'd like to be married first. Not that I'm asking yet, so don't get any idea," he said quickly to Emma.

"But seriously, Casey, I don't think you should wait," Emma told me earnestly. "Five years ago I could have had a baby, but now... things change, and I think you should just go for it. What's that expression—seize the day?"

"Carpe Diem," Coop told her. "Haven't you ever seen Dead Poets' Society?" At Emma's head shake, Coop smacked his forehead. "I keep forgetting you're just a baby."

"I'm twenty-six. That's not a baby. It's only thirteen years difference. It just seems like more because you keep bringing up movies that you know I've never seen and making me watch them on that old VCR."

Thirteen years. I was still with David thirteen years ago. I tuned out Coop and Emma's mock-fight and thought back to thirteen years ago. I was in my last year at U of T; David had already casually mentioned getting an apartment together when I finished school. I hadn't begun to start planning the trip with Brit.

If I could go back thirteen years ago and do it over again, I wonder what my life would be like.

# CHAPTER ELEVEN

"Expectant mothers should avoid as much stress as possible. Even women attempting to conceive should do their best to keep calm, cool, and collected at all times, and not worry. There will be enough stress and worrying with the arrival of a baby."

*A Young Woman's Guide to the Joy of Impending Motherhood*
Dr. Francine Pascal Reid (1941)

S TRESSING ABOUT THINGS CAN do nasty stuff to your body. I feel like crap today; I'm tired and my tummy's upset. I chalk it up to my period arriving any day now.

I had a horrible sleep—filled with nervous tension about seeing David. For some reason, at one-thirty in the morning, it got into my head that David only wanted to see me because he felt the need to tell me off about breaking his heart all those years ago. That thought would not be vanquished, as much as I tried to put it into the do-not-think-about box in my head. It's how I deal with things—mentally compartmentalize them into boxes in my head—the do-not-think-about, the too-horrible-to-consider, and my favourite, the thoughts-that-will-make–me-drink-too-much-if-I-think-about-them. Then if I have the time or inclination, I bring them out slowly when I'm ready to deal. But I don't often have the inclination, so there's a ton of stuff holed up in those boxes in my head.

Then about four-thirty (no, I didn't get a lot of sleep), when I couldn't stop thinking about poor unbabied Emma, I had the brilliant idea for David to be the father of my baby. I'm sure you already came to that conclusion, but sometimes it takes me a little longer. I mean, how perfect? I know him; I know his family; I know his family's history. I could just ask for a small jar of Jiffy Sperm, and he could go on his way. Or maybe (this thought is what kept me awake for most of the night), he got in touch with me because he's ready to give me another chance. He wants me back in his life, and then I wouldn't have to worry about the Jiffy Sperm; we could do it the old-fashioned way. It could be like the last twelve years never happened. It could be that fate led him to walk into the wine store on the day I was working. Thursdays are the only day I work late.

Normally I don't believe in stuff like fate and destiny, because if I did, then I'd have to consider that it was my fate to be alone and without a baby, and I don't think it is. I was made to be a mother. For no other reason, just look at the size of my hips!

It was still quiet upstairs when I got up Saturday morning. Because Coop and J.B. both work such late hours, mornings can sometimes blend into late morning-early afternoon, and if I'm not busy, it's easy to abide by those hours. But today I had things to do, people to see. I could start my new life with David!

So I jumped out of bed, showered, and gave my legs an extra-smooth shave, and then I rubbed scented body lotion onto every skin surface I could reach. Of course, when I was doing this, it was in front of the mirror. Naturally, I couldn't help comparing the body I see now to the body David last saw. The decade has not been kind. The hips are a little wider, the belly a little less taut. The breasts are still full and luscious-looking (one of my ex-boyfriends once told me that, and I liked the description), and while there are no stretch marks or unsightly veins, I definitely no longer have the body of a twenty-two-year-old. But that's okay, since neither will David. Not that his body was ever the attraction between us. If I recall correctly, it was okay, kind of long and lean, without any of J.B.'s muscular firmness.

Now, why should I be thinking about J.B.'s muscular firmness?

I shook the image—both images—out of my mind and got dressed. Immediately, I felt better. I know I'm not Playboy material or anything—I look okay naked, but I look a lot better with clothes on. No one has told me that; it's just my female intuition.

And then I was off to see David, to let whatever would happen, happen.

Anyone who lives in the city with a living brain cell knows not to drive anywhere close to Woodbine and Queen in the summer, and here I was—a beautiful Saturday morning in June, in my car, driving south on Woodbine, trying to make a left onto Queen Street. Impatiently, I waited for a break in the traffic. I'd waited so long to see David again. Like a sign from above, Alanis Morrisette came on the radio with "*You Oughtta Know.*" I love that song. David bought the CD for me when it first came out, and I used to play it over and over again, despite his being absolutely sick of the song. But he would always let me listen to it without complaint. He was a good guy. He is a good guy.

I was going to see David, and everything would be all right. I'd be able to have a baby. This was the right thing to do. I had no idea how things would work out; I just knew they would.

It's so nice being such an unconcerned optimist.

It was easier to find David's house than it was to find parking close by. The address David gave me was nice—a duplex, with a huge porch and a gorgeous red maple in the front yard. It was on a street directly north of the boardwalk, which explained the lack of parking. I finally found a spot three streets over. By pure luck, someone was leaving just as I drove by, but I had to reverse up a one-way street to claim the parking spot. In my excitement, I twice kissed bumpers with the Expedition behind me, but I checked when I got out and there was no damage. Not that my little Jetta could hurt a huge gas-guzzler like that.

So I was there. And despite the traffic, I was early. It wasn't even ten thirty, and David said to show up around eleven. What was I thinking coming so early? Now I had to wait around like a loser. I was actually standing in front of his neighbour's house, sort of hidden by a huge maple tree so that David wouldn't see me if he happened to glance out the window.

So either I stood out there for half an hour, went for a little walk to waste time, or headed up to David's door and hoped that he was not too put out by me being early.

I checked in a nearby car window to make sure what I was wearing was appropriate. I had on a faded denim skirt that hit mid-thigh, and layered tank tops in white and blue because it was hot for June. I might be ghostly white and covered in freckles, but at least the skin that was showing wasn't all squishy and cellulite-y. Because of the humidity, I pulled as much of my hair as I could into a ponytail—my curls always look freaked out when it's humid. I thought I looked fairly good. Okay, maybe even better than fairly good.

I was good to go. Let's go see David and get this on. Unfortunately, I still couldn't head to the door.

"Casey?"

Aw, fuck a duck. While I was standing there hiding behind the tree, who comes walking up the street from the beach with a couple of dogs (a beautiful brown Labrador and a scrappy little Jack Russell) but David? I knew I was one mass of blushes. Even the tips of my ears were warm, and I had no idea what to say.

"Hi," was the only thing that came to mind.

"I was hoping to get back before you got here, but someone," he tugged on the leash for the Lab, "insisted on taking his time." He gave me a big smile. "It's good to see you again." He pulled me into a hug that was at first awkward, but then quickly eased into being warm and comfortable. I could stay like that all day, except that David must have been running on the beach because he sort of smells a little, but I was not about to complain. I'd missed his smell. I exhaled without even realizing I'd been holding my breath.

"Let's go in," he said as he pulled away.

"I'm sorry I'm early," I told him. "I guess I misjudged the traffic coming down here."

"No problem," he told me. I watched as David pulled the dogs behind him and crossed the street.

"You live—there?" I asked before I could stop myself. I still hadn't moved. David gave me a funny look over his shoulder from the middle of the quiet street.

"Couple houses up. #104."

For whatever reason, I had it in my head that he lived at # 105. David gestured with a sweep of his arm to a duplex almost exactly across the street from where I was. "Home, sweet home."

I stepped onto the porch behind him and almost got knocked aside by the Labrador's wagging tail. This place was just as nice as the one across the street, with lots of terra-cotta containers filled with flowers and an old milking jug painted with a picture of a lake, a loon, and a dock. There was even a woven reed mat with "Welcome" on it. I felt my spirits sink as David unlocked the door. There had to be a woman around here. How uncomfortable was that going to be, if she came home to find an ex-girlfriend hanging around? I'd be pissed.

"Are you sure?" I stammered as David held the door open for me. "I mean, won't it be weird if, you know, someone comes home and finds me here?"

"Depends on what you're planning to do to me," he teased. "Get in here. I'm hot—we'll have a drink. All very innocent and unweirdlike. Don't worry."

I wished he would just say if he was married or not. It was starting to freak me out. As soon as I was inside, I began scanning the place as David pointed out the various rooms; I started to feel a little hopeful when I saw no evidence of womanly knickknacks or magazines. When there's a serious girlfriend, you can always tell. I thought for a moment I'd hit the bull's eye—then I see the copy of Us on the kitchen table, but there's a picture of Jennifer Aniston on the cover and I remembered David always liked her. There was actually not a lot of clutter, which really surprised me when I thought back to the pigsty David used to call a room. His domestic abilities must have improved some.

I told David how nice his place was. It was one of those open-concept places, with the kitchen, living room, and dining room all occupying a huge space with gorgeous, dark hardwood floors. There was not a lot of furniture, just the bare essentials—table and chairs, couch, television, and bookcases. I smiled when I noticed the collection of Harry Potter books among his tattered science fiction novels. How did I know David would have them?

"Sit down," David invited. "I'll get us a drink, and we can start to catch up."

I sank into the comfortably shabby couch and kept looking around.

There was lots of evidence of dogs, including a faint aroma like wet wool. Not very pleasant, but the dogs themselves were great, especially the Lab. He parked himself right at my feet, and I got the feeling he was telling David he approved. Yay! I'd already won over the dog.

"Oscar," David scolded as he poured my Pepsi into a glass "Give her some room. He loves making new friends," he said as he gave me an apologetic smile.

"He's beautiful." I reached down to give him a scratch, and the Jack Russell scrambled over, eager for some attention as well.

I tried to look at something other than David, but my eyes were continually drawn back to him. He was wearing tattered cargo shorts, which he kept hitching onto his thin hips. Still a swimmer's body, I thought, noticing the breadth of his shoulders and the leanness of the rest of his body. And the legs—his calves were always impressive, and age hadn't changed them much. Or the bony knees. David's knees are probably his worst body part. They're quite horrible, like upside-down muffin tins smack in the middle of very nice legs. Nice legs, ugly knees.

"So," David said, handing me the glass. I'm careful not to touch his hand. "Long time."

"Too long," I said, and immediately regretted sounding like bad movie dialogue.

We talked about the dogs for a while until David asked how I'd been. I told him about my teaching and where I'm living. I told him about Cooper, but left out J.B., since I felt weird talking about him.

And I didn't want my weirdness to ruin this wonderful comfort I was starting to feel with David. It was always so nice with him—we never ran out of things to talk about. David told me about his job, the traveling he'd done, and how much he loved living in the Beaches. I was not hearing any mention of a girlfriend, and the thought perked me up immensely.

"Um, do you mind—can I use..." I asked awkwardly, after a Pepsi and two glasses of water. Pretty soon I was going to have to start crossing my legs.

"Bathroom's the first door down the hall." David smiled, motioning to the hallway off the dining room area.

"Thanks." This was also a good time for a reconnaissance mission. I have the quickest pee on record, and then used the running water to mask the sound of me opening the cupboard doors. I found nothing more exciting than towels, extra shampoo, and toilet paper in there. Razor, toothbrush, and toothpaste in the medicine cabinet, and a bottle of Tylenol and a little jar of Tiger Balm. And only a box of condoms and a tube of KY under the sink. Okay, nothing surprising. David has sex.

Did I expect him to live like a nun? Or I guess a monk since he is a guy. The main thing I discovered was that I didn't discover any evidence of a woman. Good to know.

I came out of the bathroom with a big smile on my face to find David back in the kitchen.

"Are you hungry, Casey? I'm starving. Want a turkey sandwich?" He held up a package of deli meat.

"Um, sure, but look, I can get out of here if you have things to do."

"I thought we were going to hang out. I have absolutely nothing else I need to be doing," David assured me with a smile, while slathering mayo on whole-wheat bread.

"That'd be great," I said shyly.

After the sandwich—not up to Cooper's standards, but tasty nonetheless—David suggested a walk on the beach. At the word walk, Oscar instantly woke up, and Jack, the Jack Russell, got all yippy so that decided it for me. David clipped on the leashes, and I took Oscar as we hit the boardwalk, talking all the while.

After my calves began to beg for mercy—my infrequent exercise regime has long fallen by the wayside—we dropped the dogs at the house, headed to Queen Street, and walked along the shops. Eventually, David expressed hunger again and took me to his favourite pub for an early dinner.

"So no wife or babies yet?" I asked after our food was brought to the table. I toyed with the chicken in my Caesar salad. I had to ask. I'd waited too long, and besides, I did get to spend the day with him.

"None for me. You?" David smiled.

I shook my head, trying to mask my huge exhale of breath. "No, not yet. Soon, I hope. Real soon."

"Me too," he admitted, finishing his beer. "Does the biological clock start ticking for men, you think?"

"Maybe." There were changes in David, I noticed. I knew there would be something, but it's nothing bad. He seemed more open and less reticent since I last saw him, but that could just be because he was excited to see me. And he did seem excited to see me. I'd been very encouraged by that.

David's face was tanned. He looked well with colour in his thin face, but it also accentuated the fine lines in the corners of his brown eyes. He'd aged, but then again, so had I. He'd matured, I decided as he told me about some place in Central Asia he wanted to visit next year, but hopefully so had I. We were kids when we were together. We grew up together, as much as you can grow up in your early twenties. He was my first love, and I know I was his first lover. He was ready to share his life with me, and I gave him the boot because of a childish, spur-of-the-moment reason.

"I have to ask," David began with a smirk on his face, like he could read my thoughts. "How was Europe?"

"Oh, God," I blurted out, slapping my hands to my face to hide my embarrassment. "Oh, David, I'm so sorry!"

David waved his hand at me and laughed. "No, no, don't apologize. I shouldn't have brought it up. Ancient history, water under the bridge; I won't bring it up again."

I wanted him to bring it up. I wanted to tell him breaking up with him was the stupidest thing I had ever done and I'd regretted it every day since. But I didn't say anything because I'm a coward and because David didn't seem to be bothered by discussing how I broke his heart all those years ago. I'd be bothered if the situation were reversed. And now I was bothered because he was not bothered. I felt a sharp twinge of unease as I told him about my sister Libby and the girls.

"I can't believe how much I've missed you," David told me after dinner, with some surprise in his voice. I told him I should be going, and he walked me back to my car. The street was quiet, and I could see the lights just beginning to prick on through the leaves of the trees. Queen Street and all its bustle was barely discernible. It would be a nice place to live.

"Me too," I told him.

"Look, I really don't want you to drop out of my life again." David leaned in the car window and looked imploringly at me. "Let's get together again. How about tomorrow night? There's a new Jennifer Garner movie out."

"Okay!" I said with a little too much excitement for a simple movie invite. "I want to see that." I remembered our movie dates. David and I used to go at least once a week, sometimes twice, always sitting in "our seats" in the middle of the theatre, with a large order of popcorn and bag of Fuzzy Peaches to share, a 7-Up for him and a Pepsi for me. David was the only man I know who admits to enjoying a good romantic comedy, the typical "chick flicks." When teased, he used to say taking me to see them would get him laid, but I knew the truth. His movie collection contained every one of Meg Ryan's movies.

"Can I pick you up around seven, then?"

"Sure ... no! No, I'll... meet you there. Yonge and Eglinton okay with you?"

There was no way I was having David stop by the house until I knew exactly what was happening. That would just open up a whole can of what-the-hell-is-going-on.

David finally said goodbye, without the kiss I sort of hoped for. Earlier I had given up hope of the idea we would end the day in bed, but I thought a kiss might not be too out of line.

My mind was full of jumbled thoughts as I drove home. Most were happy thoughts, but I had a disturbing one as I pulled into the driveway. How different was the David I had just spent the day with from the David I remembered from all those years ago and the David I'd kept close to me in my fantasies? Was I missing something because my memories were clouding my judgment?

When I unlocked the door, the house was quiet. Cooper and Emma were working at the restaurant and J. B. at the bar. If I hadn't just spent the day with David, I might be tempted to drop by for a drink. But all I wanted to do was sit and think about every single word David said to me and try to interpret them. Had he been thinking of me as much as I've thought of him? Did he blame me for ending things, and did he regret not fighting for me?

On my bed, I found a folded piece of paper.

"*Hey,*" it said. "*Dinner tomorrow? I have laundry that needs to be done. J.B.*"

# CHAPTER TWELVE

"For the optimal pregnancy, the mother-to-be needs a supportive and caring relationship with the father. Even though the father may not appear outwardly affected by the vast changes in the woman as she journeys through the nine months, he will undoubtedly be as interested and anxious as the mother and may demonstrate his concerns in unusual ways."

*A Young Woman's Guide to the Joy of Impending Motherhood*
Dr. Francine Pascal Reid (1941)

I WOKE UP SUNDAY to the sublime smell of frying bacon wafting down the stairs. There's no better way to wake up. I stretched in bed, already thinking about David. Thinking about how maybe next Sunday I might not be waking up alone. That would be even better than waking up to the smell of bacon. It didn't take me long to get upstairs, and I was grinning as I hit the kitchen.

"Good morning!" I bellowed.

"I didn't know it was that good," Coop muttered from his usual spot at the vast gas stove.

"It's a beautiful morning," I told him. Actually, from the window in the kitchen, I could see dark rain clouds crowding the sky. Apparently, I didn't have a good look before I came upstairs, but that wasn't stopping me this morning.

"What's got you in such a good mood?" Coop asked with an uncharacteristic scowl.

Before I could answer, sudden footsteps announced J.B.'s imminent arrival.

"I smell bacon!" he cried as he practically bounded into the kitchen.

"Emma wanted Egg McMuffins," Cooper explained with disgust as he assembled a bacon and egg sandwich for me. "The bacon didn't work out, so she was heading out to McDonald's when I caught her." Cooper has an unexplained horror of fast food. In his opinion, if it takes less than five minutes to assemble, it's not safe to put it in your stomach. I, of course, don't share that opinion. When Emma handed me my plate, she gave me the barest of winks. Maybe I was starting to get that there was method behind her madness of trying to cook.

"You're chipper this morning, too." Emma turned to J.B. and then back to me with a suspicious smile. "Both of you in good moods, hmm." She handed him a plate, and he immediately took a huge bite out of his sandwich.

"Sorry to disappoint," I told Emma, who was looking expectantly at me, "but I spent a lovely night all by my lonesome. I spent an even lovelier day with an old friend yesterday, however."

"Who's that?" Coop asked. I was about to go into details when Cooper held up his hand. It sounded like there were footsteps upstairs.

"Is someone here?" he asked J.B.

"Well," he said reluctantly. Instantly there was a collective ah from Emma and Coop.

"You left a girl alone upstairs and came downstairs to feed your face?" I demanded with disgust. I sounded a little sharper than necessary only because of the sharp pang I felt in my heart. Not that it's any of my business who J.B. sleeps with. He can have sex with whomever he likes. What's it to me, especially when I may well be doing the same thing with David after the movie tonight. It's none of my business.

To give him credit, J.B. had the grace to appear repentant. I don't know why I've never noticed how cute J.B. is when he is embarrassed. I guess he's cute all the time, but especially when he's embarrassed.

"Well, uh, she said she wanted a shower, and girls take a long time. And I'm hungry. I could smell the bacon!" he said defensively. I noticed J.B. could barely meet my eyes, focusing intently on his breakfast. He'd already inhaled half his sandwich, and Cooper began to make him another one.

The footsteps were coming down the stairs now. Coop, Emma, and I turned expectantly toward the kitchen door. The stairs head into the hall, which separates the living room and kitchen and lead to the front door. Whoever she was would have to walk right past us.

"J. B?" a female voice called.

With a last, longing glance at his half-empty plate, J.B. headed for the hallway. I reached over and speared a piece of bacon that fell from the English muffin. If I leaned over the table enough, I could see what was going on at the door.

"What's she look like?" Emma hissed, trying to see around me.

"Blonde. Curly hair. Tall," I reported. "And she's wearing a pink shirt, so she's not a waitress."

"He stopped dating the waitresses years ago," Coop told us. "After Talia."

"Who's Talia?" Emma and I asked in unison. I sat back down. This might be more interesting, especially since all I could see was her back and one of J.B.'s hands on her shoulder, which gave me another pang I'd rather not dwell on.

"You live with the guy, and you don't know anything about him?" Cooper asked me with a raised eyebrow.

"Well, it's hard to keep track. And I don't really live with him."

"So who's this Talia?" Emma asked.

"She was one of the waitresses at the club, maybe about five or six years ago. J.B. liked her a lot."

Another pang in the heart region. Now, why is that? That was before my time!

"Anyway, he was getting serious with her—"

"What, two dates?" I scoffed.

Cooper looked at me. "There have been a couple of girls he's been serious about, you know. I remember one—what was her name? She was quiet but really sweet."

"Is that what his ex-wife was like?" I wondered. "The one who sends him a card on their divorce-versary?"

Cooper sighed. "Is she still doing that?"

"I read the one from a couple of weeks ago."

"She really doesn't want him to get over her."

"That's what I thought!" I crowed. "Is J.B. —does he...?" I floundered. Did I really want to know if he still had feelings for his ex-wife? What business of mine was it if he did?

"If he does still have feelings for her, he won't admit it," Coop said. "But it makes sense. They've been split up for twelve years or so, and he's had maybe three serious relationships. Serious being more than six months, and all with girls just like his wife—needy, clingy, and insecure."

"I don't understand women like that. Most of the time they'd be better off without a man in their life," I said.

"Like you." Emma smiled at me. "What about this Talia?" I was glad she asked because I really wanted to know and I felt guilty about her comment. I hadn't told her about David yet. How could I judge past loves of J. B. when I can't even go a month without a man of my own?

Not that David could be considered my man, only my ex-man, but after yesterday, who knows?

"She was all messed up by her ex when J.B. started dating her," Cooper was saying. "He took his time with her, helped get her self-confidence back. I'd never seen him so serious about a girl before. They were together for almost a year, I guess. They started talking about getting a place together, but then all of a sudden, the ex-boyfriend comes back into the picture and tells her he wants her back. He's gone through all this therapy; says he's a new man and all this crap. J.B. was convinced Talia would just blow him off, but then she goes back to him. She just said she owed it to him to give him another chance. Then she was gone, and J.B. refused to look at another girl twice. Well, he'd look, but that's it. Nothing serious since."

"She dumped him just like that?" Emma exclaimed loud enough for J.B. to hear in the hallway. I gave another peek—the door was open and he was standing there, still obviously saying good-bye to Ms. Blonde. "Idiot girl."

"He was pretty messed up for a while," Cooper told us slowly. "He really cared about her. He told me once that he felt betrayed by her. It was one thing for her to leave him, but he could never understand how she could go back to the boyfriend who messed her up. There were a lot of dependency issues; I think some emotional stuff, but J.B. got her to stand on her feet again, and then she goes and ruins everything by going back to the boyfriend."

"So maybe he's still hung up on her, not the ex-wife." I didn't know what upset me more. Not upset, because why should I be upset, but disappointed me? Concerned me? And why should I be letting J.B.'s love life even enter my thoughts? I had David to be concerned about now.

"What ex-wife?" J.B. asked from the hall. I didn't know who jumped more, me or Emma. Both of us glanced guiltily at each other.

"Oh, Brit," I fibbed as breezily as possible.

"Brit's not even married yet."

"Yes, but Morgan keeps saying that it's about time she started planning on how to be an ex-wife, now that she's almost married so that she can start planning her second wedding." I'm such a horrible liar that the Lord will surely strike me down someday.

I was also feeling kind of strange about the insight into J.B.'s past. It was like I was snooping inside his medicine cabinet and found he was taking some sort of secret medication.

J.B . just gave me one of those you're nuts expressions, and turned his attention back to his plate. "Did you take my bacon?"

"It was getting cold," I said in my defense.

"I was coming back."

"It wasn't fair to just leave it, like out in the cold, all alone. It needed to be eaten. It was asking to be eaten. And you took a long time saying goodbye to your friend," I added innocently.

"Gimme your bacon then. It's getting cold." Instead of handing it over, I popped the last piece in my mouth.

"Sorry, all gone," I said with my mouth full.

"You b—"

"I'll make you both more bacon," Coop said soothingly. "Geez, the two of you are as bad as children sometimes."

"Okay, back to what you did yesterday." Ever tactful, Emma changed the subject.

"Me or her?" J.B. asked with confusion.

"Casey. Who's the old friend you spent the day with?" she asked me.

"David." My face broke into a huge smile as I said his name. "I haven't seen him since university."

"Is this him? The guy?" Cooper demanded. "The one you're always mooning about?"

"I don't moon about anyone!"

"The one she dumped on his ass, and keeps on complaining about why she did it," J.B. corrected.

"That's him," I told them with a smile, not even bothered by their teasing this morning. "I hung out with him yesterday, and we're going to a movie tonight."

"A movie tonight," Emma echoed, sounding excited for me. "Sounds promising."

"Maybe."

"Tonight?" J.B. asked. "So no dinner?"

"Can I have a rain check?"

"So how did this come about?" Cooper asked before J.B. could answer.

"He just walked into the store on Thursday," I told him, happy to be back on the David topic.

"Really?" Emma asked.

"Really?" Coop echoed, but he made it sound like David innocently walking in would be the most unbelievable thing. "And that doesn't concern you?"

"Why is that so hard to believe? He likes wine. He works with one of the regular customers, and they came in after work. Not that it's any of your business."

"Right. He didn't just wander into the store? Just in the neighbourhood ..."J.B. trailed off with a questioning smile.

I clicked to what he was saying and didn't like it. "I work in a wine store, not a gay bar," I snapped. "For your information, we have tons of heterosexuals who come in every day. In fact, I seem to recall that you've been in there once or twice. Do you hear me questioning your sexuality?"

J.B. shrugged. "Had to be asked."

"No, I don't think it did. David is not gay! I would know! For your information, you could say I made him the man he is!" I gave him my best glare.

"Okay, okay." Cooper waved his arms between us. "J.B., don't be an ass; Casey, stop jumping down his throat. We're just trying to make sure everything's cool with this guy."

"Everything is cool. Everything is fine, great, terrific," I growled.

"Fine, great, terrific," Coop conceded. "Just want to make sure you're not stalking him or anything."

"Since when do I stalk anyone?" I exclaimed.

J.B. gave a cough; Cooper raised his eyebrows. "Well, last summer when George Clooney was in town shooting that movie..." Emma trailed off, giving me a little smile.

"That was George Clooney," I told them, like that explained everything.

"Do you really think it's a good idea to try and reinvent the past?" Coop asked me, this time all serious-like.

"There's no way it would work," J.B. scoffed.

"I'm not trying to reinvent anything!" I protested. "And why wouldn't it work? I may be older and maybe a little wiser and more experienced, but I'm still me. I'm still the same Casey he was in love with."

"It's been twenty years. There's no way you're the same person. Everybody changes. Look at me," J.B. offered.

"No, I think you still have the maturity, not to mention the mentality, of a fifteen-year-old, so what's your point?"

"Hey, I'm trying to be nice here!" J.B. protested. "You don't know anything about this guy anymore, do you? He could have spent the last ten years in prison for all you know. I'm just trying to watch your back."

"Thank you," I say grudgingly, only after I realize there is genuine concern in J.B.'s voice. "But I'm fine. And I doubt that David has ever seen the inside of a prison, so you shouldn't worry about that."

"How many times did you Google him?" J.B. asked with his usual smirk, the concern in his voice vanishing into smugness. I ignored the question. "It's like me trying to hook up with my ex-wife—it's a stupid idea."

Cooper turned down the burner and stepped away from the stove, which told me he had a lot on his mind because he can normally hold up his end of any conversation while continuing to cook. "Look, Casey, if you're planning on something with this guy, I really think you're opening yourself up for a big world of hurt," he began, already full into lecture mode. "So many things have changed since you were twenty. It's not going to be the same between you. I can't see how you would think it would possibly work out."

"I'm not planning anything. Yesterday was really good. Maybe—"

"Yesterday was one day," he interrupted. "He was probably surprised to see you, and yes, probably pretty happy. And he probably spent all of last night thinking about you and how great it was back then, but what if he remembered how he felt when you gave him the boot and wants to get back at you?"

"David would never do that!"

"It's been twenty years, Casey; you don't know the guy anymore!" J.B. interjected.

"Twelve," I muttered. "Only twelve."

If I were listening to my head, I would have realized the two of them were making sense, but for once my heart seemed in command.

"I need to try," I told them truthfully. "It might be my only shot."

"At what, getting pregnant?" J.B. scoffed. "You really should—"

"At being happy," I said quietly, with my face turned down at my half-eaten plate of breakfast.

"Casey, this isn't your only chance," Emma told me softly.

"No?" I asked her. "It feels like it might be."

The kitchen was quiet, and I finished my breakfast without glancing up. Yes, these were three of my closest friends and we discuss a lot and they probably know too much about me for their own good, but I've never gotten into in-depth emotional insecurity stuff. Usually, I just store that stuff in my do-not-think-about file and leave it there. But yes, now that it's out there, I believe that David might be my last chance at getting everything that I want.

I want to have a baby. I want to have a baby so bad it hurts. I want a baby to cuddle and care for and give all the love I have in my heart, all the love I'm wasting on my friends. Okay, maybe not wasting, but

I seem to be living these days vicariously through them. I'm involved in a wedding through Brit. I'm involved with kids through Libby. I'm involved with Cooper and Emma's life as they move in together. Yet I have nothing—no marriage prospects, no children of my own, no one to share my life with. Nothing. Do you blame me for thinking David might be the answer?

I went back and thought what might have been had I not broken up with David. I would have gone to Europe with Brit—David had been fine with the idea—but when I came back, we would have found an apartment together. And then we would have gotten engaged and started planning our wedding. And two years after getting married, I would have had our first baby, at twenty-seven. Two years later, I would have had our second baby, then a year and a half later, a third, so by the time I was thirty-two, my family with David would have been finished and we would have enjoyed raising them together. I'd have an eight-year-old daughter (or son) by now if that's what had happened. If I hadn't been so stupid.

But maybe it's not too late. Maybe I've got another chance at the life I've always wanted.

When I finally looked up, J.B. was staring at me with an expression in his eyes I couldn't read. It was sort of a mixture of affection and pity—and something else I'd never seen before. "What?" I muttered.

"I never thought you were the type to need a man to make you happy," he asked seriously.

"I'm not," I told him, stung by his observation.

J.B. shrugged. "If you ask me, I think you're wasting yourself on this guy. You can't fix something that happened that long ago. This guy should have moved on by now, and if he hasn't, then there's a big problem and you should steer clear of him. That's what I think."

I wondered for a moment if he was talking about me and David or himself and his ex-wife. Or maybe messed-up Talia?

"I never thought I would agree with J.B.'s advice on dating, but Case, I have to agree with him on this. Don't do it. Don't get messed up with him again. Cancel the movie—I'll take you to see it next week if you really want to go," Cooper urged.

"Go out for dinner with me tonight," J.B. offered. "You don't have to do my laundry."

I smiled at both of them. "Thanks. I'll be okay, I promise—and if not, you can both say 'I told you so' until I'm sick of hearing it. I'm going tonight, if only because this one has never felt finished, so let me see what happens."

# CHAPTER THIRTEEN

"Once the initial excitement of successfully conceiving a child colours your life, it's easy to become frustrated and dispirited about the length of the gestational period, especially during the first trimester. It's a good idea to focus on other projects during this time in preparation for the baby."

*A Young Woman's Guide to the Joy of Impending Motherhood*
Dr. Francine Pascal Reid (1941)

D ESPITE COOP'S AND J.B.'s comments and warnings, I don't remember ever taking longer to get ready for a date. I shaved my legs again, did my hair, changed my clothes at least six times, and basically wasted the day in anticipation of seeing David.

Just before I was about to leave, I heard footsteps coming down the stairs. Instead of stopping at my place, they continued into the laundry room.

"Hey," J.B. called out. "You still here?"

"I'm just about ready to leave," I told him, following his voice into the hall. I'm always surprised how a laundry room can get so dirty. Cooper bought a bright blue washer and dryer last year but still hasn't got around to taking out the old ones. The derelict machines now sit in a corner of the room, stacked with empty Tide containers, lint balls, and odd socks. I should make tidying up this room a priority.

J.B. started throwing his dirty clothes into the washing machine without separating the darks from the whites or anything.

"You look nice," he told me, glancing up from his dirty clothes. "We couldn't talk you out of it?"

"Nope." It was nice to be reassured, especially with all the trouble I'd gone through to find the perfect outfit. "Don't do that!" He'd just thrown a pair of black jeans into the washing machine with a tangle of underwear. "Colours stay separate. Do you want everything to turn grey?"

"And that's how I get you to do my laundry," J.B. grinned, stepping back and letting me take over. I just shook my head. I'm particular about laundry for some reason. And I love to iron, a trait of which Cooper and J.B., and now Emma, all take advantage.

"So who was your little friend this morning?" I asked coyly as I finished sorting his clothes.

"Aw, you know... she's, uh—Christie. Her name is Christie," J.B. managed reluctantly.

"How come you don't have a problem razzing me about the guys I date, but when I try to turn the tables, you get all stammer-y and embarrassed?" I demanded, twirling around to face him with my hands on my hips.

"'Cause the guys you're with never last for very long," he retorted quickly. "And I'm not stammer-y—whatever that is."

"To stammer," I said pertly. "And at least my guys hang around for longer than a night. I—at least—get to know them, their full names and birthdays, at least. Why don't you try—?"

"Don't go there, Casey," J.B. interrupted.

"Go where? I'm just saying I think it's time you found a nice girl and settled down." The strange thing is that as soon as the words tumbled out of my mouth, I realized that it was the last thing I actually wanted. Having him single and me—most of the time—unattached made me feel that we were sort of in this together. Like in When Harry Met Sally... and they talked about marrying each other if they didn't find anyone else by a certain age. I like the thought of having someone like that in my life.

"You know."

"Just trying to be a good friend. Cooper might have mentioned a Talia this morning..." I said before I told myself not to go there. I didn't want him to think we were gossiping about him, even though that's exactly what we were doing.

"I'm sure he mentioned a lot of things," he said wryly. "Talia, Claire, Ruby... Betsey. The wife," he explained at my expression of confusion.

"Her name is Betsey? I thought the card said Beth."

"Elizabeth, but everyone called her Betsey. Except for Ryan—the one who took her off my hands. Maybe that's why she hooked up with him. She hated the name, and he always called her Beth," he mused, like I was no longer in the room.

"There must have been more reasons than that!"

"Oh, probably, but it's too nice a day to go there. And don't you have a date or something? You do look nice, you know." He glanced admiringly at my short white skirt and purple-flowered shirt for longer than he needed to.

"You already said that." Now it was my turn to feel uncomfortable under his gaze.

"I thought it was worth saying again." He smiled down at me, and I swear my heart did this humongous flip-flop in my chest. "Too bad it's for this David guy. There's still time to bail and come out with me, you know."

"Thanks, but…" I could tell my cheeks were warm to the touch. I began to back slowly out of the room. "I've got to go."

"It's been twelve years—I think he can wait a little longer."

"Okay, enough!" I said irritably in response to his sarcasm. "I said you can do the whole 'I told you so' if nothing happens, but until then, I'd appreciate a little support. Or at least some silence on the subject."

"Look at your track record, Case. There's no way it would work even if he wasn't dredged up from your past. You have crappy luck with guys. Even without all the pressure with the baby thing, there's a good chance you'd crash and burn."

"That's not very nice! Saying that you don't think it would work out—how do you…?"

"Do you really think I want you to find someone it will work out with?" J.B. asked, turning back to his laundry.

"What's that supposed to mean? You want me to be unhappy?"

"No. Not at all," he said mildly. He leaned over and scooped up the pile of dark socks and gym shorts I'd left on the floor. "Hey, thanks for the laundry lesson."

"Yeah." To say I was confused about his words is putting it lightly. Did he not want me with David because he wanted me to be miserable or because he couldn't stand the thought of me with another man? Neither option seemed overly realistic. I gave my head a shake and vowed to worry about it later. I was going out with David, and there was no sense dwelling on J.B.'s cryptic remarks. "You really should learn to do it yourself, you know."

"Why bother when I've got you?" He smiled at me again, and I could see the creases around his bright blue eyes. He didn't shave this morning, and his cheeks and chin were covered in scruff. I couldn't help but think about how my face would be scratched if I kissed him.

"Oh. Look, I—"

"Go. Have fun. But not too much fun, you know. Make him wait a little longer, you know."

"Yeah, I guess. See you." Since when did J.B. give me dating advice? Or since when did I give him advice? You need a nice girl to settle down with. Where did that come from?

I was almost back in my apartment when J.B. called after me. "Hey, Case? You smell good, too." Which of course made me smile again, but then I tripped over the doorjamb into my apartment. J.B. was obviously watching me because I could hear his stifled laugh.

"You okay?" he called.

"Fine. Just clumsy."

As I left to meet David, I had all sorts of thoughts unrelated to David swirling around my mind. Damn him!

"Just like old times, eh?" David asked as we finally settled into our seats in the movie theatre. He gave me a wide smile that reached into his brown eyes. I wished my heart would flip-flop a little more when he smiled at me. It did a little flip, and that would have been perfectly acceptable had it not been for my earlier exchange with J.B. and the ensuing thoughts about his scruffy face. David had shaved perfectly for me. Not a trace of stubble or even any evidence of a nervous hand nicking his cheek. Stop thinking of J.B., I savagely ordered myself. Don't compare the two. David, David, David, David....

"David," I said aloud, "it is just like old times, isn't it? You, me, at the movies? Just like it was yesterday, right, David?" He looked at me quizzically at the use of his name, but only nodded in agreement.

Okay, not starting out that great.

Why do people go to the movies on a first date? I can see when you've been together for a while and don't have a need to talk and learn about each other. There was so much I wanted to learn about David, and I kind of felt like I had a deadline. Especially since I was being so easily distracted by silly thoughts of J.B. With all my might, I shoved any thoughts of J.B. Bergen firmly out of my mind and focused on David. David, David, David, David…

Despite the ease I felt around David on Saturday and how positive I'd been feeling (and how I sounded), it was at least halfway through the movie before I really began to relax. It wasn't that David made me uncomfortable, but just that I was ultra conscious about everything about him. The way his laugh boomed out unexpectedly at the funny bits. The way his eyes narrowed when he was concentrating on the suspenseful parts. How long and tapered his fingers were as they dipped into the popcorn, and the tiny sizzle of electricity I felt when he absentmindedly reached over to snag one of my Fuzzy Peaches. After that happened, I'm glad to report the creases around J.B.'s blue eyes finally faded from my mind and I didn't have to order myself to concentrate on David.

"Sorry," he whispered. "Guess I should ask first."

"It's okay." I smiled at him. That's when I finally started to relax because that's how it was with us. We would sit silently in the movie theatre, both of us concentrating solely on the celluloid world unfolding onscreen, never speaking until it was over. Even at the concession stand, it was like no time had passed. David remembered that I like extra butter on my popcorn, and asked them to shake it to make sure it all dripped into the bottom. He ordered me a bag of Fuzzy Peaches because that's what I always would get, and got himself a box of raisin Glossettes to go with his 7-Up.

David offered me his box of raisins. "Do you like them yet?" he whispered.

"Still can't stand them," I grinned.

It was like I'd fallen back in time. Is that a good thing? Can you really go back again? There are so many aspects of my life that I would dread going back and redoing, but what about the four years I spent with

David? Right now, that period in my life seems it has a rosy glow about it, giving me a lovely warm and fuzzy feeling. I was in university with David; my friendship with Morgan developed when I was with him. We studied together, argued politics and the ways of the world...

"Where were you when the World Trade Centre fell?" I asked him suddenly.

"What?" There was a car chase happening on-screen. Maybe I should have waited for one of the slow parts.

"9/11. I was just thinking about all the stuff that happened when we were together, and it just hit me that so much more has gone on since then and I don't even know..." I shrugged helplessly. I wasn't really sure what I was trying to express, but suddenly I had this need to find out all the bits of his life that I'd missed. I shared so much with David. You could say we grew up together, but did those years make him the man he was now? Did it make me the person I am now—kindergarten teacher, part-time wine store manager, with my hopeless romantic life and so desperate to have a baby? Is it because of David that I am who I am?

Is this getting way too deep for a Sunday movie night?

"Never mind," I whispered to David.

He gave me another quizzical look. "I was traveling in Europe," he said after a moment. "I was due to go home that weekend, but because of everything, it took me ten extra days to get a flight home. I was totally broke, and whenever I had to eat out, I would steal the breadbasket for the next meal."

"Where in Europe?"

"Milan. I eventually went back to Rome, because I, uh, had met someone there so I could stay..." I raised my eyebrows in the ahh expression. Okay, I knew he hadn't lived as a monk since I broke up with him. Hearing about other women isn't that bad. "What about you?" he asked.

"I was teaching. Most of the kids got picked up early by their parents. There was a lot of crying, but most of them were too young to understand. They thought it was a movie."

"Maybe it's better that way."

"Maybe." Would I like to go through life innocently believing things were just like they were in the movies? If that's the case, then things are looking good for me and David. If this were a movie, then we've already had our meet-cute moment at the wine store and are moving toward the start of the second act. Soon, we'll have some sort of conflict that we'll need to overcome before we come together for the crescendo of the movie's love song. Sounds like a movie I might want to watch.

But with David as the romantic lead?

We were good together once and could be again. I'm a better person now, more mature and better prepared for the relationship and the life we could share together. If I could go back in time, it would be the years I spent with David that would definitely be the ones I would want to revisit.

I was heartened when, after the movie ended, David and I couldn't stop talking. We started rehashing the film as we walked out of the theatre, and that led us to talking about other movies, and the next thing I knew, half an hour had gone by and we were still standing in the parking lot. Like on Saturday, it was like we'd slipped back into our twenty-year-old selves, but only more mature and worldly. I felt like I could stand there for hours talking, but all too soon, David started checking his watch.

"Oh, wow, Casey, I really have to get going," David said regretfully. "I've got an early morning tomorrow."

"That's okay. I should get home, too." I shifted uneasily. "David, I really—"

"There's stuff I need to talk to you about," David blurted out. "I wanted to tonight, but movies aren't really the best place. Are you busy tomorrow night?"

"I am," I admitted reluctantly, thinking of my long-standing date with Brit and Morgan and how I'd never broken plans with them because of a man. "I've got—"

"Tuesday then?" he asked before I could explain. "Maybe we can do dinner and talk?"

"Tuesday will be great."

"Can I pick you up this time?"

I hesitated, but J.B and Cooper both work Tuesday nights, so it was safe. "Sure. I'll text you my address." I happened to glance in his car and the very messy interior. "You really need to clean up that mess," I told him.

David smiled at me. "You always used to say that." He put his hand on the side of my head, an affectionate gesture, reminiscent of stroking a dog. His hand was large and warm and smelled of popcorn. His eyes were warm and almost liquid. Something inside me melted. The part that hadn't already melted when David first asked me out, that is.

"I did miss you, Casey," he said softly.

"I missed you too, David." Before I lost my nerve, I quickly leaned forward and pressed my lips against his. I smiled into his brown eyes as I pulled back.

"Ah," is all he said and pulled away. "Tuesday, then. Lots to say." I nodded, and he walked me over to my car. He was just getting into his as I drove away, waving.

I didn't want to think about how David didn't kiss me back.

# Chapter Fourteen

"Pregnancy is a time of discovery and new experiences, many pleasant, but some may prove to be a challenge. Enjoy all of them. This period in a young woman's life will change her forever."

*A Young Woman's Guide to the Joy of Impending Motherhood*
Dr. Francine Pascal Reid (1941)

"WHERE WERE YOU ALL weekend?" Morgan demanded as I slid into the booth across from her Monday night. It was Morgan's turn to pick where to go, and the location—a wine bar downtown—should have given me a heads-up that she had sorrows to drown. She only drinks when something is bothering her. "I called you at least sixteen times!"

"OhmyGod, Morgan, I'm sooo sorry!" With all the David drama, I had forgotten all about Morgan's breakup with Anil on Friday night. "I'm so sorry; my phone must have been turned off."

"I know it was turned off. I kept trying to call you to see if you'd turn it on. What if I needed to be bailed out?"

"Bailed out of where? Jail? Why would you need to be in jail? What happened?"

Morgan looked sheepish. "There was a little episode Saturday night."

My eyes ricocheted between her and Brit. Obviously Brit was familiar with this so-called episode, because she didn't look at all alarmed. "Morgan, what did you do?" I whispered.

"I think she was totally justified," Brit said in a haughty voice. "I would have done the same thing. Maybe not Tom's Armani suit, but definitely the cheaper ones."

It turns out Anil—Morgan's now ex-boyfriend—wasn't content with just ripping out Morgan's heart on Friday night. Since Anil had been the one who left her, Morgan felt he should be the one to move out. Seems fair enough to me, but it turned out Morgan didn't exactly have ownership of the house she shared with Anil like she thought. Anil had originally owned the house, but when Morgan moved in with him five years ago, he promised to add her name to the title of the house. But obviously, Anil conveniently forgot about doing this little task, and Morgan's name was never added to the title of the house, which means Morgan doesn't technically own any part of the house. And Anil wanted his house back.

"But you've been paying the mortgage for years!" I said incredulously. "How is that legal?"

"You're forgetting Anil is a lawyer," Brit said in a disgusted voice.

"He said it was an oversight, but of course, I don't believe him," Morgan told me, her chin beginning to tremble. "I said something about suing him, but of course, I can't—not with his whole firm behind him. And it's not like I have anything in writing. But Anil did say he was perfectly willing to compensate me for what I contributed to the mortgage, minus the cost of rent—rent! Sonofabitch! I decorated that whole house! We lived in it together! I wanted a bigger place, but Anil said he wanted to stay—and now I know why Anil didn't want to move because it wasn't my house at all! Rent! I'll give him—"

"Go back to the police part," I begged, wanting to head Morgan off before she got bogged down with the legalities I didn't understand. "Did you call the cops on him?"

"Well, no," she admitted. "I was really upset when he told me this. And I'd been drinking. A bit. Ever since he broke up with me Friday night..." Tears started to fall silently onto her cheeks.

"Oh, God." Morgan isn't really a big drinker, but when she does decide to tie one on, there's usually some serious consequences. Like the time at university when she fell asleep on the toilet at a bar. Or the time when we went to the pub on campus, and Morgan was stumbling so much she got thrown out ten minutes after we got there. Or when she decided to steal someone's Christmas lights from the bushes in front of their house. Or when— "What did you do?" I moaned.

"She took all of Anil's suits from his closet and set fire to them in the front yard," Brit supplied helpfully before Morgan could say a word. "The fire department came and everything."

"Oh, my God." I covered my eyes. And this was happening when I was enjoying myself with David? I was flooded with guilt.

"I wanted to know if she tried to hook up with one of the firemen," Brit continued. "Wouldn't that have pissed off Anil, doing it right in front of him? Especially when the police came. It's a good thing Anil didn't press charges. Did you at least get one of the cops' numbers, Morgan? They might not be marriage material, what with having to worry about them being shot and the tacky polyester uniforms, but—"

"Britney," I said, exasperated. "Were you charged with anything?" I asked Morgan. "What did they say?"

Morgan shook her head. "The one cop was really nice, and I think he must have felt sorry for me. He gave me a warning, but because Anil didn't press charges—"

"Oh God," I moaned again and grabbed Morgan's hand across the table. "I'm so sorry I wasn't around. I had no idea—I'm sorry," I told her sincerely. "I just got caught up with a few things."

"I hope they were important," Brit said in a haughty voice. "Morgan needed you." I turned to her with an expression that clearly asked *Then where the hell were you?* "I was out of town," Brit continued. "Tom and I were invited by his boss to his cottage for the weekend. I told you all about it. There's no cell phone reception up there."

"Are you okay now?" I asked Morgan. "Is the fire out? Do you need me to do anything? I feel horrible I wasn't around. Do you need to crash at my place until you find somewhere to live?"

"Brit's already offered, and no offense, but your place might be a bit small for the two of us. Anil says I can stay at the house for this week, but he would prefer I be out by next Monday. Ooh, I want to kick his ass for this! He got off easy losing only his suits."

The girl could do it, too. A few years back, Morgan got into all sorts of self-defense courses and martial arts. I know she still does kickboxing class a couple of times a week, and if she weren't so worried about bruising, I bet she'd join one of those female boxing clubs.

"Did Anil say anything to Tom about it?" I asked Brit. Tom and Anil had become pretty good friends over the last couple of years, going beyond the usual boyfriend-of-friends relationship. Tom had even asked Anil to be one of his groomsmen for the wedding, a little detail I decided not to bring up at this time.

"Tom knew nothing about it. He's so upset," Brit told Morgan. "He's going to talk to Anil."

This set off a tirade against Anil, his lack of sufficient male genitalia, and men in general, and finished with Morgan in tears again about being thirty-five, unmarried, and unloved. I signaled the waiter for another bottle of wine. This was going to be a long night.

"So what did you do all weekend?" Morgan finally got around to asking after two bottles of wine, a plate of bruschetta (shared with me), a huge bowl of fettuccini (ate it all herself), and a huge slice of cherry cheesecake (Brit had a couple of bites). Apparently, Morgan was doing the feed-the-misery thing. Her eyes and nose were still faintly red, but now her cheeks were pink from the wine as well. Even though I felt sorry for her, I didn't think it was fair that Morgan looks so gorgeous when she cries. Me, I look like a baby baboon, so it's better I save my tears for private.

"Well, actually... I was with David," I said, trying not to sound too smug.

"David who?" Brit asked, waving the waiter to get the bill.

"David David?" Morgan shrieked, a little too loudly for my liking. I nodded. "Ohmygod! Where? When? How? Details, all of them, now!"

"David Mason?" Brit asked, with more restraint than Morgan. "Where did you see him?"

"He just walked into the store on Thursday," I told them. "It was really weird, but it was him and—"

"Did you have sex with him?" Morgan screeched.

"I don't think the waiter in the back corner heard you," Brit pointed out, and Morgan lowered her voice—thankfully. Morgan gets a little over-exuberant when she's drinking.

"Did you?" she asked again, in a normal voice.

"No," I said ruefully. "But I spent the day with him and dinner on Saturday and a movie last night," I told them smugly. "He kissed me good-night." Okay, I initiated it, but a kiss is still a kiss. Even though David never really kissed me back, but I didn't think that was worth mentioning.

"Kiss, or kisskiss?" Morgan waggled her tongue at me.

"Just kiss. He's taking me to dinner tomorrow night."

"Does this mean you're off the baby kick?" Brit asked rudely.

"No. I still—I don't know," I told her truthfully. "Maybe I want to have a baby with David?"

"Oh, come on, Casey! It's been twelve years! People change. You haven't seen David in how long, then all of sudden you want him to be a daddy? I think you need to give this baby crap some more thought."

Brit rolled her perfectly shadowed eyes at me. "I was hoping you'd forget about it."

"How can I forget I want to have a baby? It's something I've always wanted. It's like me telling you not to get married."

"Like that could happen," she snorted.

"And why shouldn't I consider David as a potential father? I know his history, his family background—I know him."

"I hate to remind you—you knew him," Brit said dryly.

"I don't understand," Morgan said with a look of confusion. "Do you just want him to father a child, or do you want him back in your life? Like, for good."

"Why would you want to?" Brit asked. "Once you break up with someone, it never works out when you get back together. You're better off finding someone else. Which I've told you to do for years."

"You think Anil and I are finished forever?" Morgan's chin was back in wobble mode. And that was the end of any discussion of David and me, or me and baby, which was fine for me because I needed to give a little more thought as to just what I wanted. Or what I expected from David. Well, not from David, but what I expected from myself regarding David.

It's difficult when you look at it. I want a baby. I really think David—true, I'm basing this on the David I used to know and not the abridged, new version I still need to get to know—would be the perfect man to father my baby. What should I do—enjoy spending a little time with him before blowing him out of the water with my "Can I have your baby?" question? Or do I try for the whole shebang—hope that the feelings we once had for each other will quickly flare back up into a raging inferno, propelling us into bed at the perfect moment of ovulation, giving me both the baby and the man in one fell swoop? Is that too much of a long shot? According to Brit, it is, but that's Brit. She's just bitter I haven't jumped on the whole who-wants-to-get-married bandwagon.

Why do things have to be so complicated?

# CHAPTER FIFTEEN

"The father's role in the child's life is primarily as a protector and a disciplinarian. The new mother should not expect the father to employ a hands-on approach, only ensure there is a supportive environment and provide for the financial needs of mother and child."

*A Young Woman's Guide to the Joy of Impending Motherhood*
Dr. Francine Pascal Reid (1941)

W HEN I FINALLY GOT home, many hours later, I found J.B. in the living room watching television. Early bedtimes aren't his thing, even when he has the night off. I was not surprised to see my cat in his customary place lying on a magazine on the coffee table, surveying me with half-closed eyes. He—the cat—also didn't seem surprised to see me. I flopped onto the couch beside J.B., holding my head.

"Well, hello there," J.B. said, looking amused. "Doesn't look like you've had a good night."

"Not really. I had to listen to Morgan complain all night about what an utter bastard Anil is for breaking up with her."

"Pretty pissed, eh?"

"If I was Anil, I would not want to meet Morgan in a dark alley." I began to knead my temples. After dinner, Brit left to meet Tom, but Morgan didn't want to go home alone and convinced me to go a nearby pub and get a drink with her. I don't know how long we stayed there, but it was long enough for me to develop a monstrous headache from the noise and (no offense to Morgan) the monotony of the conversation. Normally, when I play the listener, I end up drinking way more than I should, just to have something to do between nods and sympathetic noises. But tonight I somehow managed to keep it to three glasses. I can't keep trying to make believe I'm twenty-five any longer. Thirty-six is rushing me like a three-hundred-pound linebacker, followed by the evil thirty-seven, and it's time to begin acting my age. I used to be able to spend the night drinking and then wake up bright-eyed and bushy-tailed to go to work, only to continue the cycle that night again, but I can't do that anymore. Well, I can, but I need to stop.

"Here." J.B. shifted on the couch and turned me so that my back was facing him. He began to rub my shoulders, and at that first touch, I almost swooned at how nice it felt. "She's pretty pissed, is she?"

"Who?" I asked dreamily. J.B.'s hands are big and strong, and I could feel the tension drain out of me like a slow leak in a balloon.

"Morgan. The person you spent the evening with."

"Oh, yeah. It's just that you should really think of taking up massage therapy, you know. But yeah, Morgan. She's very, very pissed," I agreed, returning with a thunk to reality. "The worst thing is that Anil's not saying why—I think it's probably some other woman, but I'm not about to tell Morgan that. I'm afraid it will put her over the edge. Mmmm," I gave a little moan, my eyes slowly closing. So much for Morgan. "That feels so good." J.B.'s hands were moving from my shoulders to the back of my neck and then onto my head, giving me a better scalp massage than even my hairstylist does.

"You've got so much hair," J.B. said quietly. His fingers were tangled in my red curls.

"I'll never know how Libby didn't end up with some of it, even the colour. And it's bad when I go out with the girls, and it's the three of us, with Brit and Morgan and their perfect blondeness and me with all this frizz. I've always understood Anne of Green Gables going on about how horrible it is to have carrot-red hair."

"Well, I happen to like it. You're like a frizzy carrot."

"Thanks, Jerk." J.B. tugged a hank of my hair in response.

"So, fun with Morgan tonight, I guess. But are you going to tell me what went wrong with the old ex, or save it for Cooper?" J.B. surprised me by asking.

"I thought you didn't want to know." I half-turned around to look at him.

"No, I said I didn't think it would work out. Hearing how you crash and burn is always worth a laugh," he teased.

"Jerk. Why do you think something went wrong?"

J.B. shrugged. "I figure that's what most of the headache is from. I think I know you well enough to tell when something is bothering you." I turned back around, and J.B. resumed his massage, to my undying gratitude. "So what happened last night? On your date? With David?" he said with more than a little sarcasm in his voice.

"He didn't kiss me back," I told him reluctantly.

Ah." His fingers tightened on my shoulders for a second. "You kissed him."

"Just a little good-night kiss. But then he pulled away and said, 'Ah,' just like you just did. What's that mean?"

"I have no idea."

"Well, what did you mean when you said it?" I urged. At the moment I had the potential for insight into a man's head, and there was no way I was stopping until I got some answers. "Ah." But J.B. didn't answer for a moment. "You still there? What did you mean?"

"Truth? I didn't like hearing that you kissed him."

I turned around again, my mouth open with surprise. "What?"

"Just being honest."

"Yes, but why?"

"You don't want me to be honest? You'd rather I lie and say I'm jumping for joy at the thought of you doing this? I don't want to see you get hurt again, as much as I enjoy teasing you about it."

"Oh." I didn't know if relief or regret was the stronger emotion running rampant through me right then. "So that's all."

"All what?" J.B. asked innocently.

"Nothing. Never mind." I gave my head a shake. "I don't know if it's a good idea to talk to you about this."

"Suit yourself. I thought it might help the headache. Are you going out with him again?"

"Tomorrow night. We're going to dinner."

"Ah."

"What's that supposed to mean?" I cried with exasperation. "You don't like the thought of what sharing a meal will do to me?"

"Okay, sorry. Ah-ha!" J.B. said in a falsetto voice, trying his best to sound jovial. It was pretty pathetic, and I had to laugh.

"Do you really think this is a bad idea?" I asked.

"I don't think it matters what I think," J.B. told me, leaning forward to grab his beer. His shoulder brushed against mine. "Sounds to me you've got your mind set on seeing how this plays out, and no one can change your mind. I just hope you're happy with how it turns out."

"You mean if David and I..."

"I got the impression that you're playing for keeps in this one, Case." J.B. turned the full weight of his beautiful blue eyes on me. "Is that really what you want?"

I couldn't turn away. I couldn't even blink. I felt like I was drowning in the blueness, and any moment J.B. would put his arms around me and drag me to shore.

"I don't know," I muttered, finally snapping out of it.

"I think you better figure out what you want." He trailed a cool finger down my cheek. "I think you're looking too hard."

I had to turn away from him. I had to move away from him because right then there was a very insistent pulse beating somewhere it had no reason to be beating. I crawled into the corner of the couch and tucked up my legs so that they were between me and J.B.

"Do you need me to keep rubbing?" J.B. asked.

"No, I think I'm okay. But look, I have a favour to ask." If I weren't so desperate to change the subject, I would never have brought this up now, but it seemed cowardly to go running off to my room.

"Shoot."

"It's for Morgan. She's got this wedding coming up and Anil will be there, and Brit suggested that she get a really hot guy to take her. And, well, the consensus is that you're the hottest guy she knows."

"She thinks I'm hot, does she?" he asked with a smug smile.

I ignored the smile and continued to plunge forward. "She does, and so does Anil. Brit thinks if Anil sees her with you, it will get him all hot and bothered and racing back to her. At least, that's the plan."

J.B. took another drink from his bottle. "You're serious about this?"

"I didn't come up with the idea; I'm just the messenger. You can say no if you want." Even to my ears, the whole thing sounded absurd, and if I hadn't promised Morgan to talk to him, I wouldn't have said a word. What was I thinking—especially asking him now? Or even anytime. It was just a bad idea.

"When is this wedding?" he asked so casually that I couldn't decide if he was for or against the idea. A big part of me hoped he was against it.

"Last weekend in July. It's a Sunday."

"My day off. Who's tying the knot?"

"Marie and Michael. I think you might have met them—Irish couple. Really nice."

"Are you going?"

"No, they're keeping it really small."

"Hmm. What do you think?"

"About you taking her? I don't know." Like I'm about to tell him every inch of me is screaming Don't take her! "She really wants someone to go with her and doesn't want the hassle of meeting someone new just for this. I'm sure Brit has another option if you don't want to go."

"I don't think I've got anything else on. Tell her I'll think about it, check my schedule, and all that stuff. Don't want her to think I'm too easy."

"No. It's just... it's nice of you to do that for Morgan."

"Morgan's a cool chick. Brit, on the other hand..." I had to laugh at his tone. I was well aware of his feelings for Brit. Neither he nor Cooper have ever understood my friendship with Brit, and my explanations don't do it justice because usually I don't understand it myself. "Plus it might make things easier for you, so you don't have to listen to her go on and on about it. Happy to help out," he continued casually.

"Thanks." I secured Morgan a date, but I was not ecstatic with the idea. But no one needed to know that. "But you, you won't... you won't, will you?" I stammered, trying not to say the words, but desperate to get my meaning across.

Luckily, J.B. isn't a complete idiot. "Contrary to popular belief, I don't try to have sex with every woman I meet," he told me rudely. Then he smiled, his wickedly white smile that makes me melt just a little when he uses it. "Just you."

# CHAPTER SIXTEEN

"Headaches and nausea are some of the minor ailments common during pregnancy."

*A Young Woman's Guide to the Joy of Impending Motherhood*
Dr. Francine Pascal Reid (1941)

MY HEAD WAS STILL aching horribly when I woke up a mere five hours later. It made my stomach feel queasy, and I was tired. It was like I had a hangover, but there was no way I should be. Over the years, I've developed a fairly healthy tolerance for wine. But if I had gotten drunk, at least my hangover would have been done and over with by ten, instead of this headache lingering for the morning and into the afternoon.

The only good thing was that it was summer and I didn't have to deal with hyper five-year-olds at school. But as bad as the morning with the kindergarten class would have been, a day working in a wine store is a hundredfold worse. Seeing the bottles of wine, talking about which red would go best with the braised rabbit, and the constant slight aroma in the store did not help me feel better.

"You're such a horrible friend," was how I answered my cell phone when I saw Morgan's name on the call display late in the afternoon.

"What did I do?" she cried. I could tell she was properly horrified. Morgan, for all her mathematical intelligence, is quite gullible.

"You kept me out too late, and now I feel like a big bag of poop," I moaned. There was no one in the store right then, so I rested my head on the counter by the cash register. There was a bunch of things I needed to be doing, but sitting with my head down seemed like a fine idea for the rest of the afternoon. "I think my head is going to explode all over these bottles of wine."

"But you hardly drank anything!"

"I know. It's totally not fair. What do you want anyway? Just to laugh at my utter, utter miserable-ness?"

"I would never do that to you, Casey. At least I wouldn't do more than giggle. I wanted to see if tonight's the night you're going out with David."

"If I survive that long."

"Are you excited?" she asked coyly. "It's been so long. Are you nervous?"

"A little—a lot," I confessed.

Especially since I still had no idea why David didn't kiss me back Sunday night. I mean, I had ideas, but I didn't like thinking about them since they involved David considering me as just an unattractive, pathetically evil ex-girlfriend, or something along those lines. And I was also trying desperately to stop dwelling on it, because that just leads me into thinking about J.B. telling me he doesn't like the thought of me kissing David. I just needed tonight to be over. Trying to prevent myself from thinking about all these different things was about to make my head explode.

"Do you really think—would you want to get back together with him? For real? What about what Brit said about it not working? And if you get together, what about the baby thing? Or would you just want to have a baby with him? And then you could marry him and not have to be alone forever. Or are you not thinking about all that, and is this some sort of catching up where you get to have sex with him?"

"I'm trying not to think about having sex with him," I said, diving right into the important question and not dwelling on the fact that Morgan predicted me having a life alone with only a baby for company. "I think that might be jinxing it. But I am going to wear my lucky unders, and I did the whole shave this morning."

"You need to wax. My girl is so good it's almost painless."

"Painless and waxing are not two words that can ever be in a sentence together. My Venus Divine does the trick nicely, and it never hurts. But back to David—I honestly don't know what to think. It's different than just a normal guy, because we've got all this history, but is that all it is? And what about the fact that I may or may not have broken his heart back then? Did he forgive me, is everything hunky-dory, or is he holding some evil bitterness inside him that's just going to explode all over me? And what about having a baby? I was all set to give up men, and now here I am getting all worked up about one again! It would be better if this was just a normal date with a normal guy, and I could just trick him into having sex with me and get the conceiving thing over and done with. This is just too huge right now for me to deal with without my head blowing up."

There was silence from Morgan for a moment. I didn't intend to go off on a vent like that, but it just needed to come out and Morgan's always a good person to vent to. "Do you think you're maybe overanalyzing this a little too much, Casey? I mean, look at it as just dinner with an old friend."

"But it's not! It's—"

"Maybe, just for now, pretend it is. That's all—just casual, sharing some food. Don't worry about everything else."

"You think I'm nuts."

"At times, yes, but I still love you lots."

I took a deep breath and prepared to calm down. "Thanks. I needed that."

"If I was there, I might have had to slap you."

"That would hurt too much. Speaking of slapping—which is what I'd like to do to that good-for-nothing Anil... are you okay today?"

"I guess." There was a catch in Morgan's voice that made me wonder if I should have played the bad friend card and just avoided the subject altogether. "It just—it hurts. It was such a surprise, you know. I had no idea. Absolutely none."

"He really blew you out of the water, didn't he? And he deserves to suffer greatly for that."

"Thanks." Yep, she was close to crying. "Look, Case, about what Brit said last night..."

"Britney said a great many things last night."

"About me going to that wedding with J.B." There was a long pause. "Are you really fine with it?"

"I talked to him about it," I told her, omitting the I'm-okay-with-it whole thing. "He said he'd check his schedule."

"Really?" Morgan said, a little too eagerly for my liking. Morgan was in a rebound mood, and if truth be told, J.B. would be a great rebound guy.

"He's not sure, so don't get your hopes up yet," I told her quickly.

"That's fine. It's just to make Anil jealous, you know, not that I'm interested or anything. I mean, it's J.B. we're talking about. It would just be nice to go with a friend."

"Why wouldn't you be interested in him?" I asked stupidly. "He's a great guy—really good-looking and smart and funny and ..."

Morgan laughed. "And listen to yourself. I figured out a long time ago that J.B. is off-limits. It's me you're talking to, not Brit, who—gotta love her—truly does believe that the world revolves around her and wouldn't notice someone's feelings unless they exploded all over her shoes. I am fully aware that me and J.B. —if ever anything, you know—that would be stepping on some serious toes. Your toes," she finished, just in case I was not getting the picture.

I couldn't help but laugh. I do love Brit and she's been my best friend for over twenty years, but it's nice to know sometimes that others see her faults as clearly as I do. But for Morgan to think that about J.B.... "We're just friends," I said lamely when I finished my giggle. "That's it."

"Why didn't you ever try again?" Morgan wondered. "Cooper has to be okay with things, now that he has Emma."

"What does that have to do with it?"

"Because Cooper was in love with you, and that's why he didn't want you and J.B. together. The whole living arrangement was an excuse—a pretty lame one, if you ask me."

"Cooper was never in love with me!"

"For a smart girl, you can sure be stupid."

"Look who's talking!"

"Now you're just being mean. But back to J.B."

"You don't know what you're talking about with Coop. We're friends—that's all we've ever been. Just like J. B. and I. Well, maybe not, but ..." I shrugged, and remembered that Morgan couldn't see me. "He's a good friend and I like being around him, and I really think that's all it's ever going to be. Besides, who knows what will happen with David, right?"

Morgan gave a little sigh. "I know what you feel about David, but don't put all the eggs in his basket, okay? I want to see you happy. For the record, I think you and J.B. would be amazing together. And you can tell me not to invite him to go to the wedding with me, you know."

"It's no big deal," I fibbed. "Besides, I'd never ask you to do that. Again. David was enough." This, of course, reminded me of how Morgan had made the ultimate friend sacrifice and walked away years ago so I could have David.

"You know, I forgot all about that," Morgan marveled. "If I hadn't stepped back, there never would have been a you-and-David. There would have been a Morgan-and-David, and since I didn't go to Europe with you and Brit, we'd still be together." She gave a little laugh. "That's strange to think about."

"Strange," I agreed. "Even stranger than you thinking Cooper was ever in love with me."

"You should ask him someday," Morgan laughed. "I know I'm right."

For the rest of the day, I couldn't quite make the thought of J.B. stay in the don't- think-about-it box. He just kept popping out, and always when I least expected it. I'd be waiting on a customer, extolling the virtues of buying a Canadian wine, when all of a sudden I'd have an image of J.B., sitting in his boxers eating breakfast with me, or laughing at me for something, or sharing a bottle of wine over dinner. I needed to stop thinking about him. It was not even worth going there. It's not—it couldn't happen. It wouldn't happen. It couldn't, so why was I wasting my mental energy thinking about him?

To get my mind off J.B., I tried to focus on seeing David later tonight and wondered what he needed to tell me. I'll get back together with David, and Morgan will meet someone, and J.B... I don't know what I want for J.B., but I'm not thinking about him anymore today. David. I need to focus on David.

By the time I got home from the store around six-thirty, my headache had faded to a manageable level. A quick shower helped, and I got dressed, hurrying because I only had a few minutes. Despite all the talking David and I had to do, I couldn't help but hope for a little action tonight, so on went my pink lace bra and thong under my black pants that make my bum look svelte. Just so you know, David fell outside the one-month-dating-before-I-sleep-with-him rule, since technically I have known him since I was nineteen.

I added my white blouse with the ruffles to the outfit. Then I took off my shirt since ruffles and dinner never go together well for me. Maybe I should wear my Capri pants, but I wanted to wear my ankle boots, so I kept on the pants. I rifled through my closet, remembering the days it was filled with the latest fashions. Those were the days when my credit cards were also filled to the brim. I'm glad I got the debt under control, but some days I really do miss the shopping.

I finally settled on a white blouse with three-quarter sleeves and my new black vest. Even though I'd be able to pass for one of the waiters at the restaurant, I had no time for any other last-minute changes. I took the two minutes until David was expected to try and tame my curls. The shower made them frizzy. I finally wet my hands and ran them through my hair as the doorbell rang upstairs. I gave myself a nervous grin in the mirror.

"Wish me luck, Sebastian-cat," I told him, giving his head a scratch. He was watching me from the comfort of my pillow. "You'll be the only one who wishes it."

# CHAPTER SEVENTEEN

"When a woman announces to friends and family that she
is expecting, she should expect some varied reactions."

*A Young Woman's Guide to the Joy of Impending Motherhood*
Dr. Francine Pascal Reid (1941)

"DO YOU WANT SOME wine?" David asked after we were shown
to our table. He'd picked a little Italian restaurant on College
Street. I'd been there a few times before, and while the pizza isn't all that
great, the pasta is superb. I nodded my agreement. "You work in a wine
store, so you pick. But I still don't like red."

David was having the mushroom risotto, and I'd decided on the pasta
with pesto and cream sauce. "How about the chardonnay?"

David shook his head. "Too..." He made a face like he was about to kiss
a fish, and I laughed.

"Dry?"

"Something in the middle."

"King of compromise." I smiled and scanned the wine list. "The pinot
grigio. You'll like that." I took a deep breath.

The evening began with the comments about our appetizers (salad for me, calamari for him) and with me comparing the food to what I'd had at Cooper's restaurant.

"And it's just the two of you living together?" David asked skeptically, referring to Coop and me. "As just friends?"

"Actually, Coop's girlfriend just moved in this weekend. I missed out on the boxes while I was with you, so thanks. And Coop's friend J.B. lives there ... with us. They've been friends forever, so he's good to... live with."

"You haven't mentioned him before."

"I haven't? Thought I did. Not that there's a lot to mention... well, there is, but we're just friends... he just lives there, him upstairs and me on the main floor. Where he never goes unless he's doing laundry. I do his laundry sometimes, actually, but... we're just friends."

"So you're not involved with either of them?"

"No! Oh, no. No. We're just friends. Even if I did want to get involved, I wouldn't. I'm not involved with anyone, but definitely not either Coop or J.B."

"Why not? I'm sure they're good guys."

Why would he say that? He should have said, "That's really good because I've been dreaming about you finding your way back to me for years," or something along those lines. I looked at him strangely and began to doubt the need for my action underwear.

"Well, because—I want to have a baby," I blurted out.

"Now?" David choked a bit. "Are you pregnant? I noticed you gained a little weight, but I just thought..."

"No, not yet, but I hope to be soon." I guessed twelve years of eating well was noticeable, but I didn't think I'd gained that much weight!

"Oh. You're not pregnant, but you want to be?" David reiterated slowly. "Do you have someone in mind to help you with this?"

"That's the funny part. Ha-ha. See, a couple of weeks ago, I was at a wedding and I broke up with my boyfriend at the time, and I got to thinking about things. I've had lousy luck with men for—for a while. Since you actually. Since I broke up with you all those years ago, which is probably the stupidest thing I've ever done. When I think—"

"Casey..."

"No, let me finish. I was dumb to let you go, and it was a stupid reason and I've always regretted it. And because of you, none of my other relationships have worked out. I've always wanted to have a baby, so why wait?"

"Who would the father be?" David had a confused furrow on his forehead, but to his credit, didn't say one word about how nuts I am.

"I'm not sure," I told him honestly. I was so tempted to chime in, "What about you?" but I just couldn't.

"I've been thinking about having children, as well," David said without looking me in the eye.

"Really?"

"Really."

"Don't you, maybe, don't you want to wait until the right woman comes along?" I asked, still using the high-pitched voice I couldn't seem to shake.

"I'm not sure if there will ever be a right woman for me."

The waiter, with absolutely horrible timing, took this opportunity to bring our food. And then he went on and on about getting me cheese and fresh ground pepper, and David asked for a glass of water, and did he want bottled or tap, until I was ready to scream before the waiter finally took off.

"Why not?" I asked, as soon as the tight-buttocked waiter sashayed off. I tried to sound casual even though my heart was thumping so loud David could probably hear it. Action undies worked their magic again! Despite the heady buildup of anticipation that was beginning all over my body, I pretended to stay cool and even forked up a piece of fusilli from my bowl and popped it in my mouth.

"I'm gay, Casey."

Unfortunately, my utter shock caused my gaping mouth to expel the piece of fusilli with such force it hit David's wineglass across the table, leaving a pesto-and-cream-sauce smear as it plopped onto the table.

"You're what?" I asked, sounding like a strangled parrot and scooping up the flyaway pasta as quickly as I could.

"I'm gay."

Instead of replying (because, really, what could I say to that?) I concentrated on wiping the sauce from the glass. David grabbed my hand, and I jerked back, almost spilling the wine. "Sorry," I mumbled. "Sorry about…"

"Casey, look at me." I did so with great difficulty. It was not that he was gay—I have no problem with homosexuality—but how could I not know? And was he gay with me? Did I turn him against women? And then there's the whole no-way-I'm-having-sex-with-him-tonight. Or apparently any other night, for that matter.

And then the worst thought hit me—J.B. was right!

I drained my glass of wine in one loud gulp. "So, uh, when did all this happen?" I asked with fake brightness.

"When I was in Italy, I met a man. Marco. He's the one—remember when you asked about 9/11, and I said I was stuck in Milan but eventually went back to Rome? That was Marco."

"So it's not something I did?"

"Of course not!" David actually laughed at that. "I've always suspected I might be different, but I've never wanted to admit it. I was happy with you, Casey, and I've had other girlfriends since then, but Marco showed me how attracted I truly am to other men. I haven't been with a woman since."

"Are you still… with… this Marco?" Who I instantly hated for calling David over to his side. David was a good boyfriend! He liked to shop and watch Meg Ryan movies! How could I have not known he was gay?

"I keep in touch with him, but he's in Italy and I'm here now." David looked forlorn, and I forgot about my misery for a minute. "Neither one of us is ready to move, so there's really no future."

"That's horrible. Do you—date—other men?" The area the wine store is located in is the predominantly gay area of the city. Most of the clientele I help on a day-to-day basis are enjoying an alternative lifestyle, but I've never really had personal conversations about their love lives with them, so this is all a bit strange for me. Plus, this is David whose love life I'm attempting to discuss, so strange isn't really the right word. Shocking, astounding, surreal, bizarre. I gave a bark of laughter. "Sorry, but this is all very weird for me."

"I'm sure it is. I've been in a couple of relationships. Neither of which lasted, because I can't seem to get over Marco."

"I know all about that," I muttered. How did this go horribly wrong so quickly? How could I be sitting there, talking to David about him being in love with another man when I had all these plans for us? We were going to be together—it was fate! We were going to have babies; he was going to make my life worth something! He was going to save me from a lifetime of dating assholes! I needed him. And—

"Dammit. He was right," I muttered under my breath.

"Excuse me?"

"J.B, J.B, my roommate. He assumed the only reason you came into the wine store—that wine store—is because you're gay. I told him lots of straight people come in. and... I hate it when he's right."

David had a bemused little smile on his face. "I'm sure they do. Sorry, but unfortunately, I'm not one of them."

"No." My little pout about J.B. took my mind off what David had told me for about ten seconds. And then it was back to—pow. David is gay. David—my ex-boyfriend who just wandered back into my life—is a homosexual. Can I not catch a break on this baby thing?

"Did you love me?" I blurted out.

"Of course I did." David pushed my bowl of pasta—which I'd lost all appetite for—aside and took my hand. "I loved you so much, and when you left, it broke my heart. Back then I was so in love with you, I wouldn't even consider I might be attracted to men. But when you broke up with me, it freed me. I was able to live with my true self. I guess I should thank you for that. But you didn't 'make' me gay, Casey."

"Oh." How was I supposed to react to this? Believe him when he said I had nothing to do with it? Keep blaming this Marco guy? Just start crying at the loss of my dream of getting married and having a child with David?

"It's really interesting you mentioned you want to have a baby," David continued, squeezing my hands tightly. "And that we bumped into each other at this point in our lives—both of us without a fulfilling relationship. So it seems that fate has stepped in. Casey, I have to ask, how would you feel about having a baby with me?"

# CHAPTER EIGHTEEN

"There is an intrinsic bond between the parents of a child, an unbreakable connection that will remain for the rest of their lives."

*A Young Woman's Guide to the Joy of Impending Motherhood*
Dr. Francine Pascal Reid (1941)

E MMA FOUND ME LATER, sitting at the kitchen table with my doggie bag full of pasta smelling up the room. Of course, I couldn't eat any dinner. After David dropped his bombs—his bombs, since the one about the baby is bigger than Hiroshima—I completely lost any appetite I had.

You'd think I'd be excited. David suggested having a baby with me, and wasn't that my ulterior motive, my master plan? Sure, but the wicked curveball—the gay thing—had thrown me into a bit of a dither. Obviously. Plus, I felt like some sort of non-woman—did I make him gay? You can see how my mind was working right then. Or not working.

Like I said, Emma got to me first, finding me sitting in the darkened kitchen with the white Styrofoam container in front of me. I found I couldn't move. I was surprised I actually made it into the house. If David hadn't insisted on driving me home, I would probably still be sitting in the restaurant with the bowl of uneaten pasta in front of me.

I couldn't stop running through my four-year relationship with David to see if there were any clues I should have picked up. Anything at all I should have noticed. I'm not the smartest girlfriend, but you'd think it might be apparent when you're having sex with a gay guy. But so far all the hints I might have gotten were his lack of assertiveness in the bedroom, which I always took for lack of experience, and silly stereotypes like listening to Mariah Carey and the Backstreet Boys and knowing most of the songs from The Sound of Music when we'd watch it at Christmas.

"Casey?" Emma said loudly. I had the feeling it wasn't the first time she called me as I sat at the table. "Are you okay?"

"Fine," I told her, still staring off in space and mentally dissecting the trip David and I took to Florida in our third year with Brit and Morgan and their boyfriends at the time. Had David been interested in one of the guys? Paul, I think that was his name, had been pretty cute. I remember the night we got drunk and played strip poker—had David been more interested in Brit's or Paul's bare chests?

"What are you doing just sitting there like that?" Emma asked gently. Either gently or like she was scared of me. Poor girl—she hadn't even been officially living there two weeks, and already I'd turned into some sort of woman-who-can-make-men-gay nutcase demanding to get pregnant.

"I'm putting my dinner away. I had some leftovers left over—I think I'll go to bed now." Leaving the Styrofoam container on the table, I got up and walked downstairs, tripping on the last step like I usually do, only this time it made me cry. Quietly, so Emma couldn't hear.

About twenty minutes later, the tears were gone, and I was back to being numb. I was just getting comfy lying in my fetal position on my bed, after ripping off my clothes, including my lucky underwear, which

I threw in the garbage when I heard Cooper's footsteps on the stairs. He didn't even knock on the door to my apartment, but just walked right in.

"Casey, what's going on? Emma says you're acting wonky." He came and sat on the foot of my bed. I could smell the odors of the restaurant mixed with his spicy-scented cologne, and I was glad I'd had the foresight to throw on my nightie. "Talk to me. What happened?"

I can only shake my head. I was remembering the times David kissed me—did I always initiate that too? Did he wish my lips weren't so soft and covered in lip gloss? Did he want me to have five-o'clock stubble on my cheeks that he could rub his face against?

"All right then," Cooper said, rubbing the instep of my foot. "First I'm going to commence the tickling until you tell me what's up. Then, if that doesn't work, I'm going to try that Dutch oven move, where I crawl into your bed and fart a bunch of times, then stick your head underneath the covers. And I'll steal your cat."

Cooper's words reminded me about how David would always blame his flatulence on our nonexistent dog, Henry.

"You wouldn't do that," I said to Coop softly. I was fighting to keep from crying again, but I wiggled my fingers to coax Sebastian onto the bed with me. Because he's a cat and I doubt he loves me, he was not offering any comfort by sitting in the doorway just watching me. But I still didn't want Coop to steal him.

"Oh, no? Try me."

I focused on Cooper with some difficulty. "I had dinner with David tonight."

"He doesn't want to get back together with you, does he?"

"How—why do you say that?"

"It's the only reason you'd be so miserable. C'mon, Case, it doesn't take a Dr. Phil freak to figure out why you always go for the jerks in the world. You pick an asshole, so there's always a reason for the relationship not to work, so you can save yourself for the day you can woo David back into your life. Right? And this whole, oops-I-bumped-into-him was your attempt at wooing?"

I gave him a ghost of a smile. "Wow, Coop, you're smarter than the average bear."

"It doesn't take a genius. So what'd he say? What's his lame reason for not wanting you back?"

"He told me he's gay."

Cooper sat back on the bed and tightened his hold on my foot. "That's a pretty good reason," he said carefully.

"I thought it would be perfect if we got together. It would solve the baby thing, because we could have a baby right away together, and then I wouldn't have to keep doing the dating thing with all those assholes. I'm so tired of them, Coop. I thought this—David—was the perfect solution. I thought it was fate or something stupid like that. How dumb can I be? And then David told me he was gay," I finished heavily. This time I couldn't help the tears filling my eyes, but kept blinking so Coop wouldn't notice. I felt like an idiot about the whole thing. Having him see me cry over some gay guy I'm hung up on would be the last straw in achieving ultimate loser status.

"Oh, Casey." Coop opened his arms and I crawled into them, resting my cheek on his chest. "Poor little idiot. Took his time, didn't he? What happened, did you come on to him, and he said, 'Sorry, I'm playing for the other team now'?" I shook my head. "Casey, you know that there's nothing you could have done that would have turned him gay, right?"

"That's what my head says. My heart is telling me a whole other story."

"You didn't do anything. People are gay from birth, not because of anything their slightly obsessed ex-girlfriend did in bed."

"I'm not obsessed," I protested weakly. Even though Cooper didn't respond, I could tell he'd raised his eyebrow at me. "Maybe a little obsessed, but not that much."

"Well, we can agree to disagree on that issue. But David being gay wasn't caused by anything you did. Or didn't do. And you know that. You're not stupid, even though you probably feel like it right now."

"I guess," I muttered into his shoulder.

"I'm sure knowing he's gay explains a lot."

"Kind of," I admitted. "He never seemed as into me as I—"

"Please. No details."

"You obviously have an issue talking about sex."

"I don't need any more images clogging up my brain. Sex aside, Case, even though I hate seeing you like this, I'm glad things didn't work out. I've never met the guy, but wow, you can really get a hate on for someone from hearing how perfect he is. This way you can finally give up any hope about you and him, because there's absolutely no hope now. It's been over ten years, so maybe you can get rid of his ghost and move on."

"He wants to have a baby with me."

"Of course he does. I've moved from hate to loathing, just so you know. What did you tell him?"

"I don't know."

"You don't know what you told him, or you told him you don't know?"

"I told him I don't know."

"Because he's gay?" Coop asked honestly. "Because that would solve your problem about getting your donor guy, even though I'm under the impression this guy is more than your usual asshole. Or is it that he's gay and you didn't know it? So you dated a gay guy—it's not the first time. Look at Liza Minnelli and Star Jones—they married gay guys!"

"The fact that you know that scares me."

"I've been living with you for years. You leave enough magazines around to wallpaper the place. I've picked up a few worthless tidbits here and there. But do I have to remind you where you work? You'd think you'd have developed better gay-dar."

"I know, I know. I mean, when it's obvious, sure, but they don't wear signs, you know." Coop laughed at me, which almost made me cry again. "I didn't know," I told him, serious again. "Honestly." If I had a baby with David and we were connected by this bond for the rest of our lives, and I had to watch him get involved with men, knowing that I wanted him involved with me but would never have the chance ... "I'm an idiot."

"No, you just haven't gotten over your first love. You haven't let yourself get over him," Cooper corrected. "It might be time, don't you think? You're thirty-five and still pining over this guy. Since you were twenty? Maybe a bit of an idiot."

"Do you think I should have a baby with him?"

"No," Coop shook his head empathetically. "It would make it too complicated, him being gay or not. You'd open yourself wide open and you'd never get over him; you'd only get hurt. I don't want that for you. If you want to have a baby that bad, I'd rather you use me than him. Let David find his own incubator."

"He doesn't think of me as an incubator." I gave a little laugh that ended in a hiccup.

"No, and that's the problem."

It felt nice sitting here with Cooper's arms around me. He's such a good friend. This thought led me back to Morgan's comment the other day. "Morgan thinks you were in love with me," I blurted out.

"What?" His voice had the right amount of disbelief, but the way his arms abruptly stiffened around me made me pull back with disbelief.

"You were in love me with me?"

"No," Coop scoffed without looking into my eyes.

"You were! How can I not have known this? Are you still in love with me?" I couldn't believe Morgan was actually right about this.

Cooper finally looked at me. "No, Casey, I am not in love with you. I love you dearly as a friend, but that's it. Maybe I once thought ..."

"Really?" My voice softened with amazement. "Why didn't you ever tell me?"

"It was obvious the interest was only one-sided."

"But you still should have said something. When was this? You should have told me! I could have ..." I trailed off. Could I have developed feelings for Cooper? It was always the friendship that attracted me to him, not anything physical. I'd always thought he was very attractive, but for me, the magical chemistry was never there, not like it had been with J.B. If Morgan were right and Cooper had been in love with me, it had probably been when I first met J.B. when I was obviously interested in him. Poor Cooper.

"You could have fallen for me," Cooper finished my sentence. "Sorry, but I wasn't about to take that chance. Either it was there, or it wasn't. It was for me—at one time. Not now," he assured me. "But it wasn't for you. I'm okay with how things turned out."

"Because you have Emma," I said uncertainly.

"Even if I didn't, I would have gotten over you. Just because you want to keep your past loves dangling doesn't mean I do. It was bad enough with you hanging around all the time, insisting that I feed you."

"That's so mean," I gasped, when his wide grin told me he was teasing.

"Besides," he began with another wicked grin, "who knows what would have happened with us? You might have turned me gay, too."

With an enormous shove, I pushed him off the bed. He was still laughing as he hit the floor.

# CHAPTER NINETEEN

"In close circles, it often appears as if women of a child-bearing age coincide their pregnancies with each other, which is enjoyable for both the mothers and the children since an attachment is easily forged under such common circumstances."

*A Young Woman's Guide to the Joy of Impending Motherhood*
Dr. Francine Pascal (1941)

THIS PUT A WHOLE new spin on things.

Not the whole Cooper-used-to-be-in-love-with-me, although that did come as quite the surprise. How did I not know about it? Maybe I'm not the most observant person—I was in love with a gay man for years, having no clue he was gay. I guess that says a lot about me and my powers of observation. I have to admit I did feel a twinge of regret when Cooper admitted he had been in love with me, but it only lasted a moment. Now what I mainly feel is relief. Cooper-and-I was never meant to be, and I'm glad he's no longer in love with me and even happier that his unrequited love didn't affect our friendship. That would have been horrible if he had stopped being my friend, especially if I hadn't had any idea of his true feelings.

But I have to stop thinking about what Cooper said or felt or still feels about me, because that is distracting me from the bigger problem. Regardless of Cooper's opinion of the whole thing, I can't stop thinking about the idea of David and I having a baby together.

And thinking about having a baby with him does sort of take my mind off the whole David-is-gay thing.

So what should I do? Despite what Cooper said, it does seem like a no-brainer to me. I want to have a baby. I don't have a man in my life. David wants a baby. He doesn't have a woman—or a man—in his life. Gay or not, I think I would love to keep him in my life. Seems pretty simple to me.

The only thing, the one little thing that holds me back from running straight to David (David, straight, ha-ha, Casey, good one!) is me. Me and my feelings. I know I'm still hung up on David. I'm not sure if I've been that way for a while (I suspect I have, and everything came to a head once I saw him again), or if it's just seeing him again that makes everything seem so intense. In any event, David seems to be a little too entrenched in my heart right now, and I'm not sure that's a good idea if I'm going to have a baby with him.

Does that make sense? That I like him too much to have a baby with him?

For now, though, I stick that thought in the don't-want-to-deal-with folder. I decide to wait until I have my period. When that comes, it will mean decision time. I'll have roughly about two weeks to get everything together—decide if David is it, and if so, just how this is going to happen. I know how I'd like it to happen, but obviously, I'm not about to get my way on that aspect. Unless David can somehow muster the strength to, you know, but I think that might be too much to ask.

I'm expecting my period any day now. No more than a couple of days. Definitely sometime in the next week. When I think of it, I don't think my cycle is at all average—some months Aunt Flo comes on the twenty-first day, other months it's on the twenty-seventh day. I think that has something to do with forgetting to take my pill sometimes. At least I'm not completely irresponsible—I always use a condom as well. But my period always comes.

So all I have to do is wait a couple more days, talk to David, and then that's it. This time next month I could be pregnant, and come March, I could be a mom! Or maybe April, just in case it doesn't work the first time. But why wouldn't it work? I'm the ultimate optimist about this now!

I focus on that and put David's new lifestyle way back on the back burner so that I can enjoy Coop's Canada Day party on Sunday. Cooper throws really good parties, but his best are the last-minute, spontaneous ones. More people show up, everyone's in a terrific mood, and the food is always incredible. This one is no exception. July 1 falls on a Sunday this year—Coop starts inviting people on the Friday night. If I did that, maybe three people would show up, and all I'd have for them to eat would be a bag of nacho chips and a jar of no-name salsa. Not so for Cooper. About thirty people give him an enthusiastic yes out of the forty or so he e-mails. Coop then spends Sunday morning creating tasty tidbits in the kitchen, while giving Emma explicit instructions about how to decorate the backyard with his chili pepper patio lights.

"Coop and J.B. throw such good parties," Brit said later as she appraised the backyard. It was almost six o'clock, and the yard was already full of music, people, and lots of food and beer. She helped herself to another tortilla chip, scooping up a healthy gob of Cooper's homemade spicy pineapple salsa. "Where's Morgan? Is she still talking to J.B.?"

I scanned the crowd until I saw Morgan standing by the bar area. J.B. was beside her, and as I watched, she laughed at something he said.

"Well, let's hope Anil will get the message that Morgan's moved on to bigger and better things and realize his mistake," Brit mused.

"She handed him a beer," I said dryly. "That would definitely get Anil all worked up if he could see them now. Have you seen her new place?" I asked, wanting to change the subject.

After Morgan spent a week in Brit's guest room, Brit introduced Morgan to her real estate agent last week, and after an intensive daylong search of twenty-six townhouses, condominiums, and semidetached houses, Morgan bought a condo in the building across the street from Brit and moving in at the end of the month. I'm not sure she'll last the month at Brit's though. I was waiting for my turn to have Morgan crash on my couch.

"It's great, same layout as mine. I'm wondering if she's moving too fast, buying something on her own. What if Anil wants her back and—"

"Anil has a girlfriend," Tom said abruptly. He'd been standing quietly behind Brit the whole time we were talking. Because Tom's so quiet and Brit's personality sort of overshadows him, it's easy to forget he's around. I'm not sure if it's good for Brit to marry such a gentle soul. She needs someone to slap her down on occasion.

"What? Why wouldn't you tell me something like that?" Brit screeched, giving him a poke with her long nails.

"I just did, dear. Please don't hit me. I just found out this morning. Apparently, she's his assistant."

Both Brit and I looked over to where Morgan was still talking animatedly to J.B. "I was hoping that wasn't the reason," I said bleakly.

"He's such an asshole to do that to her. And to do it now—just before the wedding. What was he thinking? If the whole wedding party wouldn't be thrown out of balance—I took everyone's height and colouring into consideration, you know, in planning the ceremony—I would so not let him participate in our special day. Right, Tom?"

I sneaked a glance at Tom, who had an expression of resignation on his face. "Of course, dear."

This, of course, reminded Brit of her wedding, and she started talking about the tuxedos the groomsmen were renting and how they had to complement—not match since Tom must stand out on his own—Tom's own tuxedo. I kept glancing at Tom, wondering how he fared listening to Brit, but it seemed like he'd tuned her out. Sounds like a good idea, I decided.

Shortly though, Brit switched the subject by complimenting my dress. "It makes you look really good," she told me sincerely. "I think you have lost weight. Not that you need to or anything."

"Thanks," I said. I was wearing a new blue and green sundress with a halter top. Normally I prefer not to go backless—too many freckles—but I fell in love with the dress as soon as I saw it. And even J.B. coming up behind me, poking my back with the remark about playing connect the dots, didn't put me off it. I had my hair pulled back in a curly ponytail and even took some effort with my makeup. Even I thought I looked pretty good.

"Is David coming by?" Brit asked.

"He said he might." I hadn't said anything to either Brit or Morgan about David yet. Nothing about how he wanted to have a baby with me, or that he is now gay. I was trying to come to terms with it first.

"Well, you know I'm not in love with the idea of you allowing an ex back in your life," Brit sniffed, "but I sincerely hope he can manage to get you off this baby kick."

I decided not to respond to her, because really, what was I supposed to say?

Brit—sometimes it's difficult to understand my friendship with Britney. It all comes down to two things—I know Brit loves me, since she has, unbelievable as it may seem, proved it countless times, and I'm a very loyal person. Most of my close friends have been in my life for ten, fifteen years. Coop, Emma, and J.B. are, of course, the exceptions, since most everyone else I've known since university or even high school days. I like to keep people in my life, and most of them seem okay with staying in it as well. With Brit, as little as we see eye-to-eye about things these days,

I do love her, and as of yet, she hasn't done anything horrible enough to justify the loss I would definitely experience if I gave her the boot.

"We can't stay long," Brit was now saying as Tom handed her a plate of garlic-chili shrimp hot enough to scorch the tongue. "Tom's boss is taking us out on the boat to watch the fireworks. We have to meet him by seven-thirty at the harbour."

"Isn't that your sister?" Tom asked me.

I looked over to see Cooper give Libby a hug by the gate. Coop adores my sister. He's always glad to see her, they find lots to talk about, and her open admiration of his cooking abilities always pumps up his ego. When I'm in one of my truly envious-of-Libby days, I torture myself by thinking Coop likes her more than he likes me.

I excused myself and walked over to my sister. "Hey, my big girl," I said as Maddy flew into my arms. I was just saying hello to Luke when I heard a voice behind me that made me feel like I'd swallowed the tequila worm out of the bottle.

"Well, goodness, if I'd known there'd be a party, I might have dressed up a bit."

The attempt at the pseudo-Southern accent froze the smile on my face. As my horrified eyes met Libby's, I heard Luke's "Oh, shit," and watched him abandon his children by scurrying off toward the other side of the yard, where the table full of food was laid out. Libby and I turned around in unison, to find our mother at the gate of the backyard with two men.

"Um, hi? What are you doing here?" I asked my mother, using a voice that cracked like a prepubescent boy's.

"Well, you could sound a bit more welcoming, sweetface," my mother, aka Terri-with-an-i, said with a huge lipstick-y smile. She gave one of the men standing behind her a tug on the arm. "Isn't this lovely to find both my girls here? And my darling grandbabies!" Terri reached down—difficult to do in the tighter-than-tight red skirt she was sporting—and tickled Max's foot. "Hello, Maxie baby. And where's my sweet little Madison?"

"It's Max," Libby said through clenched teeth. Our mother always has this effect on her. I value my life enough not to tell Libby that when she's pissed off at Terri, she looks just like her.

"Hi there, Mrs. Samms," Cooper said easily, like it's every day my mother shows up uninvited at one of his parties. "It's nice to see you again."

"Oh, it's Cooper, isn't it?" Terri said coyly. She gave him a kiss on the cheek—aiming for the mouth, I suspect—but Coop moved at the last moment (smart man!), then reached up to wipe the cherry red lipstick mark off his face. "You get better looking every time I get to see you. I always say my Casey is so lucky to live with such a handsome man."

"I didn't invite her," I hissed to no one in particular.

"Well, of course, you didn't, sweetface, although I'm a bit hurt you didn't think of it. No, Eric and I are heading out for a night on the town to celebrate, and we thought we'd stop in, Casey, and see if you were home. We brought along Eric's little brother to introduce to you." Terri pulled a second man beside her. "This is Derek. I thought you might have a lot in common. I thought the four of us might pop out for a drink, but seeing as you're having this little party…"

I stared at my mother for so long that I didn't even glance at Derek. "Pardon?" She was not thinking about setting me up with someone, was she? And for it to be the brother of the guy she's dating…?

"Oh, Casey, don't be rude. But I guess I should start with Eric, shouldn't I?" she giggled. Terri's attention was on me, and I noticed she'd forgotten all about her darling grandbabies. Maddy was hanging onto my leg, staring at Terri with fascination. "I've been meaning to talk to both of my girls for ages, especially now with so much to celebrate."

"Well, let's start your celebration here, then," Cooper interrupted smoothly, seeing a way to escape. "What can I get you to drink, Mrs. Samms?"

"How many times, Cooper? It's Terri, please. Especially for handsome young things like yourself." I felt like gagging. Does my mother feel the need to flirt with everyone?

"Terri. And?" he looked at the silent man standing beside my mother.

"This is Eric," she said, tucking her arm through his. "Eric Devine. You know, I would love one of those margaritas I see over yonder, and Eric here will have a beer. And Derek?" she glanced to the second man.

"Beer, please, if it's not too much trouble. Thank you," Derek said politely.

I finally glanced at him. He's not unattractive or anything. Tall, with an olive complexion and slicked-back dark hair. Nice eyes, I guess. But really, there's no way—even if she managed to bring Prince William around—I don't think there would be any possible way I could be interested in a man my mother tried to set me up with.

"Thanks, sweetface," Terri simpered.

Cooper followed Luke's earlier move and made a run for it, but with more restraint than my brother-in-law. Terri turned back to Libby and me. Libby looked like she was waiting for the execution blindfold, and I suspect I looked the same. "So, my darling girls, aren't you going to ask me what my Eric and I are in town to celebrate?"

This was not the mother I remembered, with her my darlings and her sweetfaces. My mother signed love to birthday cards, but never once said, "I love you." Libby and I provided the affection to each other because we never got any from our parents. I think my mother must be overdoing it these days, trying to compensate for depriving us when we were growing up.

"Well?" Terri demanded when she sensed she was losing her audience.

"What are you celebrating, Mother?" I asked dutifully. "Something other than Canada Day?"

"With this man we've never met before?" Libby added scornfully.

"Libby, use your manners. This is Eric," she said proudly. "My husband-to-be."

"Well, that makes it even better," Libby said sarcastically.

Eric gave us a pleasant, albeit unimpressive smile. I can't say I smiled back. This news was a bit of a shocker, but not totally out of the blue. Terri never felt the need to give us any advance notice on her engagements or marriages. (This would be the fourth marriage since my father passed, and the sixth engagement.)

Eric was short, and on the young side. I'd wager his age to be anywhere between thirty-five and fifty. It's always hard to tell with the receding hairline. That and the glasses that tinted almost black in the sunlight so I couldn't see his eyes, and the ultra-pale legs poking out from beneath his khaki shorts with the pleat ironed down the front. I had to say the younger brother was by far the better-looking one of the two.

"You're getting married. Again," I managed. "Congratulations, I guess."

"Well, of course, congratulations! I've never been so happy. Look," she waved her ring in our stunned faces. I saw nothing but a shiny glare, and then Terri grabbed me in an embrace and all I could smell was her perfume. When she finally released me and grabbed a reluctant Libby—who still hadn't said anything—Eric stepped forward.

"It's nice to meet you, Casey." He offered me his hand. He had a surprisingly deep voice for his appearance, sort of like a radio deejay. "Sorry this comes as such a shock."

"It's okay." I had no idea what else to say. I was horrified when Terri remarried so quickly after my father died—of course, to a much younger man—and stunned with husband number three, who was considerably older and much wealthier. Neither marriage lasted very long—she divorced husband #2 after a little more than three years and buried #3 after only nine months. (Heart attack. In bed. Guess what they were doing?) In between those husbands were a few boyfriends, who declared their undying love with an engagement ring, so even though Terri and Eric professed to be engaged, with my mother's track record, it didn't mean much. The shock wore off the more engagements I heard about.

"It's just happening so quick-like," Terri giggled, letting go of Libby and latching on to Eric again. "We met—we met over the Internet, you know one of those dating sites—went on three dates, and then, what do you know? Eric pops the question! We didn't even get a chance to really get to know each other, if you know what I mean."

"Unfortunately," Libby said dryly.

"When I first saw your mother, I just knew," Eric said in his deep voice, making the story sound romantic, until you remembered he was speaking about my mother. "I knew I didn't want to wait to spend the rest of our lives together."

"Which might not be that long if you're lucky," Libby said under her breath. My mother continued to ignore her.

"Isn't he just the sweetest?" Terri cooed, patting Eric's face. "And isn't he just the cutest?" She turned to Maddy, who was still standing as wide-eyed as I was. "What do you think, sweetface? Want to be in your Nana's wedding? You'd be the perfect little flower girl for me."

Cooper took this opportune moment to come back with his hands full of drinks and Morgan trailing behind. Coop passed out the drinks, which unfortunately diffused none of the tension.

"Morgan, sweetface, it's been too long!" Terri swooped down on her with a clutching hug, almost spilling her drink all over Morgan. "You're looking so wonderfully well. Eric, darling, this is Morgan, who has been friends with Casey almost forever, and... Morgan and Cooper, I'm just telling my girls my news. Eric and I are going to be married!" She gave a trill of laughter. "I think my girls might be a little surprised at the whole thing."

"Wow. Well, all the best." Cooper clinked glasses with Terri, then Eric. "Congratulations!"

"That's... great," Morgan managed. She gave me a wide-eyed glance, and I could only roll my eyes in response. Morgan knows the score with my mother, but like Cooper, she's never had a problem getting along with her, probably because she's not blood-related. But like a true friend, she takes one for the team, making all the necessary gushing remarks over the ring, which Libby and I couldn't bring ourselves to, before backing up to make her escape. But before she left, her eyes fell on Derek, standing quietly on the other side of Terri. He was smiling at her.

"Oh, no," I muttered to no one in particular.

"Hi there," Morgan said, with the most flirtatious smile I'd seen in years. "I don't think we've met."

"I know we haven't," Derek told her. "Since there's no way I could forget a face like yours."

"Oh, please," I muttered to myself.

"Morgan Riese," she told him, holding out her hand. Derek took her hand, bowing over it, and touched it gently with his lips.

"Enchante," he said with a surprisingly sexy smile. Smile or not, it was a truly cheesy move, and I fully expected Morgan to...

Giggle! She giggled.

"Oh, please." This time I groaned. "You had to find the one full of cheese, didn't you, Mom?" Of course, no one heard me, and I wrenched my eyes away from the disturbing sight of Morgan being fawned over. Not that I minded Morgan being fawned over—goodness knows, after what Anil put her through, no one deserved it more—but in my opinion, the last type of man she needed was the Rico Suave type. Especially if my mother brought him around.

Terri was still gushing to Cooper while Libby stood glowering by his side. What was happening with Morgan and Derek seemed far less nauseating, but I turned back to them in time to see Morgan leading him across the yard.

"Oh, but—" Terri called out. Then she glanced at me and shrugged. "I guess it was too much to hope for. Anyway, what do you think of our news?"

"Um, congratulations," I managed to say weakly. Libby gave me her death glare, but what could I do? Terri's eagerness and need for approval is borderline pathetic, but oddly touching.

"You're just going to accept this?" she cried. Despite her tiny frame and sweet-looking exterior, Libby has a ferocious temper. It's quick, it's nasty, and it's not nice to see. And it comes out a lot when our mother is around.

"You're just going to sit back and let her marry some guy we don't even know? But then, why shouldn't we just let her? It's not like she took any interest in our lives, just sitting back and letting our father treat us like shit. She just sat back and watched, so you know, Mother, I hope you marry someone who treats you like shit so you know what it feels like!" I think she might have continued, but Cooper put a hand on her shoulder.

"It's definitely a surprise," he said mildly.

Libby gave her head a shake and motioned to Maddy to let go of my leg. "Look at what you make me do! I never, ever swear in front of my children, and now listen to me! Don't think you're going to use my children in your wedding either. Maybe you should wait until Casey has her baby, since she's so accepting of the whole thing! Hear that, Mother? Casey wants to get pregnant without a husband or even a boyfriend in the picture, just some guy to 'donate'!" Her fingers formed claws as she made quotation marks around the word.

"Libby!" I gasped. I was sure I would get around to telling my mother about having a baby when I got pregnant, but it wasn't news to be blurted out like that.

"Oh, are you pregnant?" Terri turned to me with surprise.

"No, not yet. I'm just—"

"Well, it's no surprise if you are. I was pregnant at eighteen with you, and we didn't have to wait too long for Libby. I'm sure if your father didn't drink so much and he could have performed adequately, I would have more kids." I'm sure Libby and I have identical expressions of disgust at that comment, but it only gets worse as Terri continues.

"I would love to have more babies. In fact, another baby might be a wonderful idea, don't you think, Eric? You're just thirty-six, and I know you'd love a child of our own. I've heard of lots of women in their fifties who can carry a child. What a good idea! I'm strong and healthy, and goodness knows I'm still getting my monthlies—"

My mouth gaped open, and I had a fervent wish to have the ground open up and make me, or my mother, disappear into it. Anything that could remove those few statements from being imbedded in my mind for all time would do the trick.

"Excuse me. I feel the need to vomit," Libby said. She took Maddy by the hand and picked up Max in his car seat and stalked off. "I hope you know what you're getting into," were her final words thrown like a dart toward Eric.

I looked at Cooper standing uncomfortably beside me. To give him credit, he wasn't making a move to run away, but I was sure he didn't want to hear any of this.

"Well, I knew she wouldn't take it well," Terri said, waving Libby away. "She's always been the ungrateful, high-minded type. I'm surprised she's found a man to put up with her moods. Always been moody, that one."

"Mother!" I said reprovingly.

"Casey, you know what she's like as well as I do."

"No, actually, I don't think you know what she's like at all."

Terri looked approvingly at me as I said that. "Got some backbone, did you, Casey? About time, I'd say."

I reached forward and plucked the glass out of Terri's hand. Time I showed some backbone, then. "Too bad you have to be off, Mother. Good to meet you, Eric. Thanks for deciding to tell us about your news. Have a good night."

# Chapter Twenty

"During pregnancy a woman often forges a deeper and more intimate relationship with the father of the child."

*A Young Woman's Guide to the Joy of Impending Motherhood*
Dr. Francine Pascal Reid (1941)

J.B. FOUND ME IN my apartment, where I'd taken refuge with a blenderful of margarita, heavy on the tequila. Whereas my sister felt the need to resort to sharp words when our mother was around, I seemed okay on the outside, but often felt the need for a great deal of alcohol after she was gone. Once my mother left, dragging her latest boy toy and his besotted brother Derek with her, Coop's party lost all appeal for me.

"I thought you might be responsible for the missing blender," J.B. said mildly, taking in the sight of me flopped across my bed, with my head hanging over the edge and taking great slurps from the straw sticking out of the blender without comment.

I pushed my ponytail out of my face and looked up with red eyes. I hadn't yet figured out why I felt the need to cry over my mother's news, even though I knew indulging in a crying jag would inevitably result in a monster headache later. Another thing I could blame on my mother. That and how her visit sent me straight to the bottle, after I'd vowed to lay off the drinking.

It's not like my parents had a happy marriage. My father was an asshole, and he's been dead for years. My mother deserves happiness in her life, doesn't she? That's the good daughter inside me talking. But the other daughter—the one who remembers living in the same house with Terri-with-an-i and watching her pretend ignorance of my father's drinking and how it affected Libby and me; the one who caught her in bed with sixteen-year-old Aaron, whom I had a huge crush on at the time; the one she never managed to say good-bye to the day I left home to go to university—that daughter doesn't really think Terri deserves any sort of happiness. That daughter thinks Terri should rot in a hole with her Botox injections and her Mr. Happy Rabbit vibrator. It's not difficult to see which part of me has the better argument.

"Did you hear?" I asked J.B. scornfully.

"About your mom? Coop filled me in."

"Can you believe it? He's the same age as me. I know she likes them younger, but does it have to be so embarrassingly young? And then to bring his brother to meet me? What was she thinking?"

"That part's pretty funny, actually," J.B. said, not even trying to hide his smile.

"Ha-ha. Who wouldn't want to date their step-uncle-to-be? Ugh. Ugh!" I took another long sip from the straw. "And then she says they want to have a baby? There's a possibility my child will be older than her aunt or uncle! If I ever get pregnant, that is. Although after seeing Terri tonight, I'm starting to believe I shouldn't be anywhere near a child so I don't screw it up like she did." I took one last swallow of margarita and flipped over on my back.

J.B. lay down beside me. The warmth of his weight on the bed beside me and his potent male smell were comforting, and I fought the urge to curl up in his arms. A hug from someone would be nice right now. I couldn't even get a cuddle from my cat. He was sitting on the pillow just watching me self-destruct. It's not like he hadn't seen it before.

"Oh, I don't know. You turned out okay," he said.

I grimaced. "What do you know?"

"I know you didn't run off and get married at nineteen, just for a reason to leave home."

For J.B. to bring his marriage up instantly made me forget my pity party. "What happened with you two, anyway?" I asked hesitantly.

"There was a bunch of reasons. We were too young to get married, if you ask me. We were immature, had no money. Betsey always believed the good Lord would provide, as long as we loved each other enough. But then she got pregnant, and uh, lost the baby." He glanced at me. "She was almost four months along when they realized there was no heartbeat. That's when we both started to get pissed off with God, and I figured out he wasn't going to provide for us and I'd better get my butt in gear. I went back to school, which was fine until Betsey got pregnant again. And lost it. And then she got pissed when I wasn't upset enough that she lost the baby. I was upset because she was so upset, but she should have never gotten pregnant again."

"You didn't want a baby?"

"I was excited about the first one, but that's before I woke up and realized it would have been a disaster. I'm not glad she lost it—any of them, but there was no way we could have handled it. We were kids ourselves. Betsey could barely take care of herself—always looking for approval. And she needed constant attention—there's no way she could deal with a baby taking the spotlight from her. I was in school and couldn't find a job, so I couldn't pay for anything and the last thing I wanted was to work for my dad on the farm. That's why I left home in the first place."

"I can't see you as a farmer." I rolled over again so I was lying on my side facing J. B., who was staring at the ceiling.

"That was the whole problem—neither could I."

"So what happened? Two kids, young and in love, facing the problems of the world by themselves—and then comes baby?"

"There shouldn't have been a baby. Betsey told me she was taking birth control."

"Nothing's 100 percent, you know."

"She lied to me and stopped taking it."

"Ah. That's not good."

"Then she goes and does it again. After the second time, I started to think she wasn't as perfect as I always thought and that us being married wasn't a good idea. Plus, the good Lord wasn't providing shit, and Betsey was becoming a bit of a bitch to live with. And about that time, she started messing around with my best friend. I came home once and found them together. That's how my nose got broken."

"From your friend?"

J.B. laughed, sounding embarrassed. "I wish. No, it was her. She hit me with a book to stop me from smashing his face in. I had a bit of a temper back then."

"I don't blame you. Is that—the card said her son, the one named after you?" I didn't know how to put it delicately, but the thought of the paternity of a child out there named after J.B. had entered my mind once or twice over the last few weeks.

"Yeah. He got her pregnant, but then she tried to say it was mine. But I knew—it was easy to figure it out once you did the math." J.B. said this in a deceptively casual tone, but I could see a muscle pulsing in his jaw. Definite unresolved feelings there, I told myself.

"Wow. And she still sends you cards? I think I'd just go off and crawl under a rock someplace if I did that."

"You're nothing like her."

We lay there quietly for a few minutes, J. B. staring at the ceiling and me staring at him. I wondered if he was counting the dots on each ceiling tile like I do. I resisted the urge to run my finger down his profile, from his forehead, up the slope of his nose, touching the softness of his lips, to the arrogant jut of his chin. I resisted, mainly because this was the most intimate I'd ever gotten with J.B., even counting the times we had sex.

J.B. suddenly rolled over and caught me staring at him. "What?" he asked.

"Nothing." I could feel myself blushing.

"You're staring at me like I've got two heads."

"Just one. It's a nice one, though." I reached over and flicked his nose with my finger. J.B. didn't smile. He just looked at me. "Now you're looking at me all funny-like."

He gave a strained smile and turned his head. "You know, Case, I—" J.B. stopped short as we heard footsteps coming down the stairs.

"Casey?" I heard Morgan's voice.

"Um, down here!" Both J.B. and I leaped off the bed like we were guilty of something.

"Are you hiding?" Morgan called as she came down the stairs. I heard her stumble at the last step. The extra height of it always trips people. "Are you okay?" When she poked her head into my bedroom, she looked surprised at the sight of J.B. standing beside me. "Oh! I didn't know you were down here."

"Just rescuing the blender," J.B. said quickly, grabbing it from the floor.

"Oh?" Morgan's gaze swiveled from J.B. back to me, and then to Sebastian, still lying on the pillow taking it all in. Then she jerked her head toward the stairs, like she was trying to tell me something.

"Everything okay upstairs?" J.B. asked, noticing her gesture.

"Fine, but Casey, I found someone wandering around looking for you," she said.

"Please, don't let it be my mother or someone else she's trying to set me up with!" I begged with my eyes closed.

"Much better than that," Morgan assured me. "But maybe …"

"Come on down," I called reluctantly. There were more footsteps and another stumble at the bottom. I should put up a sign or something. I sat back on the bed, expecting Cooper and a lecture about drinking all the margaritas.

"David!" I said in surprise as he stepped into the doorway of my apartment.

"You told me to stop by," he said with a big grin. He looked good in a pair of khaki shorts and a dark green polo neck.

"That's great!" It was mainly awkwardness that made me jump into his outstretched arms. "I'm so glad you came. You remember Morgan—obviously." My laugh was a bit forced. "This is J.B., one of my roommates." I was having difficulty looking at J.B. for some reason.

"Hey." J.B. took David's hand and they shook, but he was looking at me the whole time. "David, as in—David?"

"That's me," David said a little too heartily. "Hey—that your cat?" He went to Sebastian and started giving him a good scratch.

"Ah." J.B. looked from me to David and there was not a lot of warmth in his eyes. "Well, I'll get out of here. I'll take the blender back up to Coop."

"I'll get out of here too," Morgan chimed in. "But, Casey, look, about what your Mom said—"

"I'm fine," I told her wearily.

"No, but that's good. It's about Derek." I looked blank for a moment. "The brother. I know your Mom thought maybe..." she trailed off, glancing at David nervously. I wanted to say, don't worry about giving away secrets, but I didn't. "Look, he asked for my number."

"Who, Derek? You're kidding!" I laughed.

"I kind of gave it to him," she told me in a small voice.

"What?"

"I thought he was cute," she said defensively. "And he seemed nice."

J.B. started to laugh. "Way to go, Morgan!" He draped his arm around her shoulder. "Scoop him up right under Casey's nose. You don't need me to go to the wedding with you—you'll have no problem finding your own date."

"I wanted to talk to you about that," she said to him.

"Let's go get a drink then." Without a word to me, he headed to the stairs, his arm still around Morgan. I watched him go with the feeling I did something wrong. It was like the moment on the bed never happened.

"So." David stepped away from Sebastian and rubbed his hands together. He glanced out the doorway as if to watch J.B. walk away. "That the roommate? He's pretty."

I gave his arm a sharp slap. "None of that talk, okay? I'm still getting used to the idea. I still have flashbacks, torturing myself if you thought some of our friends from school were better-looking than me."

David threw his arm around me and squeezed. I had a moment when I wished he would do more than give me a friendly squeeze, but I quickly squelched it. "Ah, Casey, I loved you best of all."

"Back then," I added. "But it's nice to know why you didn't argue with me breaking up with you."

David hugged me again. "You've always been a good friend."

"And the best girlfriend you've ever had, or ever will have, don't you forget!"

David laughed, looking at me strangely before settling on the edge of my bed. "I know this probably isn't the best time, but I was wondering if you've given it any thought? What we talked about Tuesday night?"

"You talked. I sort of sat there with a stunned expression on my face."

"Well, there was no easy way to tell you. I thought you handled it all right. Does that mean ..."

"I've thought, and I haven't thought," I told him. "Which means, it sounds like the thing to do, but I haven't figured everything out yet. I've been waiting for my period to come, and then ..."

David shuddered. "I guess I should get used to hearing about that sort of stuff," he grinned.

"Maybe."

"Maybe is pretty good. I'll give you a little more time to think about it, then."

"I should have figured it out in a day or two," I said.

# CHAPTER TWENTY-ONE

"The expectant mother should savour the excitement and anticipation once she receives the news she is indeed carrying a child. And there is always the unfortunate possibility the father-to-be might not share her joy of her being with child, especially in the beginning. Men always fear the unknown, and for male species, pregnancy and the mysterious workings of the female body is a definite unknown."

*A Young Woman's Guide to the Joy of Impending Motherhood*
Dr. Francine Pascal Reid (1941)

SINCE CANADA DAY WAS on a Sunday this year, I had Monday off like most of the country and celebrated by having a much-needed sleep-in. I'd been exhausted for the last week for some strange reason. I chalked it up to my approaching period. For once, I couldn't wait to get it. The rest of the day I spent at the house doing an also-much-needed tidying up and then headed to Libby's that night for a barbeque. I spent most of the time with Madison since a four-year-old's conversation was preferable to Libby's when she was on one of her our-mother-is-a-horrible-parent rants.

Brit, Morgan, and I canceled our weekly Monday outing, which I totally regretted late Tuesday afternoon when Morgan called me all hysterical-like. It turned out she finally found out about Anil's new girlfriend, and as I thought, didn't take the news very well. I didn't blame her, since Anil has had this girlfriend for most of the year, and Morgan had no idea. To cap it all off, the new girlfriend was demanding marriage, and I guess Anil was going for it. Poor Morgan.

Being a good friend, I let Morgan cry on my shoulder all night, and because Brit had Tom's boss over for dinner, brought her home to my apartment because I didn't want Morgan to be alone. And because I am a good friend, I didn't make her sleep on my couch, which is full of lumps, but made up the couch upstairs for her. I left a note for Coop, Emma, and J.B. that she was there and hoped Morgan was asleep before they got home. I was sure a sympathetic voice would set her off again, and then no one would get any sleep. It was after midnight when I finally tucked her in, as exhausted from Morgan's crying as she was.

Because of the drama of the night before, I was surprised when I woke up on Wednesday morning that the first thing that popped into my head was my period. Not that it had arrived—the fact that it hadn't. Like I said, my period always comes. I don't know why I never bothered to check when I had it last. Silly of me, really, but I never gave it a thought because there was no reason why it wouldn't come.

I have to backtrack a bit. The first thing that popped into my head Wednesday morning wasn't my period; it was J.B. I'm embarrassed to admit I had a particularly nice dream about J.B. during the night, if you know what kind of dream I mean. I'm not sure what brought it on, and I'm very glad Morgan slept on the couch upstairs instead of crashing in my bed with me or things might have been very awkward.

Anyway, I woke up with the thought of J.B. still fresh as a daisy in my mind, thinking wouldn't it be nice, and thinking how nice it had been the last time, and then *ohmyGod*. It hit me.

Oh, my God!

I'm so dense. Could it be possible? Could it be possible I was so stupid that, all the while I'm thinking about when I can get pregnant, counting the days and thinking all happy thoughts, when all the while I could already be pregnant, and in the worst twist ever, pregnant by a man who definitely does not want to be a father?

I'm easily distracted, but this—this is kind of big from which to be sidetracked. I mean, come on! I might very well be carrying a real live child inside me. Okay, maybe not quite a child yet, but a glob of ever-multiplying cells.

This couldn't be happening. I started counting on my fingers again, but that was too complicated so I rolled out of bed and grabbed the calendar I have stuck to the wall in the kitchen. It's July 4, Independence Day for our neighbours the Americans—and isn't that ironic that my independence might well disappear today?

Okay, I said to myself, let's see about this. I flipped back a month. Last Tuesday was that red-letter day when David rocked my world and told me he was gay. The day before that was when I went out with Morgan—good thing I wasn't drinking too much, but what about the Canada Day party and drinking all those margaritas?

Okay, no sense getting upset over nothing. I didn't even know if I was pregnant. Even so, my heart was racing and my hands were jittery. It was the week before Morgan and Anil broke up that I had sex with J.B. It was the night of the wedding. How could I have forgotten about that? Not that I forgot about it; I just didn't think it was worth remembering. Of course it was worth remembering because it was—never mind.

Could I have gotten pregnant by having sex? Duh. Did we use contraception? Yes. I went scurrying for my purse, where I keep my container of pills. If I started them on… when I opened the little pink lid,

I found to my horror there were three still in their little nests, and I took a deep breath. But I couldn't seem to remember having a period in the month of June. I must have... no, I remember I had it during the Victoria Day long weekend, because I was still with Mike then and he had talked about going away, and I put the kibosh on it because I knew he would want sex and... but that was like six weeks ago! And if there were three pills left, it meant sometime during the month I forgot to take three of my pills. I forgot one again last night, so at least four times...

How could I be such an idiot? I'm thirty-five years old. You'd think I'd have my menstrual cycle figured out by now.

But J.B. and I used a condom. I'm sure of that, because he didn't have one and I had to go rifling through my bedside table to find one. I remember there were two in there. I hit the drawer and started pulling things out, trying to find the other condom. Not that I felt like having sex now or ever, but I wanted to at least check out that the condom was worthy of protecting me from getting pregnant with J.B.

Here—purple foil wrapper. Expiry—March 2009. 2009! That couldn't be good.

I sat staring at the numbers on the back of the wrapper. Maybe the one we used was more recent, but the dread deep in my stomach didn't think so. So I had sex, possibly not as protected as I would have liked—as J.B. would have liked... There might be a little chance I could be pregnant.

How would I tell J.B.?

But first I had to check if there was something to tell him. I jumped out of bed again and grabbed one of the pregnancy tests I bought when I first thought of having a baby. Actually, I bought two, thinking I'd probably never believe the first one. Okay, I bought three. They were all lying in a Shoppers' DrugMart bag under my sink. I opened the first box—I'd already ripped it open and read the instructions several times in preparation for this moment, so I was good to go. I just had to hold the end of the stick under my urine stream for a bit, and wait until either a plus or minus sign popped up. Sounded easy enough. Then I grabbed the second box. What if the first one said I was not when I really was? Then I'd have to go through this whole rigmarole again to find out the truth. Then I'd have to wait until I had to pee again. Or what if the stick said I was, and I really wasn't? To make sure, I decided to use both at once, just to make sure. Pee on one, then pee on the other. And just to make sure the test was absolutely positive—not positive, accurate, we didn't know if it was positive yet—I grabbed the third and prepared to pee like I'd never peed before.

"Libby," I whispered into the phone four and a half minutes later. "I've got pluses. Three pluses."

"What are you talking about?" I could hear Madison yelling something in the background. "Maddy, stop," Libby responded, not moving the phone so it was as if she was yelling at me. "What's a plus?"

"On the pregnancy test I have in my hand," I told her, enunciating every word. "I didn't even have to wait the five minutes, the plus just popped right up after a minute, but I waited to see if they went away, but none of them did, and now I'm sitting here with these pee sticks in my hand, all with the blue plus on them—"

"Yeah, there's ones with the plus and the minus, but—wait a sec! Did you do a test? Why? And it's positive?"

"I think so. I did three, and they all say the same thing. The blue plus."

Libby started to laugh with delight. "Oh, my God! You really did it! You're pregnant! But when did you get pregnant?"

"I think I am. I did the test three times. It was all in the same pee, but that doesn't matter, does it? Should I do another one?"

Libby was still laughing, but I thought it was at me now. She said, "I think that's overkill. My doctor told me there's not a lot of false positives, so if one says yes, it means yes. I think you're pregnant! But when? And who? I didn't think you were going—" She stopped, and it was as if I could actually hear the wheels turning in her head. "Who? That Mike guy?"

"No, thank God."

"But who...?"

"I had sex with J.B. the night of Ethan and Darcy's wedding." I whispered my confession. "I think I..."

"Oh, oh, uh-oh. It's his? J.B. got you pregnant! Did he mean to get you pregnant?"

"I don't think so." I was still whispering, even though Libby was yelling loud enough that anyone standing beside me could hear her.

"What's he going to say? You are going to tell him, aren't you? You have to tell him. It's not right if you don't tell him—that's not nice at all, and he might be upset when you do tell him, but I'm sure he'll be so pissed if you don't and he finds out later, but I guess you could tell him it was someone else's, or that you went to get the donor stuff, but everyone knows you'd tell the world if you'd gone and done that—"

I'd never realized how obvious it was that Libby and I are sisters.

"I have to tell him."

"I guess you better. Go tell him."

"Now?"

"Yes. Then call me back and tell me what he says."

I forgot all about Morgan asleep on the couch as I ran up the two flights of stairs, tripping several times, once dropping my precious pee sticks on the stairs. I hope that doesn't leave a pee stain, I thought to myself, then started giggling uncontrollably. I'm pregnant. I'm pregnant! I'm so excited. And nervous and scared and just freaking out in general. Or I was about to freak out. I thought I was still in shock. I was pregnant without even trying to get pregnant, which meant this was totally meant to be, sort of like the fate thing I thought with David, only this was real fate, not some make-believe fantasy I couldn't get out of my mind. I was pregnant! Really pregnant!

I stopped just before I hit the top step. But I wanted to get pregnant with David. At least I was pretty sure I wanted to. I thought that's where I was heading, even though I hadn't totally made up my mind. I wished I'd made up my mind. I wished we'd done something about it so that I could say it was his instead of J. B.'s because I really didn't think J.B. was going to be happy with me ...

I wondered what J.B. would say. He had to be happy once the shock wore off, and maybe he'd want to—

Should I prepare a speech? Tell him, yes, I'm pregnant with his child, but I wasn't expecting him to take any responsibility for the baby or me. That it was an accident, totally unintentional, and he didn't have to do anything except if he—he was going to freak. Maybe I should wait to tell him.

But I was pregnant—really pregnant—and starting to get really excited, whoever the father might be, and I really wanted to tell someone. Now. And J. B.'s room was closer to the stairs than Coop's. I'd tell Cooper next.

I burst through J. B.'s door without knocking. "J.B., you won't believe it! Look at my pee—"

I trailed off when I noticed it was not J.B. in J.B.'s bed.

"Hey, Casey," Morgan said sleepily.

# CHAPTER TWENTY-TWO

"The nine months of pregnancy are peppered with joy
and anxiety; excitement and uncertainty."

*A Young Woman's Guide to the Joy of Impending Motherhood*
Dr. Francine Pascal Reid (1941)

"OH. OHHHH! MORGAN? MORGAN... what are you doing here? Here—in J.B.'s bed? Here? You were down there?" I pointed to the stairs.

"J.B. came home and took pity on me having to sleep on the couch," she told me, stretching her arms above her head. I couldn't help but notice she looked very, very comfortable in his bed. Too comfortable to have spent the night there alone.

"But you said..."

"Hey. What's with the party this early?" J.B. was standing in the doorway. I couldn't help but notice he was wearing the same red striped boxer shorts that he had on the night we conceived. The night I got pregnant. The pregnancy that he didn't know about yet, that I was about to tell him about after I got over the horrible, sick feeling I had thinking about him and Morgan.

A yawn split his face. "What's up, Case?"

"Oh. Um." I don't have to tell you how the sight of Morgan totally took the wind right out of my sails. I wanted to take my sticks of pee and run back downstairs. This was not how I pictured this. I guessed I was not the only one who was thinking about sex last night. But how could they? This couldn't be happening!

"I gotta pee," he said as he disappeared into the hallway.

"Pee," I whispered. "I've got to go." I didn't know where to look or what to say. I just needed to get out of there right now because I had a terrible feeling I might be about to cry and no one involved in this little scene needed that.

"What have you got in your hand, Casey?" Morgan called out just as I was about to make my escape.

I froze and glanced down in my hand, where I was still clutching the three sticks, each with its urine-saturated tip and a bright blue plus in the window. It was obvious what they were. How would I do this now? I should have taken a moment to prepare, even though there was no way in hell I could have prepared for this little scenario.

"I'm pregnant," I muttered, still standing in the middle of the room.

"What?" Morgan asked.

"I'm pregnant," I said a little clearer.

"Oh, my God!" Morgan shrieked. She jumped out of bed—I was happy to see that she was dressed in the pajamas I gave her to wear last night—and grabbed me in a bone-cracking hug. "Pregnant! How? Who? When? Why didn't you tell me?" Morgan was clearly over the moon with excitement, laughing and clutching me, but all I could think about was that she just had sex with J.B.

"Aren't you excited?" she asked. "What's the matter? I'm so happy for you, I could cry!" And her eyes began to get wet and weepy.

"What's going on?" J.B. asked, coming back in the room.

Morgan started to jump up and down. "Tell him, Casey, tell him, *tellhimtellhimtellhim*!"

Reluctantly I faced J.B., feeling much like I imagine Anne Boleyn must have felt as she faced her executioner that fateful day she lost her head. Fear and resignation—a sense of just get it over with. I showed him the pee sticks in my hand so there wouldn't be any question of me not telling the truth. "I'm going to have a baby."

J.B. looked confused for a moment before clarity set in. "You're pregnant?"

There was absolutely no enthusiasm in his tone. That should have told me something. I should have left then, walked right out of the room and let him process things before I made the big announcement. Since J.B. was showing no excitement at all for the fact that I was pregnant, then how was he going to react when he found out I was pregnant with his child?

"I'm pregnant," I confirmed solemnly.

Why didn't I think about how there was a good chance he wouldn't be alone? Not that I even gave Morgan a thought—why this morning of all mornings? Just when I finally put two and two together to have it equal pregnant me—why did he have to pick last night to get laid? And with my best friend?

"Wow. That's—congratulations. Why aren't you jumping up and down and waking up the whole house? What's wrong?" J.B. asked, correctly sensing I was not as excited as the situation would call for.

"When did you go and get whatever you needed to have done? I thought you would have said something. Or maybe, hey, wait, is it David's? You slut, you never said a word," Morgan cried, oblivious to the gamut of emotions I was rushing through.

"I didn't go anywhere," I added, with my eyes not leaving J.B.'s. I had to admit, my gaze must have been pretty accusatory. "Unlike you."

"Where did I go?" she asked in bewilderment. "What does—oh, Casey, no. No way."

"What are you going on about?" J.B. wondered.

"She must have been a virtual smorgasbord for you," I said bitterly. "Just lying there sleeping, all upset, so that you could take advantage of her! Being all needy and damsel in distress-y."

"Casey, don't," Morgan said. "Don't say another word."

"What are you talking about? I thought this was about you being pregnant!" J.B. asked with confusion.

I jerked my head angrily toward Morgan. Now, I like to think I'm fairly laid-back. Like my sister, I do have a temper, but it takes a lot for me to get worked up about something. Normally. But this—bursting into J.B.'s room all excited only to find Morgan ensconced in his big, comfy bed—it's obvious what went on.

To give me credit, it had been a pretty stressful couple of weeks, what with the David stuff and my mother's little announcement the other night, so I think I must have been a little on edge. I'm also guessing hormones—OMG, I'm pregnant! —were playing a part, so I was a little less rational than usual. And unfortunately for him, all this junk I had going on had mixed together into a whole bunch of pissed-off at J.B.

"Huh?" J.B. said. He didn't have a clue.

"Casey, J.B. slept on the couch," Morgan told me urgently. She grabbed hold of my arm. "He insisted on giving me his bed, but he stayed downstairs. I was up here myself the entire night. You ran right past him on the couch on your way up here."

"You woke me up, falling up the stairs," J.B. accused.

"Yes, but—oh. Oh. Downstairs."

"All night," she said quietly. "And me up here. It was nice of him to let me sleep here, but I wasn't that grateful. Or that needy."

Once her words sank in, I felt pretty stupid. "Oh. So you and him never..."

"No," she said quietly. "I wouldn't do that. I told you."

"Oh." This was so not how I pictured this. I stood in the middle of J.B.'s room still holding my pee sticks and not knowing how to continue.

J.B. cleared his throat. "I have no idea what just went on here," he said, in a voice that told me, yeah, he had a pretty good idea but he was not going to say anything. "But can we just take a step back for a sec and start again? You're really pregnant?"

"Really pregnant," I could only mumble, since I was feeling pretty stupid right then. "Sorry," I said to Morgan.

"Forget about it. So—who?" Morgan let out a gasp. "Oh, no, it's not Mike's, is it? That would be too terrible to think about," she shuddered. "But you didn't sleep with him, did you, so how could—?"

"It's not Mike's. Thank God." I turned back to J.B., but this time I could barely look him in the eyes.

"Then who?" Morgan demanded.

I could see the realization hit J.B., hit him like a knockout punch so he actually took a step away from me. "No way."

"I'm sorry," I cried immediately. "It doesn't mean anything. You don't have to—"

"What are you talking about?" Morgan shrieked. "Casey, whose baby are you having?"

"Mine," J.B. answered.

To say the whole scene was not what I ever imagined is kind of like saying Canadian winters can be a mite bit chilly at times.

"Really?" Morgan goggled at me. "J.B.?"

"I never intended—yes, I wanted to get pregnant, but I know you don't and I would never, ever, in a million years do that to you," I pleaded to J.B., who headed stiffly to the bed to sit down, with a stunned expression on his face. Morgan stared at both of us like she was watching a tennis match. "I never even thought that was the time I could get pregnant, so how could I—I mean, I know it was now, but then, when we, you know, did it, I had no idea and I—"

"Are you sure it's mine?"

J.B.'s cold words cut cleanly through my heart like a surgeon's blade. They set me back so much I didn't even have time to get pissed. I was sure I'd be pissed later, though.

"Yes. There hasn't been anyone else."

"She never slept with Mike, did you, Casey?" Morgan asked helpfully. She threw an arm protectively around my shoulders.

Now whenever I think back to this little scenario, I have a wave of love and devotion for Morgan. Not two minutes ago, I was unfairly accusing her of having sex with J.B., but instead of holding that against me—like I might in the same circumstance—she jumped in and prepared to defend me and my honour, without even knowing the whole story.

"And David?" she prompted. I shook my head. "You say it's J.B.'s?"

"But how?" he asked with more than a touch of anger. "We used—"

"They're not always 100 percent," Morgan said, sounding not unlike how my grade ten sex education teacher used to lecture the class. I didn't think J.B. appreciated the tone, however.

"But you're on the pill," he added.

"Casey's never been too consistent taking that thing, have you?" Morgan smiled indulgently at me and gave my shoulder a reassuring squeeze. She'd been privy of the many times I'd scrambled to remember what birth control pills I'd missed.

"I think it's yours," I told J.B. tearfully. "I mean, I know it is. I'm sorry."

"I don't see how—" He ran a frustrated hand through his hair.

"It was an accident, okay? I never thought—I never meant to ... with you. I never meant to with you."

"I wouldn't have gone near you if I'd known." J.B. looked at me in time to see the flash of pain cross my face. "Sorry, but you know... Jesus, Casey, what do you want me to say?"

"I don't think either of you should say anything more, in case you say something you'll regret," Morgan warned, still with her arm around me. "Come on, Casey, let's go down to your place."

I looked at J.B., hoping he'd say something positive. He was just sitting on the edge of the bed, rubbing his face with those big hands, those hands that touched me, caressed me—we made a baby together. J.B. and I made a baby. We—

"Fuck!"

He obviously wasn't happy about it.

# Chapter Twenty-Three

"Reactions to pregnancy announcements can be varied, to say the least."

*A Young Woman's Guide to the Joy of Impending Motherhood*
Dr. Francine Pascal Reid (1941)

"WHAT THE HELL?" MORGAN breathed as soon as she ushered me downstairs. "You've been holding out on me, Case."

"It was just that one time," I muttered, sinking into the couch. I felt sick, really, truly, physically sick. That did not go as I'd planned, in fact, how could I have possibly planned something like that—me getting pregnant by J.B., of all people? Who could have ever expected that to happen?

Obviously not J.B. or myself.

"When?" Morgan goggled at me. She sat down beside me, and before I could say anything, gave me a sharp slap on the arm. "That's for not telling me earlier."

"Ow. You can't hit me—I'm pregnant," I complained.

"Yes, you are!" she said gleefully, this time pulling me into a hug. "You're pregnant! You're having a baby! Oh, Casey, I'm so happy for you! Are you—are you maybe a little happy?" she asked when she pulled away and noticed my eyes were filled with tears. "Oh, Casey. It's what you've always wanted."

"But not like this," I sniffed. "I thought if I ever told a guy I was pregnant, he'd be happy and excited, just like me. Or I thought lately, there wouldn't be anyone to tell. I didn't think it would be J.B. and he'd be so pissed with me!"

"He's just upset. You kind of surprised him."

"You think?" I asked bitterly. "Am I not as surprised as he is?"

"Yes, but you wanted this, and it was the last thing J.B. ever expected, so of course there might be a difference in the reactions. But I'm sure once he gets his head around it, he'll be fine," Morgan assured me. "He's just freaked out."

"And suddenly you know him so well?"

"Well, no, but we did talk a lot last night," Morgan admitted. "When he came home, I was still awake, and we had a drink and talked. That's all, just talk. And mostly about you."

"Well, that won't happen again. I'm sure J.B. won't want to hear anything to do with me for a while." I got up to start stalking across the room. "And he won't be going anywhere near me with a ten-foot pole, not that I want him to. Asking if it's really his! Asshole!" I kicked at the couch as I stomped by.

"That was rude, and I'm not taking his side, but you really blew him out of the water—and it's not like you haven't been involved with anyone else. He doesn't know who you sleep with, does he? As far as he's concerned, you might have been doing the nasty with Mike all along instead of waiting like a good little girl, and well, there's David. You've been so closemouthed about that even I don't know what's going on there."

I stared at Morgan with disbelief that she could consider David as the dad, but then I remembered I hadn't told her that David is gay, or any of the other stuff. But now wasn't the time to get into that.

"I'm sorry I thought you slept with J.B.," I told her instead.

"Well, now I can see why you got so upset," Morgan laughed. "I would have ripped your head off if the situation was reversed."

"I overreacted, and I'm sorry." I suddenly dropped back onto the couch beside her. "Still be my friend?"

She threw her arm around me. "Of course. But you still have to tell me when it happened."

"It was after Ethan's wedding when I caught Mike. I got drunk; I got upset—"

"You got laid. It's completely understandable."

"Yes, but it was the wrong person!" I laid my head back against the couch. "Even though I don't know who the right person is."

Morgan put her head on my shoulder. "But that doesn't matter now, does it? You're pregnant! Isn't that what you've always wanted?"

Not five minutes after Morgan left, I heard the sounds of Cooper's footsteps coming down the stairs. Emma wasn't with him, so this must be serious. Was he going to read me the riot act, kick me out, call me an irresponsible slut who took advantage of his best friend, or most shockingly of all, be happy for me?

"Please tell me..." Cooper began helplessly, standing in the doorway. Obviously, J.B. had gotten to him first.

I shrugged. "What do you want me to say?" I had a horrible feeling I was going to lose Cooper because of this.

"It's true? You're really pregnant? And J.B.—he's really the father?"

"Given his reaction to the news, I really don't want to call him that," I said coolly. "But, yes, it was J.B. who got me pregnant, despite what he may think."

"What's that supposed to mean? He thinks he got you pregnant, and he's flipping out."

"Good for him."

"Hang on a sec; I don't think I got the whole story. Casey, what's going on?"

"Ask the guy whose ejaculation accidentally impregnated me." And then, of course, I began to cry again.

"C'mon," Coop said, holding out his arms.

"No. I don't want you to take sides, because then you'll take J.B.'s. I don't want you stuck in the middle."

"I'm not going to be stuck anywhere." He reached forward and pulled me into a hug. "I'm just going to congratulate you. You are pregnant, aren't you? And this is what you wanted, isn't it? So you should be celebrating, not crying. J.B.'ll come around soon enough."

By the time I showered away the traces of tears, the phone was ringing. "Morgan just called me. How could you possibly let yourself get pregnant at a time like this, when you're going to be so occupied by my wedding?" Brit raged. Her irritation at my news came across the phone lines loud and clear. "You're maid of honour, did you forget? That's a huge responsibility, did you forget? How are you supposed to give your position the energy it deserves when all you'll be thinking about is baby names and throwing up all the time? And if you dare throw up anywhere in the vicinity of my wedding dress, so help you, Casey Samms, you'll wish—who's the father anyway?"

"J.B."

"Really." There was a blessed pause as she took in the news. "Well, at least you'll have a pretty good chance of having a good-looking kid with him as the daddy."

Emma gave me quite a few hugs and told me tearfully she was so happy for me. Also that J.B. would eventually grow up, but I might have to wait a little bit for that. She told me not to give up hope.

"How could you possibly not realize you're already pregnant?" David asked with amazement when I met him a couple of days later.

"How could you not know you were gay when we were together?" I shot back. "It's not like my egg throws a party in my uterus after she's attacked or something."

David pursed his lips in an attempt not to smile. "Sarcasm. That's new."

"So is me being pregnant." I laid my forehead down on the table beside my glass of cranberry juice. No vodka for me for a while. So much for me easing off gently. It's cold-turkey time now. "I can't believe this is happening."

I honestly couldn't believe things had worked out this way. All I ever wanted was to be pregnant, and now that I was, I couldn't even be excited since absolutely no one I cared about was happy for me. Oh, sure, Cooper and Emma and Morgan said they were pleased, but I knew all three of them were totally blown away that the baby was J.B.'s.

And now David—who, being the sweet guy he is, was putting on a pretty good show—I knew I'd disappointed him as well.

It was a week after he'd asked me to have his baby and five days since the pregnancy test that rocked my world. When I called and asked David to meet me tonight, I couldn't bring myself to tell him over the phone that I was already pregnant. But seeing his face trying so hard to mask his anticipation was even worse.

I fully expected to have my hormones all out of whack being pregnant. I'd heard tons of horror stories and read even more in all the pregnancy books I own, which I now had a right to read. But I felt like a ping-pong ball all the time—I wanted to giggle, laugh with delight, cry with relief one minute, and the next I was about ready to scream with frustration. I didn't want J.B. to get me pregnant. I thought in time J.B. would prove to be an amazing father, but not now. Maybe when he was ready and willing to grow up a bit, but not now. I so wished it wasn't him. I felt like he'd ruined everything for me. And then I felt like I should be grateful to him for getting me pregnant, and then I got all confused. It had been a bad week.

"I thought this is what you wanted." David sounded confused.

"I did. I do." I sat up. "But not like this. J.B. won't speak to me—he's convinced I got pregnant on purpose to screw him over. Brit keeps moaning about how her wedding will be ruined with a pregnant bridesmaid. I told her I'll only be three months and probably won't even show, but she hates me too."

"Poor Casey. But I still don't understand how you didn't know," David repeated. "I mean, you must have known there was a chance of this happening, right?"

I shrugged. "I just never thought. I'm on the pill, but sometimes I forget to take it. And we used a condom."

"Well, then I have to ask, are you sure it's J.B.'s?"

I nodded reluctantly. "It has to be his. He was the only one I—let's just say it's been a while. And the condom we used—let's just say it was laying around for a little longer than it should have been."

"How long?"

"I had two in my bedside drawer. The one that was leftover had an expiration date of 2019 on it," I admitted, shamefaced.

"You haven't had sex since 2019!" David exclaimed a little too loudly for my liking.

"No! I said a while, meaning about four months. I don't normally bring my boyfriends back to my place," I told David. "And I can't believe I'm talking about my sex life with you of all people."

"I think I'm the perfect person," David grinned at me. "I know all the ins and outs, but have no desire to rediscover any of them."

"Thanks. You really know how to make a girl feel good." I made a face at him, and he laughed.

"Seriously, though, Casey, what are you going to do?" David asked, with his brown eyes full of concern.

"Seriously? I'm going to have a baby!" I raised my glass of juice. "And poopy on anyone who doesn't like it."

"Real mature," David grinned, but he clinked his glass against mine.

"I'm sorry," I told him. "I feel like that's all I've been saying since I found out. I'm sorry it wasn't you."

"Me too," he admitted.

"I think I was okay with the idea. I was still getting my head around it... but I think it would have worked. But now..."

"Maybe things work out for the best," David mused.

"I can't see this being the best."

"I mean me." He took a drink of his beer. "Marco called me the other day."

"Marco? Italian Stallion Marco?"

"The one and only. He wants me to come and visit. He says he misses me. I told him I wasn't sure. I thought I might be needed here."

"Because of me. And now you're off the hook, so you can be together!" In a strange way, the news made me feel better. Oh, not altogether better, because there was the twinge of thinking of David with a man, even an Italian stallion named Marco, and the surge of self-pity of being reminded how everyone in the world, including my gay ex-boyfriend, could find someone to love, but it did make me feel better about disappointing David. I didn't feel so bad about that now.

"Well, not exactly." David leaned across the table and took my hand. "Even though it wouldn't be my baby, I'd still be willing to raise it with you. If you wanted me to, that is. If things don't work out with you and J.B."

"I don't think things are going to work out," I said, my eyes filling with sudden tears. "You'd, you'd do that? You'd want to do that?"

"I would."

"You must really want a baby!" The burst of laughter wasn't appropriate but gurgled out of me.

"I do. But I also care a great deal about you."

"But it's been so long since we..."

"It doesn't mean I don't still care about you. You care about me, don't you? Enough to consider having a child with me, right? Same goes for me."

"Wow." I surveyed David across the table. "I really let a good one get away. But I guess not so good, considering the whole homosexual aspect." I gave my head a shake. "Why does it have to be so complicated?"

"It doesn't need to be. If you need me, I'm there for you."

I sat there holding David's hand and considered this. I recalled J.B.'s anger and Morgan's shock and Cooper's surprise and thought how warm David's hand was and how nice it would be to have someone on my side.

But it didn't feel right. J.B. might not want this baby, but the fact remained that it was his baby and I couldn't see him being okay with another man raising it. He might not be okay with the situation now, but that didn't mean he wouldn't come around someday.

I had to believe that.

I didn't want the fairy tale—I don't need that. I know what J.B. is like, and I know he doesn't want the happily ever after. And even if he did, he might not want it with me. So I'm not expecting anything from him. But it might be nice if he would acknowledge the baby as his, and maybe love it a little. Obviously not as much as I love it—because this thing hanging out in my uterus may only be a collection of fast-multiplying cells, but I, wow, I already love it a whole bunch. So there's no way of anyone else's love even beginning to eclipse it, but it might be nice if J.B. could possibly begin to love it. Her. Or him.

So I gave David's hand a squeeze. "You should go see Marco," I told him quietly. "See what happens there."

"So you think J.B. will change his mind?"

I shrugged. "I have no idea. But it is his baby. Maybe if I like the whole being pregnant thing a lot, you could come back and knock me up!" I joked. David gave a weak smile. "But I think I should just see how things go."

"Let me know if you change your mind," was how David left it.

I think I'm making the right decision, even though it scares me to think of raising a child alone. But then I remind myself that's what I was signing up to do had I gone ahead with the anonymous donor route. It'll just be like that, just with a different father. A father I know quite well, but who doesn't seem to want to know me any longer.

# CHAPTER TWENTY-FOUR

"While the father-to-be may not be as emotionally invested in the baby-making process or the pregnancy, he should attempt to show some excitement, as well as a great deal of care and support, and give the mother-to-be the respect she deserves while awaiting his child. After all, she is the vessel that will give life to his offspring."

*A Young Woman's Guide to the Joy of Impending Motherhood*
Dr. Francine Pascal Reid (1941)

WHEN I GOT HOME, J.B. had just pulled into the driveway seconds before me. In fact, he was still sitting astride his motorcycle taking his helmet off as I turned off my car. I sat there for a moment watching him, not really sure what to say or even if I wanted to say anything at all to him.

But then he turned and met my gaze, and I felt compelled to get out of the car. When I got out, I slammed the car door too quickly, so that my seat-belt strap caught. I fixed it and shut my door again. By this time,

J.B. was off his bike and standing by the hood of my car. The only light came from the lamp by the front door, so J.B.'s face was in shadow.

"Hey," I said coolly.

"Sorry," J.B. began briskly. "About that comment—whether it's mine or not—I'm sorry about that. I had no call to question something like that."

"No, you didn't," I agreed, my tone still cool. "And it was pretty shitty of you. Maybe since that's how you live your life, you assume others do the same. I'll have you know, I am fully aware of the name, location, and date of every man I've slept with. Except for one, but that was on a train somewhere in Europe, so it doesn't really count and it doesn't matter." I took a deep breath. "But what does matter is that unfortunately for both of us, you are the father of this baby."

"So you said."

"I did not get pregnant on purpose," I shouted. "I wanted to get pregnant, but it wasn't supposed to be with you. I didn't want you to be the father. It was supposed to be David. David and I were supposed to have a baby together, not us, not you and me."

"Sorry to mess up your perfect little plan," J.B. said angrily.

"Well, you did!" I was not about to tell him the truth. The less he knew right now, the better. Let him feel guilty about something. Let him feel guilty about knocking me up!

"When we," I used my hand to gesture at us, "got together that night—the night I was upset from the wedding—I had no idea; I had no plan; I never expected this to happen. Really. Truly. I know how you are with the idea of kids—I would never do that to you. I decided I wanted to have a baby after. Not before or during, but after we had sex. I didn't do it on purpose. I'm not your wife."

"No, you're not," he muttered so softly that I barely heard him. I, of course, took it that he meant he was happy I'm not his wife, or that never in a million years would he ever want to refer to me as his wife. Not that I was thinking I want to be his wife or anything—last thing on my mind today—but I didn't want it shoved in my face that he loathed the very idea of it.

"Thank God for that!" I retorted. "How can you be such an asshole about this?" I wanted to scream, but I managed with difficulty to keep my voice lowered to an acceptable level.

"You're angry with me about this? I had nothing to do with it—I was just in the wrong place at the wrong time. And at least I can count," he retorted hotly. It took a second to catch on that he must have been referring to my menstrual cycle.

"Fine. Be like that. I just wanted to tell you I'm sorry—no, I'm not sorry!" My voice rose again, and to my dismay, it now had a catch to it that usually precluded crying. I would not cry in front of J.B. "I'm not sorry I'm pregnant, but I am sorry it's yours. I gave up on dating so that my baby wouldn't have an asshole for a father, and now look what happens. So I'll just tell you that you don't have to have anything, anything at all to do with this baby. I'll never even introduce you as her father if that's what you want. I'll let her think that her father is some anonymous plastic specimen jar, if that's what makes you happy. Okay?"

Thinking that would make a fitting exit, I stomped past J.B. toward my door. At the last second, I remembered I hadn't locked my car and hit the button on my key chain, and it made the little *dwerp dwerp* sound. Then I had trouble unlocking my door because by then I had tears starting to well up. Of course, this was when he stopped me.

"Look, Case," he began, looming up behind me like a shadow. "I'm sorry."

"So am I," I told him automatically, trying desperately to sniff away my tears.

"It's just—I didn't want kids. I don't want kids," he corrected himself.

"Well, you don't have to have this one, either," I said stoutly, despite the wetness on my face. "I'll do all the work for you, and you'll get none of the credit. How do you like that?"

"I'll make a horrible father," J.B. surprised me by saying.

I turned around to look at him, my keys forgotten in my hand. "Since you don't want to be a father, what does that matter? You can just go piss off and have sex with whomever you want and forget you ever knew me."

"Unfortunately, I can't, because that's not the way it's going to be."

"And just how is it going to be?" I tried for as much snarky attitude as I could muster.

"We'll get married. It's the right thing to do."

Now that was about the last thing I expected to ever hear from J.B. Bergen.

"It'll have to be quick and small, and my mother will hate that, and she's never even met you, but—"

"What did you say?" I asked coldly.

"I'll marry you. It's what you want, isn't it? And it's the right thing to do. You can—"

"No."

"—move upstairs as long as it's cool with Cooper, and we can look for a—"

"No."

"What?"

"I said no."

"But—we're getting married. It's the right thing to do. It's what we have to do."

"No fucking way!" I suddenly shrieked. "There's no way in hell I'm going to marry you!"

"But you want—"

"You have no right to tell me what I do or don't want. You have no idea! There's no way I want to marry you because you think it's the right thing to do. And especially not if you're planning a small, quickie wedding that your mother would hate. Piece of advice— not the best way to propose."

"So if I said it differently—"

"No. Still no. I'm not an obligation, J.B. I'm not some poor, needy, sad, little girl who needs you to take care of me. I got myself into this situation, and I can take care of myself. I wanted to get pregnant, I want to have a baby, and I can do it myself. Myself, which means you can forget you ever knew I, or this baby, existed."

"What if I don't want that?" he asked sullenly.

"Then do something about it. Right now, as far as I'm concerned, J.B., you're not allowed any part of this baby. You've been an ass about it, and I'm through with that. I'm pregnant; you're not. You don't want a baby. So fine, you don't have one. It's all mine." I put a hand possessively over my stomach. "But if you think maybe someday you might change your mind and would like to know your child, then you better think twice about your behaviour these next few months. You'll have to prove to me that any part of this baby belongs to you."

"You want me to prove I want a baby?" he scoffed.

"I want you to prove you're not the complete selfish asshole that I think you are right now! You need to prove you're capable of loving something unconditionally and taking full responsibility for it, not because it's the 'right' thing to do, but because you want to. You've got nine months to get used to the idea. And let me tell you, J.B., you need this baby in your life. You need to learn how to love something in your life, or God help you, you're going to be alone for the rest of your life."

And with that very fitting exit line, I swept into the house.

# CHAPTER TWENTY-FIVE

"Some pregnant women are plagued with morning sickness. It is said that nausea can be looked upon as a sign the fetus is developing normally."

*A Young Woman's Guide to the Joy of Impending Motherhood*
Dr. Francine Pascal Reid (1941)

T HAT HAPPENED SUNDAY NIGHT, so the week didn't start off too well. It never got any better either.

I paid a visit to my doctor, who, after a blood test, confirmed that I was indeed pregnant. This precluded a whole panic attack, which would have led to some serious crying and then a lot of laughter because I'm so messed up. Anyway, Dr. Dennis told me I was due on or around February 16. She set up an appointment for me with an obstetrician for the first week in September. Of course, as soon as she gave me the date, I couldn't help but start to get teary-eyed, thinking it would be a few days after Brit's wedding. I wondered if Brit would be happy for me by then.

I'm going to have a baby. I wonder if he or she will look like J.B.?

J.B., who is the father of my baby; who doesn't want to be the father—and I'm sitting around wondering if the kid will look like him? J.B., who has been avoiding me so much this week that he couldn't even bring himself to enjoy Cooper's breakfasts on the weekend, preferring to head out early to bike or play soccer or some equally testosterone-fuelled activity.

Things didn't seem to be any better the next Monday either, when I woke up with a sick feeling in the pit of my stomach as I went to work. Once again, my day only went downhill from there.

There was a jumper on the subway line, so I was half an hour late to open the store. I'd decided to take a few extra shifts at the store each week. No summer vacation for me this year—I had to start planning for another mouth to feed come next year.

Being late wasn't the end of the world, since there's usually not a lineup to buy wine before ten o'clock in the morning, but it still didn't look good and it always starts my day off wrong. It also irritated me that some selfish person decided to take his life by jumping in front of a subway car during rush hour, which not only ended his life but screwed up the lives of several thousand people as well. Talk about inconsiderate. So I was not a happy camper when I finally unlocked the door to the store.

The day got a bit better as the morning wore on, but I was still forcing myself to smile. And I still felt gross, sort of like I was hungover, but without having had a drink, which was totally unfair. I kept telling myself I must be getting the flu. I was still on my own—Hannah doesn't come in until twelve o'clock—and I was ringing up two bottles of Inniskillen Riesling for a nineteen-year-old (she was actually happy to be carded), when I heard the door chime ring. I looked up with my welcoming smile—like I always do, even when I'm feeling like crap—and saw my mother walk in.

"Hello, Casey." Today Terri was dressed in a tasteful pantsuit. Tasteful for her, which meant she was not wearing anything under the jacket and was showing a little too much crêpey cleavage for my liking.

"Hello." I wondered why my mother never gives notice before she comes by. Never phones, never e-mails her intention. She always drops by Libby's unannounced, when she knows Libby absolutely hates people doing that because it never gives her a chance to tidy up. Look at what happened at Cooper's party. I wonder if she thinks we'll avoid her if we know she's coming. I wonder how many times she stops by my place without me knowing she's come by.

I finished with the customer and sent him away with a smile. Terri looked around the quiet store before teetering over to me behind the counter in her red stilettos. They were nice shoes, if you're into shoes. A little tacky, but that's Terri for you.

I was about to comment on them—the nice part, not the tacky—when Terri started in on me. The whole three-name thing.

"Casey Louise Samms, I need to know how I could have raised you to be able to show such little regard for me so that you wouldn't even have the decency to call and tell me you're pregnant. I have to find out from your sister? I'm your mother, for God's sake. How could you not tell me?" Her voice rose with each word until she was shouting at me.

I didn't remember the last time Terri was angry with me. Growing up, it was always Ed the father who was the disciplinarian. Terri's reaction to anything Libby and I did was always indifference at best. I really didn't know how to react to this onslaught of hurt feelings.

"I'm sorry?" And I was. I don't like anyone mad at me. No matter what I feel for Terri (and even on a good day, I'm not sure), she's still my mother and technically will be my baby's grandmother. I should have called her.

Terri snorted at my lame apology. "I'm sure. Any reason you felt the need to keep me in the dark about this?"

"I—" This was one of those times when a lie wouldn't help and telling the truth would only make things worse. Normally, I'd go with the lie, try to smooth things over as best I could. Today—with me still pissed at J. B. and feeling nauseated—well, the lie didn't come out quick enough. The truth did, though. "I didn't think you'd give a damn," I told her a little too bluntly for the usual conciliatory daughter. This was the bitter, resentful daughter having a bad day.

Terri made a face like a fish gasping for breath; had she been a fish, I'm sure she would have been gasping for water. Either way, I had a horrible feeling that I probably make the same expression when someone is telling me off. "How can you possibly say such a thing?" she gasped. "I'm your mother."

"Because it's true," I told her calmly. This too was a first. During confrontations, I'm more likely to become emotional and start to cry than stay calm and cool. "That's what I think. And Libby, too. When we were growing up, you were always so busy with your boyfriends to pay much attention to us. I don't call that mothering." I gave her an indifferent shrug. "It's no matter now. It's just the way things are. Both Libby and I learned the hard way that others come first with you. Yes, I should have called, since you are my mother, but I hadn't done so yet because I didn't think you'd care. And frankly, I'm sick and tired of being the only one in this world that is happy about this baby!" Now my voice was raised. I was not being fair, taking out my bad mood on my mother, but right then, I didn't really care how unfair that might be.

"I didn't realize that's how you felt," Terri replied stiffly. Her eyes rested on the bottles of wine in the store—anyplace but on me. "Well."

Nausea rose dangerously in my stomach. "Sorry." What else could I say?

"I see." Terri finally looked at me, and I was sickened by the expression of devastation on her face. I caused that. I felt horrible.

"Mom," I began, but she held up her hand.

"Casey, I know I wasn't the best mother to you and your sister growing up, and your father made things very difficult for all of us. But after—" she took a deep breath. I thought she might be on the verge of tears, but she straightened her shoulders and fought them off. "I thought you were adult enough to realize I did my best. And however I raised you, it turned you into the women you and Libby are today. Maybe I'm biased, but I think I did a good job since you turned out pretty well."

"Oh," I told her, feeling very small.

Terri nodded. "Well. Congratulations. I'll let you get back to work." Without another word, she walked out the door.

Didn't I feel like crap? I wanted to run out the door after her, but just then another customer came in, and since I was the only one there this morning, it was up to me to man the fort. I stifled a yawn. I had a horrible sleep last night.

"Morning," I said to him without my usual verve and friendliness. At least I think I greet people with verve and friendliness. Not this morning, though. Not after ripping my mother a new asshole. I'm truly a horrible person. I've screwed up J.B.'s life, I screwed up Brit's wedding, I practically made my mother cry, and all because I selfishly wanted a baby.

I've actually never told off anyone. And telling Terri off didn't make me feel empowered or take a load off my chest. No, I felt like shit. My mother came in to give me a mild scolding for being inconsiderate and not calling her, and I basically gave her the award for worst mother of the year. Nice, Casey.

The customer was most of the way around the store. I've watched people when they come in: they start with the shelves of white, move to the fruit wines, which no one really lingers at, then the sparkling, the reds, and finally the cooler with the chilled bottles before hitting the cash register. This guy was finishing the sparkling by the time I got to him. I finished another yawn—what's with me this morning?—before I got to him.

"Can I help you find something?" I asked, with a fake smile determinedly fixed to my face.

"No, well, I'm looking for a bottle of wine."

"You've come to the right place," I tried to joke, but my heart wasn't really into it. Plus, I was beginning to feel really ill. "Red or white?"

"It's for dinner." He looked at me shyly. He seemed familiar. He was wearing jeans and a T-shirt and a baseball cap. Very cute, with dark blond hair and sort of a squashed-features-Matt Damon face. It was nice I could appreciate how cute he is even while feeling sick to my stomach.

"What are you serving?" Where do I know him from? He's too young to be a friend of a friend. Maybe from Coop's restaurant? He's cute, but familiar too. It was starting to bug me.

"Steak, I think. Or salmon."

"For steak, I'd go with a nice, full-bodied red." I pointed to a row of bottles. "The Cab Franc is always nice. Or the pinot noir—a favourite of mine, but very rich, almost chocolaty. For salmon, my first choice would be white—possibly a chardonnay, depending on how you cook the fish."

"You sound like you need the whole menu." It didn't seem to turn him off. In fact, now he was paying more attention to me than the variety of wine I was showing him.

"It would help. To pick out the right bottle. Or you can pick the wine first, and then create the menu around it." I hid another discrete yawn.

"I guess I don't really know yet. My girlfriend's doing the cooking."

"Ah." Now why did that simple statement make me feel like I was about to throw up? The thought of food, or because he had a girlfriend? He looked at least ten years younger than me, and hey, I'm a pregnant woman now. So long, casual pickups, especially when the baby belly starts poking out. Darn. "Are you wine drinkers?" Back to business.

"Not really," he admitted. "I do the beer thing, and Evie likes vodka. But her parents are coming so ... are you okay?"

"Sure," I said. Suddenly I really couldn't stop yawning, and my stomach lurches were going crazy. I needed to finish this sale pronto.

"Then I would go with this—it's a nice New Zealand sauvignon blanc." I led him over to a shelf. "Can't really go wrong with this." He picked up a bottle and scanned the back label. "Can you excuse—"

"You were on the subway the other day," he said suddenly.

"I'm sorry?" I thought I needed to get to a toilet very quickly. I thought I was going to vomit.

"The subway. We were talking about Harry Potter—"

The cute guy on the subway? Of course. I'd think this was a neat coincidence if I wasn't about to throw up on his shoes.

"Oh, yeah. Listen, can you hang on a second?" Leaving him hanging there, holding the bottle of wine, I headed behind the cash register, not three feet away, at a run, where I knew there was a garbage can. It'd have to do. There was no time to go to the bathroom.

I bent behind the counter, grabbed the can, and loudly emptied my stomach into it. It wasn't much, since I hadn't eaten much all morning, but enough to make a mess in the garbage bag. Then I retched for a couple of minutes until I finally stood upright and leaned weakly on the counter. My face was damp with sweat, and I rubbed my forehead weakly. "Sorry."

The cute subway guy was looking at me with concern. "Are you okay?"

"I'm so sorry." I desperately wished for a piece of gum. I took a sip from my bottle of water. Not too much, because I didn't think it would stay down. "I'm really sorry. I just—do you want me to ring that up for you?"

"Uh, no." He placed the bottle gently on the shelf. "Are you okay? Do you want to sit down or something?"

I leaned weakly on the counter. At least my stomach felt a bit better, which was good because nothing else did. "I'm okay. I feel a little better. I'm just—sorry. This is pretty embarrassing."

"Don't worry about it. I'm actually a doctor."

"Really?" My skepticism came through loud and clear, and he laughed. He looked to be no older than nineteen. I was thinking of carding him when he bought the wine.

"Really. Why don't you sit down? Is there something I can do for you?"

"Get me a new garbage pail? I'm fine. Let me ring that wine up for you." I stood upright. The nausea was fading quickly, and only the humiliation remained. I thought my whole body must be red.

"I can come back for it later."

I gave a weak wave. "I feel better—really. I guess I just needed to throw up."

"Always makes me feel better. Do you have the flu?" He grabbed three bottles of the sauvignon I showed him earlier and brought them to the cash register.

"No," I told him, scanning the bottles. "I'm pregnant." That was the first time I told anyone I didn't know. It was the first time I admitted it to a stranger, and I smiled as I tested it out again. "I'm pregnant."

"Congratulations. Morning sickness must be a bitch."

I gave a weak laugh. "It's my first morning with it, and if the next couple months are anything like this, yes, it might be a bitch."

"Good luck with everything," he said as I handed him his bag. "It's great news."

"Thanks. You know, you saying that means more than you know. In fact, you just made me feel a whole lot better." I smiled at him, my first true smile of the morning. Despite the utter humiliation of my having thrown up in front of such a cute stranger, my Harry Potter-lover from the subway had just turned into a ray of sunshine.

"Always happy to help."

# CHAPTER TWENTY-SIX

"Relationships can often be strained during pregnancy since not all those closely connected with the expectant mother display the support they should, due to fear of how a baby will affect the dynamics of the relationship and often because of jealousy."

*A Young Woman's Guide to the Joy of Impending Motherhood*
Dr. Francine Pascal (1941)

I FELT QUEASY AGAIN when I met Brit and Morgan after work at the dress designer's for a fitting for the bridesmaid dresses. Morgan was just being zipped up into her dress when I showed up.

"It's a beautiful colour," she was telling Brit as I was shown in.

The dress was gorgeous, and I had to give myself some credit since I was with Brit when she found it. Well, found a picture of it in a magazine, but I went with her to the designer to get her to make it. It's an amethyst colour, ankle-length, with a flowing skirt and an Empire waist with tiny iridescent straps. Simple, but very pretty. Plus the colour goes well with my hair, which is why I fought against the harvest orange which was Brit's first colour choice.

"Hurry up and try your dress on," Brit told me impatiently. I decided to humour her. I'd also decided not to pretend I was happy with her lack of excitement about my pregnancy, but that would wait until later.

"So I've decided not to take anyone to the wedding next weekend," Morgan told me after we'd put on the dresses and were standing at the mirror while a seamstress bustled around us with pins. I tried to stay still so I wouldn't get pricked.

"What wedding? My wedding isn't until September!" Brit cried.

"No, Marie and Michael's wedding, remember? There are other people getting married in this world, you know," Morgan told her mildly.

"Well, it's kind of difficult to remember that, since I'm pouring my life energy into making this the best wedding ever. I thought you were taking J.B. to that one?" she added curiously.

"I was, but because of recent events, I've changed my mind," Morgan said self-righteously. "He's being an ass to Casey."

"Thank you," I said quietly.

"And this has nothing to do with the fact that Anil is laid up with poison ivy over half of his body?" Brit asked archly.

"Really?" I laughed.

"I didn't know that." Morgan didn't even try to hide her smile. "Marie told me he wasn't coming, but that's not why I decided not to bring J.B. I was actually debating whether I should invite Derek."

"Who?" Brit asked.

"You don't mean…" I trailed off weakly.

"I know, it's kind of weird for you," Morgan said apologetically. "But he's really, really nice. We've texted and talked on the phone a couple of times, and he's always sending me these funny e-mails… Casey's mother's new boyfriend's brother," she said to Brit, who was practically bouncing up and down with frustration that she didn't know who we were discussing.

"Oh, my God!" she cried with disgust. "You can't be serious!"

"He's nice," Morgan told us defensively. "You're okay with it, aren't you, Casey?"

"Other than feeling extremely nauseated, just hunky-dory."

"Really?"

I looked at Morgan and saw the disappointment in her eyes. "Do you really like him?" I asked despairingly.

"Kind of," she admitted. "I think he's waiting for me to give him the go-ahead before he asks me out. I wanted to clear it with you first."

"Oh, Morgan," I closed my eyes. "Fine. Go ahead; date the man who might be my step-uncle, but I do not want any details. And please, please, please, don't start inviting my mother to parties and stuff."

"Really? Oh, Casey, thanks! I know you'll like him when you give him a chance. Eric sounds great, too. Derek says he and your mom—"

I held up my hand. "No details. Please." Especially since I was feeling wretchedly guilty about my run-in with Terri this morning. I'm truly a horrible daughter. How was I going to be able to be a good mother if I kept messing up my own mother-daughter relationship?

"He's a nice guy," Morgan was saying happily. "I'm going to text him and ask him for dinner tomorrow night as soon as we're done here."

"At least Morgan'll have a date now for my wedding," Brit said, as always bringing the conversation back to her. "I was getting worried that my whole wedding party was going to show up single and miserable."

"I'm not miserable about being single," I said coolly.

"Whatever," Brit waved my protest away.

"Is—?" Morgan began. "Is he still standing up for Tom?"

"Who?" Brit was leafing through a magazine, impatiently waiting for the seamstress to be finished.

"Anil," I supplied, so Morgan wouldn't have to say the name.

"Well, of course," Brit said with irritation. "Tom can't dump him from being one of his ushers just because the two of you aren't together! It would screw up the numbers, and really, he hasn't got another friend he's close enough to. Do you think that would be a nice thing to do? It'd be like me dropping you because of Anil. Tom and I need to stay neutral during this difficult time with you two, until you can begin to coexist civilly. I'm really hoping that will happen by the wedding, you know," she finished pointedly.

"You're not making her still be paired up with him?" I asked, incredulous. "Because that's just mean."

"No, I wouldn't be that mean," Brit said with a roll of her eyes. "Casey, you'll be with Tom's brother Richard; then Morgan with his other brother, Henry; then my sister and Anil. Lacey's not too keen about going last," she told Morgan meaningfully.

"At least you have one of your sisters in the wedding party," I muttered. "What about Sierra?" referring to Brit's younger sister.

"More than three attendants on each side make the church look cluttered," Brit pronounced. "I'm not having a whole gang up there while I'm saying my vows. And the two of you want to be in my wedding party, don't you? Besides, Sierra's too young and irresponsible for such an important duty. Although she isn't pregnant."

Morgan raised an eyebrow at me, but I didn't rise. I was waiting for my moment. The attitude I'd been getting had been going on long enough. Morgan seemed fine with the idea of me producing offspring, although I got the picture it was making her a little skittish, but plain and simple, Brit was being a bitch about the whole thing. I'd come to the conclusion that Brit was either with me, or not. I thought it might be difficult to cut her out of my life, since she's been there for more than half of it, but if she were not with me, then changes would definitely need to be made.

I waited until the three of us were sitting at the restaurant around the corner from the shop. Brit was on a high because the dresses looked fantastic on both Morgan and me. It was too early for me to have put on any weight. In fact, I must have lost a couple of pounds in the past week since the dress was a little loose around the waist.

"So I've been thinking," I began as soon as I could get a word in edgewise. "About this baby."

"You've come to your senses?" Brit asked with a patronizing smile. She was playing with her glass of wine, and to make it worse, she'd ordered a glass of the New Zealand Sauvignon Blanc that I always get if it's on the menu. Either she'd managed to pick up some wine knowledge from me over the years, or she was totally rubbing it in my face that I couldn't drink. Tonight I'd tend to think it was the latter.

"That's exactly what I mean. I am so happy about this baby." I held my hands protectively over my belly. "It's what I've always wanted, and I'm very excited. Ecstatic. Over the moon. And so are Cooper and Emma and Libby. And Morgan. The only person who hasn't expressed any excitement or sincere good wishes or happiness for me is you, Brit—who claim to be my BFF."

"Well, J.B. doesn't seem to be too happy about it either," Brit said in a snotty voice.

"Brit," Morgan chided.

"I think I can handle things with J.B., thanks," I told her icily.

You know he'll come around, Casey," Morgan told me reassuringly. "He's just scared. He feels—he's like this big stud, right? And he feels that he's about to be taken off the market, against his will. It's like he's some stallion, and it's his time to become a gelding."

"What's a gelding?" Brit asked.

"It's a horse. A stallion is a boy horse—"

"I know that!"

"—and a gelding is what he becomes after they take away some of his boy-horse parts."

"How do they...? Oh."

"So he thinks I'm going to cut off his balls, so to speak?" I asked.

"Not you, but the baby will. Not your fault, of course. I think he'll come around," Morgan assured me. "Just give him a little time."

"How do you know about this gelding thing?" Brit suddenly asked.

"You forget I grew up in the country," Morgan told her imperiously. "You have no idea the stuff I know that you don't want to know about."

Brit waved her off. "The reason behind it doesn't matter. He's still being an ass. I think you're a fool not to just blow him off. All this he's-scared-he'll-come-around crap—stop being a martyr, Casey, and grow a pair. Tell him to step up. It takes two to tango, and you better tell him he'd better grow up and put a big fat ring on your finger pretty darn quick. It's the only way you'll ever get one now, if you insist on going through with this nonsense."

"Nonsense? This is exactly what I'm talking about," I marveled. "What kind of friend makes comments like that? It's just—really, it's shitty of you, Brit, and it needs to stop. Be happy for me, or else." After such a good start, I hit a hurdle at the end. But from the expression of surprise on her face, I think I got my point across. I took a big drink of water. Confrontations make your throat dry.

"Of course, I'm happy for you," Brit began.

I snorted. "Of course you're not. You've been a horrible friend since I told you this is what I want. I've listened to you for years about how you want the perfect wedding and plan its every last detail, so the least you can do is pretend to be happy for me. I don't even get the dignity of you faking it."

"I don't fake," she announced haughtily. "And I am perfectly happy for you. You and your surprise offspring have been taking up so much of my mental energy these days, I barely have enough time for wedding planning."

"You bitch," I say with amazement. "This is what I can expect from you when I tell you the biggest news of my life? Surprise offspring? It's a baby! My baby! And news flash for you—it's a wedding, not some last-minute G-8 summit in Israel. With your attitude, I can't believe I still call you my best friend!" My voice increased in volume with every word, so I was practically yelling at the end. But that was still not enough impact for me. Without a second thought, I picked up my water glass and hurled the remaining water right in Brit's face.

"Casey!" she shrieked, sending water droplets flying. There wasn't more than a mouthful left in the glass, and I directed most of it toward her mouth. "What the hell has gotten into you?"

"You," I told her calmly. "You make me sick. Morgan's my only best friend now." Then I ruined it by beginning to cry. Like I said, I don't do confrontations well.

"I can't believe you did that!" Brit cried. She grabbed all the napkins from the table and blotted her face. I knew she didn't wipe it in one fell swoop because that would undoubtedly ruin her makeup.

"You shouldn't have done that," Morgan said softly to me. She pushed her glass of merlot toward me. "Next time, use this." I felt a laugh bubble up and watched as she handed Brit a Kleenex from her purse, then one to me before reaching out and taking my hand across the table.

"You're insane," Brit cried. "You completely ruin my makeup, humiliate me in front of dozens of people—what has this goddamn baby done to you?"

"Brit," Morgan warned. Abruptly my tears stopped, and I glared at Brit. I pulled my hand from Morgan's and reached down and grabbed my purse. I'd had it with her.

"She threw water on me!" Brit complained. "And called me a bitch."

"You deserved it," Morgan told her. "You're lucky there wasn't food on the table."

"You damned my baby," I practically growled at Brit.

"Oh, I did not. I didn't damn anything. I didn't mean anything." Brit had managed to wipe her face without doing too much damage to her precious makeup and was now rummaging in her tiny purse for a compact and lipstick to reapply. It was an easy way to avoid looking at me directly. "Oh, sit down," she told me. "You look like an idiot just standing there." But the hostility was gone from her voice, and because I did feel like an idiot standing beside my chair, I sat down. As soon as I did, the waiter appeared with our dinners.

By the time he finished laying the plates in front of us with the usual warning about the plates being hot, Brit had fixed any damage to her face, but she was still not looking at me. I waited, my eyes narrowed, and imagined ways in which I could destroy her wedding.

"Fine," Brit huffed. "Your hormones are just insane. Maybe I haven't been as excited as you want me to about the baby. Sorry."

"Tell her why," Morgan instructed.

"What do you mean, why? I said sorry."

"Tell her why you've been such a bitch about it. There's got to be a reason, or is this just your natural bitchy side that we're stuck with? If so, I'm not happy about it either."

Brit huffed again. "Fine. You want to know why I haven't been on board? You never talked to me about it before you went and got pregnant. You just had your silly little idea, then went and got knocked up, and what about me? I tell you everything." I honestly didn't know what to say to that, but before I had a chance, Brit continued, "Then there's the whole baby thing itself. Do you realize how much this baby will change everything?" she cried, really warming up. "Did you think about that? Did you think about how I'm going to feel never being able to see you without some kid attached to you? We'll never be able to do this again," she waved her arms, almost hitting Morgan on the side of her head; "nothing will be the same. And I think that sucks."

I had to laugh. "What about the fact you're getting married? Did you think about how things will change then?"

"You have to deal with that, not me."

Morgan started laughing as well. "You are so selfish," she said, shaking her head.

Brit looked affronted. "So? I'm selfish and shallow and materialistic, and you both still love me, so what's your point?" By this time Morgan and I were practically howling with laughter. "What?" Brit asked.

We had a good laugh, which was preferable to me crying; I apologized to Brit for the water; Morgan apologized to me for not being happier and even Brit grudgingly said she was sorry. Even thinking I might have to rush into the bathroom to rid myself of the pasta I ate didn't spoil the rest of the evening.

"Now that you're not in a snit any longer," Brit said to me just before we left, "will you please tell us what's going on with you and David? I think we've talked about everything but that, and I don't know why you haven't said anything for a while. Morgan told me about him being in your room at Cooper's party. What's going on?" She smiled coquettishly at me. "What's he think of the baby thing? Any chance of wedding bells there?"

I rubbed my forehead in frustration. "Brit, how many times do I have to tell you? I don't want to get married! And if I ever have a moment of insanity and do decide to tie the knot, trust me, it won't be with David."

"But I thought," Morgan began, but I cut her off.

"David," I said dramatically, "is gay."

"What?"

"David is now a homosexual and has been one for some time. He did ask if I wanted to have a baby with him, but before I had a chance to get it on with him, I found out I'm already pregnant. He is also in love with an Italian stallion named Marco. He's going to Italy to make hot, homosexual love with him, the thought of which might excite me if I wasn't trying so hard not to vomit right now."

"Oh, you're not feeling well?" Morgan clucked at me.

"Morgan, focus on the important things!" Brit admonished. "David's gay? I knew it," she crowed triumphantly.

"How do you figure?"

"He never once tried to hit on me!"

I could only stare at Brit. As I said, there's hope for her, but she is still very much a self-centered, egotistical woman, and that's never going to change.

"Does every man have to hit on you?" Morgan asked dubiously. I was glad she said it and not me.

"Most," Brit replied matter-of-factly, without a trace of ego. "And quite a few women. And it doesn't seem to matter if they're in a relationship. Men like to flirt with me."

"But not David."

"No, never."

"So because of that, you suspected he was gay?"

"Of course. You never knew?"

"No! Why didn't you ever tell me?"

Brit rolled her eyes at me. "I'm not that horrible a friend."

# CHAPTER TWENTY-SEVEN

"Fathers often express apprehension over the impending baby. Some may even appear to resent the changes the baby will force them to make. But any anxiety or resentment the new fathers may be feeling will undoubtedly disappear when they are able to hold their newborn child in their arms."

*A Young Woman's Guide to the Joy of Impending Motherhood*
Dr. Francine Pascal Reid (1941)

D AVID CAME OVER THE next Saturday afternoon to say goodbye before leaving for Italy. I was feeling very ambivalent about the whole thing. Of course, I wanted David to be happy and I was so glad that he'd found someone to love, but there was a teeny tiny part of me that was still bitter that it was not me he was in love with. Getting back with David had been a huge recurring dream for years. And then he walked into my life like he did? I could have easily believed it was fate, but then he had to go throw a wrench into it with the whole gay thing. And not only the gay thing, but the Italian lover named Marco that he's willing to move all the way to Italy for. It's not fair, but these days it seems like nothing is, so I just have to deal with it.

"So what happens if it works out with you and Marco—when, sorry," I asked David as I was saying goodbye to him after his visit. "When you decide you have to be together, and there's no way either of you can stand being apart for one more single day? What are you going to do then? Move to Italy?"

"Casey, the romantic," David teased. "We'll have to see what happens."

"I never thought I'd be living vicariously through you," I laughed.

"Bet you never saw this one coming. But, look, I'm so happy we hooked up again. Having you back in my life means a lot to me. It's really the only thing that's giving me second thoughts about going and giving Marco another shot. Part of me wishes I would just stay put in the city and take care of you." David gave me a wistful smile, his brown eyes looking sad.

"That's sweet, David, but I'm not about to be an excuse. If there's even the slightest chance you can be happy with Marco, then you have to give it a try. I would never forgive myself if you didn't go because of me."

"I know, but I feel bad leaving you—alone and pregnant ..."

"And almost thirty-six years old and perfectly capable of taking care of myself, even if I don't know when I ovulate. Really, I'd love to have you looking out for me, but I really think that might lead to some unsuitable feelings on my part." I smiled at him to take the sting out of my words. "Really, I'll be fine. Don't worry about me. Just concentrate on wooing." I gave a visible shudder, and David laughed. "Can't get used to that image yet—I'm trying, though. You go woo Marco. And tell me how it goes."

"You, too," David urged as he gave me a hug.

"Who am I wooing?"

"Keep me posted about the baby," he said with a roll of his eyes. "Things aren't finished with you and the big guy, so let me know what's happening there."

I rolled my own eyes. "Whatever." It had been three weeks since I'd found out I was pregnant, and I had to assume J.B. was still trying to get his head around the idea of being a father. It was like he'd gone into hiding. I'd hardly said two words to him since that night he proposed. Not that it could be considered a real proposal. Did I regret turning J.B. down? No way. I know I did the right thing. I'm not sure others will think that, which is why I've kept it so quiet.

"So you haven't said what's going to happen? Will Marco come back here?" I asked hopefully, not wanting to get into a discussion about J.B.

David shook his head ruefully. "I doubt it. I think if there's any relocating to do, it's up to me to be doing it. But I'll go over and see what happens, and then come back and sort things out if I need to."

"I'm going to miss you," I told him sadly.

"Me too." He wiped a hand under his eyes. "God, this is worse than breaking up with you the first time. You can come visit, you know. We can go to Lake Cuomo and stalk George Clooney together."

"Sounds great," I sniffed.

David gave me another hug. "I've got to go, or I'll never have time to finish packing. Walk me to my car?"

When we opened the door to the hot July afternoon, I felt my stomach clench. But it was not nausea this time—J.B. was in the driveway playing basketball with three of his friends. I didn't know how I'd missed the steady thunk-thunk of the ball or loud male voices as they continually ribbed each other. I don't think I would have been so eager to walk David to his car if I had known they were out here.

"Hey, Casey," Ben, one of J. B.'s friends, called out as soon as he saw me come out the door. But it was nothing like the usual exuberant greeting I got from him. The other two—Clay and Will—said hello, but they also seemed unnaturally subdued.

"How's it going?" Clay said, but his eyes trailed back to J.B. before I could answer. J.B., of course, hadn't said a word. He didn't even look at me. I watched as he took a shot and felt partially vindicated when it bounced off the rim.

"Hey, guys," I said weakly. It was awkward just standing there, so David took my hand and led me across the lawn to the street, where his car was parked. If he hadn't, I think I might still be standing there in the doorway.

"They didn't even talk to me," I said softly to David. "They always talk to me. I know those guys; I like them and I thought they liked me, but if they're treating me like a pariah—"

"He told them he got you pregnant," David said under his breath as soon as we were out of earshot. "They don't know how to act, because it's clear he doesn't know how to deal with it."

"Well, that's obvious." Damn this—I was close to tears. Being shot down like that hurt more than I thought was possible. I was so mad at myself for letting it bother me. It was so much easier just being mad at J.B.

"No, it's obvious that J.B.'s going to come around if he's telling his friends about it," David said reasonably. "If he wasn't, you'd be his dirty little secret, and he wouldn't have said two words about it to them."

"Maybe I don't want to be anything to him," I said stoutly. "I don't need him."

"No, you don't, but it's going to be hard telling your heart that. Poor Casey," David said, wrapping his arms around me. "Poor, pregnant, little Casey."

"I'm not going to be little for long." I hugged him tightly in return.

"Take pictures. I can't wait to see the belly."

I stood on the curb waving until David drove out of sight. Then I stood there for another few minutes, getting up my courage to walk past the gaggle of hot, sweaty men playing two on two in the driveway. I prepared myself to be shot down by J.B.'s icy glare.

It was just my luck that the basketball got loose and rolled toward the street as I was walking up to the house. I stopped it with my foot and picked it up. Ben came loping up to get it from me.

"Hey," he said with a warm smile. "How's it going?"

"Good," I said stiffly. I passed the ball over to him.

"That your new boyfriend?" he asked with a frown. "I thought..."

"No, that's David. He's just a friend. He's leaving for Italy, so he came to say goodbye..." I trailed off, uncertain of why I was explaining things to Ben. Ben's a nice guy and I've known him for a few years, but it was silly to think he was concerned with my life.

"Ball, dude!" Will called to him. Ben passed him the basketball but remained beside me.

"Look, Casey, J.B. told us that..." He grinned sheepishly at me. "How're you feeling?"

"Not great," I told him truthfully.

"Yeah, Maura was sick a lot, too, in the beginning," he commiserated. He's been married for almost ten years, and he and his wife have two little boys. "It'll get better."

"I can only hope."

"Listen, she sent over a bunch of books for you to read," Ben said in a low voice. "All that getting-ready-for-baby stuff that scared the shit out of me when she made me look at them. But I'm sure they'll be helpful for you."

"Thanks, Ben, that's really sweet of you." I was so touched at the gesture I didn't tell him I probably already owned most of the books published on the subject. "Thank Maura for me."

"No prob. And Casey, take care of yourself." Ben smiled at me before rejoining the game.

I was almost to the door before J.B. deigned to speak to me. "What did he want?" he said in a voice reminiscent of a growling dog. I almost snapped back with a none of your business, jerk-off, but then I decided to be polite.

"David? He's leaving for Italy, so he came to say goodbye. I don't know when he'll be back. I don't know when I'll see him again."

"Oh." J.B. looked taken aback. "I thought you and he—"

"No, it was never going to work out. We're just friends. He's gay—now," I told him needlessly, unsure of why I was telling him this when I could barely tolerate speaking to him.

"What?" J.B. goggled. "You're kidding!" The others had resumed the game, obviously trying to give us privacy.

"Things obviously change in twelve years. You told me that."

"But I thought—you said—" J.B. stammered. I couldn't look into his eyes, afraid to see whether there was still anger there, so I stared at his chest instead. His broad, muscular chest covered by the grey T-shirt with the sweaty patches sticking to him. Most of his hair was tied back in a stubby ponytail. Even hot and sweaty, J.B. is still a helluva good-looking guy. It makes me feel that even if David weren't gay, he wouldn't have stood a chance.

"I guess I was wrong," I told him stiffly.

"I thought you were together. That he was going to—the whole baby thing..." J.B. was saying.

"He asked me to have his baby," I explained slowly. "And I might have done it, but then it was too late. I was already pregnant. So now he's going to Italy to try to make it work with the man he loves. He's disappointed because he does want a baby—and a baby with me. And I'm still pregnant, whether you want to acknowledge that fact or not. Have fun with your game," I told him shortly and continued into the house.

I forgot all about the books Ben's wife sent over for me until the next day, but when I looked in the hallway where I assumed J.B. put them, they were nowhere to be found.

# CHAPTER TWENTY-EIGHT

"Nausea in the morning is a common occurrence during the pregnancy, but normally dissipates before the second trimester. Chicken broth and crackers are helpful in relieving the symptoms."

*A Young Woman's Guide to the Joy of Impending Motherhood*
Dr. Francine Pascal Reid (1941)

"I DON'T KNOW WHY they call it morning sickness," I grumbled a week later on Sunday morning. I was eyeing my omelet with a great deal of unease. "It's morning, noon, and night for me."

I'd been plagued with it for two entire weeks. It was just like having a hangover, only worse because you couldn't promise to stop drinking in hopes you'd feel better. I was tired and nauseated all the time except just after I threw up, which was when I felt my best and tried to eat as much as possible, which would inevitably return to haunt me within the hour.

"Do you want me to make you something else?" Cooper asked sympathetically, standing at the stove.

"No, I want this. I'm hungry. But I know I'm going to throw it up after. And I'm sure regurgitated eggs aren't as nice coming up as they are going down. I still have no stomach for chicken or rice." I was trying to retain my cheerful demeanor, but it was difficult at times. And this had only been two weeks. I had many more to go.

Emma made a face. "I don't think I could handle throwing up all the time."

"I think I must be getting used to it," I told her, taking a bite. "I'm calling Dr. Dennis tomorrow. Apparently there's some wonder drug that will help."

I pushed my plate away. I'd eaten about a quarter of my omelet, and that was about all I could do. Sebastian was sitting on my feet, waiting for the scraps. While I was probably going to be losing weight by not being able to keep anything down, my cat was going to be quite fat eating what I couldn't manage. I scraped most of the omelet into his upstairs food dish and smiled gratefully as Cooper handed me a plate with hot buttered toast. I could eat toast without it popping back up five minutes later. Toast and French fries and crackers. Everything else was iffy.

"So I think I'll go shopping this afternoon," I told them. "Brit's wedding is coming up, so I won't have too much free time until that rigmarole is over. I'm going to need some maternity clothes and baby clothes and diapers and a crib, a stroller..." I ticked the items off on my fingers. "I've got lots to buy."

"How far along are you?" Emma asked.

"About eight weeks. Although it really doesn't seem that long. I mean, they calculate from—"

"Don't you think you should wait a bit?" Emma interrupted gently. "I mean, there's a reason people wait until three months to tell people, isn't there? Not that I want to put a damper on your excitement or anything."

I gave her my best condescending smile. "Nothing is going to happen to this baby," I said, with my hands over my belly.

"I'm sure it won't but—"

"It won't. It can't. I won't let it. End of story."

"Okay." Emma smiled at me. "At least don't go buying everything right away. There are things called baby showers, you know."

"Oooh, presents." If there is anything I love, it's getting presents. Not that this baby isn't present enough. Then my stomach gave an uneasy lurch, and I stood up. "But right now I think I have to deal with a throwing-up present. Thanks for breakfast, guys, and I'll see you later," I told them as I rushed downstairs.

Later that morning, I was pulling my wet clothes from the washing machine to toss them in the dryer when I discovered someone had forgotten to take his clothes out of the dryer. Cursing under my breath, I started pulling them into my empty basket. I'd done J.B.'s laundry enough times to recognize his boxers and gym shirts. I guessed this was what happened when I stopped doing his laundry for him.

When my clothes were safely tumbling dry, I took the basket with J.B.'s clothes back into my apartment. I was tempted to just go and dump everything onto the floor of his room, but realized at the last moment that it would just be a childish way of expressing my bitterness toward him.

I had to get over my resentment and anger at J.B. After all, he didn't want to have a baby. This wasn't planned between the two of us. Sure, it's what I'd always wanted, but obviously J.B. wasn't sharing my feelings on the matter, and I knew that all along. And he did try to do the right thing, even though he made a huge cock-up of it. There was really not much I could do. I couldn't force him to be happy about a baby he didn't want. What it came down to was that I wanted—I expected—him to be happy about the baby. I thought once he got over the initial fear, some sort of paternal gene would kick in and he'd be happy and excited, like me. I never expected the anger or him coming with his tail between his legs to propose a quick and small wedding only to have his mother hate me. It all came down to the fact that I was disappointed in J.B., and there was no one I could blame for that but me.

But I missed him. I missed him a lot. I missed our friendship and just hanging out with him and even the simple conversations with him. And I missed the flirtation between us and the constant bickering and teasing. He didn't come down for breakfast again this morning—Cooper said he left early to go bike riding, but I knew he was avoiding me. He didn't know what to say, and so he was choosing to hide his head in the sand. Childish, sure, but what could I do about it? I wished I didn't miss him so much.

While I was standing here cursing J.B. and his dickheadedness, I'd been mindlessly folding his laundry. I was holding a pair of red striped boxers in my hand, and I stood there with them for a long moment. These were the pair he was wearing that night, the night this whole mess began.

"Are things ever going to go back to normal?" I asked my cat. Of course, he didn't answer. I picked up the clothes I'd folded and put them back in the basket to take upstairs.

"Where's J.B.?" I asked Coop, who was still at the stove. I swear, it seems some days Cooper never leaves the kitchen. This time, there was no egg smell or other breakfast-like aromas wafting around. It was another smell entirely. My stomach tossed restlessly. Whatever he was making didn't smell all that good for me.

"Why?" Cooper asked. "What are you going to do to him?"

"I folded his laundry," I said defensively. "And now I'm tempted to go and dump it into the compost heap in the backyard."

Cooper laughed. "That's more like it. You start being nice to him, and I'll think there's something going on. Something more than there already is…" he trailed off with a pained expression.

"I'm not mad," I began, then slapped a hand against my nose. As Cooper stirred, the room was filled with an odour of…

"What's that? It smells like—" I peered at the stove.

"Brownies with raspberry shiraz jam…" he trailed off, with a confused frown at my hand still holding my nose. "You like chocolate."

"Why is this happening to me?" I cried. Cooper started to laugh. "Stop laughing! How would you feel if the smell of the one thing you love more than anything is making you feel like you're going to puke? Fuck a duck!" I howled. I backed away from the stove.

Cooper was still chuckling. "Get out of here before you get sick then. J.B.'s not here. He's still out with Ben."

Ben. Ben and the books. I forgot all about the baby books Ben brought over for me. "Have you seen a pile of baby books around lately? Maura sent some over last week," I asked from the doorway, still with my hand over my nose.

Coop shook his head absentmindedly. "Haven't seen them. I think you might have enough of your own, though, don't you?"

"Probably." I'd been trying to breathe through my mouth and hold my nose, but it was not working. The rich chocolaty smell was getting through. "Goddamit!" Normally I'd be practically drooling by now. "It's not fair to take chocolate away from me! I won't have anything left! I gotta get out of here," I cried and raced out of the kitchen with the basket banging against my hip and Cooper's laughter ringing in my ears.

"It won't be forever," he called after me.

By the time I reached J.B.'s room upstairs, I really was ready to throw all of his clothes outside, hopefully to be trod on by an army of ants and pooped on by a dozen birds with diarrhea. How dare he get me pregnant? I'm carrying his child, unable to drink wine or even stand the smell of chocolate, and where is he through all of this? Riding his bike. What does he know about morning sickness? I wished a plague of morning sickness on him. I hoped he'd vomit every day for the next nine years and that the smell of garlic and beer and all lovely things he likes to smell, like women's perfume and the exhaust from his motorcycle, would make him want to throw up every time he was around them and...

My rant ended as soon as I stepped into his room.

There, sitting on the floor beside his bed in a neat pile, were the missing baby books. There, sitting on the floor, like they were waiting to be read, were copies of *The Baby Whisperer*, *Girlfriend's Guide to Pregnancy*, *The MOMMY of all Pregnancy Books*, and more. And there, lying face down on his pillow was *What to Expect When You're Expecting*.

I placed the basket of clothes gently on the bed and reached over and picked up the book. It looked like J.B. was reading this—was he really reading this? A book about what to expect when you're expecting? Really?

I flipped the book over. The Fifth Month. Oh, my God—did this mean…

I burst into tears at the thought.

# Chapter Twenty-Nine

"It is said that a woman becomes a mother when she conceives a child, but a man becomes a father when he holds the child in his arms."

*A Young Woman's Guide to the Joy of Impending Motherhood*
Dr. Francine Pascal Reid (1941)

T HE DISCOVERY OF THE baby books in J.B.'s room sent me into a tailspin for the rest of the day. J.B. was reading baby books—did that mean he wanted to be involved? Or was he looking into all the scary stuff that's going on in my body and all the truly frightening aspects of life after the baby to justify running scared? I was so confused. I didn't even want to hope. I didn't know what to hope for!

But finding those books in J.B.'s room brought everything to a head and forced me to do something drastic. Something I do my best not to do more than once every few months.

I cleaned my apartment.

And I mean cleaned. I did the floors, the windows, the closets, and the cupboards. I disinfected Sebastian's litter box and scrubbed the shower walls, all the while singing along at the top of my voice. I may be tone-deaf, but it stops me from thinking about anything, and at least I have a super-clean apartment.

About seven-thirty, I finally called it quits, because the only thing I had left to do was organize my clothes and I didn't have the energy for that. But as soon as I turned off my stereo, I heard footsteps on the stairs. It was J.B.

"I think we need to talk," he said, running a hand nervously through his hair. I leaned against the doorway between the living room and the kitchen and looked at him. He was barefoot, with his unattractive feet on display, wearing a battered pair of jeans and an AC/DC concert T-shirt that was once black, but age had faded it to an ugly grey-brown. He looked overdressed compared to me in my gym shorts and ratty T-shirt with holes under both arms and a slash across the front that exposed an inch of not-too-taut midriff. I suddenly realized I'd yet to shower today. I didn't need a mirror to tell me I was looking pretty bad right now!

"You think?" I asked lightly, even though my heart was going a mile a minute. "Come in."

As soon as J.B. sat down on the couch, Sebastian crawled over to him and started butting his hand with his head. J.B. looked around the room. "You tidied up." There was a note of amazement in his voice.

"I do that every once in a while. What do you want to talk about?" There was no way I was going to make things easy for him. Not unless he'd come prepared to grovel, and grovel well.

J.B. cleared his throat. "I think I screwed things up," he admitted slowly. I sat down and waited for him to continue. This definitely had the potential for groveling. "You having a baby—me having a baby—I wasn't ready for it."

"Nooo," I said. "Sometimes it's hard to be ready for that. That's why they give you nine months to get used to the idea."

"You seem to be fine with it."

"I'm able to take responsibility for my actions," I told him coolly.

J.B. winced. "I deserve that. Look, Casey, I'm sorry. I screwed up. You told me and I—I freaked out. I got angry and scared. I'm sorry. I've been an ass."

"You have," I admitted.

"The thought of having a kid freaks me out. It was worse than it was with Betsey—back then I was just pissed off. I was pissed off for about a minute when I thought you did it on purpose."

"I would never do that."

"I know. You didn't hear me—I was only pissed off for about a minute before I realized you would never do that."

"Good. I wouldn't do that."

"I know. And then I practically forced you to marry me—I don't know what I was thinking."

"Me caveman, you pregnant woman?" I suggested lightly.

"Yeah, maybe," he said with a little chuckle. "I know you can take care of yourself—you've been doing it forever—but I thought that you thought I needed to do that."

"I don't."

"Yes, I know. Why didn't you tell me about David?" he asked abruptly. "You made it seem that the two of you were all hot and heavy and I was standing in your way for your 'one chance at happiness.' And then you lay it all out last weekend about him being gay?"

I blinked with surprise at the sudden switch of topic and at J.B. quoting me—it's exactly what I said the morning after David stepped back into my life, when I was convinced he was part of my future and I had no idea Italian Stallion Marco existed.

"You make it sound like he's some sort of criminal," I protested.

"This is nothing about his sexuality," J.B. roared. Well, not roared like a lion roars, but almost a shout. I blinked with surprise again. "I couldn't give a damn about that! I'm pissed because you made me feel like shit because I screwed things up between the two of you. I beat him to the post, or whatever stupid thing you said. And now you tell me he's gay, so there wasn't any hope to begin with for the two of you."

"Well, no," I said meekly. "I mean, yes, I said that, and yes, he's gay. But I didn't know that when I first went out with him."

"The first time twenty years ago, or the first time a couple of weeks ago?"

"Both. He told me the day after I kissed him and he didn't kiss me back."

"So you knew he was gay when you got pregnant?"

"Well, yeah," I admitted. "When I found out I was pregnant. I can't believe Coop didn't tell you this."

"He didn't. What was the point of making me feel I was in the way?"

"Well, you were. Sort of." Okay, I'm not supposed to be the one feeling guilty about anything here. I could see a thundercloud of annoyance and confusion pass across J.B.'s face, and I hurried to explain. "David wants a baby too, so he asked me if I would have a baby for him. Or rather, with him. He thought we would raise it together. He would be the father, and I would be the mother."

"I get how that works, thanks."

"And I was trying to decide if that's what I wanted to do—when I got pregnant. When I found out I was pregnant," I corrected. "By you. Or with you, whatever the proper grammar is. So David and I couldn't have a baby together, so technically you did get in the way. I guess I should have told you this, but—I was kind of pissed off at you, you know! And I didn't want to hear you say, 'I told you so.' So I didn't say anything about it to you."

A snort of what might have been laughter came from J.B., and with it some of the fire and brimstone that had been blowing out his ears. He sat down on the chair across from me. "So you keep me in the dark about this guy, make me go on thinking that the two of you are all hot and heavy and he's probably going to be the one raising my baby, all because you're pissed off at me? Do you know how pissed off I was this last couple of weeks—thinking about the two of you? Thinking that you're making all these plans about my baby and I wasn't going to have any say in it?"

I bit my lip. Suddenly I thought back to that night when J.B. told me he hated thinking about me kissing anyone else. If he got that upset just thinking about a kiss, then he must have been going crazy with all this running through his head. No wonder...

"I'm sorry," I whispered. This was not how I had pictured the groveling part of it!

"I thought he was taking both of you," J.B. said gruffly to the cat curled up in his lap. "Were you going to have a baby with him?"

"I don't know," I told him honestly. "I talked to Coop and he didn't think it was a good idea, but you have to admit it was the perfect solution. It would have got me the man and the baby without having to deal with the rest of the stuff."

"Some people want the rest of the stuff, you know."

"I know. I just want to be a mother. I want a baby and now I'm having one, and no matter what you feel about it, I'm so happy I can just cry."

"You doing a lot of crying these days?"

"I'm hormonal," I told him stiffly. "Get used to it."

"Yeah, well, I guess I better," he muttered. And yet again, I blinked with surprise.

"What's that supposed to mean?"

"It means, you want me to prove something to you, I will. I'll prove that I can take responsibility for things and that I want this in my life. I'll prove that I'm not a complete selfish asshole."

"I don't really think you are," I admitted faintly. "I just think there are some assholic tendencies that flew out there for a bit. But, J.B., I can do this on my own. I want to."

"You don't want me involved?" J.B. asked stiffly.

I shrugged helplessly. He sounded serious, like he really meant it. I know he's not an asshole, and deep down, I think he would make a good father, despite what he might think. Of course I would want him to be involved, but I don't want him to take part because he feels some obligation, some pity for me. I want him to want it.

But then I think about the baby books up in his room. I had to assume he was reading them, or else they made a handy nightstand.

"I do want you involved," I told him simply, with my hand back on my belly. "But—"

J.B. gave my hand a squeeze. "I'll prove it to you," he vowed, all very serious-like. "I'll show you this is what I want. Okay?"

"Okay," I whispered, with a sudden, fervent wish that J.B. would kiss me right then.

But he didn't.

# CHAPTER THIRTY

"The excitement of a pregnancy often overshadows the exhaustion of the first trimester."

*A Young Woman's Guide to the Joy of Impending Motherhood*
Dr. Francine Pascal Reid (1941)

I MET WITH BRIT and Morgan Monday night. The only thing I said to them about J.B. was that we had a talk and he seemed to be okay with the baby thing now. Morgan was happy for me, but of course, Brit started muttering about marriage and never finding another man. I was glad I hadn't told them he actually proposed. If that's what it was. Half-assed attempt, if you ask me. But still... it was nice to know I'm not alone in this now.

The three of us ironed out plans for Brit's stagette. The wedding was a month away, and it was time to start the celebration. I just wished I felt more like a party.

A surprise party wasn't an option since Brit made that perfectly clear back when she and Tom first got engaged. And there was not much to plan, since Brit knew exactly what she wanted with everything concerned with this wedding. I wondered if Tom got a say in anything. I know Brit suggested golf as a way for him to start his bachelor party.

Anyway, Brit came up with the idea for her perfect bachelorette party before she even got engaged. She wanted a whole day of togetherness, with the three of us shopping at her favourite stores in the morning; followed by a quick lunch at her favourite Thai restaurant; on to her favourite spa for facials, manicures, and massages; and then dinner at the private room at Coop's restaurant, which isn't quite her favourite, but she likes it and I do have some pull, which comes in handy making reservations for sixteen. She even has a guest list ready, with phone numbers and e-mails included.

We decided to have the stagette two weeks before the wedding—which was going to be on the Saturday of the Labour Day weekend—because both of Brit's sisters would be in the city then. Lacey lives in Vancouver, and Sierra, the younger, had been traveling in Europe for the summer before she headed to graduate school.

I was officially sharing the role of maid of honour with Morgan when it came to planning the party, mainly because she's so much better at it than I am. At least I had more of an idea of what Brit wanted than her sister Lacey does. Lacey is still quite the party girl, living it up in Vancouver, working part-time as an actress. She's been e-mailing me for weeks with suggestions for the hen party, which is what she calls it.

Anyway, over the last few weeks, Lacey's given me some of the more traditional ideas (male strippers), the supernatural suggestion (a coven of Wiccans will brew a love potion for Brit to ensure a happy marriage), and the exotic (some guy teaching us how to give the best blow job ever). Not that it would be useful for Brit, because in her words, and I quote, "There's no way in hell I'm ever being caught kneeling between a guy's legs. He'd have to go down on me for a good long time to have me be suitably grateful enough to do that." So we were just going with Brit's own idea. It's always easier that way.

The day of the stagette arrived, and I met Morgan and Brit, as instructed, in front of Pottery Barn in Yorkville. We managed to do quite a bit of damage in quite a few stores. I was even pleasantly surprised by Brit allowing me to enter BabyGap. I couldn't help buying something from the store, even though I was still days away from being three months.

It seems there's this magical thing that occurs at the end of the first trimester for some women. All of a sudden they're allowed to start talking about their pregnancy like it's just happened. Sure, I understand about the threat of miscarriage and everything and I'm definitely not going to start telling the world even when I'm eight and a half months along, but the way I look at it, I'm pregnant and very happy to be so. I'm going to enjoy every moment of it, and if something happens, God forbid, then I'll deal with it then. I don't want to be afraid to be excited about my baby.

Anyway, I ended up buying a little sleeper from BabyGap with little yellow ducks and a hat to match. It's very gender-neutral. Right now I was very ambivalent about finding out the sex of the baby, but that might change.

Brit spent an absolute fortune in a very short time (not in BabyGap though), and Morgan didn't do too badly either. Of course, it's not that difficult when you have their salaries. I was in a buying mood despite my much smaller bank balance, but it was really frustrating wanting to buy a pair of end-of-season Capri pants, knowing I wouldn't be able to fit in them for much longer. I bought them anyway. There's always next summer, right? Brit's new gesture of tolerance and acceptance did not extend to browsing in maternity wear. But it was a nice day even though I used the lunch break to throw up. The bathroom in the Thai restaurant was absolutely disgusting and made me vomit a second time, although I didn't mention that to the waitress, who was very attentive to us when she noticed Brit's mountain of shopping bags.

The visit to the spa that afternoon was to die for—I even enjoyed the manicure and the pretty pearly pink my nails were painted. And my toes had never looked so nice. I was cleansed, exfoliated, something wonderful was done to my pores and then I almost fell asleep under the firm administration of Olga, the masseuse. One of my recurring fantasies involves Pedro, the horny massage therapist who can't control his raging libido when confronted by my nakedness under the thin cotton sheet, but I was thankful Olga didn't seem interested in making that fantasy a reality. But that's way off-topic. There was no use thinking about Pedro or any fantasy since I had no one but me to scratch that particular itch. Despite the lackluster "proposal," I doubted J.B. would want to come near me for a good long time. Look what happened last time!

After the spa, I was almost too relaxed (read tired) to continue with the evening, but Brit and Morgan were raring to go. I drove—since I was the only one who was guaranteed not to be drinking. I don't like being the DD. I'd never done it before. We headed to Coop's restaurant Galileo to meet up with the rest of the party. As soon as I left the parking lot where I'd left my car for the day, Brit grabbed her cell phone from her trendy little purse and called Tom, who was having his own bachelor party tonight.

"Is Anil there?" Morgan demanded as soon as Brit hung up, first making Tom say he loved her and promised to be good.

"Of course. I'm sorry, Morgan, but they are friends."

"How is he?" Morgan sounded a little too eager for news of Anil for my liking. I met Brit's eyes.

"Why do you care?" Brit asked without an iota of sympathy.

"Because... because I don't. I'm just curious. It's hard not to wonder." When I glanced in the backseat, I saw Morgan staring out the window.

"What happened with Derek?" I asked warily, taking pity on her. She did spend years with Anil and was doing her best to get over him. "I thought you had dinner with him." Morgan gave a sigh. "What happened?" I groaned. "I should have known my mother would pick a man with an asshole brother. I wish she'd never introduced you."

"No, no, there's nothing of an asshole about him," Morgan protested.

"Then what—"

"Who are we talking about?" Brit interrupted.

"Derek," Morgan and I said together. "The brother of the man my mother is engaged to marry," I added, trying to stifle my distaste for the idea.

"He's a great guy, nice and smart and caring and considerate," Morgan told us eagerly. "And I can talk to him about anything and everything, and we talk all the time. The main problem is that he doesn't want to be the rebound guy."

"Well, he would be," Brit put in bluntly. "You haven't been with anyone since Anil. It's like you're stuck in a rut, just licking your wounds. I mean, there are a ton of guys—"

"Brit, it hasn't been that long," I chided her. "They were together for six years. How would you feel if you and Tom broke up?"

"Well, that's not going to happen, since we're getting married in two weeks," she reminded me cheekily. "And I'd be too busy worrying about going to prison for murder, since I would plan on making the bastard suffer greatly if he ever treated me like Anil treated you."

"So Derek doesn't want to be rebound guy," I said hastily, trying to get the subject away from suffering and Anil's misuse of Morgan. "What does that mean?"

"It means," Morgan said shyly, and when I glanced in the mirror at her, I thought she was blushing a little, "Derek thinks we have a future together but wants to hold off because I may still have unresolved feelings for Anil."

"And do you?" I asked, already knowing the answer.

"I don't know. Probably. Derek says I need to explore these feelings so that I can exorcise—"

"Exercise?" Brit interrupted again.

"Ex-or-cise. Rid myself of the ghost of Anil. However I need to. I'm supposed to do this, and then give it a try with Derek."

"There's something to strive for," I muttered, wishing I could sound more encouraging.

"Is that why it's suddenly all Anil, all the time? You haven't mentioned him in weeks," Brit demanded.

"I'm just trying to resolve my feelings," Morgan said defensively. "Instead of trying to ignore he exists, I thought I would focus on Anil and try to talk myself out of being in love with him. If I still am."

"That's fine, that's fine," I told her. Interesting logic, I thought to myself. Not sure I'd go that route, but if it works, it might be something to think about to get J.B. out of my head. "Good luck. I'll try to get over the nightmare of you resolving all over my possible future step-uncle."

"No more talk of relationships other than mine!" Brit barked.

"Yes, sir," I muttered.

"And no more baby talk. I let you talk enough about this baby this morning. Need I remind you tonight is all about me? Me, me, me!" she sang.

"No, you don't have to remind us," I grinned.

"Be nice, Brit, 'cause if you piss us off, the pregnant one is likely to throw a glass of water on you!" Morgan threatened with a giggle.

"Don't tempt me. I'm still hormonal."

"Well, if you try that tonight, you're definitely out of the wedding party," Brit said, and I could tell she was not exactly joking. How long is it until this wedding is over?

# CHAPTER THIRTY-ONE

"An expectant mother can almost always be assured of
being the centre of attention at a gathering."

*A Young Woman's Guide to the Joy of Impending Motherhood*
Dr. Francine Pascal Reid (1941)

WHEN THE THREE OF us showed up at Coop's restaurant, Emma
showed us to the table in the back room. That's another reason
I thought Galileo might be a good choice—the private room in the back.
There was always the possibility (certainty with Lacey here) that a group
of women could quickly turn obnoxious, especially when there were
copious amounts of wine involved and the prospect of X-rated gifts. I
thought if we were tucked away in the back room, it might be nicer for
the other diners.

Most of Brit's guests were already there, seated with drinks in front of
them, and Brit was greeted with hugs and tons of gift bags overflowing
with coloured tissue paper. It was a combined shower/stagette since
Brit is vehemently opposed to the potential cheesiness of the traditional
bridal shower. Her aunt Claudia threw her one last month, and I was

invited. Brit got an amazing amount of presents (enough to make me want to reconsider my whole not-wanting-to-get married idea), but the shower games we were forced to participate in almost took all the fun away from the gifts.

"So you're having a baby?" Brit's sister Lacey asked me first off, plopping into a chair beside Libby. There was a great deal of skepticism in her voice. I preferred to think of it as skepticism rather than disgust. Lacey turned to Libby. The two of them are the same age and used to be quite close when they were young. "Is she nuts? Oh, I forgot, you popped out a couple too, didn't you?"

"I have two, yes." From the frosty note in her tone, I could tell Libby was not keen on renewing her past friendship with Lacey anytime soon.

"Crazy. Who's the guy?"

"A friend of mine," I told her, reluctant to talk about J.B.

"Sucks you can't drink," Lacey laughed, filling up her glass from the bottle on the table. "Is he hot, at least?" Lacey's been living in Vancouver for the last ten years, but within five minutes in her company, I could tell she hadn't changed a bit from the annoying teenager I remember. Still selfish and self-centered, and now that she's over thirty, she's even more juvenile. Her outfit was something I would never be caught dead in, but since I've been shopping with Brit for years, I had no trouble recognizing the expensive quality and designer names. And I never would have believed it possible to walk upright in heels that high had I not seen her stride across the restaurant, the last to arrive.

"J.B. is hot and with a body to die for," Libby cut in. Knowing Libby and her competitive nature the way I do, her comment was more of a jab than a piece of gossip. She was basically telling Lacey that her big sister (me) could pull a better-looking guy than Brit (Lacey's big sister). Nice of her to be so biased toward me (J.B. is way cuter than Tom, by the way!) but I'd rather have the topic of me and J.B. swept right under the table and stepped on by all of the obviously expensive footwear. But it's not meant to be. Lacey has a bone and wants to gnaw on it for a while.

"Maybe hot but doesn't sound too bright. And you! Brit told me you wanted to get pregnant? That this was intentional? What's that all about?"

"It wasn't intentional, but it's not unwanted," I said shortly. I really didn't want to get into it. Unfortunately most of the table—there were sixteen of us—seemed to be paying rapt attention to the conversation. And Lacey couldn't stop laughing. Like a hyena, I think the saying is, and it's true. I could even see some fangs come out, if hyenas have fangs. They have sharp teeth at least.

"So is this someone you were dating or just some guy you pulled off the street?" asked one of Brit's friends from work. Not that it was any of her business.

"Did he ditch you when he got you knocked up?" I think that was from her neighbour.

"Apparently J.B. wants nothing to do with the baby," Brit told the enthralled audience.

"J.B. will do the right thing," Morgan defended him. "He's just..."

"Scared shitless?" Libby asked dryly. "I've always thought he was a great guy, but really, the way he's treating Casey, he's proving to be an ass. This isn't all Casey's fault. It's not like she did it on purpose."

"How old are you anyway?" Lacey demanded. "It's all fixable, you know. If you don't want it—"

"Don't tell Casey that," Brit cut in. "Remember, she wants a baby. I try to tell her there's no way she'll ever find a husband—you'd think unmarried mothers were still pariahs these days—but she won't listen. And since she was sleeping with J.B. for quite some time, it was bound to happen sooner or later." No wonder her sister was giving me the third degree if this is how Brit talks about me!

"Thank you," I told her sarcastically, which was, of course, lost on her.

"Oh, so he's some sort of friend with benefits thing," Lacey said knowingly. She winked at me lasciviously. "I've got a few of those tucked away myself. Of course, I'm not about to let one of them get me pregnant. But I thought you were going out with a gay guy?"

"I'm not dating anyone, actually," I replied slowly.

"I didn't say she was 'dating' him," Brit hissed to Lacey. "I said she tried to get back together with him." What? Why? Why is it my life that is being spread out in front of the table like some sort of tasty treat? I had no idea how to change the subject as younger sister Sierra picked up the interrogation.

"Did you know he was gay when you started having sex with him?" Definitely sex-obsessed.

"No," I told her between gritted teeth. "And I wasn't having sex with him. David and I went out a long time ago and recently bumped into each other again. That's when he told me he's gay."

"He was gay when you went out with him?" Lacey asked, with her blue eyes as wide as they could be. I'm sure some women look sweet and innocent when they do the wide-eyed thing, but not Lacey. She looks feline, if hyenas can be feline. Nevertheless, I was wishing we hadn't waited until Brit's sisters got home to have this stupid stagette.

"Apparently, since most homosexuals are that way since birth."

"But he was still in the closet? Or did he have a guy on the side?" Lacey persisted. I could clearly remember why I always went along with Brit's torture of her sister. We used to dunk the heads of her Strawberry Shortcake dolls into Jell-o, so Strawberry would turn into Grape Girl. I wished I could dunk Lacey into something now.

"No. Yes. Isn't it time for presents now?" I asked desperately. Lacey only laughed.

"It's not my fault your life got really interesting. For years all I hear about is all these guys you're going out with and now this. I have to say, all I wanted was to be you when I grew up, all the guys, all the partying. You've sort of been my inspiration. And Brit's been keeping me posted, but in person is so much better. So dish. Who are you bringing to the wedding?"

I looked around, hoping to avert this discussion. I'm her inspiration? Sure, maybe I might have been considered a little wild in my twenties, but I've grown up now and don't need the reminder. It's been years since I considered myself a party girl, and there's no way I was ever anything like Lacey! I wonder how… my eyes fixed on one of the wine bottles on the table. If I hit her over the head with an empty bottle, would Lacey stop talking?

I shifted uncomfortably (full bladder again) in my chair and made a motion toward the bottle.

Libby grabbed my wrist. "No," she whispered, reading my mind in that scary sister way. "There'd be too much blood."

I laughed out loud. "Can you believe it?" Lacey asked, thinking I'm laughing at another one of her stories. I'd hoped she'd given up on me. She was doing her best to claim the majority of the attention tonight, which resulted in a silent battle of wills between her and Brit. Forgetting about me for the moment, Lacey started regaling everyone with tales of the acting jobs she'd been on and the famous people she'd met. Frankly I don't think drinks with Jared Leto is much to write home about (according to Us, who hasn't he had drinks with?), but the others seemed enthralled. Of course, they'd had a lot more to drink than I had. Lacey was always a brat, but she's become so self-absorbed and materialistic she makes Brit look caring and considerate.

Speaking of Brit, before dessert was served, Emma (who thankfully for her, was not our waitress tonight) poked her head into the private room and asked if everything was okay, and commented the chef would love to meet the guest of honour. So then, in came the executive chef, Jonas, and his arrival shifted the attention from Lacey as the whole table (even Brit's mom!) prepared to pay lip service to him.

I'd met Jonas a few times, and while unarguably he's a kick-ass chef, he's also an arrogant asshole. He truly believes he's God's gift to women, which from the reaction of Brit's friends (even her mom!), he might well be. I'm embarrassed to admit I once found him attractive, and there's a story about me and him in the freezer that Cooper loves to bring up when he really wants to embarrass me, but Jonas does nothing for me these days. Tonight, all of his charms are focused on Brit. Maybe she's right. Maybe all men do find her irresistible. There's a great deal of laughter and hair-flipping by her until Jonas reluctantly heads back into his kitchen, where no doubt, Coop is up to his elbows preparing food that Jonas gets credit for. Another reason I can't stand him.

"Brit! You're getting married in two weeks!" one of her friends admonished her after Jonas—with a last look at Brit that's as hot as his entrées—leaves.

But Brit never got a chance to respond, since Lacey realized she'd lost her audience, and with impeccable timing, turned back to me. "So who are you bringing to the wedding, Casey?" She twirled the dregs of her red wine in front of my face, just to torment me, I'm sure. "What are you doing for sex? I mean, obviously, you've had some—" she pointed to my stomach, eliciting laughter from a few, "but who are you dating? You used to always have the hottest guys. But now..."

I instantly picked up on her assumption that no one—hot or otherwise—would prefer me now. And I couldn't help but think she was right. Sure, I'm cute and bouncy when I'm not exhausted, but I can't compare to Lacey. Here I am dressed in the same halter dress I wore to Coop's party because my boobs seem to have grown overnight and most of the tops I would wear out are a little too tight around the bosom for my liking—and here is Lacey, dressed in this season's hottest pants and a low-cut, sleeveless top displaying her golden shoulders and super-toned arms.

"I'm not into dating right now, so I'm not bringing anyone to the wedding." I didn't intend to, but I came across sounding like a bad case of sour grapes. I could tell Lacey thought so too because I saw her raise a perfectly waxed eyebrow at Morgan. I know she waxes her eyebrows because earlier, while we were waiting for the appetizers to arrive, she told the table how she waxes every part of her body, including her nether region. In fact, she went on to describe the almost pleasurable agony one receives from the Brazilian wax.

When I glanced back toward Lacey, I had this horrible thought that I was looking at myself. Or how I used to be. Even on my worst days, it was not possible for me to be the bitch that Lacey was capable of being, but the lifestyle she was living—that was the same lifestyle I was happy with not very long ago. Oh, sure, Lacey does it better with her designer duds and her Jared Leto lunches, but how she irresponsibly cavorts through life, the string of casual relationships, the drinking, the partying—that was me. That was all me.

If I was so condescending toward Lacey, did that mean I was demeaning my own life? Well, not now, since I have cleaned up in the last few years. But the way I was before?

Looking around the long table littered with sixteen women, with an average age of thirty-three, I was guessing all of them were either married or planned to be soon. Well, maybe not Lacey. It'd take a brave man to take her on. Libby was telling some story about Luke, and Brit was basking in the glow of being almost married. Everyone had someone. I'd never before felt the profound weight of being a single woman.

"Have you thought about throwing a paternity suit against the father?" one of Brit's coworkers asked me suddenly. I was not sure if she'd just awakened or something, but the last thing I wanted was to discuss my life any longer.

"No," I snapped. "Things are fine. J.B. is fine with everything—he even asked me to marry him." As soon as the words were out of my mouth, I wanted to suck them back in.

The transformation of Brit was fascinating to watch. She was sitting across from me, so there was no way she didn't hear me. Her eyes went huge, and she gasped loudly, almost like she was trying to inhale all of the available oxygen in the room. "Casey!" she exhaled. "You should be mortified that you are announcing your engagement at my party, but I'm just so *happpppeeee*!"she shrieked. "*Omygod!*"

"Why didn't you tell us?" Morgan gasped, clapping her hands with glee.

"Why didn't you tell me?" Libby demanded.

"I said no," I whispered, wishing I could sink under the table.

"Whaaat?" Brit screamed so loudly I was afraid for the wine glasses on the table. "You said no?"

"Why?" Morgan breathed.

"You idiot," Libby put in.

I threw up my hands. "I don't want him to feel obligated to marry me," I told them.

"But what if he wants to marry you?" Morgan demanded.

"He doesn't. Maybe someday, but he doesn't now."

"How can you tell?"

"I just can," I said lamely. "Can we please change the subject?"

Brit gave me a look like she was washing her hands of the whole thing, but I knew that was not possible and that this wasn't the last I'd hear about it. "Well, I hope you'll acknowledge your stupidity when you're forty years old—alone–and pushing a baby stroller. Alone." And luckily, that was the last she said about it that night.

But after dessert, when most of the girls were discussing going to J.B.'s club, I quietly said my goodbyes to Brit and Morgan, claiming fatigue and an overwhelming urge to throw up. I knew Brit wasn't happy, but Morgan smoothed it out for me, giving my belly a pat and telling me there'd be time enough to party when I wasn't pregnant anymore. Morgan didn't say anything about my impromptu announcement, but she didn't meet my eyes either. I could tell she thought I was making a huge mistake.

But I'm not, I kept reassuring myself. J.B. just got me pregnant—I'm not about to trap him into a marriage he doesn't want. We don't have to be married to raise a baby together.

Libby left with me, and as we walked to the lot where I parked my car, we idly discussed the evening.

"Lacey's turned into such a bitch," she exclaimed.

I had to agree. I was very glad the day was finally over.

# Chapter Thirty-Two

"Pregnancy forces every new mother to reevaluate her life in preparation for the momentous responsibility of caring for another life."

*A Young Woman's Guide to the Joy of Impending Motherhood*
Dr. Francine Pascal Reid (1941)

THE MORNING AFTER BRIT's party was a bad one. First of all, I was awakened at eight o'clock by Brit calling on the phone. I got a huge guilt trip about leaving early, and when she deigned that I'd apologized sufficiently, she proceeded to give me every last detail about the rest of the evening, including gossipy little bits about those in attendance. Then, when I was practically falling back asleep, she started in about J. B., demanding more of an explanation about why on earth I would refuse his marriage proposal. An hour and a half later, I finally managed to get off the phone because of a sudden need to vomit. It was the first time I'd thanked God for giving me morning sickness.

After that, I began to get hungry since I was too awake now to try to go back to sleep. I headed upstairs to scrounge some breakfast. But Emma was already there, and as I opened the door to the kitchen, the sound of the smoke detector and the smell of burnt eggs sent me rushing back down to the washroom again.

I decided to have a shower before breakfast to give the kitchen a chance to air out.

"How was your little hen party?" Cooper asked when I returned upstairs. The windows were still open and the kitchen smelled much better. Cooper had made a lovely ham and mushroom frittata, but I really wished he would lay off the eggs. They were not that good coming back up, and even when they were not burnt by Emma, the smell gets to me.

"It wasn't little, but I guess it was okay," I told him, sliding into a chair.

"You don't sound convinced," Emma smiled at me. "You all sounded like you were having a good time last night."

"It was fun," I said firmly. "Brit had a good time, and that's all that matters. They went out to a club afterward, but I bailed and came home."

"You can still go out dancing and stuff when you're pregnant, can't you?" Cooper wondered. "I would have thought that would be right up your alley. You haven't been out dancing in a while."

"I know." I pushed a piece of mushroom around my plate. "But I was tired and—I really didn't want to," I told them suddenly. "I knew all of those women last night, and the majority of them are my friends too, and I've gone out with them dozens of times, but I just had no desire to do anything with them last night. They irritated me all night with their silly talk and gossip—Brit's sister was the worst of them. I just... I didn't want to be with them."

"Aaaw," Cooper smiled. He went over to Emma and draped his arm around her shoulders. "Em, darling, our little girl is finally growing up!"

I was about to ask what he meant by that when J.B. made an appearance. And he was gripping How to Baby the New Mommy in his hand.

"Do you know about this?" he demanded, waving the book in my face.

"Probably if I knew what you were talking about," I replied irritably, trying to avoid a book to the head.

"This. This huge needle thing!" J.B. showed me the page, and I got a quick glimpse of the heading Doctor's Visits. "They have to stick this needle into the baby! Do you know about this?"

"Amniocentesis. Yes, I am well aware of that, thank you."

"They stick it in the baby!" I wasn't sure if this was coming from a hidden fear of needles or if he was really concerned about the baby. "It can cause a miscarriage!"

"Yes, but it's important in determining whether there may be a birth defect, which can be more prevalent in older mothers. And they don't stick it in the baby; they just need to get some of the amnio fluid. They do stick it in me, though, in case you're wondering."

"Oh. So you did know. Aren't you worried?"

"I'm actually hoping I won't need to get one since I'm still thirty-five and normally they don't give them until the mother is older. I've got to talk to the doctor about that."

"Oh. So you might not have to have one?"

"I'll have to ask the doctor," I told him patiently.

"Oh." Some of the steam went out of J.B., and I hid my grin as he sat down. "I just wanted to make sure you knew about it," he told me lamely.

"I know a bunch of things," I said. "But if you find something you don't think I know, you can come talk to me about it, okay?"

"Okay." Emma set a plate down in front of him. After he thanked her, she turned to me and mouthed, So cute! "How come you didn't come with the others last night?" J.B. asked me.

"Where?"

"The club. Morgan and Brit, all those women," he grimaced. "Drunk, dancing on tables, and trying to make out with boys young enough to be their kids, women. You missed out on a great time." His expression told me differently.

"So Brit told me."

"I think they hit a couple of places before they stumbled in. What happened to you? Everything okay with..." His eyes shifted lower, to my midsection, before they met my surprised gaze again.

"Fine. It's just—I just got tired. I didn't really feel up to a lot of rumpusing with the wild things last night."

I got up and took my plate to the sink. "That sitting all right?" Coop asked when he noticed the plate was empty. I'd left nothing for Sebastian this morning. He was weaving around my ankles, threatening to trip me in hopes of getting some scraps.

"Not bad. So far anyway. The fact that there was only a little bit helps." I rinsed my plate and set it in the dishwasher. "Thanks."

"Anytime. What are you up to today?"

"Not much. Laundry to start. Then maybe a nap." I laughed.

"Oh, the life of a mother."

"That sick stuff," J.B. ventured suddenly, "I read that won't last too much longer, right? It's supposed to end in the second trimester, and what? You're ten weeks now?" I had to say I was a little startled hearing those words coming out of J.B.'s mouth. Referring to the pregnancy in weeks, not months, and talking about trimesters?

"I'm eleven weeks along," I corrected. "And yes, the nausea is supposed to end at the end of the first trimester."

"I forgot to tell you," J.B. said as he opened the newspaper to the sports section. "My sister told me about this weird combination of stale Coke, ginger, and something else you freeze that helps when you feel sick."

"You talked to your sister about me?" I asked in amazement.

"Yeah, I called her about a month ago. I meant to tell you—"

"A month ago? Before you talked to me?"

"Well, yeah, I thought I'd let her know that she might have a new niece or nephew coming, and she—"

"You talked to your family before you talked to me? You told your family that I—that we were having a baby before you talked to me?

Before you apologized for being such an ass? What if I told you to fuck off?" I cried.

J.B. lifted his shoulders in a shrug. "Thought you'd come around. Face it, Case, you don't hold a grudge too often."

"You ass!"

"Ah, the sweet sound of insults flying across the table. I have to say I missed the two of you bickering," Coop mused in a singsong voice.

"We don't bicker," I argued. "Bickering is for old married couples." Coop raised an eyebrow at me but didn't say anything.

# Chapter Thirty-Three

"Hearing the heartbeat of the baby is one of the most magical moments of the pregnancy. It should be something treasured by both the mother and the father."

*A Young Woman's Guide to the Joy of Impending Motherhood*
Dr. Francine Pascal Reid (1941)

WITH BRIT'S STAGETTE FINALLY over, I could get back to the more important things in my life, being, of course, my first doctor's visit. My baby doctor. I was going to hear my baby's heartbeat. My appointment took place the Tuesday before Labour Day, the weekend of the all-important wedding.

I felt a little weird when I arrived at my appointment and found the waiting room packed with couples. I was the only expectant mother sitting alone in the waiting room. Everyone else had a supportive partner to go along with their beautifully swollen belly except me and my still unnoticeable bulge. I felt like I'd wandered into an Expensive Shoe Club meeting wearing Payless specials.

Being alone was what I had planned for. If everything had gone according to my schedule, I would have been artificially inseminated with a stranger's semen, and I would be planning how to raise my baby alone, as a single mother. But J.B. and I... I may still be a single mother—and despite Brit's opinion on the matter, I'm quite okay with that—but I may not have to go it alone.

I smiled at J.B. as he walked nervously into the waiting room. I couldn't help but notice him goggling at all the baby bellies. As soon as he came in the room and sat down beside me, he grabbed one of my hands and held it in both of his. I didn't know if he thought I was nervous and he was trying to reassure me, but I was just excited. The handholding was doing more for him, especially since I couldn't even flip through a magazine.

"You okay?" he asked for about the tenth time.

"I'm fine. Are you?" We'd been waiting for twenty minutes, and I didn't think his body had stopped moving. Either he was tapping his foot or patting his knee or fingering my hand.

"Sure, no problem," he waved my question away. "Piece of cake."

I laughed aloud at his show of bravado. "You're full of shit."

"Hey," he narrowed his eyes at me. "Watch the potty mouth. Lots of babies in here." But he gave my hand a squeeze.

Ten minutes later, we were finally called into the doctor's office.

"How are you feeling, Casey?" Dr. Morrissey asked. She was a tiny, grey-haired woman, with glasses perched on the end of her nose, and somehow managed to appear ferocious instead of motherly. It was like the grandmother and the big bad wolf from "Little Red Riding Hood" morphed into one. My beloved GP, Dr. Dennis, referred me to her, saying that she was highly respected in the field of obstetrics at Women's College Hospital, which was where I'd decided to give birth. Dr. Morrissey might be highly respected, but I was not getting any warm and fuzzy feelings about her right then. Maybe it was just because I was a little nervous, but I felt irrationally afraid of this woman. Maybe it was because I felt she held the health of my baby in her hands. A baby I was already very attached to.

"Okay," I stammered slightly. I was sitting ramrod straight in the chair across from the doctor. This time I'd rammed my hands between my knees, so J.B. resorted to clutching the arms of the chair he was perched on. "I mean, I've been sick and I throw up a couple of times a day, but other than that, I feel fine."

"Morning sickness is unfortunate, but very common," she said without looking at me. She was reading my file. At least, I hope it was my file. "I'll give you a prescription which should help. And you're the father?" she asked J.B.

"Well, uh... you see, I...um..."

"Either you are or you're not," Dr. Morrissey said with an amused smile. "Makes no difference to me."

"Yes, I am the father," J.B. gulped. He glanced at me with a sheepish expression. I hoped it would get easier for him to admit that as time went on.

"Glad we cleared that up. Let's get started, shall we?"

We had a short chat about my periods—to J.B.'s obvious dismay—and she told me my due date was February 16, which Dr. Dennis had already told me. Then Dr. Morrissey asked me to hop up on her table and we'd listen to the heartbeat. This was the moment I'd been waiting for. I jumped up so eagerly, I tripped over my purse on the floor beside me.

"Should I... do you want me to leave?... I don't need to..." J.B. floundered. I saw his eyes go wide as he noticed the stirrups on the edge of the examining table.

"It's probably nothing you haven't seen before," the doctor told him briskly.

"It's okay with me if you want to stay," I tried to smile reassuringly at him. He only managed a faint one in return and hovered at the side of the room, near the door so he could make a quick getaway if he needed to.

I lay on the table, and the first thing Dr. Morrissey said after I pulled up my shirt did nothing to improve my first impression of her.

"A bit on the chubby side," she commented absentmindedly as she pressed on my stomach. "Baby doesn't give you a free rein to snack, you know?"

"No," I murmured. Chubby! I'm not chubby! So I hadn't been exercising lately. And maybe I'd put on a couple of pounds. It's hard when the only foods I could keep down were carbohydrates. Babies are chubby, not me! Nasty old bat.

"These will only get bigger," she told me next, with a curt nod at my breasts.

"Really?" I groaned. "I'm not going to be able to fit into my wedding dress this weekend." I was already overflowing my quite substantial D-cup, and I couldn't imagine how big I'd be when this thing was over. Double F-cup maybe.

"Are you getting married?" Dr. Morrissey asked politely.

"Oh, no, I'm just the maid of honour for my best friend—I'm not married. I don't want..." I paused for a second before I added, "Is it a problem if I'm not married?"

"Not for me," the doctor replied in a tone that implied that being unmarried might well be a problem for me.

Then Dr. Morrissey did the whole stick-her-fingers-up-my-who-who and poked around a bit. I could feel J.B. cringe across the room. "Your pelvis is a bit narrow," she said, still absentmindedly.

"No, it's not," I couldn't help saying.

"It is, through here." She poked one of my hips.

"Is that a problem?" The way she said it, I felt I must have an irreparable defect.

"Again, not for me," she told me, withdrawing her hand and pulling off the latex gloves. "But I doubt you'll be able to have a vaginal delivery."

"What? How am I supposed to get it out?"

Dr. Morrissey squinted at me like I was some kind of idiot. I admit it didn't make me appear to be some Rhodes scholar, but what did she expect? She was not being at all nice to me. "In all probability, you'll have a long and difficult labour that will not result in a vaginal delivery. This is without knowing how big the baby will be, but based on your size, I'll most likely schedule you for a Cesarean delivery."

"What? What if I don't want a C-section?" I cried.

"Do the words long and difficult mean anything to you?" She lifted a grey-haired eyebrow.

"It's okay, Casey." I knew J.B. was trying to soothe me, but it was difficult when I could hear his voice shaking. "My sister had a Cesarean, and she was fine."

Dr. Morrissey began pressing on my belly while I lay pouting. First I'm chubby, and then my pelvis is too narrow to give birth. What kind of doctor is she? I want a new one. I pulled my arm up, cradling my head; my shirt pulled up and my pants pulled down to reveal the expanse of my belly and its slight bulge. After spending a few minutes pushing down on my belly, Dr. Morrissey coated the skin with a jelly-like substance and ran a microphone thing over my stomach. I held my breath. It was about time for some good news.

"You can breathe, Casey," Dr. Morrissey told me with doctor disdain. I let out my breath in a whoosh and tried to breathe normally—when I heard the faint thump- thump.

"Is that it?" I practically yelled. J.B. quickly moved closer.

"No, that's you." She moved the microphone a little to the right. "This is your baby."

"That's it?" I could hear the quicker thump-thump-thump, and to my embarrassment, my eyes filled with tears. "That's my baby?" I could feel J.B.'s hand against my arm, and I glanced up at him. "That's our baby."

"Wow," he said, staring at my belly with awe. "That's really it. It's really in there."

"It really is." J.B. clasped my hand, and this time I was so glad he was there to hold it. I was picturing myself holding a little creature swaddled in blankets and J.B. smiling down on us, when I noticed the doctor frowning. "What's wrong?"

She moved the roller to another part of my stomach. "And it seems this is also your baby."

"It moved? Already?"

"No." She moved the roller all over again. "I think we should get you in for an ultrasound right away. Seems like you've got two of them in there."

"Two of what?"

Dr. Morrissey actually laughed at that. "Twins, Casey. I think you're having twins." She listened for another moment, moving the roller around. "Goodness. Did you take any fertility drugs?"

"No. Why?" I could hear the note of hysteria creeping into my voice. At the word twins, J.B. paled, and now he was a ghostly white colour.

"What are you talking about?" he croaked.

"Is there any history of multiple births in either of your families?"

"How am I supposed to know that? I don't even know his family!" Dr. Morrissey blinked at my outburst. "Why? What's going on?"

"I can't be positive..." The doctor moved the roller around on my belly some more. "One, two... Casey, I think there might be three babies in there, actually. Let's get an ultrasound for you right away."

After almost casually mentioning that I was about to be a mother to triplets, Dr. Morrissey left J.B. and me alone for a couple of minutes—the worst thing she could have done.

"Is she serious?" J.B. whispered. "Are there really three of them in there?"

I was almost in tears and wouldn't let go of my belly, as if that was going to prevent any egg from splitting into thirds—too late, Casey! I couldn't for the life of me figure out how on earth I could possibly raise three children. Not all at once. Sure, I'd love to have three kids, but not all at once, and I definitely needed some time in between. I was a bit of a basket case already when the nasty old bat of a doctor returned, pushing a computer on a cart.

"I gave the lab a call, and they are fully booked for the day. We'll have a little look here to confirm what's going on."

"So it's not triplets?" I asked, like someone asking, "So it's not diphtheria?"

"Oh, I'm pretty sure you're having triplets, but it's always nice to double-check these things."

She was right, of course. There were three tiny alien creatures growing in my uterus. Having actual aliens growing inside me would have been less of a shock than having three babies. Dr. Morrissey pointed them out on the screen, but it was like I was back in math class, trying to figure out equations. Plus, I couldn't see much through my tears, but I got the gist of what the doctor was telling me. In about six months, I was going to give birth to three babies.

How on earth could this possibly happen to me?

It's all J.B.'s fault. That asshole put not one, not two, but three goddam babies in me! Three! In me! How...? What...? Oh my God!

"How did this happen?" I asked weakly.

Dr. Morrissey gave me a look like she was concerned for my mental health, but I was beyond caring. All I could think about was how I could possibly raise three babies by myself.

"Either you had one egg split after it was fertilized, or you released three eggs, all of which were fertilized separately, which means you would have fraternal, rather than identical—"

"I know all that," I snapped.

"I don't," J.B. said quietly.

"Maybe you should have figured it out before I let you and your super-sperm anywhere near me!"

"How is this my fault?"

"It's not," Dr. Morrissey said so firmly I was scared to argue with her. "Please listen, both of you. You are having a multiple pregnancy, which means you're a high risk. There's a greater possibility of severe nausea and vomiting—"

"Now you tell me!"

"—and premature delivery. You'll also have a higher weight gain, and I want you to make sure you take your vitamins."

I tuned out the rest of the lecture until the doctor suggested I come in to see her again in a month. In the meantime, I should get an ultrasound as soon as I could. I was trying to take all this in, but all the while Dr. Morrissey's words *here's your baby... and here's your baby... and here's another one...* were ringing through my head. I chanced a glance at J.B. as we were leaving. His face was white with shock. I could hear his ragged breathing. For once I didn't give a good goddamn how he was reacting, because as far as I was concerned, this was all his fault.

"Whoa," was the only thing J.B. said as soon as we were out of the office. Like I was some sort of horse.

"Is that all you can say?" I asked, still with that note of hysteria evident in my voice, even to me. "We get this horrible news—"

To make things worse, as we left the building and I was doing my best just to breathe, I was not looking where I was going and I bumped into an elderly man on the sidewalk and practically knocked him down.

"Casey, watch where you're going," J.B. chided me as he helped the man to his feet.

"You should have watched what you were doing," I suddenly snarled. "I can't have these babies! I did not sign up for this! There's no way I can do this. Why did I even think I could have a child? I don't know the first thing—"

"Casey—"

"—about raising a child properly, let alone three! How the hell can I have three kids? That's, that's a whole family already. How will I fit them in my car? I need a minivan. Did I ever tell you I hate minivans?

They're nothing but slow-moving boats for suburbanites! There's no way I can fit three carseats in my car. Three babies! What if I have three girls? Oh my God, what if I have three boys? I can't do this! What was I thinking? thinking can just go get some sperm and that'll make me this wonder mother who can do everything herself when—" By this time I was standing in the middle of the sidewalk yelling at J.B. People were crossing the street to avoid me, but I was still getting quite the audience.

"Casey, slow down. Let's just go home. Talk about this. Calm down."

"I can barely dress myself some days. How can I think I can handle one kid, let alone three of them? Three of them!"

"Let's get out of here."

"I have to get rid of it. I have to get rid of them! Women used to drink a bottle of gin or vodka or something and sit in a bathtub—I can do that. I'll go home and try that. Or I can fall down a set of stairs—women always used to miscarry after that. Or I can just go throw myself under a bus, that should do it, because the way my life is these days—"

"Casey! Shut up!" J.B.'s words finally registered in my hysterical brain. "Let's just get out of here."

"She said I'm having triplets!" I screamed at him, so loudly people across the street stared at me. I made a face at them. "She said I'm having three babies! 'There's your baby,' she said, and then, 'There's another one! And whoops, there's one more!' Three! Three friggin' babies! I didn't sign up for this! What am I supposed to do?"

# Chapter Thirty-Four

"While the idea of multiple births may seem daunting, it truly is a blessing."

*A Young Woman's Guide to the Joy of Impending Motherhood*
Dr. Francine Pascal Reid (1941)

"WHAT'S WRONG?" EMMA DEMANDED with horror. I was surprised to find myself at Coop's restaurant. J.B. didn't even bother trying to put me in the car; he just dragged me the six blocks to Galileo.

"I didn't know what to do," he was telling Emma bleakly.

"Oh my God," she breathed. "What happened? The baby..."

"I'm having three fucking babies!" I snapped. Emma blanched.

"The doctor thinks she's carrying triplets," J.B. translated.

"Three!" Emma actually jumped up and down in delight. "Three of them? That's wonderful news!"

"For whom?" I yelled.

"For you. Or not for you? Oh, Casey, it's a surprise, but this is so great. I have to tell Cooper." And she ran into the kitchen.

"We're having three babies," J.B. said glumly to a passing waiter.

"Congratulations!" he chirped in return.

"No, it's not congratulations." I was back to snarling again. "It's the worst news ever!"

Cooper stalked out of the kitchen with a look of irritation on his face. I cringed, thinking it was directed at me, but all he did was pull me into his arms. "Really, triplets?" he asked into my hair. I nodded. "Three babies are better than one. Everything will be fine."

I burst into tears.

"I didn't know what to do, man," J.B. explained in a low voice. "She just lost it. I think she's hysterical."

"Everything will be fine, Casey," Emma told me with a pat on the back. I was still crying.

"I don't know what to do," J.B. repeated. I wished he'd think of something to do, or at least something else to say.

"Everything will be fine. Just calm down." I didn't know if Cooper was talking to J.B. or me, but I think his words worked on both of us. I finally stopped crying, and J.B. ceased his pacing through the restaurant.

Emma brought me a glass of wine and led me to a table already set for dinner. "I'm sure the doctor will say this is okay," she assured me.

"I have a Valium in my purse," offered one of the hovering waitresses. I remembered her from the night of Brit's stagette. I'd have said hello, but I was not capable right then.

"I have a joint," someone else offered. That sounded even better. I held out my hand for the drugs.

"She's pregnant," snapped Emma.

Well, as soon as she said that, I got plied with congratulations and best wishes and cries of "That's so wonderful!" from the staff who didn't witness my initial outburst. It's hard to have a pity party or a scared-out-of-your-mind party when that's going on, so I had to pull myself together. I finished my wine in about two gulps.

"I'll take you home," J.B. told me.

"You're not taking me anywhere," I told him savagely. "This is all your fault."

"You can't mean that." Emma laughed.

"You think I'd do this to myself?" I retorted.

J.B. opened his mouth to speak, but Cooper raised his hand. "Casey, you're not making sense. You're understandably upset. J.B., you have to go to work. Em, why don't you call Casey's sister and see if she can meet her at the house? I'll get her in a cab, and Case, you can go home and have a nice bath—"

"Without any gin," J.B. said quickly. I made a face at him.

"Without anything like that. Lots of bubbles," Coop said. "And all this will feel better in the morning. Sound good?"

"I'll try to get off early," Emma promised after she called Libby for me. "Call me if you need anything."

"Everything will be okay," Cooper told me as I was getting into the cab.

"Casey?" J.B. called to me. His face was white and set, and I still didn't care. Yes, it may be irrational blaming him, but at the moment, it seemed like the right thing to do. I stalked out to the waiting cab without another word to him.

Libby was there when I got home. I was about to start off another rant as soon as I saw her, but she easily derailed me with three little words, "Shut up, Casey." Then she made me the decaffeinated tea I'd been drinking lately, and I told her everything Dr. Morrissey told me—about the chubby and the vaginal/pelvis stuff, everything I could remember. After the doctor hit me with the news of three babies, it was hard to remember much more after that. I did remember disliking her with an intensity that was unusual for me.

Anyway, with Libby taking over from what Coop and Emma began, I finally decided that throwing myself under a bus wasn't a viable option at this time. Libby kept telling me how Dr. Morrissey didn't know shit from shat and I could give birth any way I wanted to. She also surprisingly made me see that none of this was J.B.'s fault. By the time she left, even though I was still scared poopless about the prospect of triplets, I felt a great deal better. My babies are going to be loved by so many people, I thought to myself as I drifted into sleep.

I woke up hours later, absolutely starving. Normally I had a strict policy about not eating in the middle of the night—if I did that, I'm sure Dr. Morrissey would be calling me more than chubby—but because I'm pregnant, I felt it was my duty to indulge. Plus, I'm not often hungry. I was sure I'd end up throwing it up later, but a little food now wouldn't hurt.

I went upstairs because Coop had made some homemade bread the other day and I thought it would make wonderful toast right now. So I headed up without turning on the light in the stairway, almost tripping on the cat, which wouldn't be a good thing since in the movies, women always have miscarriages when they fall down the stairs. And now that I was calm, cool, and collected, I didn't want one little thing to go wrong with these babies. Even earlier, when I wasn't so calm and collected, I still didn't really want anything to happen to them. I might not have gotten pregnant the way I planned and I might be having more babies than I intended to... I just realized absolutely nothing involving this pregnancy was going according to plan. I should just throw away any preconceived notions about what I was doing and how I was supposed to act and how everyone else was supposed to act. But the bottom line was that I would die if anything happened to these little kidlets I'm carrying within me. My babe-lets. My babies. Oh my God, there are three of them!

I made my toast and then went back downstairs, holding onto the wall again so I wouldn't be tempted to trip. The toast tasted great and I managed to keep it down, but it also woke me up; the way my mind was racing, I was not sure if I'd be able to go back to sleep.

Triplets.

Who has three babies at one time? How could my uterus accommodate three babies at once? Women look like they have an oversize basketball under their shirts when they're pregnant with one kid—what am I going to look like with three? Like I have three basketballs under my shirt? That's just too lumpy to even contemplate. How is my body ever going to go back to normal? I'll be all stretched and saggy, like my deflated exercise ball sitting at the bottom of my closet. That's why I'm chubby according to Dr. Morrissey—because all my exercise stuff is at the bottom of my closet. Stupid, hobbit-sized bitch for calling me chubby.

Okay, so I'm a little irrational—emotional, illogical, crazy—at the thought of having triplets. Three babies. Me with three babies! Eventually, I do want more than one child, but not right away! I thought I could take some time and figure out what I was doing. I could make my mistakes with the first one so that when number two came along, I'd have everything down pat. And by the time the third rolled around, I'd be an expert.

But now—chances are these are all the kids I'll ever have because who is going to want to date a single mother with triplets, let alone marry her and have more? What are the chances of me having another multiple births after the first one? I could, like, end up with sixteen kids by just being pregnant a couple of times, like one of those horror mothers from the reality shows. I should ask the doctor about it. Chances are this is probably it. So if I screw up, I screw up all of them at once. It's a scary thought.

What is also scary is that if these babies are the only ones I will ever have, then I will have no other children by anyone other than J.B.

I wonder if I would be having triplets if David had been the father or Mr. Anonymous Donor? Is it my fault, or is it J.B.'s supersperm that did the trick? It must be supersperm if it managed to get past the condom (probably not the most effective use of latex since it expired over three years ago) and my birth control pill (also not that effective when you don't remember to take it constantly). But—wow. Somebody upstairs sure wanted me to get pregnant. Probably sick of hearing me go on and on about it, so it's like, let's give it to her with both barrels to shut her up.

But looking at it that way does do the trick in making me feel better. I'll be okay. I'll be better than okay—I'll be great. I'll have my babies, and maybe it won't be the easiest thing in the world to raise them, but you know what they say about what doesn't kill you makes you stronger? Well, I'll be superstrong after I finish raising these kids. Superstrong, like J.B.'s supersperm. The thought makes me giggle.

I can't imagine how I eventually fell asleep, but I managed, probably because I was so exhausted by the hysterics of the day. I was awakened later by the sounds of the stairs creaking, then footsteps. Whoever it was, they were doing their best to be quiet, so it was hard to tell. Probably Cooper, I decided, coming down to check on me. I heard a shuffle on the carpet outside my bedroom, and then I could smell him. The smell of beer, cranberry juice, and olives tried to overpower his cologne.

J.B.

I didn't move. I lay still, trying not to breathe too loudly as I waited for him to say something. Maybe he'd just come down to check on me—make sure I didn't electrocute myself or something, just to get rid of the babies.

Instead of speaking, J.B. came over to my bed. Then he lay down, curling his long body beside mine and slipping an arm around me. All the air I'd been holding in came out in a little gush.

"Are you awake?" J.B. whispered.

"No," I told him.

"Oh." His arm tightened around me. "You okay?"

"Not really."

"I'm sorry," he said cautiously. "I didn't mean to give you three babies."

I had to smile at that. "It's not your fault," I admitted. I could feel his arm relax around me. "I'm sorry I kept going on about that."

"It's fine. Blame me for whatever you want. You're the one who has to take care of these things."

"Just me?" Icy fear clutched my heart. Was that it? Was J.B. running scared at the thought of three babies?

"Well, for now, because they're sort of inside you, but I'll do what I can. I mean, I'll try to."

"You're not leaving?" I asked tearfully.

"I'll stay the night if you—oh." He took a deep breath as he realized what I meant. "No, I won't leave you, Casey." I could only nod and clutch at his arm slung over me. J.B. gave a little chuckle. "Guess you think I've gotten rid of some of my inner asshole then." ·

"Maybe a little," I whispered.

We didn't say anything for a while. I could feel him cuddle closer to me.

"I'm glad you were there," I said softly.

J.B. gave a low chuckle. "Me too. You probably would have knocked that poor old guy over and started screaming at him in the middle of the street if I hadn't been."

# CHAPTER THIRTY-FIVE

"Having the care and support of friends and family during this exciting time makes the pregnancy even more memorable for the expectant mother."

*A Young Woman's Guide to the Joy of Impending Motherhood*
Dr. Francine Pascal Reid (1941)

WHEN I WOKE UP in the morning, J.B. was gone. I thought I dreamed the whole thing. The only proof I had that he was there was an imprint of a head on the pillow.

Triplets! Three babies! Who has three babies at once? Here is your baby, says stupid doctor, and here is your baby, and oh, yeah, here is another one! Three babies.

The concept takes some getting used to.

After throwing up my breakfast, which Cooper brought downstairs to me, I did the thing I should have done months ago. I called my mother. As I was waiting for her to pick up, I decided it was a good thing I wasn't with Terri in person, since I still hadn't brushed my teeth since throwing up and most likely had the worst breath.

"Mom? It's Casey." I almost called her Terri, but thought it was time I started calling the grandmother of my children by her rightful name.

"Hi, there, sweet—hello." The welcoming voice changed quickly but I chose to ignore it. I was mending bridges, not redigging old ditches. Yes, I'd been a horrible daughter and hadn't spoken to her since the day she came into the store and I gave her the worst mother of the year award, but it was time to move on. There was no way I could take back what I'd said, so I just decided to gloss over the fact and pretend it never happened.

"I just wanted to call—I thought you'd like to know—I went to the doctor's yesterday and found out I'm having triplets. Three babies."

"Oh, Casey!" The warm and welcoming voice instantly returned. "Triplets! Oh, sweetface, how wonderful!"

"Is it? I'm pretty freaked out about the whole concept."

"I'm not surprised," Terri laughed. "You know, my mother had twins. I've heard these things skip a generation."

"She did? What—what happened?"

"Uncle Michael. He had a brother, but he died after only a few days."

"That's so sad." And so scary. It was the first time I'd ever given a thought to something happening with my babies.

It was like my mother could read my mind. "But nothing like that will happen to you, Casey. It was a long time ago, and things are different now. I remember when I found out I was pregnant with you. I went into denial for about two weeks. I refused to believe it, not because I didn't want you, but because I was so scared. Then I started throwing up all over the place and couldn't deny it any longer."

"You had morning sickness?"

"Morning, noon, and night. It was horrible. How are—"

"I've got it too! It started the day—the day you came into the store." There, that gave an excuse for me behaving like a bitch if she wanted to bring it up

Terri sighed. "You poor thing. Just keep reminding yourself it will come to an end. And the funny thing is I never got it with Libby. Just you."

"So I might not have it again?"

"You want to have more than three kids?" Terri asked, and I could tell she was smiling.

"I'll get through these first. Um, how are you and, um, Eric?"

"It's nice of you to ask. We're just fine. He's been after me to decide on a wedding date. Says he won't move in without a ring on my finger, isn't that funny? Usually it's the woman who pushes for it, but not this time. I'd be okay just living together, but not Eric."

"He must really love you," I said slowly. It was strange to think of my mother as being loved by a man. It was strange to think of her as lovable at all.

"I think he does," Terri said lightly. "It's nice."

"I guess." There was a pause. "Do you remember that book you gave me?" I asked suddenly. There was dead silence, so obviously she didn't remember. "It was a pregnancy book from the forties. A Young Woman's Guide—"

"To the Joy of Being a Mom, or something like that? Of course. I read that when I was pregnant as well. I remember there was a lot of bullshit—"

"Exactly!"

"But there was some helpful information in it. I gave it to you because you kept talking about having a baby, and I thought it might be interesting for you."

"Oh." So much for my theory she was just being a bitch trying to rub salt in my non-baby wound at the time. I feel pretty bad thinking that for so long. Maybe I should have just asked her. Maybe I should have—

"Why?" Terri asked.

"No reason. I've just been reading it. There's a part in there about not trying to conceive after a woman is thirty-seven."

"Aren't you glad you're pregnant now, and not yet thirty-six? You still have time for another one if you want!"

"Don't think so!"

"I was eighteen when I got pregnant with you," Terri reminisced, "and I remember reading that part and thinking thirty-seven sounded so old. Now it seems so young. There are so many women these days having babies later in life. You'll fit right in. Whoever wrote that book obviously couldn't predict how things would change in the future."

"I guess not."

"Thanks for calling," Terri said. "If you need anything, anything at all, you just have to ask. I'll do whatever you need, get you a crib or babysit or... Triplets. It's so wonderful. My baby is having her own babies." Terri's voice sounded thicker suddenly, and I had a feeling she might be ready to cry.

"Thanks." I was not sure how to deal with an emotional mother. "I'll let you know—I'll call you. Let you know how things are going."

"I'd like that." Okay, definite tears there. "Bye, sweetheart."

"Bye, Mom."

I think it might have been the nicest conversation I'd ever had with my mother, and I felt pretty good about myself.

# CHAPTER THIRTY-SIX

"Swollen breasts are often one of the earliest signs of pregnancy."

*A Young Woman's Guide to the Joy of Impending Motherhood*
Dr. Francine Pascal Reid (1941)

I COULD PROBABLY HAVE wallowed in my fear and self-pity for a while, but that option was taken away from me by Brit. Brit's response to learning that I was about to become a mother to not one, not two, but three babies was to raise one perfectly plucked eyebrow. "Wow. So look, about the wedding ..."

But I forgave her because Brit's name was on the card that came with the three dozen roses Morgan sent to me the day after I found out about the triplets. For the sake of our longtime friendship, I had to believe she was a willing contributor, and Morgan didn't just sign her name.

After the stagette, Brit had suddenly switched the wedding planning into high gear, and it got worse the closer the wedding got. The week before the wedding, she was barely off the phone with me. Listening to her go on and on about how everything needed to be perfect was quite effective in getting one's mind off how many babies were currently expanding one's uterus.

On Thursday, two days before the wedding, she discovered a massive flower crisis—apparently the florist had ordered pale lilac roses for the boutonnières, not the pale lavender Brit demanded. I had no idea there was such a discernible difference between lilac and lavender, but I guess Brit has a much better eye for colour than I do and she was furious that such a mistake could be made. So furious, she managed to guilt me into hunting down a florist who had lavender roses for her. I had to do it because, according to Brit, it was my duty as the maid of honour, and because Brit was indisposed at the time getting her legs waxed. Plus, since I was out of school for the summer, she assumed I must have the time.

After doing my duty for the flowers, I then had to spend all Thursday night with her sorting out the seating arrangement because Brit forgot Anil was bringing the new girlfriend and she had to find a suitable seat for her. Once that was done, I made a last-minute run to the printers' Friday morning to get another seating chart made. This made me late for work at the store, but it didn't really matter—not to Brit anyway, since she called me every hour on the hour with some mini-crisis through which I needed to hold her hand. You'd think after planning this wedding for twenty years, things would have been straightened out by now. I was exhausted by the end of the day, but there was still the rehearsal and dinner to get through that night, which thankfully went as planned and were free of any pre-wedding drama.

Luckily for everyone involved, the day of Brit's wedding dawned as bright and blue as if she had ordered it especially from her Pottery Barn catalogue. I was so glad it had finally arrived because I'd been forced to listen to her plan the stupid thing for years and it was about time the big day had finally arrived. It was the eighteenth wedding I'd been to in the past five years, and the tenth in which I'd been a member of the wedding party. But it was also the wedding of my oldest and sometimes dearest friend, and despite everything, I had to remember that it was a privilege to stand up for her as maid of honour. At least, I hoped it would be a privilege. I may love Brit like a sister, but she was being a royal pain in the ass, and right now I felt like stuffing my lavender roses down her throat.

"There's no more material to let out, Casey," an exasperated Brit told me as I struggled to zip up my bridesmaid's dress with Morgan's and Lacey's help. "You've got to fit in it, or you're not walking down the aisle with me."

The gorgeous amethyst dress I helped pick out because the colour went so well with my hair and the fit and style flattered every body type did not fit me. Two weeks earlier when I last tried it on, it still fit perfectly, but today—well, let's just say my breasts must have become a wee bit fuller in the last fourteen days. In the last couple of weeks, despite the still constant vomiting, I knew I'd put on a couple of pounds—or so the bathroom scale said—and apparently the extra weight had gone right to my boobs. I'd read breasts do get swollen during pregnancy, but I could never imagine this much. I was blaming it on the fact that I'm having three babies.

"Don't tempt me," I muttered, but Brit didn't hear me, which was a good thing, since the term Bridezilla now fit Brit to a T. I was contemplating pulling out my camera and videoing her for YouTube. Last week I was amused by her precise attention to detail. Today, I was truly scared of her.

At approximately one hour and fifteen minutes before the limo was to pick us up and take us to Glenview Presbyterian Church—according to Brit's preparation plan—Lacey, Morgan, and I were supposed to unzip the garment bags containing our dresses. Brit had allocated us fifteen minutes to put on our dresses and touch up any hair and makeup mishaps. The hair and makeup was done at the salon earlier this morning (appointments commencing at 10:30 for Lacey and Brit and 11:15 for Morgan and me).

Then we were to spend the next hour in her childhood bedroom in her parents' house—only six streets away from where I grew up—getting

Brit into the mass of silk, satin, ruffles, and lace she called a dress. After this, it was time for quiet reflection and meditation on our duties, as well as the supreme importance of this day for Brit. I swear, that's really what is said on the copy of the "Wedding Day Schedule" Brit handed me this morning. Not to be confused with the "What Needs to Be Done the Week Before the Wedding Schedule" I received last week or the "Wedding Rehearsal and Dinner Seating Plan and Schedule" I got last night. The girl had gone completely overboard with this.

"Okay, just suck it in a liiitle more," Morgan urged as she gently tugged up my zipper.

"I can't suck in my boobs," I protested, already holding my breath for everything it was worth. I was trying to flatten my boobs or push them down onto my stomach—anything to let the dress up.

"Pull them up," Lacey suggested. "So they're sort of overhanging." She grabbed my breasts in the dress and tried to demonstrate what she meant, and I'm sure I looked properly horrified, not only having Brit's little sister practically feel me up, but by showing off so much of my breasts. Even when I'm not pregnant, my breasts are on the large side, but this—they were huge! Two days ago, I woke up to find that none of my bras fit, and I've had to wear my exercise bras until I have a chance to buy some new ones. I guess I should have thought about the dress maybe not fitting then, but I pretended to Brit that this was an overnight thing.

"You have to admit, you've got absolutely gorgeous tits now," Lacey told me. She rubbed her hands across the aforementioned gorgeous tits and actually gave them each a cheeky squeeze. There was no "practically" now—I'd just been officially felt up by Lacey. "Fan-fucking-tastic! I'm so jealous. And kind of turned on." She gave me a wink and reluctantly dropped her hands when Morgan cleared her throat.

"Maybe now's not the time for that, Lacey."

"You've got to admit, Morgan—just look at them! Touch them." Lacey reached forward, but I gave her hand a quick slap.

"I'm trying to cover them up so the whole congregation isn't tempted to touch."

"Why did you have to go and get fucking pregnant before my wedding?" Brit suddenly shrieked, stamping her foot. "Aaahh! Everything is supposed to be perfect, but you can't even fit into your dress! You are the fucking maid of honour, for fuck's sake! You're supposed to make sure everything is perfect for this fucking wedding so I can sit around on my ass and enjoy getting fucking married. Because that's what I've always fucking wanted! And that's what you signed up for, fucking best friend! You weren't supposed to get fucking pregnant! And you," she turned furiously to Lacey, "leave her fucking tits alone! The only one who is allowed to have gorgeous fucking tits today is me. Me! Fuck!"

The three of us could only stare at her. The sight of Brit, red-faced and clad only in ivory lace bustier, panties, and garters, stamping her foot with frustration, was something to see. I would have laughed if I hadn't been so horrified. Brit's hands flew up to her head to clutch at her hair, but were stopped by the gallon of hair spray that was keeping her elaborate hairstyle in place.

"Don't touch!" Lacey gasped.

"Aaahh!" Brit screamed again. Not shouting or yelling, but an actual scream. She paced around the room like a cat on a leash.

"Everything okay, Britney?" I heard her mother call from down the hall. Brit banned Mrs. Spears from the room earlier, when she started crying after seeing Brit return from the salon with her hair and makeup done.

"Just pull it up, Morgan," I whispered out of the corner of my mouth. I held my arms out straight, Lacey pushed up my breasts (which I was not thrilled about, but now was not the time to get prudish), and Morgan finally got the zipper pulled up.

"Done," Morgan gasped, stepping around to survey. "I don't think you'll be able to take a deep breath, but at least it's done up." I glanced at the seams under my arms and saw them straining. I prayed they didn't burst. I prayed I didn't burst out the top. I'd never seen myself look so voluptuous. I looked like I was wearing a corset to make my breasts overflow out the top of the dress. I could keep my lipstick and a pack of Kleenex down there, and no one would notice. I tried to stick a little more breast down the dress and prayed my nipples stayed covered.

"You look lovely," Brit said sweetly, as if her tantrum had never occurred. She preened in front of the mirror, tucking a stray piece of hair back in place. "You all do. Now it's time for my dress. You can come back in now, Mother," she called. "But no crying. You'll have a minute to do that before I get in the car. After I go, bawl all you want."

It was not the first Jekyll and Hyde episode of the day, and I feared it wouldn't be the last.

But we made it to the church. In the limo Lacey had suggested champagne to relax Brit, who agreed and drank half a glass, but then freaked out because her breath smelled like alcohol. I passed around the cinnamon Altoids I was instructed to have with me all day, and the crisis was quickly averted. Morgan and Lacey finished the bottle of champagne.

I spent the ride to the church teaching myself how to breathe in my dress. Shallow and slow, I told myself, hoping the fabric of the skirt didn't wrinkle too much. I had to scramble into the limo after a last-minute run to the bathroom to puke—a false alarm, but I've learned that if something wants to come up, I've got to let it. I'm thirteen weeks pregnant, which means I've entered the second trimester, the magical part of the pregnancy when everyone says I'll feel better.

I managed to pull Morgan aside just as we headed up the church steps. "Are you okay with the whole Anil thing?" I whispered as Lacey tried to assist Brit and her gargantuan dress into the church without getting screamed at for her efforts. It's a beautiful dress but very high-maintenance (quite like the woman wearing it), and Brit looked a bit like one of those Barbie birthday cakes, with the doll sticking up from her skirt-cake.

Lacey could deal with Brit for a minute. I hadn't had a chance to talk to Morgan about this all day. In a few moments she was going to walk down the aisle of a church where her ex-boyfriend was standing at the front. They wouldn't be in the positions she originally planned for them, and I was sure it had to be upsetting since for six years all Morgan ever wanted was to marry Anil.

"It was a little awkward last night at the rehearsal dinner," Morgan admitted to me in a low voice. "I'm just glad he didn't think to bring his new little bitch of a girlfriend."

Last night at the wedding rehearsal was the first time Morgan had laid eyes on Anil since she found out about the new girlfriend. And it was the first time Morgan had spoken to him (without a police presence) since the little episode with the bonfire on the front lawn of the house. But they were surprisingly civil toward each other, which to me, was sort of the calm before the storm.

"And Derek? You didn't want him to come?"

"I did, but he said he'd feel too awkward and it might take some of the spotlight off Brit if Anil and I both brought new significant others."

"And he's your new significant other?"

"I think so," Morgan told me with a shy smile. "I'm sure by the end of today, any residual feelings I still might have for Anil will definitely be gone. I just have to get through the church part, and then I can get drunk and everything will be fine."

"Ah, but look what happened to me the last time I got drunk at a wedding." I pointed to my overflowing breasts, and Morgan broke out in laughter.

"So what was that with Lacey earlier?" she asked, with an expression of delight on her face. "I totally thought she was about to plant one on you, but was too afraid of Brit having a hissy fit about both of you ruining your lipstick!"

"I know!" I exclaimed.

"You know if you can't find a guy, with those tits you can always switch and go for the other side!" Laughing, she poked at my overflowing chest area. \

"You're such a bitch!" I told her, poking her in the boob in return.

"Casey! Morgan! Stop touching each other!" Brit screeched as she was about to enter the church vestibule. Even with the heavy doors closed, I'm sure everyone inside heard her. Morgan and I, both with our eyes downcast, hurried to her side once again.

At the front of the church, I took slow, shallow breaths and tried not to fidget as Brit took her time walking down the aisle to "Here Comes the Bride." I was conscious of the packed congregation and happy no one was looking at me. I was also happy that for the first time in my life, I didn't have to try to suck in my stomach standing in front of this many people. I thought I looked pretty good, until I caught sight of Morgan and Lacey, both of whom are maybe a size two. So then I started thinking about how soon—in about six months—my size eight would seem positively anorexic, so I felt better. But I had to say, even feeling self-conscious, my breasts looked so much better than either one of theirs. Even Brit in her overpriced Manolo Blahnik shoes couldn't compare to my chest today.

The ceremony itself went off without a hitch, just as perfect as Brit expected it to be. Tom looked like the picture of a perfect groom in his grey morning coat and had tears in his eyes as Brit walked down the aisle. It was a long service and I felt an onset of nausea hit about the halfway mark, but I managed to keep the pasted smile on my face. Not one cough, sneeze, or baby cry marred the ceremony, and I knew Brit would literally kill me in the church if I did something that wasn't according to her carved-in-stone plan—like rush to the washroom to vomit. So I did my best and managed not to throw up as Tom and Brit were named husband and wife. Not that seeing Brit get married made me want to vomit—not that I'd blame myself if I was nauseated, since that was all I'd been hearing about for the last twenty years! I wondered what Brit would find to obsess about now that her wedding day was finally here.

After the wedding party filed out of the church, there was a cool breeze, which made me feel better as I stepped outside on Tom's brother Richard's arm. "Whew! Glad that's over."

"I thought it went very well," Richard replied with a frown. Tom is a sweet and unassuming type of guy and often so quiet you forget he's in the room. Last night at the rehearsal dinner was the first time I'd met his family, and I have to say Tom got the lion's share of the personality in his family. Richard and the other brother, Henry, are, well, bland. They run an accounting firm together, never have been married, and still live at home. Not sure how Brit fits in with that family. Christmas might be interesting for her.

Richard dropped my arm and made a beeline for Tom, leaving me teetering on the stairs in my high heels. I argued with Brit about wearing them—along with the constant threat of throwing up, I didn't want to have to worry about falling over in the four-inch heels. I was surprised I'd made it through the day so far, using halting little steps to try to keep my balance. Richard's quick release threw that precarious balance out of whack, and I started to sway on the stairs.

And then I flashed back to the last wedding I was at—wearing yet another bridesmaid's gown (albeit not as nice as this one—sorry, Darcy) and standing outside the church, looking around for Mike, boyfriend at the time. Who, if you recall with perfect clarity as I was doing right then, was in the coatroom, getting nasty with someone other than me. This, of course, led to me getting drunk and J.B. comforting me in the only way he knew how.

"And that's how I got you," I said aloud, one hand resting on my stomach.

"Are you okay?" J.B. asked. I hadn't even noticed him in front of me. But there he was, standing in front of me with Cooper and Emma, all three with concerned expressions on their faces.

"Fine." I could feel myself blush a little, embarrassed to be caught talking aloud.

"You're holding your stomach," J.B. pointed to the area in question.

"I'm fine." I went to take a step down, but my heel caught in a tiny gap in the stone and I literally fell into J.B.'s arms. "Sorry."

"Can't say I mind," he said, and when I looked up, he was staring at my chest.

"Stop that." I knew I should push him away, but I found myself enjoying the feeling of being in his arms.

"Do you blame me? They were great before, but now—wow!"

"Stop that!" Cooper ordered with a wince. "It's bad enough I'm getting this constant reminder of the two of you together. It's actually worse than walking in on you."

"Did you really do that?" Emma wondered as J.B. stood me upright. But he kept his hand on the small of my back.

Cooper passed a hand across his eyes. "Unfortunately, yes."

"Oh, come on," I told him defensively. "It wasn't that bad. Nothing was happening—we were fully clothed. Well, we were under the covers. You didn't really see anything."

"I saw a partial breast, and the image of it still haunts me to this day," Cooper said painfully. J.B. gave him a friendly punch in the shoulder.

"Enough about her image, dude," he told Coop. "Speaking of which," he turned to me, "you look great." Leaning over, he brushed my cheek with a kiss. His lips were soft.

"Thank you."

"You do look terrific," Emma told me. "Really sexy, with the..." she gestured at my chest.

"Thanks." The breeze was threatening to pull out some of my curls. The other three—all blondes—went with sleek updos, but I asked the hairstylist just to pin up my curls in a less formal style, definitely more me.

"Are you feeling okay?" Emma asked me.

"I almost lost my breakfast a couple of times, but I managed to hold it in."

"I thought you were taking some drug for that?" J.B. asked.

"It makes me tired and bitchy, so I'd rather keep throwing up. I don't do bitchy well."

"No, you don't," J.B. agreed with a grin.

I stuck my tongue out at him. "Be nice, or I won't tell you how nice you look," I said. I noticed Cooper and Emma glance at each other. I was sure they would be happy if things got back to the way they were. The way they used to be, with three big differences—babies—but you know what I mean.

"Are you sure that dress isn't too tight? You look ready to burst. In a good way, of course," J.B. added, giving my ever-expanding breasts another once-over.

"It was a little tense getting it on," I admitted, with my hand trying to cover the overflow.

"It looks nice, though," J.B. said sincerely. His eyes held mine for a long moment.

"Thanks," I whispered with a shy smile.

"There you are," Morgan swooped, interrupting what could have been a very nice moment. "Hey, you all look great. Casey, Brit wants us for pictures. I think we'd better get over there before she starts screaming again."

"Casey, Morgan!" Brit screeched from the sidewalk in front of the church.

"Oops, too late," Morgan grinned at me. "Gotta go."

"Have fun," J.B. told us.

"Are you serious?" Morgan asked. "This is going to be torture. I feel bad for the photographer to have to put up with Brit. Apparently she has a list of poses she wants done. I'm never going to be able to do this without a drink."

"I'll have one waiting for you at the reception," J.B. promised her. "For both of you. Nonalcoholic, for you, of course," he teased me. He winked, and I stuck my tongue out at him again.

With a death grip on Morgan's arm, I toddled over to Brit, still unsteady on my heels, but feeling much better.

# CHAPTER THIRTY-SEVEN

"Pantyhose should be worn at all times to avoid swollen ankles."

*A Young Woman's Guide to the Joy of Impending Pregnancy*
Dr. Francine Pascal Reid (1941)

DESPITE EVERYTHING, IT WAS a beautiful wedding. A beautiful day, even though I couldn't really breathe naturally because my dress was like a steel band around my lungs and I had a constant fear of throwing up.

At the reception, my seat was at the head table, trapped between Tom and an already-intoxicated Lacey, who was determined to flirt with every male in the place, including the sixteen-year-old waiter who cleared her plate. Plus, she kept making inappropriate comments about my breasts, which was embarrassing to me; but Anil, on Lacey's other side, found the comments hilarious. The reception took place downtown at the Royal York Hotel, in the historical Imperial Ballroom, where prime ministers and royalty have dined and danced. Or so Brit says. It is a beautiful room and the dinner was lovely; I managed to eat a few mouthfuls. The speeches, usually a bore at wedding receptions, were tolerable, and even the one Brit's father made welcoming Tom into the family was amusing, in part because Mr. Spears was well on his way to being three sheets to the wind, just like his daughter Lacey.

As maid of honour, I had to say something, and I didn't have the luxury of a drink or two to soothe my nerves. Speaking in public isn't a favourite pastime of mine, but I thought I did okay, producing a couple of laughs and a collective aah from the guests as I finished with a poem by Christopher Marlow. After Brit and Tom had their first dance, and after Brit danced with her father and the wedding party all joined in, I finally escaped my duties and headed over to the table where Coop and Emma were sitting. J.B. had been seated with them, and I wondered where he was.

"Ah, freedom," I sighed with relief as I sank into a chair beside Emma, propping my sore feet up on the next chair.

"You did great," she praised. "I liked your speech. Your feet okay?" she asked in a worried voice when she noticed me inspecting my ankles.

"I think they're swollen," I told her incredulously. "I'm only three months. Does that mean I'm going to swell up like a balloon by the time this is over?"

"I'm sure you won't," Emma soothed. "You've been on your feet all day and in those shoes. Even my feet hurt."

"No more shoes for me tonight," I decided, slipping them off my feet. "I should have brought my Uggs to wear."

"Oh, I'm sure Brit would love having you galumphing around in that dress and your boots," Coop said sarcastically.

I tilted my head back on the chair. "I'll be sooo glad when this wedding is over," I said to the ceiling. "I need my life to go back to normal. Not that I know what normal is going to be like," I said suddenly, with my hands over my belly.

"At least it will be interesting," Emma smiled at me.

"I can't even imagine what those babies are going to do to my kitchen," Cooper muttered. "Don't they, like, go through drawers and everything? And no way am I getting childproof locks on the cupboards!"

Emma and I laughed. "I think you might have a little time before we have to start worrying about that," I giggled. "Who knows where I'll be when they're running around being little holy terrors?"

"You're not moving out, are you?" Emma asked worriedly.

"Eventually," I told her. "But no plans right now."

"Good. I'm kind of excited about having a baby around all the time," she said shyly. "Or three of them."

"I can see that wearing off after the hundred or so diapers I get you to change," I teased. But I also gave her hand a squeeze as I heaved myself to my feet with difficulty. The tightness of the dress inhibited ease of movement.

"Where are you off to?" Coop asked.

"I think I'll go throw up now, so have fun."

"You can just decide like that?" Coop asked in surprise.

"Pretty much. I feel the need to vomit most of the time, but I've found out it's fairly easy to control. If I have the time and a decent bathroom, I throw up. Or if I want to feel better for a bit. Brit gave me the key to the bridal room just in case, so I have the decent bathroom and I think now's a good time."

"That's... odd."

"But very helpful. I'm thinking of making it into some sort of a party trick, what do you say?" I gave a smile and a little wave as I headed off across the dance floor.

I think most of the two hundred guests were on the floor, including Brit's father, who was doing an odd version of the Chicken Dance despite the song playing not being the Chicken Dance song.

"Casey!" Will Spears bellowed across the floor at me. "Come on and dance with me!" Because the reception was in full swing and Brit's father had been full swinging into drinking, it sounded like, 'C'mon dans w'me!'

"Not on your life," I said under my breath and cheerfully waved. Mr. Spears waved back and accosted someone else. I could see Lacey doing her best bump and grind with J.B. She saw me and gave me a coy wave, but J.B. rolled his eyes and gave me a pleading look.

"Save me," he mouthed. There was no way I was going over there because I was sure Lacey would try and pull me into whatever action she was trying with J.B. I wiggled my fingers at him and kept moving across the dance floor.

I began to weave my way around another group of dancers until someone stepped directly in my path.

"Why do you keep showing up like this?" asked a male voice. It took me a moment to recognize him. It was the cute guy from the subway, the one I threw up in front of at the wine store the day the nausea began. I didn't recognize him because he looked smart in a black suit.

"Hey! What are you doing here?" I blurted out. "Sorry, that's really rude. But really, what are you doing here?"

He smiled, which made him look less like Matt Damon but still cute. "My girlfriend is Tom's assistant. There's no need to ask what you're doing here."

I dipped into a brief curtsy, which at the last minute, I realized gave him an amazing look down my cleavage. "Maid of honour, at your service."

"Are you feeling better then?" he asked. "With the whole pregnancy thing?"

"Not really, actually. It hasn't gone away. The throwing up, that is. The pregnancy hasn't gone away either. Other than that, I feel great. Other than the fact I found out I'm having triplets."

"Wow! Triplets? That's—"

"Very scary."

"I was going to say amazing. And you look—great. I mean, I don't know you very well, but I'd say pregnancy agrees with you." I noticed his eyes dip down to my chest.

"It agrees with my breasts anyway. Since you're a doctor, I can say that, right?"

He gave a little cough. "Sure. I'm Adam, by the way." He held out a hand.

"It's nice to put a name to the stranger who keeps popping up," I laughed. "I'm Casey."

"I know. I read the program at the church. Eve, my girlfriend, thinks—"

"Your girlfriend's name is Eve?" I asked skeptically.

"I know. I call her Evie, makes it a bit better. Look, I better get back to her. She only knows Tom and a couple of people from work. They put us at a table with—over there." He pointed to the table I was just at with Cooper and Emma.

"This is way too weird. They're my roommates."

Adam gave a nervous laugh. "Okay, this is getting a little too strange, so I'll be going now. But I bet we'll bump into each other sometime again."

"Probably," I agreed. "See you."

Strange, I thought as I left the dance floor. And nothing against Adam, but after talking to him, I really felt the need to throw up, so I headed directly to the bridal suite, ignoring all eye contact with people who might want to stop and talk to me.

I finally made it to the bridal suite on the second floor above the ballroom, and I rested a minute after I did the vomiting thing. It was cool and quiet in there, but I could still here the thump of the sound system below as it headed into some retro eighties' song. I saw Brit's going-away outfit hanging in the closet, and her makeup had already been strewn across the vanity.

I couldn't believe Brit was married. I was there, I watched it happen, but it was only hitting me now. My oldest friend was no longer Brit Spears, but now Mrs. Tom Smith.

Brit was married. Because it had been an emotional day—an emotional month—I started to cry a little. I wondered if I'd ever get married. I know I always say I'm not into it, but hey, every girl really wants a fairy tale, doesn't she? For the first time, I began to wonder if I did the right thing refusing J.B.

I think this must be why men assume single women at weddings are so easy to pick up. They're desperate for some reassurance they won't be alone forever.

But I won't be alone for long. I've got three babies that will occupy my every moment, and if I have any left over, there's always J.B. He proposed to me. The enormity of that was finally reaching my baby-addled brain. It had taken almost a month and for me to actually take part in someone else's wedding, but it finally hit me. J.B. Bergen, whose conquests are numerous and legendary, asked me to marry him.

And I said no.

I said no because, honestly, I don't want J.B. to be stuck with me just because I happen to be having his babies. It's like being the last one picked for a team—you know they don't really want you, but they had to take you. I don't want to feel like that. And I definitely don't want J.B. to start resenting me, thinking it's my fault that I've clipped his wings. This way is better, I keep telling myself. We're having the babies together, but both of us are free to live the lives we want. That's the way it should be.

But then when I'm repeating this over and over and over again, there's a little voice that keeps interrupting—what if his proposal wasn't just about the babies?

But why would it be about anything else? I'm attracted to J.B. more than any other man I know, plus I like J.B. more than any other man, save Cooper. I'm not sure what goes on inside J.B.'s head concerning me, but my self-esteem isn't damaged enough for me to believe that it's only convenient sex that draws him to me. There's something between us that I can't explain, but I think it's more than sex. Is that a good enough reason to marry him?

I wiped away the traces of my tears and checked my makeup, borrowing Brit's lipstick since mine was long gone. I would have liked to fix my hair, since it felt like it could collapse down my neck at any moment, but there was so much hairspray I couldn't really move it. Good to go. I smiled in the mirror at myself, hoping I didn't look as forlorn and melancholy as I felt. I could just chalk it up to hormones if anyone asked. Not that I really thought they would. This was Brit's day and I was just standing in the shadows, but there's no sense crying in the shadows.

I got up and, after a final glance at myself in the mirror, decided I'd better get back out there. I was sure Brit had something for me to do. But when I pulled open the door of the bride's room, I saw J.B. on the other side, his hand raised as if to knock.

"Hey," he said.

# Chapter Thirty-Eight

"During the pregnancy, the expectant mother should make a conscious effort to remain calm and relaxed in order to ensure the health of the baby and herself."

*A Young Woman's Guide to the Joy of Impending Motherhood*
Dr. Francine Pascal Reid (1941)

"You okay? Coop said you weren't feeling well."

"Um, yeah, but I'm okay now. Just had to toss my cookies."

He made a face. "Ah. Great. Is it this bad every day?"

"Most days, but I'm getting used to it."

J.B. remained in the doorway, casually leaning his shoulder against the doorjamb, his arm stretched across, like he was preventing me from leaving. "Do you want to lie down or something?"

"No, I'm fine. Do you want to lie down or something?" I teased. He'd loosened his tie but still had on his jacket. "Have a nice time with Lacey?"

"Man, she's a piece of work." His hair fell in tousled waves, looking exactly like Lacey ran her fingers through it. "I practically had to fight her off." Eyes narrowed, he glanced at me. "You jealous?"

"Of Lacey? She's harmless."

J.B. guffawed and came in the room. "I don't think she's harmless. Doesn't she, you know, know about—well, us? About the babies and stuff? Aren't you two friends?"

"I don't think it would matter to Lacey if you had two wives and sixteen babies. She likes to play. She tried to play with me this morning."

"Really?" he asked with interest in his voice. "Now that might be something to see."

"Men are so predictable." I sat back on the bed and wished fervently to be able to take a deep breath.

"When it comes to two women, definitely. So how's it going?"

"Good. Only a couple more hours to go."

J.B. sat down on the bed. "I feel bad that you have to go through all this," he said, looking as guilty as he sounded. "All the throwing up, not being able to eat what you want to. Coop told me about the chocolate."

"It won't last forever. My mother said she had it too, so it's one more thing I can blame her for."

"Are you really okay?" he asked, leaning closer and running a finger down my nose. "You've been crying. It gets red when you cry."

"A little," I admitted. "It's just Brit—seeing her get married and everything. We've been friends for a long time."

"Is she being nicer to you about the babies? 'Cuz I'll really have to hurt her if she isn't."

"Oh, Brit just likes to be the centre of her own universe," I said. "My getting pregnant just disrupted her orbit for a bit. Morgan more than makes up for it. And Cooper and Emma and Libby and... and you."

"Now."

"Now is all that matters. There's no point living in the past." J.B.'s hand was resting on his leg and I picked it up, rubbing his palm before linking my fingers with his. "Seeing David again taught me that."

"Glad it taught you something." He gave my hand a squeeze. "You know, I always thought I'd lose her if she went ahead and had a baby.

Betsey," J.B. said suddenly. "I thought a baby would split us up. And it did, only not in the way I first thought it would. Ironic, isn't it? And that was then. You'd think I'd grow out of it—this being selfish and childish, but the thing is, I can't help this feeling. And with you…" he trailed off here and took a deep breath. I could see his Adam's apple bob, and it's not even that pronounced.

"But with you," he continued slowly, "it's like it's bringing us closer together."

"Do you think that's a good thing?" I whispered.

Instead of answering, J.B. raised our hands, still clasped together, and kissed my fingers, all the while looking into my eyes.

My pulse was racing and my heart was hammering loudly in my chest…

No, that was the door. Someone was pounding on the door.

"Casey, are you in there?" It was Brit, shrieking loud enough for the party to hear her downstairs. "Open the door."

"She's got great timing," J.B. murmured.

"It's her room." Reluctantly, I pulled away, slipping sideways as J.B. tried to grab hold of me. "She won't go away."

"I'll make her go away," he grumbled.

I smiled over my shoulder at him as I pulled the door open. "What's the matter?" I asked. Brit was holding up her voluminous skirt and was red-faced, like she just ran up the stairs. I never thought she could run in her dress, or her shoes for that matter.

"Get downstairs right now and stop Morgan from ruining my wedding!" Brit screamed in my face. She looked like she was about to burst into tears.

"What's she doing?"

"She's telling off Anil in front of everyone! All I wanted was for everyone to get along today, and then she can do what she wants to the little dickhead, but no, she can't do one little thing for me. Go downstairs and make her stop!" Then she burst into tears, noisy sobs that had her chest heaving and sounding like she was about to hyperventilate.

"Okay, okay, don't cry," I said hastily. I pulled her inside the room. "Come in and calm down, and I'll go down and fix things. Everything's fine. J. B.," I looked at him beseechingly. "Could you stay—?"

"Not on your life," he said, and quickly jumped off the bed. "I'll come with you. You might need my help with her."

"Okay, Brit, just calm down," I said soothingly. Brit's breathing was still coming in quick gasps, like she couldn't take a deep breath. "Do you need a paper bag or something? Try to breathe slowly—"

"Stop her!" she shrieked. Then she looked up and noticed J.B. and the rumpled state of the bed. She shot him an icy glare. "I sincerely hope you are not trying to make a move on her during my wedding and using my bride's room. I would gut you like a fish if you did that."

There was not much J.B. could say to that.

"Go stop her! Now!" Brit shrieked, and I headed out of the room at a run, J.B. right behind me.

"I hope she doesn't pass out or anything," I said as we hit the stairs. I was glad I took off my shoes downstairs, or I'd be more worried about me falling headfirst down the stairs than Brit's breathing. "What could Morgan be doing that's so bad?"

As we reached the doorway to the ballroom, I could quickly see what Morgan was doing. It wasn't so bad, but it was causing a bit of a stir. She was standing in front of Anil, who was seated at a table with his new girlfriend and a few mutual friends. Morgan is a tall girl, so I could see her through the crowd gathered around them—a crowd gathered obviously to hear the venom that Morgan was spouting.

"Oh, Morgan, don't," I pleaded. Of course she couldn't hear me. "He's not worth it." I headed straight for her.

"Tell me how this isn't about to get really funny?" J.B. asked, reluctantly following me. "He deserves everything he's going to get."

I couldn't hear what Morgan was saying, but as I moved closer, dodging the interested wedding guests grouped together, all of a sudden Anil's new girlfriend rose up from her chair. "Go away!" she shouted at

Morgan. She was short and dark, very cute, but no match for Morgan, who could eat her for breakfast. She also seemed, based on unsteadiness on her feet and serious slurring of words, to be very drunk as well. "Can't you just leave us alone? It's bad enough he's had to stare at you and your fake hair and your fake boobs all day. Can't you just leave us alone?"

Oh dear. Angry and drunken girlfriend feeling insecure. That can't be good. I braced myself for the drunken catfight. Brit was going to love this. No wonder she was hyperventilating. Was I just thinking about how she was getting the wedding she'd always wanted? I pushed myself through the crowd and finally reached Morgan.

"Her boobs aren't fake," I said, but no one was listening. Now the group gathered was ducking for cover as the new girlfriend began to throw wineglasses at Morgan. Not just the wine, but the entire glass. There were quite a few glasses on the nearby tables, so there was plenty of ammunition for her. I jumped back as one hit Morgan on the side of the head, leaving a splash of wine on her shoulder. Luckily, Morgan's hair took the brunt of the attack, so she was not cut. People scrambled to get out of reach, and the deejay stopped the music as he ran over to get a closer look at the action.

"You psycho bitch!" howled Morgan as she sidestepped another glass. Luckily the girl's aim wasn't very good. Smash went another glass on the floor, but not before my dress was splashed with red wine.

"Hey!" I cried out. J.B. attempted to move me out of harm's way, but I was not leaving Morgan. "Stop that!"

"Did she hit you, Casey?" Morgan asked and turned to me, just as a glass hit her right below her mouth. I don't know how it didn't break on impact, but it must have hurt like hell. There'd be a bruise tomorrow. "Do not hit Casey! She's pregnant!" Morgan screamed, and striding through the growing pile of glass like some sort of avenging Amazon, she landed a beautiful right hook against new girlfriend's face. The girlfriend instantly went down, landing on her bum on the floor. Anil was so stunned he didn't even have a chance to try to catch her. I always said

Anil wouldn't want to meet Morgan in a dark alley, and I guess I was right. He looked like he was ready to abandon the girlfriend and get the hell out of there. But before he did, Morgan turned on him and, with a quick jab, popped him right in the nose.

"You son of a bitch," she cried. "That's for the six years I wasted on you!"

In the instant of silence that followed, all we could hear was Brit's cries.

"What the fuck are you doing to my wedding? Casey, I told you to stop her for God's sake!" She pushed herself through the crowd, holding armfuls of dress. "You're the maid of honour! Do something!"

I couldn't help but start to laugh at this. The look on Brit's face was priceless—horror and rage and fear all mixed together with perfectly applied eye shadow and long-lasting lipstick. Then there was Morgan, with her heavy breathing and obviously very sore fist, but glaring at Anil with a triumphant expression on her face. I was laughing too hard to look at anyone else. Sure, make the pregnant woman clean everything up. After this, I thought my maid-of-honour duties would finally be over.

"Great wedding," I overheard someone say.

# Chapter Thirty-Nine

"Proper pre-natal care is effective in assuaging some of the irrational fears and concerns of the first-time mother."

*A Young Woman's Guide to the Joy of Impending Motherhood*
Dr. Francine Pascal Reid (1941)

So Brit was finally married and on her honeymoon. I wished Tom all the luck with her. Morgan swore she was over Anil—telling him off at the wedding was the last thing she needed to get him out of her system, and the quick jab to the nose didn't hurt. I reluctantly gave her my blessing to get involved with Derek. My friends were happy, and I was happy for them.

As for me, I had no idea what was going on with J.B. I kept thinking about the look in his eyes when he kissed my fingers. But that was all I did. I didn't want to push; I didn't want to rush. I'd just coast along and see if I could figure out where things were going. If they were going anywhere. I mean, technically, nothing needed to be going on. Lots of parents lead separate lives. Just because I was having his baby didn't mean I had any claim to J.B. But I had noticed the lack of overnight visitors in the house in the last few weeks.

I really didn't know what to think. One minute J.B. was kissing my fingers and telling me this baby was bringing us closer together, and then he backed right off. It was confusing. Was it a man thing, I wondered, or was he reconsidering things between us? What did he want from me? As with anything that confuses me that much, I did my best to stop thinking about it. It was not easy, but at least I had a pretty good distraction.

The week after school started, I had an appointment for my first real ultrasound, as opposed to the one Dr. Morrissey gave me. I was going to see my babies again. I settled impatiently into a chair in the waiting room of the lab, shifting uncomfortably because of a very full bladder.

"Hey," said a voice. I looked up to see J.B. standing in front of me.

"Find it okay?" I asked as he sat beside me.

"No problem." He drummed nervously on his leg.

"Are you nervous?"

"No! 'Course not. It's just—look what happened the last time I came to one of these things with you. We ended up with triplets."

I had to smile at his logic. "Unless they find another one hiding in there, it can't be that bad. You do know what they're going to do to me in there, don't you?"

"They're going to do something to you? Something bad? Will it hurt?"

"Well, they're just taking pictures, but they're like, pictures of the babies. Is that what you want to see? Not that they'll look like babies yet, they're really just—well, they're babies, but I'm only sixteen weeks, so..." I trailed off when I realized I was babbling. "Is that okay? You want to see the babies?"

J.B. gave me his slow smile, the one I hadn't seen since before this baby stuff started. I had to admit it gave me a bit of a thrill to see it. So much for not thinking about him. "Well, I thought I'd just have a chance to see your bare belly and all," he drawled. "And maybe those other things that look like flotation devices." I gave a bark of laughter and covered my breasts with my arms as he grinned at me.

"Aren't they huge?" I whispered. "And the doctor said they'll only get bigger."

We sat in the waiting room for over half an hour. J.B. waited patiently, leafing through a magazine, but I couldn't sit still. It might have had something to do with the two liters of water currently on hold in my bladder and anxious to escape. Finally, they called my name, and J.B. stood up with me. The nurse/technician put up a hand to stop him.

"Perhaps your husband can wait here for a few minutes," she began, with such a strong Scottish brogue it took a minute for me to understand her.

"Oh, he's not my husband!" I told her a little too loudly. "He's not—he's just the father."

"I'm a friend," J.B. cut in grimly, with a disgusted look at me.

"He's a friend," I repeated lamely. I gave J.B. a sickly smile.

"Well, anyhow, I'll see that he comes in after I do my tests." She raised an eyebrow at J.B.

"Thanks." Without a word to me, he sat down.

I followed the woman—who looked sturdy enough to walk across the entire Scottish Highlands without stopping—down a dim hallway into a curtained cubicle with a bed and a computer. It was very dim, with the screen providing the only light in the room, and very warm.

My Scotswoman gestured to the bed. "Hop up there, dear, and we'll take a little look-see." I complied, and after a brief tussle with my pants, allowed her to help me pull them down so that my stomach was exposed. She then slathered it with the jelly stuff Dr. Morrissey used, only much more of it, talking all the while, but with such a thick accent, I could only understand about every third word she said.

"When did your doctor say you're due?" The way she said due sounded like doo. It made me smile. She placed the roller-ball thing on my belly.

"February 16. Dr. Morrissey said—"

"You have Dr. Morrissey?" the technician tried to hide a smile. "She's a verra good doctor."

"She scares me," I admitted. I didn't want to say she was a bitch, but that was exactly what I was thinking.

"She scares everyone." The technician smiled, and I saw that her name tag read Jeannie.

"That makes me feel better. I think—"

"Ah, now, here's your wee one. Wee ones, I guess?" All talk of the scary Dr. Morrissey was forgotten as the computer screen was filled with squiggles and shapes I assumed were my babies. Just like when Dr. Morrissey did the ultrasound in her office (which, based on the equipment Jeannie was using, was very low-tech), I couldn't make out heads or tails of them. I hoped they didn't have tails!

"Three of them in there," she mused. "Hope you'll have some help?"

"I do," I said, thinking fondly of J.B.

For the next little bit, I was not sure what Jeannie was doing. She ran the roller-ball thing over my stomach, back and forth, all the while muttering things I couldn't make out. I didn't want to ask her what the matter was since she appeared somewhat annoyed and I was afraid it was something I'd done. So I lay and watched the screen and the shapes moving crazily across it. It made me dizzy to watch, but I hung on, trying to catch sight of something I might recognize as my babies.

Finally, Jeannie stopped, and the screen went blank. "Lovie, I can't get the measurements I need. The wee ones are wiggling all about. I'm afraid I'm going to have to do an internal to get what I want."

"An internal what? Oh! Oh." I watched as Jeannie pulled out this two-foot (okay, maybe it was not two feet, but it was long) thing that looked a bit like a thermometer. "Um, that's going where?" I asked as she unrolled a condom onto the skinny head of it.

So that was how I underwent my first (and hopefully last) transvaginal ultrasound. It didn't hurt. I actually didn't feel much; it was just the knowledge something was sticking out of me. At least Jeanie was quite pleased with the results and made sort of a happy clucking noise like a chicken as she murmured into a microphone.

By the time she was done getting all her measurements (whatever measurements they were), I had quite the headache from watching the computer screen. But I still couldn't tell what part of the babies were which.

"Now, lovie, would you like your young man to have a boo?" Jeannie beamed at me. I nodded, not wanting to tell her again that he's not my young man. "I'll just go grab him. What's his name?"

"J.B. Bergen."

"Be right back." I liked the way she rolled her r's. I lay there on the narrow table with my shirt hiked up and one leg kicked free of my pants. There was a thin sheet covering everything south of my pubes, which was a good thing since I didn't make an appealing picture with the ultrasound camera-thingy sticking out of my who-who.

But that, of course, was how J.B. found me.

He looked at my face first off, with a smile, and actually looked pretty excited. Jeannie bustled in after him, and with a very businesslike manner, pulled up the edge of the sheet and adjusted the camera between my legs. J.B. watched her with confusion, and suddenly, as if he realized what he was seeing, his eyes went wide and he looked at me with something akin to horror. I couldn't help but laugh, even though that was not the funniest part of the whole thing.

"I thought—" he stuttered.

"I'll explain later," I told him.

The funny part, although I doubted it was funny to J.B., was how about ten minutes of both of us staring fixated on the computer screen as Jeannie pointed everything out to us, J.B. started to sway. I didn't notice right away. Like I said, watching the movements of the babies on such a small screen was making me dizzy, and I was lying down. But J.B. was standing, in the very small and now very hot curtained cubicle.

"Sit yourself down, laddie," Jeannie said suddenly. With a firm hand, she pushed J.B. onto a stool in the corner. "Head between your legs."

"I don't..." I'd never seen J.B. so white. Even his lips were pale.

"Head down," Jeannie ordered, and J.B. complied.

"It's so hot in here."

"It's for the bare bellies." She winked at me. "Happens all the time."

"Really?" J.B. had his eyes closed as his head was hanging limply between his legs.

"Not really," Jeannie admitted, with another wink at me.

"Fuck." He said it quietly and I didn't think she heard it, but I could see Jeannie smiling as she pointed out one of the babies' legs. After a couple of minutes with his head down and some deep breaths, J.B. finally hauled himself to his feet again.

"All better?" Jeannie asked solicitously. J.B. made a sort of growling sound, and this time Jeannie tried to hide her smile. "All done! Would you like a video and a picture of your wee ones?"

When we got home, J.B. stuck the picture on the refrigerator with a magnet that was advertising twenty-four-hour beer delivery. Cooper found the whole thing hilarious, but Emma got misty-eyed when she saw the picture.

# CHAPTER FORTY

"Deciding on a baby's name should be a quick and instinctive process and should only be done once the child is born."

*A Young Woman's Guide to the Joy of Impending Motherhood*
Dr. Francine Pascal Reid (1941)

I HAD MY SECOND ultrasound when I was twenty weeks along. It was not nearly as eventful as the first one. J.B. was really taking these appointments seriously and told me he'd pick me up from school. As I waited outside the school in the warm October sun, I suddenly wondered how that was going to happen. There was no way I should be riding on his motorcycle. That just screamed irresponsible mother, and if you considered how I got pregnant, I was sure I'd have enough to do to get rid of that moniker. A shiny black Pathfinder pulled up beside me.

"Hey," J.B. said as he lowered the window. He had a huge grin on his face. "Get in."

"Whose car is this?" I marveled as I settled in the passenger seat. It was brand-new since it still had that new-car smell. I ran my hands across the dashboard and the dark leather seats.

"Mine," J.B. said as he pulled out of the school driveway.

"Yours? But—did you sell your bike?" J.B.'s motorcycle is his favourite toy. He thinks he's so cool when he's riding it—okay, he is pretty cool when he's riding it.

J.B. just gave me a look. "Don't be dumb. I sold the car." J.B.'s second favourite toy was his car—a shiny blue two-seater Lexus that he drove when inclement weather forced him to keep his bike at home.

"You sold your car?" I asked quietly.

"I thought it was time I got something bigger," was all he said.

Whoa. This was big—and not just the SUV. This was huge. This was—my eyes actually welled up when I realized this was one of J.B.'s ways of proving to me that he was up for taking responsibility for our babies.

He looked over with a quizzical glance. "What's wrong?"

"You sold your car for the babies," I told him, sniffling a bit.

"It's not that big a deal. It was just a car."

"It was your car."

"Yeah, and these are my babies. Sort of. Yours and mine. Besides," he said with a smile of embarrassment, "you think I want you driving around with the babies in that tin boat you call a car? You can fit three car seats in the back. Now you don't need a minivan."

"You remember I hate minivans!" Now the tears were starting to flow.

"Hey, hey, it's okay. Are you going to be okay, or is this some sort of hormonal thing?" Now he looked nervous, and I smiled through the tears.

"Hormonal probably." There was no way I was going to admit I was bawling because he sold his car. Because it was something like a husband would do, or at least a person in a committed relationship, expecting a child with the woman he loved. But since it was J.B. we were talking about and he was not in any sort of committed relationship, it was probably just hormones making me cry. "Get used to it."

"Great."

I was surprised at how light my heartfelt as we sat together waiting for my name to be called for the ultrasound. For the first time, it really felt like we were in this together. At the last ultrasound and the doctor's visit, J.B. was there with me, but still separate. Before today, I had always considered myself a single mother planning on raising triplets on my own with the help and support of friends. I always included J.B. as one of the friends. But now—now I was a woman preparing to raise my babies with the help and support of the father. And our friends. It was like we stepped into this new level of togetherness.

Considering how only two months ago, J.B. was dead set against being a father, he'd come a long way. I thought he was really okay with it—better than I was some days. There was no hesitation nor visible fear, other than what was to be expected. It was like once he found out—and after he was a dick about everything, but luckily that didn't take too long—he got his head set on straight and jumped right in. If he was not quite ready to be a father yet, I knew he would be when these babies were finished cooking.

"So you really want to find out what I'm—we're—having?" I asked, stumbling a little over the word we're. I hadn't drunk as much water as last time, but I was still finding it difficult to sit still while we waited. Compared to fidgety me, J.B. was calm and cool, leafing through a magazine like he didn't have a care in the world.

"Since we're here, why not? The doc seems to think we might be able to have a good look."

"I'm not sure if I want to know," I admitted.

"You don't?" J.B. asked with surprise. "I figured you'd be dying to find out."

"I don't know," I shrugged. "I might like the surprise."

"Isn't having three babies enough of a surprise?" he asked wryly.

"Yeah, maybe," I smiled. "It would help pick out names, though. What do you think about Kaitlin?"

"Aren't there a lot of Kaitlins out there?" J. B. put down his magazine. "I think I dated a couple."

"Well, that will make things more difficult," I teased. "If we can't name them after someone you dated."

"I think that can go both ways," he pointed out. "Your list is fairly long as well."

"I think we can agree on no significant others? For me, someone I dated for longer than three months; for you, if you knew her last name."

"Hey!" J.B. looked offended, but I was laughing too much to care. He gave my shoulder a shove, which made me laugh even louder. "I'll have you know I know lots of last names."

"What's mine?" He looked like he was about to growl at me, but I kept laughing. "Please tell me you don't keep a list of all these last names."

"Do you mean my little black book, volumes one to ten?" I rolled my eyes. "I don't have a black book," he added patiently.

"Anymore," I said darkly.

"I never did," he said quietly. I met his eyes and something wiggled in my stomach. I didn't think it was the babies yet.

"Speaking of which, I haven't seen any long, tall, blonde things popping up over breakfast in a while." I had to congratulate myself on being able to say this so casually, especially with the way he was looking at me.

"Nope," J.B. was just as casual.

"No? Hitting streak over then?"

"I thought I'd just take a little time out on the bench, that's all." He glanced at me out of the corner of his eye. "Thought it was a good time to do that."

I gave a careful nod. "Oh. Maybe."

"Maybe what?"

"Maybe it's a good time to do that."

"I thought so. What about you?"

"Oh, I started my bench warming the night this happened," I told him, with my hand on my belly. "Remember?"

"Except for David," J.B. said with a tiny note of scorn in his voice. If I hadn't been listening to it, I might have missed it.

"Yes, but that didn't last too long." When he grimaced, I tried to hide my smile. "Are you still mad at me about that?"

"Why should I be mad?" he bluffed.

"No reason. In case you were curious, David is in Rome with Marco. I got an e-mail from him—he's not sure where things are going, but they're taking it slow. I guess Marco's family is an issue."

"The whole being Canadian thing?"

"No, more likely the whole being gay thing."

"Parents should accept who their children are and be happy for them," J.B. pronounced darkly. This, of course, surprised me more than a little.

"It's nice you have such a tolerant approach when you're on the cusp of being a parent yourself. I guess things change when you face life-altering events."

"I've always been tolerant. My best friend growing up was gay. I was the first person he told."

"I—I didn't know that. Why didn't I know that?"

"It's not something I felt the need to bring up in everyday conversation. There are things you don't know about me, Case."

"I think there's a lot I don't know about you. And I think I might be looking forward to finding out more," I told him shyly.

We sat in silence for a few minutes, but it was a good, comfortable silence. The lab was packed, so our wait was longer than before, but today I didn't seem to mind.

"Back to baby names?" I finally ventured. "I like Sarah."

"Not bad."

"What do you think? Boy and girl."

"Well, I like Ben, for a boy," J.B. finally said slowly. "For a girl, I kind of like Dorothy."

"Dorothy?" I repeated. "Really?"

"Kind of."

"She might need a pair of ruby slippers and a dog named Toto." I gave a little laugh, not knowing how serious he was about the name. "But I guess we could call her Dot."

"I was thinking Dory," J.B. said defensively.

"Dory," I echoed. "Like the fish."

"What fish?"

"Haven't you seen Finding Nemo?" At the shake of his head, I smiled. "We better get you watching some kid movies."

"I guess. So maybe not Dory. What about Sam, if it's a boy?"

"Sam Samms. I don't think so. Sort of like Bob Roberts."

"The last name's going to be Samms?" J.B. asked.

"Well, I guess. It is my name. I hadn't really thought..." It was then that I got called in for the ultrasound. I left J.B. sitting in the chair without any resolution on the last name of our children. It was not bad enough that I—we—had to figure out so many first names; now there was going to be confusion with the last name as well.

There was no problem with seeing the babies this time, and the technician got all her measurements without using the internal probe. This one wasn't as nice or talkative as my Scottish Jeannie, so I just lay on the table with my mind wandering until she asked if I wanted her to call in the father.

"Please. His name is J.B. Bergen," I told her. Bergen-Samms, I wondered to myself. Or Samms-Bergen. Sam Samms-Bergen still didn't work.

J.B. followed the technician in, and I smiled when I saw his eyes flicker to the sheet covering my lower body. I knew he was looking for the probe sticking out from between my legs again. "Just the regular one this time," I told him as the technician squeezed another dollop of gel on my belly.

"It's bigger," J.B. said, and for a second I thought he was talking about the babies. Then I saw him looking at my stomach.

"This is nothing," I smiled. "I'm going to be huge."

"There's one," the technician interrupted, pointing to one of my—our—babies on the screen. Both J.B. and I eagerly leaned forward at the same time, and I ended up bumping my head on his chest. For a moment I breathed in his cologne, and then moved away.

Despite the technician's best attempts, our babies were modest today, and there was no way of discovering if they were girls or boys. Not that she could tell us, I was informed, but later J.B. said he was sure he saw something like a penis on one of them. I replied that it must be wistful thinking, and the way he is, it would serve him right to have three daughters. The bad thing about not knowing what we were having was that I still had to figure out a lot of baby names.

# CHAPTER FORTY-ONE

"Feeling the babies move is one of the most magical moments of a pregnancy."

*A Young Woman's Guide to the Joy of Impending Motherhood*
Dr. Francine Pascal Reid (1941)

I LIKED BEING PREGNANT. Actually, I loved it, as you may have expected. I was born to have babies—maybe not three at once, but this is what I was made for. I mean, look at the size of my hips, small pelvis or no small pelvis.

It was fun being pregnant. Every day I seemed to get bigger and noticed new strange and wonderful things happening to my body. And some not so wonderful, like the constant flatulence, but we don't need to get into that. Despite the nausea and urge to throw up all the time, I loved being pregnant and everything about it. Well, maybe not the heartburn I'd been getting at night. That was another new and not so wonderful thing. Or the leg twitches that kept me awake, or the continually full bladder and the constant need to empty it. But I loved it. I was looking forward to when the babies are born, but I really liked being pregnant.

Even the maternity clothes weren't all that bad. Except the underwear, which I did draw the line at. My bikini panties worked just as well.

It turned out I'm one of those women who loved people touching their bellies, talking about them, and just giving me loads of attention for being pregnant. Plus, when I told people I was having triplets—which I did a lot, especially on the subway—I got tons of sympathy.

I finally had to tell the kids at school after one of them rudely informed me that my belly was getting really big and maybe I needed to go on a diet. Some of them thought the idea of me being pregnant was pretty cool, but most of them ignored the belly unless I couldn't manage to fit at one of the tables. Except for the one little darling who seemed to come in every single day with a new and horrifying tale of his little baby sister, usually regarding how often and loudly she cried or how often and messy her bowel explosions were. I have no idea what his parents were feeding the kid, but remind me not to get feeding tips from them.

I was lying quietly in bed one Sunday night after spending the day with Libby and the kids. Normally a day spent with the kids tires me out, but I was surprised just how exhausted I was. I could have slept for hours.

I felt something strange in my belly. At first I thought it might be some new form of gas, since it felt like bubbles popping in my stomach. I didn't give it much thought other than letting out a huge burp, but then it hit me. It was a baby moving. Somewhere down in the bowels—well, not the bowels, obviously—one of the babies was getting busy. Someone was awake.

"Hey, there," I said gently. "You awake down there? Which one are you?"

I lay there with both hands on my belly and started to laugh. They were moving! My babies were moving.

"I can't wait to meet you," I said aloud in the dark room. "I can't wait to be your mom. Not that I'm not your mom already, but I don't really have much to do right now. I'm looking forward to you coming out. It'll be a lot of work, and maybe I shouldn't tell you this, but I have no idea what I'm supposed to do with you. It's not like you come with a manual, you know. That might be a good idea. Plus, there are three of you in there, in case you didn't notice. That was a bit of a surprise—a nice surprise—" I assure my belly, quickly glossing over my first freak-out session, "but I wasn't really planning on so many at once. But I guess I shouldn't tell you that in case you get a complex or something."

I suppose this seems strange, me lying in the dark talking to my babies. I wondered if they could hear me. I wondered what they thought of me. Did they know I'm their mother and that I already love them so much? "You're going to be so loved," I told them, giving my belly a rub. One of them kicked in response, and I let out a delighted laugh through my tears. I was crying with happiness and joy and love for my babies. I was going to be a mother, and it doesn't matter if I don't know what to do in every circumstance. I'll figure it out.

"I'll have lots of help," I promised. "It'll be okay. Aunt Libby will know what to do. And I guess your grandmother—we don't have to talk about her right now. I think I'll need to explain a few things about her. But Aunt Libby will be great, and Max and Maddy will be your cousins and they're so excited to meet you, too! And Cooper and Emma—what should we call them? Should they be Uncle Cooper and Aunt Emma? I'll see what they want to be called. And Aunt Morgan and Brit—you might not see Brit too much, but I'm sure she'll love you in her own way. And your father... your father. Daddy. J.B.'s excited to be your daddy."

I really believed that. It took awhile and it was hard at first, but I really thought J.B. was there. This wasn't the way it was planned, but this was how it turned out, and I thought J.B. was making the best of it. He was ready to be a father to my—our—children.

But what was he to me? That was something I didn't know yet, and I didn't know if he did either. It was true that we had grown closer, closer than we ever were before, but it was the platonic kind of friendship I always tried in insist on but had trouble sticking with. Now—anything more than friendship wasn't an issue. He treated me like—like a friend.

All the fun little flirtation we so enjoyed for years was gone. And so was the teasing. True, we had had the little moment at Brit's wedding, but that was it. I knew me being pregnant frightened him a little—and the idea of labour totally freaked him out—but it was like he had forgotten about the woman part of me.

Which was a problem since these days I felt like all woman, all the time. Like a very ripe, needing to be plucked, woman. But I couldn't talk about that in front of the babies.

"Let's go show Daddy what you can do," I suggested to my stomach and heaved myself off the bed.

"Where's J.B.?" I panted as I came across Cooper and Emma cuddling on the couch. There seemed to be a lot more stairs these days.

"Upstairs, I guess. Are you okay?" Cooper asked anxiously.

"I felt the babies move," I called, already halfway up the stairs.

I stopped just short of rushing into J.B.'s room, remembering what had happened the last time I did that. I knocked politely, and immediately the door was pulled open by J.B. A freshly showered J.B., wearing only a towel.

"Um, hi." I had to literally tear my eyes away from his chest to make sure he was alone. Such a broad chest, with a fine coating of reddish brown hair. The books I'd been reading said your energy returns in the second trimester, which wasn't exactly true for me yet, but they were dead-on about the increased sexual arousal. I couldn't stop thinking about sex. This wonderful glimpse of an almost buck-naked J.B. would keep me going for a while.

I gave a little sigh and managed to look J.B. in his blue eyes.

"What's wrong?" he asked.

"I felt the babies move," I told him proudly. "At least one of them. It's hard to tell because—"

"Really?" he asked, amazement written all over his face. "Can I feel?"

"If they do it again." He led me into the room, and we stood there for at least five minutes with his hands on my belly. His hands are so big they almost covered the whole of my stomach. I had a sudden image of those hands tenderly holding one of our babies. "Sorry," I said apologetically when he finally dropped his hands. "Maybe next time."

"Yeah." He seemed sincerely disappointed. "What did it feel like?"

"Like bubbles. Or butterflies."

"You make it sound so pretty. Being pregnant suits you. Hang on a sec." He grabbed a pair of boxers and disappeared into the bathroom.

"Maybe I can spend some more time upstairs so when they do it again, you can be close by," I offered loudly so he could hear me. "Once I get further along, they'll be moving all the time, I think. I read that—"

"Can I see your belly?" J.B. interrupted, reappearing in front of me in his red boxers. "Your bare belly, I mean. I never have before. Only during the ultrasound, but..." He was silenced as I obligingly raised my shirt.

I caught my breath as J.B. ran his hands across my swollen stomach. It looked huge, but Dr. Morrissey assured me it was the right size for someone almost seven months along with three babies inside. "You didn't have this before," he commented, fingering the dark line of hair on my abdomen that had appeared. "It's so cool," he mumbled, his eyes never leaving my belly.

"It's just a belly." I was embarrassed, not because of his interest, but by how turned on I was getting! I hadn't been touched in, well, a long time. And this was just my stomach!

"It's not," J.B. murmured. "It's our babies." He finally looked up and took my flushed cheeks for embarrassment. "Sorry." He immediately dropped his hands.

"Don't be." I grabbed one of his hands and put it back. "You can scratch it a bit—that feels good," I told him.

J.B. ran his nails over the expanse. "What was that?" he asked suddenly. "Did they move?"

"That was me. I'm hungry," I confessed.

He laughed, and now both of his hands were running over my belly again. "It's so amazing. Big." Our eyes met, and I couldn't help but think again how glad I was that he was here to go through this with me. It wouldn't be the same if I had gone with the anonymous donor. I couldn't wait until my babies could know their father, and I was happy their father is J.B.

And right now I'd be happy to know J.B., if you know what I mean. I took a deep breath and boldly took J.B.'s hands and moved them onto my breasts.

There was a sudden silence in the room. J.B. just stared at my chest. "These have changed too," he finally commented.

"Apparently they do," I joked. I joked because I was practically orgasmic just from J.B.'s hands on my breasts, and if I didn't make a joke about it, I was afraid I might just eat him alive right then. "I didn't know if you wanted to check them out too."

"Mm hmm," was all he said. One of his thumbs brushed against my nipple, and I closed my eyes and tried not to groan aloud.

But then, just as I was leaning closer, with my eyes half-closed, readying my lips for what I was sure would be a gentle, yet hungry, kiss, J.B. did the unthinkable.

He moved his hands.

Moved them right off my breasts, right off my body, and held them nervously at his sides.

"It's probably not a good idea," he told me.

"Why not?" I demanded. Do not beg, Casey, I ordered myself. Do not beg.

"Well, because, you know... that's what got us in this mess in the first place." I knew he was trying to joke, but at the moment, I didn't think it was at all funny. J.B. took a step back from me as if just having a penis in the vicinity of my uterus would crowd the babies or something.

"You don't want to. I get it." I stiffly pulled my shirt down to cover everything. "That's fine."

"Casey, it's not that I don't want to." J.B. grabbed my arm as I turned to leave.

"I get it. I'm the size of a baby humpback whale, and it would disgust you to see any more of my nakedness. I get it."

"That's not it. I think you're beautiful when you're pregnant. It's just..."

"Whatever." I snatched my arm out of his grasp because the heat from his hand was making me feel like I was about to explode. It was like I was back in high school and had a severe crush on my science lab partner, and I'd just told him how I felt and he didn't return the emotion. I was humiliated and embarrassed—and my feelings were hurt. Not good emotions when you're almost seven months pregnant.

Without another word, I stormed out of J.B.'s room and down the stairs.

"What did he do now?" Cooper called from the kitchen.

"Should have got a sperm donor," I muttered mutinously on my way downstairs to pull out Morgan's gift that she gave me for my birthday a few years ago. I hoped I had enough batteries.

# CHAPTER FORTY-TWO

"Anticipation over the arrival of a child is often contagious to even the most stalwart of cynics."

*A Young Woman's Guide to the Joy of Impending Motherhood*
Dr. Francine Pascal Reid (1941)

TIME ACTUALLY FLIES WHEN you're expecting, and I was amazed to wake up one morning and realize I was twenty-six weeks pregnant.

I was twenty-six weeks pregnant, and I had turned thirty-six last week. My birthday was a bit of a nonevent, but I didn't really mind. Brit and Morgan took me out, but since I couldn't drink and I got tired by about nine thirty these days, it wasn't much of a celebration. Cooper and Emma and J.B. did a nice dinner for me on the Sunday night, but I threw most of it up and couldn't even stand to touch the cake, so that wasn't much fun either. But I got some really nice things for the baby, and J.B. went out and bought me a ton of maternity clothes because I complained once or twice about being bored with what I had to wear. Turning thirty-six wasn't as traumatic as I fully expected it to be, probably because

I was pregnant. If I weren't pregnant, I most likely would have drowned my sorrows in whatever alcohol was readily available and hooked up with a totally unsuitable stranger. With that as the other option, I much prefer this way to celebrate me being born. Plus, me turning thirty-six and being pregnant was sort of like flipping Dr. Francine Pascal Reid the bird.

I looked pregnant now. I looked really pregnant, but considering there were three of the little darlings in there jumping around, I was just the right size according to Dr. Morrissey, whom I still haven't developed much of a fondness for. She kept reminding me that pregnancy wasn't an excuse to snack, which I found ironic since I was still throwing up all too often. The pills the doctor prescribed made the vomiting stop, but also left me tired and bitchy—not a good combination for a kindergarten teacher. It had been over six months, and I had learned to live with the nausea. I kept telling myself it wouldn't last forever. Luckily, I had discovered an array of foods that didn't cause me to throw up everything, but unfortunately, most of them involved high levels of carbohydrates.

A couple of weeks after my birthday, two things happened. One, I slipped and fell on some ice outside the store, which led to a nasty bruise on my hip; and two, I had my first Braxton Hicks contraction.

Of course, I freaked out at the false labour the first time it happened, which unfortunately was in the middle of library period with my kindergarten class. Luckily, the librarian has had four children and was very helpful in explaining that I was not in labour before I could call 911.

"Are you sure this isn't the real thing?" I asked Mavis, holding my side and panting like I imagined I would be doing when I went through the real thing. A few of the kids watched me intently, but most were more concerned with their books. "It feels like the real thing. It hurts a lot. The doctor said I'd be having premature labour so I could really go anytime, you know."

Mavis shook her head at me with a beautiful smile. "Casey—trust me. You'll know when it's the real thing. You won't be asking anyone about it."

I questioned Libby about labour pains when I visited her that Sunday afternoon.

"Oh, sure, labour sucks. It feels like your insides are being pushed out your bum. But it's awesome."

"How could something being pushed out of your bum be considered awesome?" I wondered in all seriousness.

"Don't worry about it." Libby brushed my worries away with a wave of her hand. "I thought you were having a C-section?"

"That's what Dr. Hobbit said, but I'm still not convinced. I mean, look at my hips! How can they possibly be too small?" I stood up with difficulty to pick up Max, who had rolled off his play mat and gave him a cuddle before putting him back in the middle. He thanked me with a gurgling smile that warmed my heart. Imagine—I had three of these inside me!

"I think it's the pelvis she's referring to. Are you just going to ignore her and try popping out the three of them when she's not looking?"

"No. I haven't figured it out yet. But my way of looking at it is that this is probably the only chance I'll have to have a baby and I'd like to see what all the fuss is about."

"Trust me—you don't. The end result is great, but face it, if you can avoid pain and ripping and tearing and—" Libby laughed when I winced. "Oh, yes, all of that and more. Haven't you read any books? Are you signed up for prenatal classes?"

I perked up when she asked me that. "J.B. and I are both taking them. He insisted. I signed us up for a weekend course at the end of December."

"Sounds like things are going well with the two of you." Libby smiled as Max rolled over and grabbed the toe of her sock. "Don't try and eat that, my silly boy."

"Other than he refuses to touch me, things couldn't be better," I told Libby. I was still embarrassed about what happened the night the babies first kicked, and I've managed to avoid him as much as possible.

"Touch you, touchyou, or just regular touching."

"Not the regular touching." I gave her a brief recap of what had happened in his room because I was feeling sorry for myself.

"Ah. Well, what do you expect? He's scared of you. You're a woman, you're carrying his child—children—and all these things are going on in your body that he doesn't understand. If I was a man, I wouldn't touch you either."

"I was hoping he could move past that stuff," I grumbled.

"All men go through the same thing," Libby said knowingly. "I mean, you've heard the saying that men want to have sex with the slut and marry the girl next door, or however that goes, right? Imagine how happy they are when they get her home and realize the girl next door is a dynamo in the sack. I know Luke thought he was pretty lucky."

"Didn't need to know that."

"Well, anyway, you got the guy all happy for a couple of years because he's got the best of both worlds, and then his girl next door goes and gets pregnant. Big dilemma, here. It was hard enough at the beginning to go from thinking sweet girl to slut in the bedroom, but now sweet, slutty girl has morphed into one and she's having his baby. Does he go back to treating her like prized porcelain or keep on with the getting everything that he wants from her?"

I made a face at Libby's attempt at an analogy. "The only prized porcelain J.B. has is the new dishes they just got for the restaurant. And I'm not the girl next door; I'm the girl downstairs. And he's never really treated me like a slut."

Libby rolled her eyes. "You know what I mean. Luke had trouble—"

I held up my hand to stop her. "I think if you continue, whatever you say will fall under the too-much-information category. I love Luke, and there are certain words I don't like being associated with him. So let's just say I get your point and move on."

"If you're worrying about this, does it mean something's going on with the two of you?" Libby asked curiously. "More than just the normal you're-having-his-babies thing?"

I leaned my head against the couch. "I don't know, Lib. I don't know what I'm supposed to feel. All I kept hoping the first couple of weeks was that J.B. would come around and maybe be a little happy I was having his baby, and that was it. Then he got all excited about stuff. He's reading all these books and did this research to try and find the best triple stroller and everything. It's really nice. So do I just leave it there, or press my luck and hope for something more?"

"How does he feel?"

"That's like asking if I have any memories of being in Mom's uterus."

"Not a nice image, thanks."

"Well, you know. J.B.'s changed, but not that much."

"You could ask him. Maybe ask what his intentions are. Like, does he intend to ever have sex with you again? Just so you know, logistically, it's going to get pretty difficult. I always found doggie style to work, or you'll have to get on top. Missionary is out for a while, which was okay for Luke because—"

I raised both my hands in alarm. "Please don't tell me what's okay for Luke!"

"For someone who's had so much sex, you're a real prude."

"I am not, and I'm offended by that comment. I'm okay with everyone having sex, but for some people—your husband included—I just don't want that image in my head. Especially now when it seems sex is the only thing I think about. Do you really want me to start thinking about your husband in that way?"

"Go for it," Libby laughed. "He'd get a kick out of it. He'd feel all manly, which might bode well for..."

"Stop it," I cried, and Libby laughed.

"Getting back to J.B. I think you should lay off the whole 'I never, ever want to get married' thing, you know. Just in case he's got ideas and you're scaring him off."

I sighed. "I want him involved for the babies' sake, as well as his own. I'm not looking for a husband out of this. If I was, I would have jumped at him when he asked me before. Or I would have moved to Alaska years ago. Apparently they have tons of single men there. I was thinking of suggesting that to Morgan before she met Derek." Now it was Libby who winced. "Oh, c'mon, Lib, give him a break. He is a nice guy, and it's not like Mom is going to start hanging out with Morgan or anything. And she really likes Derek."

"Who? Mom or Morgan?"

"Both. Mom thinks he's terrific. She originally wanted him for me, but figures Morgan is almost as good. I guess she never considered it might have been a little awkward with the whole mother-daughter-dating-brothers thing."

"Definite eww."

"I know. But Derek seems nice, and he treats Morgan like a princess, which is what she needs. And he's already stayed over a few times. Morgan says—"

"Do not go there," Libby instructed sternly, holding up her hand like a traffic cop, much like I did. "I beg you. You don't want to hear about Luke, and I can't deal with listening how Morgan might be getting it on with the brother of our soon-to-be stepfather. That's our step-uncle or something!"

I laughed. "I know. She gave me a few too many details. But give Eric a break next time, will you, Lib? It's not his fault our mother is a cradle-snatcher."

It was still snowing when I got home. I saw the giant black Pathfinder in the driveway and knew J.B. was home. Even if I didn't, J.B. called down from the kitchen as soon as I closed the door behind myself.

"Hey! Casey, c'mon up, will you?" Apparently he was not still embarrassed about the other night, if he ever was. J.B.'s probably had too many women throw themselves at him to bother counting. I had a sudden, intense wave of hatred toward any woman who was throwing herself at him, but told myself to stop.

After climbing the stairs, which leaves me out of breath these days, I could barely get in the kitchen for the plastic shopping bags scattered around. "What did you—Toys R Us?" I asked in wonderment. There must have been six or seven bags sitting on the kitchen floor. "What did you do?"

"You got to see this stuff!" Clearly J.B. was still feeling the adrenaline of the shopping high every woman knows as he started pawing through the bags. "I know you don't want to breast-feed, so I got all these bottles and a bottle warmer and a sterilizer, and there's this bunch of toys called Baby Einstein and they make videos and it's all educational—it'll teach the babies about music and art, so I got them some of that, and this really cool musical train with these animals and these teething toys and stuffed animals and..."

I started to laugh then. "J.B., you bought so much. You don't have to, you know. There's time." I glanced down at the train and the videos he'd pulled out to show me. "They won't be using these for a bit."

"Doesn't matter," J.B. shook his head. "You know, I've never been in that toy store. It's awesome. The girl who was helping me showed me these bouncy seats, and they vibrate and play music so the babies can even sleep in them." He pulled out a brightly coloured box. "I had to get three of them, so they wouldn't get upset about having to share."

This time I had tears in my eyes as I laughed. "I don't believe you," I told him softly. "All this stuff."

"I know I probably went overboard, but I couldn't help myself," he said sheepishly. "Next time you can come with me. But look—look what I found." Out of one of the bags, J.B. pulled a stack of DVDs. "That Finding Nemo you told me about, plus Cars and Ratatouille and this Dora the Explorer. There were tons of them, so I guess she's pretty popular."

"Pretty popular," I echoed. My niece Madison had enough Dora memorabilia to stock her own store.

"Want to watch one tonight?" J.B. asked eagerly. "We can eat and then watch a movie?"

"Okay," I told him. I couldn't stop smiling.

J.B. made a quick pasta dinner for us, and then we headed to the living room to watch Finding Nemo. I'd seen it a few times with Libby's kids, but it's one of those movies I don't mind seeing again. Sebastian the cat settled in his usual perch on the ugly wagon-wheel coffee table, watching J.B. with half-closed eyes.

About two-thirds into the movie, when the pelican flies into the dentist's office and tells Nemo his father is looking for him, I had another one of the Braxton Hicks' pains.

"Ugh!" I said aloud and held my side tightly.

"What's wrong?" J.B. jumped to the other end of the couch so quickly that he frightened the cat, who bolted out of the room.

"Ugh, just—nothing. It's just false labour. Nothing to worry about—hurts though."

"Braxton Hicks," J. B was nodding his head authoritatively.

"How do you—you're still reading those baby books, aren't you?" I accused.

"Well, what do you expect? I like to know what's going on with you," he said defensively.

The pain abated, and I took a deep breath. "If something like that is going to hurt that bad, then I wish it would just be the real thing," I complained.

"I really hope it's not the real thing," J.B. said. "We haven't got a crib or car seats or a stroller..."

"We've got lots of time," I told him, snuggling back under my blanket. "At least two more months."

"Have you felt the trips kick a lot?" J.B. asked eagerly. It was Cooper who first called the babies the trips, and the nickname stuck. Cooper also began trying out new and unusual names—he would lean up to my stomach and start calling out, "Mabel, Maxim, Mohammed—anybody awake in there?" Or my favourite, "Xander, Xavier, Xorianda—stop kicking Mommy's bladder."

"I honestly think I might have the next David Beckham in my uterus. I'm going to blame you for that. They really get going when I'm trying to sleep or sitting still."

"Can I... touch... you?" he carefully asked. I just knew he was thinking about the other night.

"If you like." I moved closer and so did he, so that we were sitting shoulder-to-shoulder on the couch. J.B. put his big warm hand on my belly, but this time didn't ask to see it naked. He scratched it gently.

"I'm sorry about the other night," he said quietly after we'd been sitting like that for a few minutes. "When I—when you..."

"It was my fault," I told him. "Hormones and stuff."

"It's not like I didn't want to," he assured me. "Or that I didn't want you."

"I get it." I could feel the blush start at my neck and work its way up through my face. I wished he'd stop talking about it so I could stop thinking about it.

"I thought," J.B. stammered, "I thought we could take things slow."

"Slow?" I couldn't help the snort of laughter. "I think we're past the slow part."

"I was thinking," J.B. said slowly, his fingers still moving along my stomach. "We'll be kind of busy when these guys come out..."

"Kind of," I smiled.

"Well, I was thinking, maybe you'd want to go to a movie or something before they're born. Maybe dinner and a movie one night. Or something," he paused, keeping his attention on the television.

"It sounds like you're asking me on a date," I whispered.

"I guess I am. Trying to get to know you a little more before we jump into anything. There's a lot we don't know about each other."

I bite my lip trying not to laugh again. Jump into anything? "Okay," I whispered.

"Why are you whispering?" he asked, also in a whisper.

"I don't—I don't know," I said in my normal voice.

"How about Tuesday night?"

"I'm working at the store until six, but after... okay."

"Okay. We'll do dinner and save the movie until next time."

"Next time," I parroted.

"Well, yeah," J.B. said, turning to me with a smile. "I thought we should maybe go out a couple of times before we become parents. It's a little backward, I know, but it still works for me. If you want to, that is." He suddenly sounded nervous.

"Okay" was all I could bring myself to tell him. But I couldn't stop smiling.

# Chapter Forty-Three

"Grandparents are a wonderful source of knowledge and support for the expectant mother. They will be eager and excited to meet the new arrival and often want to provide care for the entire family."

*A Young Woman's Guide to the Joy of Impending Motherhood*
Dr. Francine Pascal Reid (1941)

T HE NEXT DAY, MONDAY—THE day before my first official "date" with J.B.—was a bad day. Technically, it wasn't my first date with him, because we had those couple of dates when we first met. This was like the first date the second time around. Or I could call it the first date after he impregnated me.

Anyway, it was snowing, which always gets the kids at school excited, and today they all flipped between being hyper and whining in the blink of an eye. Added to this, the babies had been kicking me all morning, I'd thrown up twice before breakfast and once at lunch, and I'd had a bad backache for the last couple of days. For the first time, I was tired of being pregnant.

Despite constant nausea—which had gotten a little better, but was still around—and the throwing up, I'd already gained thirty-five pounds, and today it felt like I was carrying even more than that. I had two more months of this, and right now I couldn't for the life of me think why I had signed up for it. Oh, that was right—I didn't. This is all J.B.'s fault.

I fought the snowflakes as I walked the few blocks to the store from the subway. The first snowfall always got me in a Christmas mood, even if it was in November. This year I'd have to watch out for ice on the ground. I was even more uncoordinated than I usually was. My hip still ached from when I fell last week.

Not ten minutes after I got to work, the door swung open with a gust of cold air and in walked my mother. Luckily, she seemed in a much better mood than the last time she came for a visit.

"Casey! Sweetface!"

"Hi, Mom." I looked with surprise at the way she was dressed. She was wearing a grey tweed skirt and a black leather jacket. I loved the coat, but that was not the surprising part. Her skirt wasn't too tight; all of the buttons of her blouse were done up without showing cleavage; and for Terri-with-an-I—or too-tight Terri—she looked quite respectable.

"You look nice," I told her honestly. I wasn't sure the last time I said that and meant it.

"Why, thank you, sweetie! And look at you! C'mere and let me get a look-see at that belly."

I stepped out from behind the counter and let Terri have a rub. "What's up?" I finally asked.

"How would you feel about taking a little trip next weekend? Like to Vegas?" Terri asked in a singsong voice.

"What's in Vegas?"

"Only my wedding!"

"Oh! Your wedding—you're really getting married. I mean, I knew that, but... um, can I fly being this pregnant?" I wondered.

"Of course you can. I'd really like you there, sweetface. I'd love for Libby too, but with the kids..." And since she's barely said two words to you since you told her you were getting married, is what I didn't say. "It might be hard on her, leaving the kids. Will you talk to her? Please. She listens to you."

Libby refused to listen to anyone but herself. "I'll try."

"Will you come?" In all my thirty-six years, I had never heard my mother sound so vulnerable. She sounded like she actually, truly wanted me there. "And you don't have to worry about the plane tickets—Eric said it was an early Christmas present from him."

"Really?"

"Really. Having you there will make my wedding day just perfect! I know it's short notice ..."

"Okay," I told her. "I have to check with my doctor, but okay."

"Okay?" my mother cried with such happiness in her voice, it made me happy. "Really?"

"Sure. Why not?"

"Oh, baby!" Was my mother crying? "You know, sweetface, if there's anyone you'd like to bring... are you dating anyone?"

"Well..." I paused, "I have a date tomorrow night."

"With who?" she gasped.

"J.B.," I admitted shyly.

"Well, that's nice. Go have your fun now before the babies are born because you sure won't have a lot of time then. Unless, of course, you ask me to babysit!"

Mom left after giving me several heartfelt hugs, and I was left with a warm and fuzzy feeling. It was not often I've made a difference in Terri's life, but she seemed so happy that I agreed to be at her wedding, I couldn't help but be glad too.

After about an hour, though, the nice feeling wore off. Not for any particular reason, but I just started to feel sick. Today, though, it was worse than usual. Different. I tried making myself throw up, which sometimes helped, but not this time. By three-thirty, I was feeling so ill that I had to leave work early. Along with my perpetual nausea, today I had heartburn, a nasty backache, and a cramp in my neck. A nice lie-down would fix me right up, I decided, and I might even have time to watch a little T.V. when I got home. I had PVR-ed Downton Abbey and had gotten a few episodes behind.

The lives of Victorian-era gentry had faded from my thoughts by the time I reached home. Literally dragging myself there, I'd never felt this awful during the whole pregnancy. I even had to jump off the subway twice because I was convinced I was going to vomit. I didn't, mainly because I had no desire to lean over the disgusting garbage cans on the platform and heave my guts in front of tons of people. Then with the thought that some fresh air would help, I got off a station early, but I was so tired and my back hurt so much, I had to stop at least half a dozen times before I made it home. I should have called someone to pick me up, or at least gotten a cab. I kept looking for one as I stumbled home, but they're never around when you really need them. And, of course, I'd let my battery die on my cell phone.

When I finally opened the door about forty-five minutes after starting out, I was so relieved to be home I felt tears spring into my eyes. And I'm not a crier.

"Casey? Is that you?" Emma called from the kitchen. "What are you doing home so early?" She came to the top of the stairs to see me leaning against the wall, unable to take my shoes off. "OhmyGod! What's wrong? Is it the babies?" In a flash, she was down the stairs, with Cooper and J.B. right after her.

"You need to lie down." Cooper pushed open the door to my apartment and steered me inside, his arm firm around my shoulders.

"What's wrong? You look horrible. Is it the babies?" J.B. asked from my other side. I'd never seen him look so worried. I opened my mouth to speak and found I couldn't. I had to vomit, right then. I pushed Cooper away and lurched forward. The contents of my stomach spilled noisily onto the ceramic floor inside the door. After it all came up—it feels like it took forever—I was still kneeling on the floor, still retching. And I was crying for real now. J.B. had his arm around me, which I usually can't stand when I'm throwing up, but today I couldn't care less who was touching me. Emma was pressing a cold cloth to the back of my neck, and Coop was nervously hovering. I give him credit for staying—I know he's a sympathetic puker.

"Sorry," I mumbled to no one in particular after my stomach stopped heaving. Then everything started to go dark, and my eyes rolled back in my head. My last thought was that I hoped someone caught me before I landed in the puddle of my own vomit.

# CHAPTER FORTY-FOUR

"It's important for the expectant mother to be aware and mindful of her health, as a minor ailment can easily become more serious when carrying a child."

*A Young Woman's Guide to the Joy of Impending Motherhood*
Dr. Francine Pascal Reid (1941)

IT TOOK A FEW minutes to realize where I was when I finally woke up. In fact, I honestly didn't know and did the whole "Where am I?" mumble.

"The hospital," J.B. said from the chair at the side of my bed. "We brought you to the hospital. You kept throwing up, and then you passed out. How are you feeling?" He took my hand.

I wet my lips. "Thirsty."

J. B. found a glass of water somewhere in the room and handed it to me, first positioning the bendy straw for me. "Just take sips," he instructed. "I don't want you to throw up again."

After I took four tiny sips, he took the glass away from me. I leaned back on the pillow and closed my eyes, feeling J.B.'s warm hand on my clammy forehead, smoothing away my hair.

"You're so pale," he said.

"How long have I been here?" I managed to ask with some effort. I still felt horrible. Then an even more terrible thought: "Babies?" I gasped.

"They're fine," J.B. soothed. "They put you on some sort of monitor, and everything's fine. So don't worry. It's almost six now," he continued as he checked his watch. "I think it was about four thirty when you got home. You came to in the car on the way here, but you were still pretty out of it, and then you passed out again when we got here. I've never seen Em drive so fast," he laughed. "It was fucking scary!"

That got a weak smile. "What's wrong with me?"

"Why don't you tell me?" he countered back. "The doctor checked you and the babies out, but you weren't exactly helpful, just lying there."

"Sorry," I said.

J.B. leaned over and pressed his lips on my forehead. "You scared me," he muttered almost inaudibly. "Don't do that again."

I scrabbled on the covers for his hand, and clutched it. I could feel my eyes closing. "I don't want to miss our date," I moaned. Then I fell asleep.

When I woke up again, J.B. was still there. It turned out I was suffering from extreme dehydration. Like the time on Survivor, when those guys kept throwing up and you saw their eyes rolling back in their head. Like that. That was me. The doctor read me the riot act, and to piss me off, decided I needed to stay overnight for observation. Apparently, all of the throwing up I'd been doing had made me severely dehydrated. He gave me strict orders to take the pills the doctor prescribed, no matter how tired and bitchy I became. And he used the word bitchy, too. I promised Dr. Bode I'd start taking them again. I much preferred this guy to Dr. Morrissey. He thought my pelvis was just fine! Plus, he was young and not bad-looking, which was weird thinking about when he was giving you an internal exam.

The only time J.B. left me was when he went and told the nurse I was awake, and once to go to the bathroom. But he made sure Libby was with me then. Cooper called her as soon as they got me into the hospital, and she came right over. It took a couple of hours until I was feeling human again. I had an IV (I was so grateful I was unconscious when they stuck that in me!) pumping some stuff in me, and the nurses kept sticking their heads in and telling me to take little sips of my juice. That was all they'd let me have.

It was after eight by J.B.'s watch by the time I noticed Coop and Emma were getting antsy. Luckily, I'd been put into a private room, but with four people, plus me and the bed, it was getting quite crowded. I was impressed Coop had managed to last this long—ever since his sister had cancer, he's avoided hospitals like the plague. I was telling them it was all right to go home when the faint sounds of a cell phone interrupted.

"No cell phones in here," J.B. said irritably, looking from Cooper to Emma to Libby.

"It's not mine," Emma retorted, checking her purse.

"I think it's mine," I told them. I recognized the ringtone. "Did you bring my bag with you?"

Cooper pulled it out from under the bed and handed me the phone. I answered without checking who it was.

"Where the hell are you?" Brit screamed over the phone. She didn't really scream scream, but it was pretty loud. But before I could tell her what had happened, I was blindsided by a tirade.

"I'm sitting here in the bar you wanted to go to by myself! Morgan is late, and neither of you has the consideration to call and tell me. Instead, you probably love the idea of me sitting here all by myself. I thought you were a better friend than to—"

She was yelling so loud that J.B. had no trouble hearing the entire conversation from his seat by my bed. He plucked the phone from my hand before I'd had a chance to get a word in edgewise.

"Shut your mouth, Britney!" he yelled into the phone. "If you'd shut up for a goddamn minute, Casey could tell you the reason she isn't there listening to you moan about your pathetic excuse for a marriage is that she's in the hospital!"

Silence on the other end. Or maybe she was speaking quietly now. But no. "OhmyGod!" I heard her cry. "What's wrong? Was it an accident? Are the babies okay? Is Casey all right? What happened?"

"She's at Women's College, room 415. Come and see for yourself. And if you start to bitch about anything, I myself will throw you out on your bony ass, so make sure you behave yourself!" With that, he clapped my phone shut. Cooper actually applauded.

"Good for you!" he cheered. "I've wanted to do that forever to her."

"Felt pretty good," J.B. grinned. "Sorry, her being your friend and all."

I couldn't say anything since there have been many a time I've wanted to do the same thing.

"She used to be such a nice girl," Libby mused. "When she was in high school, remember the metal she used to have in her mouth, Case? Horrible. I wonder if there's any correlation to her becoming gorgeous and a bitch at the same time."

"She's not a bitch." I felt the need to defend Brit against such adversity. "She's just..."

"Spoiled?"

"Shallow?"

"Selfish?"

"A cow?"

"She's not a cow," I said weakly.

"Yes, she is," Libby said, straightening my blanket. "I think she'd be very difficult to live with. Very high-maintenance. I'm sure poor Tom is finding that out now."

I didn't say anything because things weren't going well with Brit and Tom, but now wasn't really the time to get into it. Turns out Brit has a serious case of post-wedding blues, which is compounded by a schoolgirl crush she has on Tom's boss, so long story short, marriage wasn't turning out to be all she imagined it would be. I think she had more fun planning the wedding than actually being the wife.

Brit made it to the hospital in record time. She oohed and aahed about my situation, but I could tell she was miffed at the lack of enthusiasm her rush to the hospital generated. Coop was dead-on about the selfishness. But Brit's minute in the spotlight was cut short by yet another visitor.

"Mom," I said weakly, shooting a how-did-she-know glance at Libby. Libby's apologetic shrug told me she called her.

"Sweetface!" Terri cried as she rushed to the side of my bed that J.B. gave up for her. "I knew something was up as soon as I saw you this morning. I hope the news of the wedding didn't upset you?"

"I'm dehydrated, Mom," I told her dryly. "I need water. That's it."

"You need to take care of yourself," she chided, full of motherly concern for the first time in years. "You have to take care of my precious grandbabies in there." She rested her hand, with its inch-long pink nails, on my stomach. Luckily, Libby had adjusted the blanket, or I'd be worried about her talons poking right through me into my uterus.

"You take care of those babies. Triplets," Terri breathed, her other hand against her chest. "Oh, Casey, what a gift. You'll have three beautiful children. And you won't need to have anymore." J.B. turned a guffaw of laughter into a cough, which brought Terri's attention to him. "Oooh," she said skittishly. "You're D. J., aren't you? The daddy-to-be?"

"J.B.," he corrected. "And yes, I am."

Terri jumped up and engulfed him in her perfumed embrace. "Well, how sweet you're here with my baby," she told him, kissing him full on the lips before he could escape. "I feel like we're already family." She turned back to me. "What a hunk!" she said, sotto voce.

It might be possible to repair my relationship with my mother, but unfortunately, I couldn't change who she was—the oldest flirt in the world. Well, maybe not the oldest, but a huge flirt nonetheless. And the oldest in the room.

After ten minutes of incessant chatter from my mother, my head was pounding, and I felt like throwing everyone out. Everyone except for J.B., that is. I loved how he was handling my mother, deflecting her questions and attempts at groping with his usual charm. Even with Eric in the room, my mother couldn't keep her hands off a good-looking man. Eric obviously turned a blind eye. After his sincere, "Are you sure you're all right? Is there anything I can get for you?," Eric stood at the back of the room, talking quietly to Cooper and Emma.

"I'm sure Casey told you all about our upcoming nuptials," Terri said loudly, this time her left hand pressed to her chest so the engagement ring was visible. "We're eloping to Vegas," she giggled. "I doubt you'll be coming now," she told me mournfully.

"Vegas?" Libby asked skeptically. "When did you decide that?"

"Just on the weekend. I told Casey today, and she was going to convince you to come too."

"You're going to Vegas?" Libby turned blazing eyes on me.

"Not anymore she isn't," J.B. cut in. I've been in many relationships with men where they felt they could tell me what to do, but no one has done it with such affection and concern in his voice. "I think she should stick close to home until these little guys are born."

I must have been still woozy, because I'm embarrassed to admit I was close to swooning at the look J.B. gave me. I could only shrug apologetically at my mother.

"Well, drat," Terri said. She actually stamped her foot, not that a size five makes much of a stamp. "I wanted both my girls at this wedding. Since it will be my last," she simpered, batting her lashes at Eric.

"That's all right," Eric agreed. His agreeableness and tolerance with my mother was beginning to grow on me. "We can either plan some sort of ceremony for the spring, or go down to city hall when Casey's feeling better."

"I want to get married now," Terri pouted. "And not at city hall."

"How about having it at our place?" I was gobsmacked to hear Cooper suggest that. Just gobsmacked. (Isn't that a terrific word? I should use it more often.)

"What? Coop, you don't—" I started to say.

"How lovely!" Terri clapped her hands together. "Oh, Cooper, what an absolute sweetheart you are! We accept!"

"No, you don't. Coop, you don't—" I tried again, but this time it was Cooper who cut me off.

"It's fine, Casey," he said gently. "We can have it the day after our Christmas party, on the 14, if you like. That way the place will be all decorated for the holidays."

"That's too generous of you, Coop," Libby told him mutinously.

"It's in the spirit of the holidays," Cooper told her. Then, while my mother was congratulating herself with Eric, I heard Coop whisper to Libby, "Will you help me? Casey's awful at organizing anything."

# Chapter Forty-Five

"A common ailment in expectant mothers is dehydration, especially with morning sickness. It can be dealt with easily with constant and continual hydration, but when left unchecked, can prove serious and may result in hospitalization."

*A Young Woman's Guide to the Joy of Impending Motherhood*
Dr. Francine Pascal Reid (1941)

C OOP, EMMA, AND LIBBY finally left, with Mom and Eric, and Brit right behind them, not that I was at all sorry to see them go. For the last forty-five minutes, all I'd heard about was wedding this and wedding that; and after Brit's rigmarole not too long ago, I was sick of the subject. Morgan called three times, twice on Brit's phone and once on J.B.'s, and told me she'd come to see me tomorrow. Finally, the room was quiet, with only J.B. left.

"Why don't you go home and get some sleep?" I told him. My face cracked open with a huge yawn.

"Maybe later," he said. "You should get some sleep, though."

I nodded and flexed the fingers of my left hand, the hand that had the IV. I hated the things. I'd much rather get countless needles than have one stuck in and not be taken out. "I had my little catnap earlier." J.B. shifted in the chair, the plastic leather creaking underneath him. "You're going to be so stiff. Go home."

"I'm not leaving you here." I was sure he meant well, but it came out more stubborn than sweet.

I yawned again. "Just remember, I gave you the option. So I've been reading my baby name book, and I'm up to the letter V—Victor, Vivian, Viridian—"

"I don't think we'll be having a Viridian. Is that a boy or girl? You should just skip the rest of the alphabet if that's what you're coming up with. I don't think it'll be much help."

I smiled tiredly after him. Maybe if we kept talking, I might stay awake. "You don't think we should consider Xavier or Yvette? What else do you like? We need three, you know. And middle names."

"I know. I kind of like Cameron. And Jacob."

"Jacob's too popular. But Cam—I like that. Ben and Cameron if we have two boys. Have you thought of girls' names?"

"I like Lucy. I don't think I've ever dated a Lucy."

"Well, that's good. What about Sophie?" I couldn't stop yawning. I found that I yawn a lot before I'm going to be sick, but now I thought it was just because I was really tired. "What time is it?"

"Almost eleven. Go to sleep."

I took his advice, although it took a while for me to fall asleep. I think it had something to do with being so conscious of J.B. sitting beside me. It's not like he was doing anything to keep me awake, but it was nice knowing he was there. And it was nice—sort of like he was taking care of me. It had been a long time since someone had taken care of me.

When I woke up in the middle of the night, J.B. was still there, sitting in the uncomfortable-looking chair beside my bed, with his long legs propped up on the mattress and reading a two-year-old magazine. But I didn't see him at first, since I was in the middle of one of those dreams I'd been having lately. I was in between sleep and awake as I started plucking at the blankets covering me.

"You okay?" J.B. asked with concern. "Are you cold?"

"I can't find one of the babies," I mumbled. "They were all right here, and I can't find one."

"The babies are right here," he said with a warm hand on my belly. "They haven't gone anywhere. I think you might have noticed if they had. Casey? Wake up, now. You're freaking me out."

His voice brought me back from the dream. "Oh." I leaned back against the pillows. "Sorry."

"Are you okay?" J.B. asked again.

I rubbed my eyes to wake myself up. "I've been having these dreams when I'm in bed; I can't find one of the babies," I told him. "One of them is tangled up in the covers, and I can't find them and get so scared."

J.B.'s hand was still resting on my stomach, and he gave it a little rub. "The babies are fine. You're not going to lose them."

"I'm going to be a horrible mother." I was still so wrapped up in the dream that I was not even embarrassed when I started to cry in front of J.B.

"How do you figure?"

"Look at how I got pregnant," I cried. "Look at before I knew I was pregnant—all I could think about was getting pregnant. I have no idea what to do with these babies! Plus I drank too much and I didn't take care of myself, and now look at me—I'm in the hospital, for God's sake! How can I be a mother if I can't even take care of myself?" I gave a big sniffle and wiped my nose on the sleeve of my hospital gown.

"Hey, c'mon," J.B. soothed. "This is hormonal stuff, and you know I can't handle it."

"I can't handle anything!" I sobbed.

"Stop," he said, a little firmer. "You'll be fine. You're a great teacher and an awesome aunt to Libby's kids, so how much harder can it be raising a few of your own? I'll give you that it didn't start out all that well, and you were kind of stupid to end up in the hospital, but there's no damage done. The babies are just fine—they're like me, they're tough little critters. But you're going to start taking care of yourself better, and I think you should stop working after Christmas. Both jobs. You're going to need all your energy when these babies come, especially since you told me I don't have to do the late-night feedings."

"I didn't say that." I sniffed again, but the tears were slowly drying up. How could I ever have thought J.B. was nothing but a juvenile playboy? "Besides, you'll be upstairs, so you won't even hear them."

"Yes, but you'll be up there with me. I talked to Coop and Emma, and they agree—you're moving upstairs with the rest of us. And after the restaurant is up and running and I have a little time, we'll go out and get a place of our own. You and me and the babies. The five of us."

I must have still been sleep-raddled because I couldn't have heard him correctly. "You want to move in together?" I asked carefully.

"That's normally what people do when they get married. Coop and Emma love us, but I don't think—"

"You don't have to marry me," I told him weakly, without any of the heat from my earlier refusal. I must have been still asleep or all hormonal right then because marrying J. B. wasn't sounding like a bad idea.

J.B. looked at me with exhausted blue eyes. He hadn't left my side since I was admitted. He hadn't left my side since I told him I was pregnant with his baby. True, there were a few dicey weeks there, but on the most part, he'd been right there for me. He'd proved to me that he wanted these babies, but only in my deepest dreams did I ever hope he would want me as well.

He put up his hand just as I was about to speak. "Let me do this the right way since I made such a cock-up the last time." He slid off the chair and amazingly dropped to the floor. "I was going to do this after the babies were born, but I don't want to wait any longer."

"Get off the floor," I murmured.

"Casey Samms, I love you," J.B. announced in all seriousness. "Even without these babies, I would love you. It just might have taken me a while longer to figure it out," he finished sheepishly.

"We haven't even gone on a date yet," I whispered. "Or we haven't since before. It was supposed to be tomorrow night."

"You can call this our first date if that's what you want. Our second first date."

"You don't want to get married," I finally managed to croak. "You told me you didn't. You want to take things slow. This isn't slow."

"I said I wanted to take the time to get to know someone. I think I know you pretty well now. And I didn't want to have a baby either, but there are three of them coming and that's turning out to be a pretty good idea."

"You really want them?"

He got up off the floor and stood beside me, stroking my cheek gently. "I really want you. The babies are just an added bonus."

I closed my eyes to hide my tears, but a few trickled out. "I don't want you to feel—"

This time he put two fingers against my lips. "Stop arguing. Just say yes. You know you want to."

I looked into his eyes. Now that I let myself, I could see the love. "Say it again. Tell me you love me."

"I love you," he said with urgency.

"Since when?"

"Since forever. Since you moved into the house. Since Cooper told me this awesome chick with amazing hair and these funky eyes was moving in and I was to leave you alone. Since the first time I saw you." He shrugged self-consciously. "I just didn't let myself admit it."

I closed my eyes again, but it didn't stop the tears. And now my chin was starting to quiver. I was really going to be a basket case in a moment, but it was okay because it was not from sadness but from this huge bubble of happiness and love that was about ready to explode in my chest.

"Me too," I whispered.

"Me too, what?"

I opened my eyes to see J.B. smiling down at me. "I love you, too."

"And..."

"Yes. I'll marry you."

Maybe I wasn't that sick of the subject of weddings after all.

# CHAPTER FORTY-SIX

"While the labour and delivery of a baby might seem daunting, it is truly a wonderful experience, the act that finally brings a mother and a child together."

*A Young Woman's Guide to the Joy of Impending Motherhood*
Dr. Francine Pascal Reid (1941)

COOPER WAS TRUE TO his word, and my mother got married in his living room, soon to be my living room as well, a week before Christmas. It was a nice little wedding, but I thought the best thing about it was that it really brought me and my mother closer together. Which, of course, was Cooper's main intention.

Christmas came soon after, and J.B. and I divided our time between Christmas Eve with Cooper and Emma and Christmas Day with Libby and Luke. And then I slept most of Boxing Day. And the next day. If the little stint in the hospital did anything for me, it was a wake-up call that I'd been working too hard. I wrapped up at school the day before the holidays began. It was hard saying goodbye to the kids, but I told them I'd bring the babies in to meet them. I was going to work part-time at the wine store until the first week in January, and then it would be nothing but sitting with my feet up and watching mindless hours of television while I waited for these babies to be born.

And that's exactly what I did. That, and move upstairs into J.B.'s room. He had a much more comfortable bed than I did. And then, even though I had weeks to go, one Sunday morning, J.B. and Cooper set up the cribs in the spare bedroom, the one Emma had just finished painting a sunny—and very gender-neutral—yellow.

January 12 came, and I had a doctor's appointment. Dr. Morrissey told me I had to come in every week for checkups now until I gave birth. I'd been pregnant now for thirty-five weeks, and I still didn't like the woman.

"So does that mean I'll be giving birth early?" I asked hopefully. I felt like a balloon stretched to the limit with helium.

"It's quite possible. Most multiple births are premature. I think next week we'll see about scheduling you for a Cesarean section."

"I don't want a C-section," I pouted.

"I don't think you'll have a choice. Your cervix has softened a bit, but you're not even dilated," she told me after an excruciatingly painful internal examination. I was glad J.B. wasn't here to see this, especially the way the doctor had to heave me up into a sitting position. "I doubt it will be anytime soon."

"Soon sounds good," I said, sliding off the table, still with her help.

"You're doing wonderfully," Dr. Morrissey surprised me by saying. "And congratulations, by the way." At my look of confusion, she pointed to my left hand. The hand that now wore not one, but two rings. Rings I couldn't take off because my hands were so swollen.

"Thanks," I told her.

Two days ago, J.B. and I got married. Yes, married! I'd still be over the moon with excitement if I could go longer than forty-five minutes without having to pee. Yes, I timed myself.

My wedding was a quiet ceremony, held in J.B. and Cooper's new restaurant which opened on New Year's Eve. I didn't like them closing for an entire Saturday, but Coop insisted. So the wedding—my wedding. When I married J.B. With a handful of guests looking on, I became Mrs. Jeremy Bergen. Actually, just Casey Bergen, since I hate the whole Mrs. So-and-So stuff. It sounds so 1950ish. But I'm still married. Married to J.B.

Libby was my matron of honour, and Maddy was both flower girl and ring bearer because Max can only take a few toddling steps before falling. Coop stood up for J.B. Brit was there—alone, because Tom had filed for divorce. She stood with Morgan and Derek, who looked very happy together. Mom and Eric were there (she thankfully has given up any wild idea about having another baby). Emma was there, looking fondly at Coop in his suit. I could tell her head was filled with ideas for her wedding in July. There were a few other friends of mine there. David and Marco were in town spending the holidays with David's family, and I invited Darcy and Ethan, whose wedding I was in—remember? That was how this whole thing started. I thought it was only fitting they come. J.B. invited some of his friends, but thankfully no ex-girlfriends. Everyone seemed nice, once they got over the surprise of J.B. getting married and having a baby all at once. Having three babies.

J.B.'s mom was there, with his sisters Carrie and Beth and her husband Dennis. They lived in Vancouver. J.B.'s dad and Alec, Carrie's husband, had to stay in Paris Flats to mind the farm. They didn't actually say "mind the farm," but it sounded like something they would say. Mrs. Bergen was planning on coming back when the babies were born to help out. I wondered if I'd ever be able to call her Gerta now that I was a Mrs. Bergen as well. She said I was to call her Mom, but I haven't been able to do that yet. I didn't really call her anything at all yet. It might be interesting getting help with diapers from a woman I barely know, but she's more qualified to help than my mother is. My mother kept buying wildly unsuitable baby clothes, without even knowing what we were having.

So J.B. and I got married. It was a nice ceremony, lots of flowers and good food, which I barely ate because there is no longer any room for my stomach to expand, and lots of wine and champagne, which I was permitted a lowly glass of. When these kids pop out, I told J.B., I want a bottle of Dom Perignon all for myself. I can have it, since I'm not planning on breastfeeding. While in theory breastfeeding sounds wonderful, the state of Libby's nipples (cracked and bleeding) after Maddy got through with her, and even the sight of her formerly perky breasts after two kids turned me right off. Plus, I'm having triplets, and while I might convince myself I will be an okay mother, I was well aware I was no supermom and couldn't imagine trying to nurse two babies at once like some pictures I had seen.

It was hard to hide my excitement with Brit, which I tried to do since Tom left her three weeks ago. Turns out she did more than talk about Tom's boss, and Tom found out about it. She tried to put on a good front, but I knew she was miserable without him. I guess she really did love him, only it was too little too late.

"I thought you didn't want to get married," Brit accused when I met her and Morgan later the night after my doctor's visit for dinner. I tried to feel sympathetic towards Brit but she made it difficult at times.

"I didn't know I did," I admitted, going pink in the face.

"You didn't know you wanted to marry J.B.," Morgan explained with a smile. "I knew you were in love with him." Morgan was very happy for me. I think a lot of that has to do with the fact her and Derek were happy together

By the time I got home, I had a headache from trying to cheer up Brit and a wicked backache from the uncomfortable chairs we had to sit on at the restaurant. It wasn't uncommon for me these days—the backache, not the uncomfortable chairs. My back was hurting so much that the almost twenty-five minutes I spent driving home was almost unbearable.

"How did it go at the doctor's earlier?" Emma asked as I waddled into the kitchen. There was no other word but waddle to describe my lumbering, thoroughly ungraceful walk. I was absolutely huge, and I still had five more weeks to go. I could only pray I'd deliver early. I pulled open the refrigerator and looked longingly at the chilled bottle of white wine, and grabbed a bottle of water instead.

"Oh, that." My mind was still on Brit's sorry state. "I have to go once a week now to see that horrible woman." I leaned my hand on the fridge and drank deeply from the bottle. "I think she might be growing on me, other than the fact she's still telling me to plan on having a C-section. I told her—"

"Did you spill your water?" Emma interrupted in a strange voice. I looked down to see a small puddle forming at my feet. "Or not go to the bathroom when you should have?"

"No." I stared at the puddle intently. "No. Do you think—? Well, holy shit! And I was just at the bloody doctor's, who didn't have a clue I was going into labour! Did you miss some key points in your training there, Dr. Morrissey?" I cried. "Stupid cow!"

"Does this mean you're in labour?" Emma all but whispered.

"Guess so." I finished the bottle of water in a few gulps while Emma stood staring at me. "I'm going to go clean myself up."

"Shouldn't you, shouldn't you go to the hospital?" she cried. "You're having the babies!"

"Not right now," I smiled indulgently at her. "The classes said it can take a while, and I haven't even had a contraction yet. I think there's a bit of time." I knocked on my belly. "Hello, guys. I was just at the hospital. Couldn't you have started a bit sooner? Then I would have missed miserable Brit."

"Casey," Emma said in a strangled voice. "You're having the babies!"

"I am." I could see my joy mirrored on Emma's face, hear it in her voice, and it made my heart sing. "I'm going to be a mother!"

"It's what you always wanted." She gave me a tearful hug, being careful not to squeeze too tightly.

"I'm going to be a mom," I said, beginning to be a little tearful myself. "I have to call J.B."

"He won't want to miss this."

"I hope it doesn't take too long," I mused.

But it did. By the time my contractions started in earnest three hours later, I was safely ensconced in a narrow bed in the triage department of the hospital, with a dreaded IV stuck in my arm. J.B. was with me—unable to sit still, he'd taken to hovering by my bed, asking inane questions. It started out oddly endearing, but I could see it getting old real fast. Cooper and Emma were sent up to the waiting room outside the delivery room to wait for Libby. I'd talked to both Morgan and Brit, who wanted to come, but I told them not to since it could take all night. I knew they were waiting impatiently by the phone. Surprisingly, I was the calmest one in the bunch, a fact Emma made note of several times.

The doctor between my legs stood up. And you wouldn't believe who it was!

"No offense, but could I maybe get another doctor?" I asked with a smile. It was Adam, the cute subway guy that I kept bumping into. I knew he said he was a doctor, but I never imagined he was a doctor working at the hospital I was giving birth in, let alone being the attending in triage when I went into labour. It was scary the way he kept popping up into my life. "It's sort of weird now, considering you have your hands up my who-who."

"Sorry," Adam told me, stripping off his latex gloves. "Duty calls."

"She's going to have the babies, then?" a clearly nervous J.B. asked.

"Looks like we're moving right along here," Adam told me. "You're seven centimeters, so I suggest we get you up to delivery. A little ahead of schedule, but these gaffers are impatient. Everything seems fine, so we're good to go."

I was going to have my babies now. Three babies. In a short time, I was going to be a mother. I was going to become the one thing I'd always dreamed about. I was going to bring life into this world, and I was so excited my teeth were actually chattering. I was going to be a mom. I couldn't help but shed a few tears.

Eleven hours later, my excitement had worn off, but my teeth were still chattering because of the pain. I couldn't even remember what stage I was in according to my pregnancy books, but I was trying to push and it hurt! The contractions were nonstop, and they (nasty doctors!) had reduced the wonder drugs in my epidural to help me push. Adam was gone, and I'd heard talk that Dr. Morrissey had been paged. J.B. was exhausted and worried, but still supportive and had never left my side.

"Casey, we're not making much progress here," the nurse—I forget her name—told me. I'd been pushing for well over an hour, waiting to hear the magic words, "I can see a head!" to no avail. "Your pelvis is quite narrow, and I think we'll have to go for a C-section. The babies aren't in distress yet, but I don't want to wait much longer to get them out of there."

Which was exactly what Dr. Morrissey had told me, and I quote, "You will have a long and difficult labour, which will not result in a vaginal delivery."

"Damn you, Dr. Morrissey," I said through clenched teeth. Then I collapsed against my pillows. "Get them out of there."

So despite my best intentions, my babies were born not with the pointy, bruised heads of those traveling through the birth canal, but with the round and perfect heads of Cesarean babies. Well, Ben's head was a little cone-shaped. And at the last minute, Dr. Morrissey made it to the hospital to deliver them. I finally decided to like her after she handed me one of my daughters.

"Ben and Sophie and Lucy." I smiled tiredly at J.B. and the little bundle he held tenderly in his arms.

"Sophie, Lucy, and Ben. They're perfect. Thank you." He leaned and kissed my lips. "Happy? You got what you wanted."

I could only nod, and I closed my eyes so he couldn't see the tears of happiness flooding my eyes. "Even though it didn't really go according to plan."


The End

Find out how things work out for Casey and J. B. and the babies in

Unexpectingly Happily Ever
And keep reading for a sneak peek of the first book of my women's fiction, Sisters in a Small Town series

Coming Home

# Sneak Peek!

## Coming Home

### Chapter One
### Brenna

There can be no situation in life in which the conversation
of my dear sister will not administer some comfort to me.

—Mary Montagu

B RENNA EBANS WAS FINALIZING the paperwork for a 2.5 billion
dollar acquisition for one of her most problematic clients when
Kayleigh's call interrupted her train of thought. She looked longingly at
the neat file on her desk; she loved her sister but...

Brenna had been surviving on pure adrenaline for the past three days,
trying to get the deal done and to everyone's amazement but hers, she'd
succeeded. One little loophole and the power was back in her client's
hands. She loved her work.

At least, that's what she told herself.

The extension blinked accusingly and Brenna punched it with a sigh. "Kayleigh. Hi."

"You're a tough woman to track down."

"And yet you managed it. What's up?"

Brenna listened to her older sister's gossip with half an ear as her assistant Crystal poked her head into the office. She had a big smile on her face when she dropped off another file with two yellow post-it notes; Call them ASAP with a happy face and I'm leaving in 10 mins with an even bigger happy face.

It was already five-thirty on a Monday; Brenna was going to have to cancel yet another dinner with Toby.

At first, Brenna enjoyed working for the same law firm as her husband. But now it only seemed to create more tension every time she got inundated by work.

Which was becoming almost a daily event.

She wasn't sure how Toby did it. How did he manage time for friends, the gym and fancy dinners? Out of the last six attempts, Brenna managed to make it to one dinner with her husband. One.

As Kayleigh reported on the town gossip with the seriousness of a TMZ reporter, Brenna snapped her fingers to catch Crystal's attention. She covered the handset and motioned to her assistant. "Can you find Toby for me?" Brenna jerked her head towards the paperwork on her desk with a sorrowful expression. "I can't make dinner tonight. I have to finish this."

"I'll tell him," Crystal promised with a distracted smile.

She probably thinks I'm a horrible wife.

Maybe I am.

I should tell him myself.

"Are you coming home for Addison's wedding?" Kayleigh asked, pulling Brenna back to the conversation. "Maggie said you haven't sent your RSVP back."

Addison was getting married? Brenna didn't remember Addison being engaged, let alone planning a wedding. Who was the groom? Rummaging through her inbox, she could swear she hadn't received an invitation. She'd remember a wedding invitation to my own niece's wedding. There was nothing in the work inbox. With a frown, she combed a year's worth of paper out of the inbox marked 'personal.'

"Oh, Kay, work is just so crazy and—"

There was the invitation; still unopened with her name written in sparkly green ink, along with a credit card bill and an invitation to join the newest fitness center in the area. "It's been really bad—really busy," she corrected. "I'm doing this deal and no one thought it was going to come together but I managed it and—"

"You're always busy. You work over Christmas and you never take vacations. Look at how late it is and you're still there."

"There's a three-hour time difference between Vancouver and Forest Hills," Brenna reminded her. "So, actually, it's not that late."

"It's been years since you've been home, Brenna."

Here it came. Sooner or later, all Brenna's conversations with Kayleigh took a sharp right down Guilt Lane.

Yes, it had been fourteen years since she had left home. Yes, she realized she hadn't been back since.

Brenna rolled her eyes as Kayleigh warmed up. "You never update Facebook, so I don't even know what you look like these days."

"I look like me. Tall. Kind of scrawny. Red hair." She ran her hand through her hair and remembered she missed her last two salon appointments.

"Brenna..." Kayleigh sighed, her exasperation flying from the tiny town in Northern Ontario to settle heavily on Brenna's shoulders. "Just come home. Please. Addison's wedding is in two weeks. Maggie needs you to be there. It's her oldest daughter. It's Maggie."

Brenna winced in resignation as Kayleigh threw the sucker punch. She knew any mention of Maggie was a sure way for Brenna to feel the maximum guilt.

Their father had abandoned the family when Brenna was three; their mother died ten years later. Eldest sister Maggie had been the rock of stability, taking on the roles of both mother and father to her sisters.

Everyone in the tiny town of Forest Hills knew the five Skatt sisters. Everyone felt sorry for them.

Reluctantly, Brenna ticked off on her fingers what she needed to do if she was going to make the trip back home. Who could cover her cases, how long she could be away from the office, what to tell Toby...?

Toby!

She had to make sure Toby knew she was running late. The last time she forgot to tell him, he ended up waiting at the restaurant for almost an hour.

"I'll call you back," she told Kayleigh hastily.

"Brenna!"

"I will. I'll see what I can do, I promise. I'll call you back, but really – I have to hang up now. Call you right back-" Brenna hung up with Kayleigh's protests still ringing in her ears and hurried out the door of her tiny little box of an office.

Davis and Daniels Attorneys at Law occupied three floors of a high-rise in downtown Vancouver, and Toby, being next in line for partner, had one of the cushy top floor offices. Brenna headed for the elevator, hoping to catch her husband before he left.

They'd been fighting steadily for weeks – months really – about Brenna's inability to make time for him. They weren't exactly fights; Toby was too passive-aggressive for that. He would make snarky comments that Brenna would pretend to ignore, things would be awkward so Brenna would spend even more time at the office. Last Sunday they had a heated discussion about her choice to work rather than enjoy brunch with him, but Brenna left the condo before resolving anything. Toby hated it when things were left hanging. He needed things packaged up with a neat little bow.

She used the short trip between floors to respond to an email that Crystal should have taken care of. Brenna realized her assistant wasn't the most efficient, but she was cheerful and friendly and would always bring Brenna a latte when she got one for herself.

Brenna's thumbs flew across her phone, responding to another email as the elevator doors slid open. This should have been done hours ago. What was Crystal thinking?

Crystal had seemed especially smiling that afternoon. Brenna wondered wistfully if there might come a time when the two of them could be more than boss slash assistant. Friends, even. Brenna could ask for advice about Toby and Crystal could tell her about the men she was dating...

Who was she kidding? She couldn't even make time for her husband, let alone someone she could talk to about him.

She checked another email between the elevator and Toby's office, pausing with her fist poised to knock as she skimmed the request. There were texts she hadn't got to –

Toby. Telling him dinner was out of the question.

Brenna couldn't remember if she'd knocked and tentatively pushed open the door. "Toby, I – "

"Brenna!" Toby cried in a strangled voice. He was sitting at his desk by the window.

There was a thump from under his desk.

"Toby? You okay? What was that?"

"What are you doing here?"

"I wanted to tell you –"

And then Crystal crawled out from under Toby's desk. "I was telling him for you," she said with a spiteful gleam in her eyes.

"Thanks...what...?"

It took Brenna a moment to comprehend what she was seeing.

The sight of Toby jumping out from behind his desk, his slim-fitted pants bagged around his ankles, fully exposed and suddenly very flaccid, cemented it.

"Oh, my God!" The cry didn't seem strong enough for the situation. "What the fuck?"

"I can explain," Toby said urgently, pushing Crystal aside. His handsome face was flushed with fear and annoyance, as he fumbled to pull up his pants.

"How can you possibly explain this?"

Inexplicably, the urge to laugh bubbled up and Brenna took a deep breath, swallowing the hysterical giggle. Toby favored an eclectic style of fashion and the image of him wearing a sweater vest, pants around his ankles, and blue and orange argyle socks pulled up was something she wouldn't soon forget.

"Brenna –" Toby proved it was impossible to discretely pull up pants.

"What the hell are you doing?" She noticed how his close-cropped hair had become more silver than brown of late. Toby was seventeen years older than Brenna and getting caught with his pants down—literally—suddenly made him look every day of those fifty years.

"Let me—" His pants were still undone when he stumbled out from behind the desk. Brenna beat a retreat to the door, eager to keep her distance.

"I know what you were doing. You were in her mouth! How do you expect to explain that? And in your office, of all places?"

"Brenna, you know things haven't been great between us."

"This is my fault?"

Crystal snorted as she scrambled to her feet, face flushed with rage rather than remorse. "How can someone so smart be so incredibly stupid? Things are horrible between you two! Everyone knows it but you." Brenna stared in horror as the girl continued. "You're a terrible wife! I've been taking care of your husband for weeks now and you're so busy with your head stuck up your ass you haven't even noticed a thing!"

Brenna flinched at the crassness of Crystal's attack. "Should I be thanking you for taking care of him, as you so eloquently put it?"

"I've done a better job than you ever could!"

One of the straws holding Brenna's control snapped. "And look where it's gotten you. I suggest you get your things out of this office because you're fired. And you," Brenna turned to a silent Toby. Anger and disappointment raged within her, and as she looked at her husband, disappointment won. "How could you do this to me? With her – here? You know what this job meant to me."

"You're upset about a job?" Toby said incredulously.

"No, I'm upset about you. Walking in on you with my assistant hasn't been the highlight of my day. It's just – how could you do something like that, Toby." She didn't wait for a response. "I can't be married to you anymore."

"Brenna, wait. You're over-reacting."

"I don't think so. I think it's time I do some reacting." She turned to leave but decided a parting shot was necessary. "We're over."

Was that all she had?

"Your penis is pathetic and I've had better sex with my vibrator," she added in a rush. "Plus your socks are stupid and that vest makes you look like a dork. So there."

Brenna swept out of Toby's office with her head held high.

Hang on, she told herself, vowing not to break down until she was alone.

How did this happen? How could she have not noticed what was going on?

How stupid was she?

Brenna punched the button for the elevator, praying it would arrive before Toby did. She fully expected her husband to rush out after her.

To fight for her.

Except he didn't.

She held her stomach, sick with disappointment. How could she miss what was going on? Toby and Crystal? How could he?

Brenna remembered how Crystal had always found an excuse to bring in a file or message whenever Toby had been in her office. She laughed at his jokes, listened to his stories.

Tears pricked her eyes and she pushed away from the wall as the elevator arrived.

On her way back to her office, Brenna paused at the pod of desks in the middle of the floor that Crystal shared with three other assistants. One of her client files was open on the desk, paper spread haphazardly, along with a half-empty mug of tea and Crystal's iPhone.

"Can I help you with something, Brenna?" The woman across from Crystal's desk asked, her eyes wide with confusion.

Brenna realized she didn't even know the names of the people she worked with. No wonder she never noticed a cheating husband.

"Did you know she was fucking my husband?" Brenna asked conversationally, carefully tucking the papers back into the file on Crystal's desk.

"What?" The protest was so thoroughly insincere that it left no doubt she and Crystal had spent many hours discussing Toby, Toby and Crystal, Toby and Brenna, and her complete and utter ignorance of the affair.

"Could you hold this for a sec?" Brenna asked politely, passing the file over the dividing wall to the woman before picking up Crystal's phone. "Do you think she has pictures of him on here?"

The woman gaped at Brenna, who shrugged and smashed the phone against the corner of the desk.

And again.

"What are you doing?" The fear in her voice was sincere but Brenna saw no need to answer. The phone still looked somewhat functional so she threw it on the floor and crushed the screen with the heel of her shoe, grinding it like a bug.

"Brenna! Stop!"

Looking up, Brenna saw Toby, with a red-faced Crystal right behind him, hurrying down the hall. She snatched Crystal's new hot pink Coach tote bag sitting innocently under her desk and punted it toward them like a football. The contents of the open purse flew out in every direction, pens, and tampons flying through the air like miniature Scud missiles.

"Brenna!" Toby shouted. A tube of lipstick hit him in the head.

"I'm calling security," the woman wailed.

Brenna snatched up the mug, which had Be Mine emblazoned in pink and threw it at the PC, the sizzle of wet electronics chasing her down the hall along with Crystal's shrill scream and Toby's shouts, her breath coming in panting gasps.

She locked the door behind her and stood for a minute, with a hand over her eyes, waiting for the tears.

Her phone, still clutched in her hand, rang.

"Kayleigh, I'm coming home."

Keep reading
Coming Home

# Also By

**Suitor Science**
Falling for The Suitor
Hating The Chemistry Teacher
Fraternizing with the Ex (June 2022)
Marrying the Billionaire Best Friend (Oct 2022)
Loving the Wrong Guy (Jan 2023)
**Don't**
Don't Tell Me You Love Me
Don't Want to Be Friends
Don't Stop Me Now
**Charlotte Dodd series**
The Secret Life of Charlotte Dodd
The Missing Files of Charlotte Dodd
The Best Worst First Date Ever
The Hidden Past of Pippa McGovern
The Last Stand of Charlotte Dodd
**Sisters in a Small Town**
Coming Home
Hanging On
Stepping Up

**Love and Alliteration**

Perfectly Played

Beautifully Baked

Pleasantly Popped

**Oceanic Dreams**

I Saw Him Standing There

Unexpecting

Unexpectingly Happily Ever After

Absinthe Doesn't Make the Heart Grow Fonder

**Kid Lit**

The Dragon Under the Mountain

The Dragon Under the Dome

Manufactured by Amazon.ca
Bolton, ON

27772025R00219